THE OCTOPUS OF PARIS

THE
OCTOPUS OF PARIS

BY
GASTON LEROUX
Author of "The Phantom Clue" etc.

WILDSIDE PRESS

INTRODUCTION,
by John Betancourt

Gaston Leroux (1868–1927) was a French journalist and novelist best known for *The Phantom of the Opera* (1910), but his contributions to detective fiction were equally significant. A former court reporter and investigative journalist, Leroux applied his keen eye for mystery and intrigue to fiction, creating one of the most notable early fictional detectives, Joseph Rouletabille. Like Sherlock Holmes, Rouletabille relies on logical deduction rather than brute force, making him a precursor to later greats like Hercule Poirot.

Leroux's *Rouletabille chez les Bohémiens* (1922)—translated into English as *Rouletabille among the Bohemians* (1923), *The Sleuth Hound* (1926), and sometimes *The Octopus of Paris* (1927)—is the final book in the Rouletabille series. In this adventure, the young journalist-detective is drawn into a conflict involving a group of so-called "Bohemians." The term bohémien in French historically referred to the Romani people (gypsies, though this term is no longer in use due to negative connotations with it), based on the mistaken belief that they originated from Bohemia (now in the Czech Republic). In reality, the Romani came from northern India, but European misinterpretations led to the persistent confusion. By Leroux's time, the term was still commonly used, both to describe the Romani and as a broader reference to unconventional, artistic lifestyles.

In this novel, Rouletabille attempts to recover a stolen sacred book and confronts the sinister figure known as "La Pieuvre" (The Octopus). Like much of Leroux's work, the story blends mystery with adventure, taking readers through a world filled with secret societies, hidden identities, and high-stakes intrigue. Though less well known than his earlier works, Rouletabille among the Bohemians showcases Leroux's flair for suspense and his deep engagement with the detective genre, solidifying his legacy as one of early crime fiction's great pioneers.

THE OCTOPUS OF PARIS

THE OCTOPUS OF PARIS

Part I

CHAPTER I

IN WHICH "THE OCTOPUS" IS MENTIONED FOR THE
FIRST TIME

JEAN DE SANTIERNE darted up the staircase
to Joseph Rouletabille's flat at such a pace that
despite his youth and devotion to every form of
sport, he stopped a moment at the door out of breath.

The famous journalist of the *Epoque* had lived during
the last two years in this old house in the Faubourg
Poissonière to which he had retired after the tragic death
of his wife.

Jean rang the bell. Some time elapsed before the
door was opened. At last a man servant appeared. He
was a flat-faced man whom Rouletabille had brought
back with him from the Balkans. Taciturn, with a
perpetual look of gloom on his face he was a slave to
orders.

"Monsieur is not at home," he declared.

"Don't talk nonsense, Olajaï," protested de Santierne
in a tone of irritation. "I know that he's here. Let me
in."

"Monsieur is not at home to anyone," retorted the man.

But de Santierne had already thrust him aside and
with a masterful air opened the door of Rouletabille's
study.

9

He had no sooner entered it than he uttered a dull exclamation and stammered a confused apology. A woman was in the room which seemed to have been put to the sack. Books had been thrown to the floor in heaps; partially opened letters and papers lay strewn here and there; the drawers of the desk seemed to have been forced; and yet de Santierne was less surprised by this extraordinary disorder than by the sight in that room of the woman who seemed to be the cause of it and to rule over it.

She was not beautiful, but, as the saying goes, she was worse than beautiful. Still young, in the thirties, an uncommon face was crowned by a fringe which was cut straight across the forehead, covering it to the eyes which she blinked in the manner of shortsighted persons, and which held a disquieting light that stole with a seeming indifference over people and things. She was clad in a light gray tailor-made costume of perfect simplicity but faultless style.

She cast a hostile glance on him and at once turned away, slipping behind the desk, and disappearing through a door which connected Rouletabille's bedroom with his study. Quickly though she had fled, de Santierne had none the less recognized a form whose appearance in that room rooted him to the spot.

"The Octopus!" he murmured with a catch in his breath. "The Octopus here! Ah, that explains many things."

When he had recovered his composure he went into the entrance hall and called Olajaï.

"How is it that the study is in this state? Is your master moving house?"

"He will be back soon," replied the man and left him without another word.

Almost immediately afterwards, Rouletabille came to him in the study. He held out a somewhat feverish hand;

made certain of the fastenings of the door, and asked him in the friendliest way what had brought him there. Such an effort of composure was merely on the surface. De Santierne was not the man to be deceived.

"First let's talk about yourself," he said. "What's happened here? You must forgive me for forcing my way in."

"My dear Jean, I'm going to tell you something that I determined to keep from everyone, and I ask you, for the present, to regard it as a dead secret. To be frank, what has happened is that Rouletabille's flat has been broken into."

"Broken into!"

"Yes."

"I hope you know by whom and why."

"I have no idea and I can't make it out."

"Rouletabille, when I came in just now," went on Jean in a low voice, "I found a woman here and my presence seemed to embarrass her."

"Forget that you saw that woman," returned Rouletabille in decisive tones. "You've got to. No one must have seen that woman in my flat."

"For my part, I am particularly sorry to have seen her here," returned Jean, sinking his voice.

"Why are you sorry?"

"On your account . . . Madame de Meyrens here! Do you know what that woman used to be known as?"

"Yes," returned Rouletabille with a smile that Jean did not like. "She has told me the story of her misfortunes."

"You mean the misfortunes of others! We called her 'The Octopus.' I hope that I am sufficiently your friend to say: Rouletabille, be on your guard. Wherever that woman has shown her face disaster has followed. She has invariably left ruin and despair in her train. . . . At Vienna and Petrograd where she had access to the best society, for she had official support, she was said to be in government pay. She disappeared after the war. Some people even suggested that she was shot with her back to the wall in Schlusselberg. . . . And I came across her here, in your flat, as though she were at home, and a close friend of yours! Look here, Rouletabille, I know that during the last few months you have had a love affair, but I was far from suspecting that it was with her. . . . And yet now that you have told me of this burglary, nothing surprises me."

"Has she ever done you personally any harm?"

"No, because when I was an attaché at the embassy the ambassador said to me: 'Look out for yourself!' At all events I hope that you are not in love with her!"

"I?" returned Rouletabille. "Don't worry. I loathe her."

"And she?"

"She loathes me."

"Has it come to that?"

"Yes, but let's change the subject. Tell me what brought you here."

"Tell me first how you were burgled."

"I'm ashamed to tell you, but here goes! . . . You are aware that I am in the habit of working late at the office. I scarcely ever get back here until two o'clock in the morning. Last night by chance I went to bed at ten o'clock. I felt tired, worn out, I can't say why. I have even wondered since if anyone gave me a sleeping draught without my noticing it."

"Where and with whom did you dine?"

"Calm yourself. Not with her, but here."

"Can you depend on your servant?"

"As a matter of principle I never depend on anybody, but from the logical point of view I had to reject the idea of a drug. Even presuming that my man was in league with my burglars, it was to their interest to see me go out as soon as possible and not to keep me in my own place even asleep. No: they were as greatly surprised to see me here as I was to see them. . . . Well, I went to bed. It might have been half-past twelve or one o'clock when I awoke. A strange noise, a continuous grating like that of a file on a lock, roused me from my torpor and suddenly I heard a creaking and after that nothing.

"It seemed to me that some article of furniture had been forced with a jimmy. That was, perhaps, merely a delusion and the sound was naturally caused by the cracking of the wainscoting. I sat up in bed feeling rather limp. You know that I am not lacking in courage. Well, at night time I have often been as nervous as a child at the mysterious sounds which things make in the dark.

"Perturbed, the perspiration breaking out on my temples, I thrust my hand into the drawer of my bedside table. My revolver was not there. I remembered leaving it in a pigeon-hole in my desk. The noises, as it happened, came from my study. They were being renewed; the grating sound began again; it grew more distinct and in the face of this unmistakable sound, I at once completely recovered my self-possession.

"I slipped out of bed and cautiously opened the door of my room. A gleam of light flickered at the foot of the door leading to the entrance hall. I called to mind a knotted club which lay in the umbrella stand. I armed myself with it and put my ear to the study door.

"I heard the whisper of voices in a language which I did not understand. My man sleeps on the floor above. I was alone against a gang who would not hesitate to lay violent hands on me. I determined to leave the flat if there was still time and warn the concierge; but at that moment the study door was opened, there were some exclamations of surprise quickly stifled and three men flew at my throat.

"In no time, I was knocked down, gagged, carried into my bedroom, bound firmly with my bedclothes and rendered helpless. The men had, of course, switched off the light, but I had the consciousness that they were still moving round me. What was the nature of their job? Suddenly the front door bell rang and they made themselves scarce like a flight of villainous night birds.

"Heavy blows with the fist were being rained on the door and I heard the stentorian voice of my friend La Candeur shouting:

"'It's me! Open the door, Rouletabille. You're wanted at the office. We've tried to ring you up. Why have you left the receiver off? The editor is furious.'"

"I for my part was fruitlessly straining every nerve to get free and to make myself heard. La Candeur went downstairs again cursing. On consideration, I was by no means sorry that he failed to see me in that plight. I, Rouletabille, to allow myself to be caught like that! I was ashamed, and annoyed. That was the feeling which was then uppermost in my mind. . . . My man released me this morning. I threatened him with jail if he ever breathed a word about it, and as far as you are concerned I feel certain that I can rely on you not to give me away."

"But after all, what does such an attempt mean?" asked Jean de Santierne, who forgot his own anxieties as he listened to Rouletabille's extraordinary experience.

"Ah, that's just it," returned Rouletabille, making a sweeping gesture towards the study in disorder. "I have tried to find out. Those fellows obviously came here to steal certain papers, but what papers? I've been making an inventory, and can't find that a single one is missing. It struck me for a moment that there was some connection between last night's incident and my articles

a couple of days ago on the trading scandals in Bengal,
but the papers have not been tampered with. . . . It's a
mystery!"

"Still, you must have some idea. Weren't you able
to catch a glimpse of those fellows?"

"Yes, for a second, but you can bet they didn't take
long to switch off the light."

"What did they look like, your thieves?"

"Like thieves. Far too much like thieves. Their faces
were hideous, too hideous. Their clothes were too dirty;
their caps too awful."

"How did they get away?"

"Over the balcony. The flat at this side is empty.
They forced their way in by the back staircase. Here
they sawed through a shutter and broke a pane of glass
—it was quite easy!"

"Haven't you informed the police?"

"No."

"But, Rouletabille, don't you suspect anybody?"

"Yes."

"Whom?"

"The police. It is possible that they were hunting
for something that they will never find here. I shall
soon know what to think about it."

Jean took time to reflect, his face overcast.

"Rouletabille, I say again: Be on your guard against
the Octopus."

"Didn't you mention that she was connected with the
police?" asked the journalist chaffingly.

"So I've been told."

"Well, I shall get to know from her whether the police
did the deed," he returned, lighting his pipe.

Jean stood up.

"Look here, I can see that there's nothing more to be
said to you. . . . Good-by." And he added somewhat
craftily, "I won't worry you any more."

Rouletabille did not at once answer but picked up his hat and stick.

"I'll come with you for I see that you shrink from speaking of Odette under the roof which shelters Madame de Meyrens," he said.

"How do you know that I wanted to talk to you about Odette?"

Rouletabille shrugged his shoulders and drew him to the staircase.

"You've had news from Camargue . . . bad news. Hubert de Lauriac never leaves Odette. He is becoming more persistent, almost threatening."

"How did you get to know all this? Who told you?" asked Jean, taken aback.

"You! The whole thing is written there." And Rouletabille tapped him on the forehead.

"What is your opinion of de Lauriac?"

"I think he is capable of anything, but I confess that it is not he who worries me as far as you are concerned. Have you spoken to Callista?"

"No, I came to ask you to speak to her."

"I like that," exclaimed Rouletabille, who seemed to conceal under a bantering mood the annoyance which de Santierne's request caused him. "I like that. I was nearly strangled last night, and to-night I am to have my eyes torn out!"

CHAPTER II

CALLISTA

"I REALLY do not know how to tell Callista about my marriage to Odette." Rouletabille repeated to himself his friend Jean's words while Jean, seated at the piano in the boudoir, played Beethoven, and Callista whose legs were bare under flying black draperies bedecked with leaves of gold, was dancing.

It was a strange scene, shrouded in partial darkness. Jean himself was in the shadow. He was heard but not seen. The jingling of Callista's bangles could likewise be heard when her movements became accentuated. The three spectators, Rouletabille, the bear's cub and the parrot, were as silent as their images reflected on the wall.

Of course Callista was dark, but nothing could be seen of her save her dazzling legs, which flashed on the carpet like running fire. Suddenly the movement of her limbs under her frills was stilled, she sank to the floor, and from her waving hair, which flew loose over her shoulders, a lovely face wearing an expression of fierce sorrow could be seen.

"She has never danced so tragically," thought Rouletabille. "One might almost think that she foresees the calamity. We have a difficult time ahead of us."

Rouletabille's mind harked back to the day when he first saw her dance. That was two years before. It was in Carmargue, near Les Saintes Maries where he and his friend Jean had gone to shoot wild-fowl.

Callista came out dancing from a gypsy's caravan, which was stranded between two clumps of evergreens, and they were arrested by the delight of this biblical scene in the open air.

Their presence was observed and the dance came to a stop. They were driven away by the gypsies' unspoken hostility. And then the following day, as they were lunching with others—a merry crew who knew how to enjoy life it must be said—in a small rustic inn in the neighborhood, within a stone's throw of a river, they beheld in the midst of their modern diversions—some one playing a shimmy on the piano—the apparition of a faun giving chase to a naiad.

They recognized in the half-nude young girl the gypsy whom they had seen the day before, and the faun was the man with the guitar. He was in a terrible passion, and had snatched up the poor child who struggled as she shrieked and bit him. And he was about to carry her off when Jean and Rouletabîlle and their friends made a rush at him. The gypsy was forced to yield to superior numbers. He slowly made off, turning his head from time to time towards the girl who continued to load him with her imprecations.

Panting for breath she placed herself under Jean's protection:

"My name is Callista. That man is Andréa. He is a Spanish gypsy but does not belong to my tribe. My father is dead, and he wants to take me away with him. He is nothing to me."

An hour later, to avoid fresh complications, Jean drove off in his car with Callista amid the acclamations of his friends. And that was how Callista and Jean became lovers and why Callista still loved him.

She adapted herself to her new life with the zeal of a convert to whom the joys of a new religion of unsuspected charm is revealed. Though she remained at heart a gypsy, she quickly transformed herself into an odd sort of Parisienne, dressing elegantly and in ultra-fashionable style. It really seemed as if she were bent on forgetting her antecedents. For Jean alone, and for Rouletabille who was reckoned as of no account, she sometimes danced her Spanish gypsy dances, and, as we have seen, Jean set them to Beethoven's music. . . .

Callista was now laughing, but her laughter sent a shudder through Rouletabille. The parrot and the bear cub also began to laugh.

Jean closed the piano and endeavored to explain to Callista that it was essential for him to leave her early that evening:

"Rouletabille will keep you company."

She did not answer. She offered him her forehead as cold as marble, and he made his escape stammering his excuses. Rouletabille would have given a great deal to go with him.

Callista sat down on the divan.

It was she, however, who spoke first:

"He wants to leave me does he not?"

Rouletabille coughed again.

"Rouletabille, repeat what I say to Jean. Girls of my race who wear a bangle on the arm—a bangle which bears this sign—are true daughters of Romany. They cherish constancy in love and never forget a wrong. And now go quickly. . . . Go, I tell you. Go to your friend!"

There were three to drive him out, for the bear's cub and the parrot united their forces with Callista's and the parrot was not the least formidable of the three.

CHAPTER III

OLAJAÏ

AFTER turning over the pages of a railway guide which lay on his desk, Rouletabille walked up to one of the large road maps of Europe which hung on the wall, between the bookcases, and spread their variegated puzzles before him.

With a deliberate movement he ran his finger, which pointed to "Avignon," along the line of a road on the map and then turned to the telephone:

"Has Monsieur Jean de Santierne returned yet?"

"No."

"I've been waiting an hour for him. I want to see him very particularly. If he doesn't come back within twenty minutes from now I will telephone you my final instructions." He hung up the receiver without giving the least sign of trepidation.

He wore the check suit and cap by which he was so well known; and a portmanteau carefully covered with gray canvas proclaimed that he was about to start on a journey. He took a revolver from a drawer, placed it in his pocket, sat down, and closed his eyes.

For those who know their Rouletabille—his usual animation, his natural high spirits, which often concealed the gravest anxieties, his constant longing to be on the move, to be up and doing—his aspect at that moment spoke volumes.

Rouletabille never worked so hard as when to all seeming he was doing nothing. Nature is never more still than when she is preparing to launch her thunderbolts. What

20

new adventure was Rouletabille meditating? Obviously
he foresaw some considerable task which would need all
his reserves of self-possession. What momentous events
was he dimly glimpsing behind the veil of his closed
eyelids?

Suddenly he opened his eyes. He sprang from his
chair. He recognized Jean's tread. The latter darted
forward uttering cries of delight:

"To-night I am burying my life as a bachelor. I
invite you to be present. You know that I settled everything wonderfully well with Callista. Upon my word,
I don't know what's the matter with you, you take
things so seriously. It's Madame de Meyrens who makes
you see the dark side. Since you have associated with
that woman you have completely changed. . . . But to
return to Callista, old man. She behaved first-rate. I,
too, was first-rate: 'You know how much I loved you.
I shall never forget you. But life is life. . . . I've got
to marry and settle down.' In short a little coaxing talk
and a decent settlement."

"Did she accept your money?"

"I left it on the mantelpiece. I hope it will be some
consolation to her."

"Perhaps the money is still on the mantelpiece."

"Well, old man, I shan't go back to have a look. I
might meet her again, and I don't want to think of anyone but Odette—Mademoiselle Odette de Lavardens who
will soon be Madame Jean de Santierne."

"You run no risk of meeting Callista at her flat,"
returned Rouletabille frigidly. "She is not there now."

"Where is she?"

"At Lavardens."

Jean gave a start.

"What's that!"

"If she's not at Lavardens she's no great distance
from it. She started for Les Saintes Maries."

"Callista at Les Saintes Maries! Are you sure of that?"

"I rang up her maid and she told me so."

"When was that?"

"About twenty minutes ago."

"And you tell me that with a calmness—a calmness that terrifies me."

Jean now observed the portmanteau and the check suit.

"Are you going away? Do you intend to leave me at a moment like this?"

"Really I must. I'm going to leave you to bury your life as a bachelor."

"Oh, stow that. Will you tell me where you are going?"

"I have no secrets from you. I'm off to Lavardens."

"Rouletabille!"

Jean flung himself into his friend's arms and embraced him, but Rouletabille quickly released himself.

"Don't let's give way to emotion. Do what we will, we shall be twenty-four hours behind her. May we arrive in time!"

"Let's hope so," muttered Jean. "We must strain every nerve to avoid a scene."

"Scene!" echoed Rouletabille with a disquieting smile. "Ah, my dear fellow, you should have heard her throw in my face those words: 'Go, repeat what I say to Jean. Girls of my race who wear a bangle which bears this mark . . .'"

"Yes, you are right. We have everything to fear. I'm going crazy."

"This is not the moment, if you want to save Odette."

"Save Odette? Is it as bad as that?"

"First of all we must not miss the two-ten train. We shall be at Avignon to-night at two-fifty-one. Here we shall have to take a car, and we shall reach Lavardens

as light begins to dawn. And now go and pack your
bag. Meet me at the station. I have still an hour to
spare. I can manage in that time to call at police headquarters."

"Why are you going to police headquarters? About
that burglary business of the other night?"

"Perhaps. By the way, I am without a servant now."

"Have you sacked him? Quite right. His face always
filled me with distrust."

"I didn't sack him. When I got home last night I
found the keys of the flat with the concierge and a letter
lay on my table."

"A letter?"

"Read it."

"Well, he writes very fair French your man of the
wilds:

"MONSIEUR,—I offer you my apologies for leaving your service so abruptly. It may be that I shall
never see you again, but I shall aways remember the
many kindnesses that I have received at your hands.
—OLAJAÏ."

"Here's another of those funny names."

"Yes, he signs himself Olajaï," returned Rouletabille
in a strained voice. "And do you know what that word
means in the language of his country? It means a
curse!"

"It's weird," said de Santierne making a movement
towards the staircase.

Rouletabille stopped him by a gesture.

"Yes," he returned, "it is weird, especially as Olajaï
also took the train last night to . . ."

"Where to?"

"Les Saintes Maries."

De Santierne gazed at Rouletabille with eyes wide with
wonder.

"But what does it all mean?" he stammered. "It can't be simply a coincidence. What is at the back of it all?"

"I don't know what's at the back of it all," returned Rouletabille, "but at least it shows us, that we are all being driven there by some necessity, and are struggling in a vortex of mystery in which your affairs and mine are involved. *Olajaï!* . . . This Olajaï is a gypsy from the Balkans, and I don't believe that he went off to Les Saintes Maries merely to offer a prayer at the shrine of Saint Sarah."

The young men parted on these gloomy words.

Three-quarters of an hour later Rouletabille saw Jean come along the platform of the Gare de Lyon looking paler and more anxious than when he had left him. He held a letter in his hand.

"Look, old man. Read it."

The letter was from Odette:

> *"Come as quickly as you can. Come at once. I am afraid on your account. I am afraid for myself. Can it be that you do not love me but another? And then Hubert de Lauriac frightens me. And father also is anxious. Oh, do come at once. I cannot say more."*

"The villain," growled Jean who could scarcely contain himself. "There is no room for doubt. He has told her about Callista."

Rouletabille drew his friend into a carriage and shut the door. They were alone.

"You must tell me everything you know about Hubert de Lauriac," he said.

"You saw him one afternoon in his own surroundings and you know as much about him as I do. You saw a pretty rough customer."

"That's too general a way of putting it," objected Rouletabille.

"It's the man himself," returned Jean.

"Oh, forgive me, but I thought that his character was much more complex than you have made it out to be."

"When it is a question of the means by which he attains his object, perhaps, but I assure you that when you have seen this big fellow on horseback among his drovers, brandishing his fork behind his terrified cattle, you carry away not only an impression of him physically, but you have sounded the depths of his psychology. . . . And then he, too, perhaps is an artist 'in his own line.' "

De Santierne gave expression to a mournful laugh. Rouletabille could not be mistaken. He had before him a jealous man—jealous to the point of tears. And it was as much, indeed, as Jean could do to restrain his tears under cover of his laugh for he was a tender-hearted man was Jean—quite unlike Hubert—and under his apparent dandyism lay a fastidious spirit sensitive to an almost morbid degree.

It was the art of Mozart and Beethoven which had brought about the engagement between Jean and Odette de Lavardens, but de Santierne was fully aware that before he met this exquisite flower of Camargue, Odette, as a child, had been subject to other influences which though they were more rustic were none the less formidable. It was Hubert de Lauriac who had taught Odette to ride.

"You must understand," explained Jean, "that in those days old Lavardens also was attracted by Hubert de Lauriac. But when this country gentleman—I mean de Lauriac—whose only means consisted of his house and his herds of cattle, asked him if he might look forward to receiving the hand of Odette—that was four years before—Lavardens answered: 'Make money first and

we will talk about it again when Odette is old enough.'
Well, Odette is now old enough, and Hubert de Lauriac
has acquired wealth, but Odette and I love each other.
I hoped to challenge him to a duel, but it seems that
persons don't fight duels nowadays. The coward has
preferred to tell Odette about my affair with Callista.
It's infamous."

"The dear little girl! What with de Lauriac and
Callista I pity her," exclaimed Rouletabille.

"Odette is very fond of you," returned Jean pressing
Rouletabille's hand.

"And I have a sincere affection for her because she is
to be your wife."

A short pause ensued. Then Jean continued:

"Look here, when we get there leave de Lauriac to
me while you see Callista."

"It will be better if I take everything on myself,"
objected the journalist. And as Jean made a gesture of
dissent: "Now please do exactly what I tell you. I
assure you that we haven't a moment to lose, and if we
make the least false step we are done for."

"For all that they won't kill her."

"No, but I am afraid that events will move quickly."

Events did indeed move so quickly that we cannot do
better, in order to show their rapid sequence, than set
down in all their brevity a few extracts from Rouletabille's diary which were written during that tragic night.

EXTRACTS FROM ROULETABILLE'S DIARY

"*Lyon, eleven-forty p.m.*—Jean raised the question
of whether it would not be better to alight here and
cover the rest of the way by motor-car . . . gain of
time problematical. . . . I decided to adhere to my first
plan. Jean is growing restless with impatience and worries me.

"*Avignon, two-fifty a.m.*—From Avignon by car.

Jean drove in mad fashion; he will break our necks.
. . . I insisted that he should give place to me at the
wheel.

"*Château de Lavardens, four a.m.*—Roused the
gardener. Everything quiet. Monsieur de Lavardens
and his daughter retired to rest at an early hour. *Four-
ten a.m.*—I am leaving Jean at Lavardens and starting
off in the car along Les Saintes Maries road. *Four-
thirty-five*—A shot in the road. A back tire burst. A
man sprang up before me with a carbine in his hand. I
recognized Olajaï. He was breathless and stared at me
with wild eyes: 'Don't show yourself in Camargue!
Don't leave Lavardens!' he shouted, and plunged into a
clump of tamarisks. While changing the wheel I
thought over Olajaï's warning. It was sound advice.
I returned to Lavardens.

"*Six o'clock.*—A few minutes after reaching the
château I saw a crowd of excited peasants bringing in
the dead body of Monsieur de Lavardens which they
had found at the other end of the park near the bound-
ary gate leading to de Lauriac's land. Monsieur de
Lavardens had received a terrible blow on the temple.
A cursory examination of the body convinced me that
the murderer would never be brought to justice.

"*Seven o'clock.*—Hubert de Lauriac has been arrested.
Meanwhile it was discovered that Mademoiselle de
Lavardens was spirited away during the night. Jean
has completely lost his head. Dear little Odette! I will
save you. . . ."

CHAPTER IV

THE MIDI AND CAMARGUE STIRRED

THE few lines which Rouletabille hurriedly scrawled in his diary merely set forth in blunt language tragic incidents which the police on the one hand, and the newspapers on the other, would soon endeavor to reconstruct down to the smallest detail.

Let us, therefore, follow his movements step by step, after he was driven in such strange fashion from the Camargue road by the phantom-like apparition of Olajaï. Rouletabille drove back to Lavardens. It was not at the exact moment of his return that the discovery of the murder was made, but, as he noted in his diary, some few minutes later.

Jean was waiting for him on the front steps of the Viei-Castou-Nou—the old-new château—as it was called in the district when mention was made of the spacious country house, in the Provençal style of architecture, which the de Lavardens had built at the beginning of the last century.

The house stood on the Arles road, to the north of La Camargue, a country of cool and shady places which after leaving the marshy plains, luminous as a flashing mirror, grows surprisingly like a Normandy landscape with its grassy paths, its fields of wheat, and its tall, leafy trees with their moss-covered trunks.

Rouletabille at once observed that Jean's expression was entirely reassuring. For himself, smarting under the extraordinary incident on the road, he was far from feeling as easy in his mind as his friend. He allowed

28

himself to be taken to a small reception room where Alari, an aged man-servant who had been in the service of the de Lavardens family for thirty years, had laid a table with early morning breakfast.

"We are fools," exclaimed Jean. "Everything is quiet in the house. I have questioned Alari. De Lauriac has behaved in the most extraordinary way, and I understand that Odette was greatly upset."

"All the same," said Alari, after pouring out the coffee, "If I were in your place, Monsieur Jean, I should keep my eyes open. There are days when that fellow is like a highwayman."

The old servant left the room repeating with a tremulous motion of his head, "like a highwayman."

"Another thing," Jean went on when Alari was out of the room, "I know now why Callista came to Les Saintes Maries."

"Speak out, old man, let's have it," returned Rouletabille, whose mind was still occupied with Olajaï.

"Why, it's very simple. You know that under her frivolous Parisian ways Callista still remained a gypsy with all the prejudices and superstitions of her race."

"Too much of a gypsy; much too much, my dear Jean, for our peace of mind."

"You don't follow me."

"You mean that you don't follow me which is not quite the same thing."

"But listen to me, if you don't mind. You like to hear yourself speak, but you never listen to anyone else."

"That's your imagination, Jean. To listen to you I have no need to hear you speak."

"Oh, you talk like a Southerner. Besides, you are chaffing. Our affairs are improving."

"No, they are not improving. But you were saying that Callista . . ."

"Is superstitious," returned Jean, somewhat out of

countenance. "You know her devotion to St. Sarah . . ."

"Well, of course. St. Sarah is the patron saint of these people."

"Yes, but you don't know how far that goes with Callista."

"What then?"

"Then, you know, on the twenty-fourth of May every year gypsies make a pilgrimage, in honor of St. Sarah of Les Saintes Maries, to the crypt of the church, which was built on the very spot where, according to tradition, Mary of Bethany, Mary the Mother of James, and Mary Magdalene landed with Lazarus, and Sarah their servant."

"Anything else?"

"I'm getting on your nerves."

"No, you are merely wasting my time with your history lesson. I know all about that as well as you do. What is it that you really want to say?"

"This: Alari tells me that never before at such a celebration has Camargue been so overrun with gypsies of all kinds. They are here from every part—North, South, Italy, Spain, and even farther afield. Rumor in the district states that the twenty-fourth of May this year fits in with a prophecy from which the whole race expects great things. That being granted, it follows that to an enthusiast for St. Sarah like Callista . . ."

But Rouletabille was no longer listening. He had pushed his cup aside, and wrapped in thought walked over to the window filling his pipe.

"Alari tells me that such a sight has not been witnessed since the Queen of the Sabbath was crowned . . ."

Without turning round Rouletabille said in the faraway voice that he assumed at times as though he were speaking from another room, a room in which he alone was entitled to enter, and to which he seemed to have retired taking with him his imprisoned thoughts:

"A few weeks ago I wrote an article about the trial of certain Romanys. These were a body of 'your money or your life' thieves. I dealt in this article with the curious destiny of this race, and ended by stating that the People of the Road had not in fact lost faith in their future."

"Where did the article appear? How is it that I didn't see it?"

"It appeared in the *Revue de la Langue d'Oc* and was written in the Provençal dialect. I came to the conclusion that the subject was an opportune one," Rouletabille replied in his far-away voice, the voice that seemed to come from another room.

Suddenly he turned round and went back to Jean.

"I also said in that article that St. Sarah had given her people the promise in so many words it seems—don't smile—that in the near future their one-time prosperity should return to them."

"Well, old man, it was to perform her devotions at the shrine of St. Sarah that Callista came to Camargue."

"My servant also came to Camargue to perform his devotions. By the way, I came up against him."

"Olajaï?"

"Yes, Olajaï. He burst one of the tires of my car with a carbine shot. He wanted the opportunity to advise me to return here immediately and not to leave Lavardens."

"What does that mean?" exclaimed Jean, rising from the table.

Rouletabille shrugged his shoulders.

"Well, what could it mean unless it meant that danger hangs over Lavardens?"

"Danger of what? Lavardens has nothing to do with gypsies."

"No, but possibly Callista has something to do with Lavardens, and Olajaï knows it."

"So Callista has a secret understandnig with Olajaï?"

"I don't think Olajaï is inspired by any ill will towards me; and yet in certain respects his behavior is unintelligible and gives me cause for anxiety. I saved his life in the Balkans. . . . But if there is no understanding between them there may be something worse."

"And you, you frighten me," exclaimed Jean. "Let's get out of the place. Let's go quickly and leave these gypsies and Callista and Olajaï and that ruffian de Lauriac far behind."

"Well, go then, and the sooner the better," said Rouletabille.

"What about you?"

"I shall stay."

CHAPTER V

LOU CABANOU

JEAN stared at Rouletabille in surprise.

"Might I ask what will keep you here when I am away?"

Rouletabille was obviously in no hurry to answer for he at once asked Alari who had come into the room:

"What is happening at Les Saintes Maries?"

"God knows, m'sieur. But it's not for nothing that people call their mass the devil's mass."

"Gypsies are good Catholics, you know."

"*Quésaco.* What then? That does not do away with the fact that they say mass in the crypt the wrong way."

"How do you mean?"

"Well, their priest faces instead of turning his back to them, and, besides, the altar is turned round. But that's a trifle, I assure you. It's what takes place afterwards. Ah, it wouldn't do for an ordinary man to fall into their hands at such a time."

"Would they eat him?"

"No, but they don't look upon it as a proper festival in that crypt unless blood is shed."

"Who told you so?"

"Everyone in Camargue knows it."

Jean shrugged his shoulders.

"Why, monsieur," went on Alari, "I came up against one of those infernal people yesterday and asked: 'Where are you going with that big knife?' He looked at me out of the corner of his eyes and answered: 'To cut their heads off. I'm the executioner.'"

33

"Meanwhile what was he cutting?"

"Osiers for making baskets."

"You see, my good man, you are a bit simple-minded."

Just then the sound of voices was heard in the entrance hall, and Alari went out to see what was happening. He returned with a look of bewilderment, holding in his hand a light blue silk wrap which he showed to them.

"Old Tavan found Mademoiselle's wrap in Monsieur de Lauriac's garden," he said.

Jean became deadly pale. Rouletabille rushed out of the room. In the hall he ran into Estève, the lady's maid. She was a native of Arles, and had not long been in service at the Viei-Castou-Nou, and he asked her in a harsh voice if Mademoiselle Odette was in her room.

"I should think she was in her room! I've come down to fetch her breakfast," answered the girl, somewhat taken aback by Rouletabille's manner.

"Did Mademoiselle Odette go to Monsieur de Lauriac yesterday?" he asked.

Estève who was growing more and more offended by this brusque examination flushed, and burst out:

"How should I know whether mademoiselle went to see Monsieur de Lauriac? It's too bad. Am I here to keep watch over mademoiselle? Let me pass. *Quésaco.*"

Jean came into the hall with Alari at his heels and said to Estève:

"Take this wrap, which this man found in Monsieur de Lauriac's garden, to your mistress."

"In his garden!" echoed the maid obviously disconcerted.

"Yes, in his garden," interjected old Tavan, a day laborer who occasionally worked at odd jobs for the de Lavardens, but more often still for Hubert de Lauriac.

"Were you working for Monsieur de Lauriac this morning?" inquired Rouletabille.

"Yes, I went there to start work and saw the wrap

on the ground in the pathway," he returned. "I recognized it at once. The young lady was wearing it over her shoulders yesterday. I went and knocked at Monsieur de Lauriac's door, but no one answered me. So I brought the wrap here."

"Now, Tavan, where was mademoiselle yesterday, when you saw her wearing that wrap? Not at Monsieur de Lauriac's, I suppose?" questioned Alari.

"No; she was out for a walk with her father about five o'clock."

"In that case," interposed Rouletabille, "she must have lost the wrap during her walk. Monsieur de Lauriac must have seen and picked it up, and dropped it in his turn on his way home."

"Unless Monsieur de Lauriac met monsieur and mademoiselle on their walk and purloined the wrap by way of a joke," said Alari.

"A queer sort of joke," snapped out Jean. "Still Monsieur de Lauriac will tell us all about that. Thanks, Tavan, and God bless you."

Meantime Rouletabille had not lost a shade of the play of facial expression round him. Estève had disappeared to the kitchen. Tavan had the features of one of those shrewd old peasants who seek to hide their real cunning by affecting a look of innocence.

"I'll go off with Tavan," said Rouletabille. "He will point out the place where he found the wrap."

Jean, whose mind was greatly perturbed, went after them and Alari brought up the rear.

They went along the road to the gate leading to de Lauriac's small estate. De Lauriac's house, which was not very imposing, stood on the edge of the de Lavardens' park. Alari always referred to it in contemptuous words as *lou cabanou*, "the shanty," though Hubert had spared no expense to impart a modern appearance to it and to furnish it in some style.

They made their way into the yard and Tavan pointed out the spot where he found the wrap. Rouletabille was by this time on all fours, and soon left the path to follow up a trail, newly marked in the soft garden soil, which led to the rear of the house.

Alari, who watched Rouletabille's movements with a look of admiration, murmured between his teeth an old witticism:

"One of these days when it is night people will wear a tail with an eye in it which will whirl about in a thousand ways and be able to see at ten paces the veins of a flea."

The wall which ran along de Lauriac's yard was somewhat low at this point. Suddenly Rouletabille cleared it in a couple of leaps and dropped into a sunken road ending in a blind alley. The others made a movement to follow him, but he appeared again almost immediately with a thoughtful look on his face and one word on his lips:

"Car!"

"What is it?" asked Jean.

"Stand aside," said Rouletabille to Alari and Tavan. "I want to talk to Monsieur de Santierne."

"Well?" inquired Jean when the others had moved away a few steps.

"Odette did come here."

"Odette came to de Lauriac's place?"

"Yes."

"By herself?"

"Certainly, by herself. But what disturbs me, you know, is not that she came here, but that I can't see how she left the place."

"That's your fancy. Where can you see traces of Odette's footsteps? Show them to me. I should like to see them."

Rouletabille took him to the place where Tavan

alleged that he had found the wrap. Here, in fact, the imprint of a small pointed shoe could be discerned; an imprint which was suddenly lost. This imprint turned towards de Lauriac's house—after that nothing.

"Nothing," echoed Rouletabille sinking his voice. "Those footprints show that she came here but did not return. And they are joined there by a man's footprints, and this man's footprints lead to the wall. And do you know what was behind the wall? A motor-car. If Odette is not in her room we may assume the worst."

"The worst that we may assume," gasped Jean who was suffering tortures, "is that Odette came here alone. All else is of no consequence. No one carried her away. No one tried to carry her away, otherwise she would have told us about it, don't you think. Besides, you know her."

"Yes, I know her," returned Rouletabille gravely.

"And yet you can imagine Odette coming at night time to de Lauriac's house? Why, you must have sworn to drive me out of my mind."

"Pull yourself together. Odette is an angel and you are a poet. Let me get on with my business of examining the marks which were made by persons in moving over the ground."

CHAPTER VI

A PIECE OF ORANGE-COLORED MATERIAL

"WHAT does it all prove?" growled Jean. "Why shouldn't there be a woman's footprints in the garden? How can we tell who came here to see de Lauriac? And why are you so keen on showing that these marks were made by Odette's shoes?"

"For three reasons," returned Rouletabille, wiping his forehead. "First, because I saw them near where the wrap was found; secondly, because they are the exact size of Odette's shoes; and lastly, because they came from over there."

And Rouletabille pointed to a small door in a rather low wall, which divided de Lauriac's domain from the old château.

"The partition door," exclaimed Jean with a laugh. "I believe the partition door has been permanently closed for ever so long."

"Well, see for yourself," returned Rouletabille, and he had but to give it a push for the door to open.

"Oh, I am stifling," cried Jean.

He turned and walked a few steps towards de Lauriac's house, his whole body expressing menace, but Rouletabille stood in his path. He pointed to Tavan, who was standing not far away slyly taking in what was being said.

"Restrain yourself, I entreat you."

"I will kill this man de Lauriac," Jean muttered, grinding his teeth and shaking with passion.

Rouletabille shrugged his shoulders and beckoned Alari

to come to him. He had but to point to the door for the old servant to grasp the position.

"I can say for certain that last night the door was still locked and bolted. You can see that lock and bolts are covered with rust. The door hasn't been unlocked and unbolted for years. As a matter of fact, not since the death of Monsieur de Lauriac's father."

"Where was the key kept?"

"Indeed, monsieur, I couldn't tell you. You should ask monsieur or mademoiselle."

"Very good, Alari. You can go back to the château, and I know you well enough to feel that you'll hold your tongue about all this."

"Certainly, monsieur, but what about old Tavan?"

"Leave old Tavan to me."

He hurried Alari into the park and went into it himself with Jean. From that side he could see the key in the lock. He made sure also that a very considerable effort must have been required to push back the bolts. Jean, who was staggered by the thought of Odette visiting de Lauriac of her own free will the night before, watched him speechless and dazed as he tried the fastenings.

Suddenly ominous cries rang out, in which Alari's voice rose above the others.

Rouletabille and Jean darted forward and, turning the angle formed by a dense wood, discovered a number of persons standing round Alari, who was on his knees.

On pushing aside the panic-stricken group, the young men found themselves in the presence of a dead body, the face of which was covered with blood. Jean uttered a great shout:

"Monsieur de Lavardens murdered!"

Alari was shedding tears. Old Tavan, who also had come hurrying up, declared that the "poor man" was already cold.

Rouletabille waved him away, forbidding him to touch the body. He at once noticed a ghastly wound in the temple. At the same time he noted on the victim the marks of a struggle which had obviously been desperate. Monsieur de Lavardens' clothes were in disorder, the neck of his shirt was torn, and in his clenched hand he held a piece of orange-colored material.

"Why, that's from Monsieur de Lauriac's tie," exclaimed Alari.

"Yes it is. Yes it is. It's from Monsieur de Lauriac's tie," the others standing round cried in unison.

"Are you positive?" demanded Jean in a hoarse voice.

"I should think I was positive," declared Alari, rising to his feet. "And old Tavan, too, is positive about it. Why don't you say something, Tavan?"

"Because this is beginning to be a matter which is no business of mine."

"What is your business then?" inquired Rouletabille sharply.

"To look after my garden," returned Tavan. "I should certainly have done better if I had stayed in my garden this morning."

"That wouldn't have prevented your master from being murdered," exclaimed Jean.

Jean rushed into de Lauriac's estate, the others following him.

Rouletabille, however, did not go with the crowd. After briefly examining the appearance of things near the body, he hurried off in the opposite direction.

He encountered Estève, the lady's maid, in the hall as she was coming up from the kitchen.

When Estève beheld the journalist again she could not repress a start of uneasiness.

"What fresh news is there, monsieur, that you look so upset?"

"Go upstairs. I'll come with you."

She shrugged her shoulders with annoyance and mounted the stairs.

"Be good enough to tell your mistress that I must speak to her at once."

She tried to make some protest, but Rouletabille gave her a look which silenced her. Then she knocked at the door of the room and entered. She came out again almost directly, white-faced, seeking to control her too obvious emotion and speak in a firm voice:

"Mademoiselle will see you presently. She cannot see you just now."

Rouletabille pushed her out of the way, opened the door without waiting for permission and entered Odette's room.

The room was empty. . . . The bed had not been slept in.

He turned sharply to Estève, who tried to make off, but, seizing her by the wrist and closing the door, he said:

"Now to business."

CHAPTER VII

ESTÈVE

"WHAT have I done? What have I done?" cried Estève, in a state of extreme terror.

"I swear that you shall tell me," Rouletabille rapped out in her face. "To begin with, you knew that your mistress was not in her room. Don't lie. You deceived us."

"I swear to heaven I thought she was in her room. Lord preserve me! . . . I swear to heaven."

She lifted her wide-open eyes to him appealingly. Rouletabille looked into their depths and then let her go as though he were relenting.

"Why were you so put out a little while ago?"

"How do I know?" she returned. "Your eyes frightened me."

"You're not speaking the truth, Estève. You know something that you choose not to tell me, but listen to me—your mistress was kidnaped last night. I have sent for the examining magistrate, and you will be arrested as an accomplice."

"Kidnaped! Kidnaped!" cried the poor girl, and she sank weeping to the foot of Mademoiselle de Lavardens' bed. . . . "Oh, why did you run away?"

"Estève, I believe you to be a good girl," went on Rouletabille, "and you may have been guilty of an act of carelessness which will be forgiven if you honestly speak out. Did you not enter into conversation yesterday with certain persons whom we do not as a rule see at Viei-Castou-Nou or hereabouts?"

"No, monsieur. No, monsieur. Not a soul. . . . But stay . . . yesterday morning the garden gate was open. I was tidying the room when I noticed opposite the gate a rough-looking fellow. As it happened mademoiselle passed in front of the gate, and I heard the good-for-nothing have the cheek to call out to her."

"What did mademoiselle do?"

"She went out and talked to him very nicely for some time, believe me. She is always too good to those vagabonds, especially when they are like this one, who looked a real brigand and stared at her with his wicked eyes."

"Did mademoiselle say anything to you about it when she came in?"

"No, but I asked her. I was curious to know what this man wanted. 'He is a dog-clipper,' she told me. 'He asked me if I had any dogs to be clipped.' That was all. Then I went back to the window, but the man was gone. No matter, I didn't like the look of him. That's the man, certainly, who did the deed. . . . Oh, poor mademoiselle!" moaned Estève. "She was so trusting, so kind to everybody."

Just then Jean came along like a whirlwind. They heard him rushing up the stairs shouting:

"Odette! Odette!"

Rouletabille bundled Estève into a small dressing-room and turned the key, exclaiming:

"You are my prisoner. I haven't done with you by a long way."

Then he opened the door to Jean and had but to point to the bed which had not been slept in.

"Oh, the villain!" Jean bellowed.

"Whom do you mean?" asked Rouletabille frigidly.

"You ask me that!" exclaimed Jean. "Why, I mean the man who murdered de Lavardens and kidnaped Odette. Oh, Rouletabille, Rouletabille, you know that

Odette has been carried off and you are not yet on her tracks!"

"Who told you that I am not on her tracks?" returned the journalist, losing patience. "Who says that I am not going after her more quickly by remaining in this room than if I were flying over the ground in a motor-car. My poor fellow," he added, going up to him. "You are running after de Lauriac. Every step you take is leading you away from Odette."

"You defend de Lauriac now," gasped Jean. "Well, here, read this. This is what I found in a room at his place, which was turned upside down last night by this dreadful business. Read it. Read it, I tell you."

Rouletabille read the letter, which was all crumpled:

"Mademoiselle,—The treatment that I have received at your house in defiance of your pledged word, and the attitude which, alas! your father and you have adopted towards me, have roused my indignation. I must see you. I shall expect you to-night at 10 o'clock in the garden, near the partition gate. If you fail to come, I will not be answerable for the consequences.

"Your sorrowful
"Hubert de Lauriac."

"Do you understand now," cried Jean excitedly. "I assure you that there is no necessity to go down on your hands and knees to grasp the meaning of this letter. . . . Odette received a letter and tried to prevent some rash action on de Lauriac's part. She went to the garden. The villain compelled her to go to his house. The poor dear cried out. Her father heard her, took down a dog-whip which I have here"—and Jean thrust in the journalist's face the dog-whip which he had likewise picked up at de Lauriac's—"and made a rush at the scoundrel. . . . There was a terrible scene. . . . He tried to bring his daughter home. The struggle was continued in the garden and park, and de Lauriac did not shrink from murder in order to carry off Odette. . . . And now heaven only knows where she is or what steps we must take to rescue her. . . ."

Rouletabille bit his lip until the blood came. He knew that Jean was, as a rule, as gentle as a young girl, but as impulsive and headstrong as an artist or a poet. Rouletabille took his two burning hands in his:

"Don't let us waste our time in talking at random. You must understand that it was not Odette who was the first to go to de Lauriac's place, but Monsieur de Lavardens. And the letter which I have just read proves it, and corroborates all that up to now I have been able to picture of the tragedy."

"You forget that the letter was not addressed to Monsieur de Lavardens, but to Odette."

"You compel me to say that I know Odette better than you do," returned Rouletabille with a sad smile. "I am positive—mark you, I am positive—that when Odette received that letter she took it to her father. Do you follow now why Monsieur de Lavardens was the first to go to de Lauriac's house, and why Odette, in her alarm at his failure to return, went after him?"

"What do I care about all that?" said Jean distractedly. "The fact remains that de Lauriac murdered him. Oh, I want to get at him, I tell you."

Rouletabille endeavored to hold him back.

"Jean, it was not de Lauriac who committed the murder."

"Rouletabille, you are no longer a friend of mine," retorted Jean, as he wrenched himself free and ran like a madman to meet the examining magistrate, who had now arrived.

CHAPTER VIII

IN WHICH THE FATAL SIGN AGAIN APPEARS

ROULETABILLE went to the dressing-room and took Estève back to Odette's room.

"Mademoiselle de Lavardens received a letter from Monsieur de Lauriac yesterday," he began, "and you brought it to her."

"I swear I gave no letter to Mademoiselle Odette."

"I did not say that you gave her the letter. I said that you brought it."

"I didn't bring anything. I didn't bring anything," she cried, wringing her hands, a prey to despair which was not simulated, but the result, perhaps, of remorse for her falsehood. Rouletabille interpreted her attitude rightly. He determined to play a bold stroke, and pointing through the window to the officials who were beginning their investigations:

"See!" he said. "There are the magistrates who are here to arrest Monsieur de Lauriac on the charge of kidnaping Mademoiselle Odette and murdering Monsieur de Lavardens.

Estève drew herself up, electrified. "Monsier de Lavardens murdered!" She swayed and would have fallen but that Rouletabille held her.

"Yes, murdered, and woe betide the man or woman who does not speak the whole truth!"

"Well, I will tell you . . . I will tell you," the hapless woman cried in a choking voice. "I was wrong to take money from Monsieur de Lauriac. If I had only known! Lord, if I had only known!"

46

"Why did he give you money?"

"To tell him what Mademoiselle Odette was doing and whether she was receiving any letters from Monsieur Jean, and even from you—in short, everything. I oughtn't to have done it. Heavens, if I had known! In the end I was obliged to do as I was told. . . . I was passing yesterday along the footpath when he jumped over his wall and gave me a letter for Mademoiselle Odette. And he gave me more money. So I did as he wished, and placed the letter there, on the chest of drawers."

The poor girl stopped for a moment, choked with sobbing.

"Come, come, now," urged Rouletabille. "What took place after that?"

"After that I wondered what would happen when Mademoiselle Odette found the letter. . . . Well, she saw it that evening when she went to her room. I kept an eye on her from the head of the stairs. She at once went to her father's room."

"Of course," muttered Rouletabille.

"I expected them to ring for me. I was dead frightened. But mademoiselle returned to her room a few minutes later and I heard nothing more. So I went to bed, but I couldn't sleep the whole night."

"What time was that?"

"About half-past nine."

"As you couldn't sleep, didn't you hear anything unusual?"

"Yes," confessed Estève, with a shudder. "I heard a cry and seemed to recognize mademoiselle's voice."

"What then?"

"And then I buried my head in my pillow. Later I said to myself that I must have been dreaming. I couldn't really believe that mademoiselle would leave her room. For all that, the reason of my being so upset this morning was that it was getting late and she hadn't rung for her breakfast. So I went downstairs to look for her, for I was inwardly quite scared, because of the cry in the night. . . . Oh, when I saw the wrap my blood ran cold, and I went down to the kitchen. . . . Then my knees gave way beneath me, and I hadn't sufficient strength to go up again. . . . Oh, when I saw that her room was empty! I don't know how I had the courage to come out and lie to you. But I had to do it, hadn't I?"

"Monsieur de Lavardens died a violent death as a result of this letter, not to mention that Mademoiselle Odette is probably also dead," declared Rouletabille.

"Heavens, you'll drive me crazy."

"The chief culprit in these two crimes is you."

Estève gazed at him haggard-eyed and asked in a breath:

"Shall I be sent to prison?"

"Not if you tell the truth when I question you."

"But what about the magistrates?" sobbed the poor woman. "What must I say to them?"

"Oh, you needn't tell the magistrates anything, for, as you may suppose, they would put you in prison at once—you may be quite certain of that. But you must tell me . . . me who won't have you put in prison if you speak the truth . . ." And he bent over her and fixed her with a piercing look: "You must tell me where this thing came from."

As he spoke he flashed before her eyes a curious ornament which he had taken from the partly-open drawer of a work table. His attention, always on the alert, had been attracted by the fantastic beauty of an oriental frontlet which exhibited the mysterious sign of the Romanys —the cross and crescent shaped like a dagger.

"Yes, where did it come from?" he repeated, brandishing the chain which, since it was found in Odette's room, so fully corroborated his suspicions and confirmed his investigations that he could now surely say to himself: "I see the hand of Callista in this!"

"That was a present to Mademoiselle Odette."

"From whom?"

"Monsieur de Lauriac."

Rouletabille gave a start. He was unable to conceal his dismay.

Under the same date the following entry appears in Rouletabille's diary:

"Estève was speaking the truth. She cannot lie to me. But her answer involving de Lauriac dashes to the ground the entire superstructure which I had built up. I am quite at a loss . . . unless . . . unless. . . . But then, whither are we tending? Beware of the Octopus!"

CHAPTER IX

HUBERT DE LAURIAC

A LUCKY chance had willed that certain magistrates, who were proceeding to Les Saintes Maries to hold an inquiry, should be in the neighborhood of the Viei-Castou-Nou when the murder was discovered.

When Rouletabille went down again into the garden he found himself in the presence of men whose minds were made up. To use the language of the country, "the service was over." Young de Santierne had strengthened the conviction of each one of them when he informed them of Odette's abduction. The examining magistrate who had conducted a brief investigation and taken the depositions of the first witnesses, was holding Mademoiselle de Lavardens' wrap in his hand.

"We find, therefore," he declared, "that neither Monsieur Hubert de Lauriac nor Mademoiselle Odette de Lavardens slept in their rooms last night. This wrap was picked up in Monsieur de Lauriac's garden and establishes the fact that Mademoiselle Odette and he met. Everything goes to prove that Monsieur de Lauriac was guilty of abducting Mademoiselle Odette, just as everything goes to prove that he murdered Monsieur de Lavardens. All that remains to be done is to take steps to effect Monsieur de Lauriac's arrest. What do you say, Monsieur Rouletabille?" ended the magistrate.

"Monsieur Rouletabille says," returned the journalist, "that you may possibly arrest Monsieur Hubert de Lauriac, but that you will never arrest the murderer."

50

"What? We shall never arrest the murderer!"

"No, you will never arrest him because you will never discover him."

"According to you, therefore, Monsieur de Lauriac is not the man?"

"You assert that everything goes to prove it, while I say that nothing goes to prove it. The scrap of his tie found in the victim's clenched hand no more proves him to be the murderer than the wrap in the garden proves him to have abducted Mademoiselle Odette."

"Rouletabille is crazy," cried Jean. "But, look here, why do you defend this scoundrel whom everybody else accuses?"

"Precisely because everything seems to incriminate him."

"You will never allow yourself to agree with other people," retorted Jean. "That method has sometimes stood you in good stead, but to-day your pride will have a fall, and you are making yourself the defender of a murderer."

"And you, Jean, are blinded by love and jealousy."

"But, after all, let's have this out," burst forth the examining magistrate. "Monsieur de Santierne is right. Explain yourself."

"You must ask the man himself for an explanation," returned the journalist. "Why, there he is! Come on, boys, come on!"

And he started to rush toward the partition gate. The others quickly followed him into de Lauriac's garden. They arrived to see Rouletabille come up to de Lauriac at the moment when the latter, looking like a thief, his clothes in disorder, without tie or collar, was stealthily entering his house. He had leaped the wall at the spot which Rouletabille a few minutes before had cleared, as he followed up the trail leading to the sunken road behind the house.

Jean was the first to arrive and he heard Rouletabille say to de Lauriac in a muffled voice:

"Monsieur de Lavardens has been murdered. There's only one thing that can save you, and that is to tell the whole truth."

At the same time Rouletabille was the first to lay hands on him. Jean sprang forward next and, in spite of Rouletabille, seized de Lauriac by the throat. The gendarmes had much ado to separate the two.

"You villain, where is Odette?" he shouted in his face. "What have you done with Odette?"

The magistrates ordered every one to stand back and prepared to open a preliminary examination. Rouletabille strove once more to calm Jean who, after his first contact with the enemy, was shedding bitter tears.

"Why did you have him arrested? If you think he is innocent why did you arrest him yourself?" he cried.

"So that he might clear himself," returned Rouletabille.

The examining magistrate had by this time come to grips with de Lauriac.

"The fact of your return here, monsieur, in this condition, considering you had every reason to fear that Monsieur de Lavardens' body had been discovered, shows that you must have been impelled by very powerful motives. I do not ask what they were. We already know them. They form the evidence of your guilt which, in the aberration of the moment, you left behind, and you came back to look for them. They consist of this whip, which was Monsieur de Lavardens' property, and this letter addressed to Mademoiselle Odette. . . . We also have Mademoiselle Odette's wrap. These things were found at your place with other evidence of your guilt. Confess that you were carried away by a fit of passion."

The prisoner, who wore the hunted look of an animal at bay, stammered:

"Odette kidnaped!"

"You know nothing about it?" asked the examining magistrate. "Perhaps you are equally ignorant of the murder of Monsieur de Lavardens?"

"This gentleman told me," gasped de Lauriac, indicating by a motion of his head Rouletabille.

"So you deny everything?"

"Yes, I do. I deny everything," he cried, foaming with rage.

"Let him be confronted with the body of his victim," ordered the magistrate.

"I entreat you, monsieur, to concern yourself first with Odette," cried Jean. "Where has the villain taken her? That is the most urgent question."

De Lauriac cast a look of deadly hatred at Jean.

"I don't know where she is," he shouted in a hoarse voice, "but wherever she is I'm glad she's not with you. And if I am to be condemned for a crime which I did not commit, may she never be found again!"

The de Lauriacs, men of family who had fallen on evil days, had settled some considerable time before in Camargue, where they maintained themselves by breeding horses and cattle.

Hubert's father had at length acquired a small fortune and retired to the "old shanty," as Alari called it, in Lavardens, near Arles, leaving to his son the management of his "farm".

Thus the de Lauriacs and de Lavardens became on visiting terms. The lord of the manor was a great hunter and angler and had at once taken a liking to young de Lauriac.

Odette, who as a little girl was brought up somewhat unconventionally—Madame de Lavardens died when her daughter was a baby—had also yielded to the influence of this big, rough, country fellow, who taught her how to ride.

Hubert had at once fallen in love with the little girl. "Oh, she is but a child," he would say, "but she is all the more beautiful on that account." She seemed extremely frail and yet no one was more fearless. At one time she was haughty and proud like a young queen, at another free and unconstrained. She was fair as ripe corn, with eyes the color of the sea. The child became a young girl and every year, every day, grew taller and prettier. De Lauriac could hold out no longer, and when his father died he boldly asked Monsieur de Lavardens for Odette's hand.

Monsieur de Lavardens so little expected such a proposal that at first he was at a loss for an answer. He treated the matter lightly while dwelling on Odette's extreme youth. She was then fourteen.

"If you tell me to wait ten years for her I will wait ten years and even longer," de Lauriac rejoined. "The main thing for me is to know that she belongs to me."

"That's plain speaking, my boy, and I will be equally plain with you. I don't believe that you would suit Odette or that she thinks of you in that way."

"Ask her," suggested de Lauriac.

Monsieur de Lavardens left him with a shrug of the shoulders, muttering:

"At the most he would suit her as a servant."

But he lowered his tone after acquainting Odette with the strange story. Without displaying the least concern she made answer.

"I shall have to get married one day and Hubert is the bravest man in Camargue. No herdsman is a match for him in the branding fêtes, and no bull can withstand him."

When Monsieur de Lavardens met de Lauriac again he said:

"You have done nothing to deserve Odette, and you are a poor man."

"Must I become rich?" asked Hubert.

"You won't make a fortune at Camargue," returned Monsieur de Lavardens. "After what has passed between us, you would be better to try your luck elsewhere."

"Suppose I come back a rich man, will you give me Odette?"

"If you come back a rich man and Odette consents, you shall marry her."

"That's all right. I don't ask for anything more. Will you allow me to wish Odette good-by?"

"Yes, my boy."

On the day of de Lauriac's departure Monsieur de Lavardens left them together. Odette shed tears. Hubert asked her to pledge her word to him.

"Father has made me swear by the saints not to pledge you my word. Wait until you return."

De Lauriac left Camargue with a light heart, resolved to get rich quick by any and every means. Odette did not nor could she love him. Then Jean de Santierne appeared upon the scene.

Jean belonged to an old Provençal family and had succeeded to a considerable estate. He frequently appeared at Les Saintes Maries attracted by Odette's beauty. Rouletabille was in his confidence and he too became an habitual guest at Monsieur de Lavardens' table.

Jean was an artist and poet and soon succeeded in showing Odette her true self. She was swept off her feet by him. Hubert de Lauriac had given her an insight only into the life of action. Jean provided the inspiration which transforms a being, and helps to discover a world beyond the world of visible things.

The full weight of disappointment fell upon de Lauriac when he returned a rich man. Moreover, it came as a thunderbolt to Monsieur de Lavardens, who, knowing the young man's nature, was prepared for the worst. Odette, on the other hand, was in no way perturbed.

Monsieur de Lavardens entreated the young people to keep the engagement secret for the time being, but the country round about had by this time informed de Lauriac. He, too, resorted to subterfuge. He paid the usual visits of ceremony, resumed apparently, without ulterior motive, the friendly life of years ago, and even invited the young people and Rouletabille to his "farm."

It was not until de Santierne and Rouletabille returned to Paris that he opened the attack. It was direct as usual. Wealth seemed to have made no change in him. He had made inquiries about Jean. He spoke of him to Odette with contempt, as a youth of easy morals who was living in Paris with a dancer called Callista. Odette left him distraught. She told her father that the sight of him had become unendurable, and begged him to allow her to go with an old servant and stay with an aunt in Avignon. Monsieur de Lavardens welcomed the suggestion with relief, and Odette took the train that morning. To her father's intense surprise she returned two days later upbraiding herself for having acted very foolishly. She had been thinking things over, she explained, and she refused to allow de Lauriac to assume that she was afraid of him.

That evening, after Monsieur de Lavardens had questioned the old servant who accompanied Odette, the servant was discharged.

A few days later de Lauriac indulged in wild excesses. He took to drink, and in a company of herdsmen, to whom he was standing treat at the Saintes Inn, he declared that Odette de Lavardens would be his wife or else before long "they might look out for something in Camargue."

De Lauriac had resolved to bring matters to a crisis and called upon Monsieur de Lavardens two days before the murder, but since we enter at this stage directly into the conflict, we will leave the accused to speak for himself. It may be mentioned that when he was confronted with Monsieur de Lavardens' body, he in no sense changed his attitude.

"I will tell you what happened within my knowledge," he said. "When I have finished you will know as much as I do. But I will not speak here. You can keep me before this body a thousand years and I will not say more than this: The murder was not done by me. I am, I repeat, innocent. Let that be understood once and for all!"

A few minutes later he told his story to the examining magistrate in one of the rooms of the château to which he had been taken.

"The day before yesterday I called at Viei-Castou-Nou. I saw Monsieur de Lavardens and Mademoiselle Odette. Mademoiselle Odette wanted to leave us. I begged her to remain because I had brought her a small gift. I asked her to be kind enough to accept it as a souvenir of my travels. It was a somewhat rare jewel—a gold chain bearing an oriental design, which Monsieur de Lavardens and his daughter greatly admired. But I had not come for a mere trifle of that sort.

" 'Four years ago,' I said to Monsieur de Lavardens, 'when I asked for your daughter's hand, you told me that she was too young and I too poor, but after talking it over with her you finally promised that if in four years I came back a rich man and Mademoiselle Odette was still willing to have me, she should be my wife. Those four years have elapsed, and I have come back a rich man. I am ready to prove to you that I am a rich man; and I am more in love with Odette than ever.'

"When she heard me speak out so bluntly Mademoiselle de Lavardens did not even wait for a sign from her father, but rose and left the room; but she heard what I intended her to hear, which was the main thing, and I was left alone with her father, who gave me an evasive answer: 'Your abrupt call upon us comes as a surprise,' he said.

"It was not the first time since my return that he had put me off with these lame excuses; nor was I pleased either with the manner in which Mademoiselle de Lavardens had left us, considering the old understanding between us. I said to the old man plainly: 'I left the country. I made my fortune. I claim my rights.' Thereupon he rose from his chair with a black look on his face and declared: 'There was no definite promise. I must tell you that my daughter is engaged to Monsieur de Santierne.'

"I felt the full force of the blow. I bowed and cleared out. . . . I sent Mademoiselle Odette the letter which is in your possession. I was mad enough to think that she would keep the appointment. I waited for her some time and then went back home. Suddenly I heard a noise in the garden. The door was being shaken. I opened it and found myself confronted by a veritable wild animal.

"Monsieur de Lavardens had my letter in his hand," continued de Lauriac. "He threw it in my face and, foaming with rage, cried: 'How dare you write in this way to my daughter! What do you take her for?'

"He accompanied the question with the most offensive insults. Seeing the state he was in I did my utmost to keep myself under control.

" 'I made a mistake,' I replied, 'in asking her to meet me. But there is some excuse for a fellow who has lost his temper. I adore your daughter and you have broken your word to me.'

"He made answer that I ought to have known from the first that he would never have given me Odette, for I was not good enough for her, being only a groom and so forth. In fact, he went so far in this sort of compliment that I could contain myself no longer, and I laid my hand on him to turn him out of the house. He had a dog-whip with him and tried to thrash me. We at once closed with each other in the most savage manner. It was at this moment that he must have torn a piece out of my tie. At last I got the better of him and bundled him into the garden with all the more force, since he was hanging on to me in a passion of rage.

"Then I shut the door again. I could hear him shouting curses as he went away. For my part I was overcome, staggered less by the violence of the scene than by a feeling of certainty that I had lost Odette forever, and I remained some time without stirring a limb. When I came to myself from a sort of lethargy which lasted, perhaps, for some hours, I rushed out of the house like a madman and wandered aimlessly about the country.

"I must have covered a good distance. Where did I go? Which way did I take? It would be impossible for me to tell you. It was not until daybreak that I began to recover my mental balance, and see for myself my pitiable plight; so much so that I hid myself from every person I met in order to avoid entering into any explanation. And this was how I tried to get back home without being seen, to change my clothes and think over such decisions as I should have to make. But then you arrested me, and thus I learned of Monsieur de Lavardens' murder and Odette's abduction."

When he finished his statement he sat silent and the examining magistrate could not get another word out of him that day.

"And, perhaps, she too is dead," said the magistrate. "For, after all, since you will not tell us where she is we are compelled to suspect the worst. Did you carry her away alive or dead?"

To the last question, which the magistrate persisted in putting, de Lauriac replied with a shrug of his shoulders, casting a diabolical look upon him.

He was taken to prison that same evening by a circuitous route, for the police desired to escape the populace, which was greatly incensed against him and seething with excitement. De Lauriac left in Camargue a number of enemies who, since his return, had spread the most malevolent rumors about him and the manner in which he had acquired his fortune.

The truth was that nothing was known of him during those four years.

When he found himself confined in a prison cell, as though it were the end of his untold efforts, he fiercely shook his shoulders as if he longed to rid himself of the weight of his ill-fortune, and his parched throat gave forth the snarl of a hunted animal.

Suddenly his attention was roused by a continuous noise which came from without; a rumbling sound which penetrated the walls which held him prisoner. A word or two in a foreign tongue fell on his ear. He rose and lifted his eyes. Above him, high in the wall, was a dingy square of glass in a narrow window, which transmitted a gleam of the pale light of night. He placed his stool on his mattress and raised himself in this way to the opening, which was protected by iron cross-bars.

The pane of glass was not fastened. He had but to open it and the voices outside grew more distinct. Amid the cracking of whips and the trampling of sandals, odds and ends of sentences which were certainly not Provençal but pure Romany, as spoken in Wallachia, struck his ear. Thus a child's voice fretted aloud several times, *Mec naxim tegalitsia*—"I want something to eat"—and her *raya*, her mother, sent her to *beka*, that is, to the devil. Then the sound of singing drifted by, in which was a pleasant invocation to *debla*, the sun; and next voices were raised in abuse, among which recurred an irritable shout, *Ushela!*—"You dog!" De Lauriac understood every word.

At the same time his eyes fixed themselves in the distance on the road whitened by the moon, dotted with shadows of a procession returning to the North, a procession of slatternly men and women, creaking caravans, and lean but unwearied horses which had worn out their shoes on the great roads of the world. Still nearer, black shadows turned for a last look at Les Saintes Maries, to which they had come impelled by a dream which had, perhaps, been realized. So near were they that de Lauriac could see the dark gleam in their jade-like eyes. . . . And it seemed to him that not all those faces were unknown to him.

A name repeated with noisy satisfaction threw him back into the gloomy abyss of his prison.

"Sever Turn !"

Then, on the impenetrable screen which he had set up with so much unyielding obstinacy between the past and the future, certain pictures seemed to appear, sulphurous pictures which began to take shape like a vision of disaster, devastation and desolation, in which lingered an unholy figure strangely suggestive of de Lauriac himself. In the depths emerged the falling towers of a doomed city, laid waste by old-time catastrophes—invasions, pestilence. . . . Sever Turn! Sever Turn!

After the destruction of Babylon, the gypsies—for such was their Egyptian name—the most ancient people on earth, flocked from the prehistoric Atlantide to the west, whence they came and sought asylum at Sever Turn. But after the first disaster which in the Mohammedan era, fell upon the city, they fled from it terrified, and were unable to find sanctuary in any country; and other people called them derisively Bohemians, though they had never dwelt in Bohemia.

They were driven out from country to country and knew not where to lay their heads, yet it might also be asked where they buried their dead, for the grave of a gypsy was never seen, and thus a legend sprang up that they changed the direction of the bed of streams and buried their dead therein to save them from desecration by alien hands.

Throughout the centuries, their forefathers maintained that their calamities were a punishment for their cowardice. They ought never to have abandoned the sacred city; in that city alone, in that city still, lay their salvation.

Why was this ungodly figure of de Lauriac lingering in this country, once again devastated by pestilence? He was a pitiable sight, dissimulating a form consumed with fever under the habiliments of a gypsy to escape from a people which in its adversity denounces the stranger. Let us see him as he saw himself two years before, finding sufficient strength to mount a stolen horse and fly this country of the dead. Suddenly an arm is raised on the road—an arm which beckons him. An old man richly clad in the manner of officiating priests in the Russian or Greek Church, stands before him in his death agony, stricken by the scourge. He offers him an object in a leather covering, which he was clasping to his breast. He collects his last breath to whisper:

"You are of our people. Come, take this. It is the Book of Ancestors."

According to an ancient custom an old man was appointed to carry the Book to the neighboring tribes, and by the fervency of his prayers to battle against the contagion.

Before the old man breathed his last he said to de Lauriac:

"The plague has struck me down. You must take the Book to the chief of the nearest village three miles from here."

De Lauriac accepted the object that was entrusted to him. When he drew the book from its covering he saw that he was in possession of a veritable gem. The binding

was inlaid with the most precious stones. Henceforward
de Lauriac was a rich man, or rather he possessed the
wherewithal to become rich. He hastened, with his
treasure, to quit a country which was a sort of open sore
in the world.

How came it that he was in the country? He had once
heard someone tell his father that the de Lavardens
were not formerly so wealthy, and that old de Lavardens
traveled a great deal in his younger days before he
achieved fortune, the foundation of which lay, according to rumor, in the acquisition of certain petroliferous
lands on the borders of Transylvania. One day, indeed,
de Lauriac's father had questioned de Lavardens, who
answered vaguely that he had merely passed through the
country which was, indeed, one of the richest in oil in
the world, but its inaccessibility, the difficulties of transport and the ill-will of the inhabitants rendered the ex-
ploitation of the oil wellnigh impossible.

De Lauriac, who was at the end of his resources and
with whom nothing had succeeded, had just entered Hun-
gary. He made a wide detour in order to ascertain for
certain what foundation there was for the rumors that
the surface of the soil of this wild country was oozing
with oil products. But in order to obtain admission to
the forbidden zone, he was compelled to live for many
long months in the country, to adopt the habits of the
primitive Tziganes of the mountains, and to learn their
language. And in the end he was forced to abandon
his project because of the plague, and, as we have seen,
to leave the country. But he brought away with him the
Book of Ancestors.

What was the present state of the book shamefully
despoiled of its erstwhile magnificence? In the gloom
of his prison de Lauriac saw it as when he first received
it, luminous as a book of fire! The amethysts, topazes,
beryls, chrysoberyls, emeralds, rubies, with which it was

encrusted were like so many drops of blood, blazing as though they would scorch him. But that which blinded him most in this phantasmal vision was not the magnificence in which the sacred text was encompassed, but the first few lines which he had read inside its cover:

Whoso shall reverence this Book
Preserve it if it be in peril,
Restore it if it be lost,
Shall be given a fitting recompense.
But whoso shall steal this Book,
Or mutilate it,
Shall be chastened and suffer the pain of death.

Superstitious, like every self-respecting herdsman, de Lauriac was never able to forget those words. Sometimes, when least he expected it, they rose up before him from the depths of his too tenacious memory. Sometimes a supernatural force seemed to project them outside himself so that he could see them with greater clearness, and they began to dance before his bewildered eyes . . . and his terror-stricken face . . . as they were dancing that night, for the name of the accursed city rang in his ears that night; he beheld once more the people of Sever Turn, beheld their dark faces, their jade-like eyes, their gestures of execration. And was not the prophecy in the very process of being fulfilled that night? Was he not marching along the road which led to chastisement and death?

These people had, in very truth, entered into a compact with the devil, with their *debla!* All that had befallen him since was anything but natural; was, indeed, supernatural. To begin with, these people had changed the character of "his Odette." He no longer recognized her. When he left her she was his—"all his." By what species of witchcraft had it come about that she refused to look at him when he returned? And then the incidents which had ensued! Everything had turned against him in an extraordinary way. Then came that infernal night when, instead of Odette, he had encountered her father . . . her father who next day was found murdered! By whom? By himself perhaps. He did not know!

He, so clever, so crafty, who by dint of quiet cunning had got the better of more than one person, had suddenly acted like a man possessed. He had seen red; in other words he was incapable of seeing things as they were. Why had he forgotten that the very last thing to do, in spite of all, was to raise his hand against Odette's father? He had seen red; he had struck him a blow and perhaps killed him. When de Lavardens raised his whip against him he had, perhaps, seized a dagger which lay on his desk ostensibly for the purpose of cutting the pages of his books. . . . But de Lauriac never read books. This dagger was more or less an absurd ornament, but assuredly, in his hand it might have carried death with it. What had he done with the dagger? He did not know! His memory seemed to have become detached from the struggle. From a certain moment onward his mind had fallen into a dark void and when he recovered at daybreak he found himself wandering about the country like a madman. What had become of that trifling object bought at a bazaar, that insignificant paper-cutter shaped like a dagger? What had he done with it? His mind was a blank. . . . It was chaos and witchcraft! . . .

CHAPTER X

THE venerable church loomed up from the lagoon, its blackened walls standing erect on the edge of the waters, its machiolated towers and patrol pash path silhouetted on the skyline like a mediæval citadel, silhouetted on the skyline like a mediæval citadel, and its apse seeming like the veritable donjon which, in the days of old, repulsed the assault of the Saraces. . . . Now the marching rabble of gypsies found cover within its shadow.

Suddenly Jean caught sight of the van of the army coming towards him. It was made up of gypsies from Germany and the Carpathians, who were the first to return to their distant homes. This year the mysterious rites had been quickly concluded. There were years, like this year, when the Romanys leave the country before the Provençal fêtes begin, years when they refuse to mingle with the "alien," and when, as they leave the crypt after their fantastic devotions to St. Sarah, they flee as though they had committed some crime.

The retreating army were more cheerful than sullen. They were singing in their caravans. Young women with laughing eyes and the faces of old hags greeted him with gay gestures. "This is where Callista came from and where I ought to have left her," thought Jean. "Why is she back again among this crew? Rouletabille is perhaps right in being troubled about it." But as the thought led him away from Odette, following a line of reasoning which brought him back to de Lauriac, he soon ceased to think of Callista.

He reached Les Saintes Maries as dancing was beginning to the music of guitars and accordions. The main street, which was so narrow that no two vehicles could pass each other, was illuminated with Venetian lights. Canvas awnings spread from one roof to another, diffused their shade in the passage during the day, but now lay inert over an oppressive atmosphere filled with the reek of wine which the waiters were serving at the tables on the pavements.

An air of liveliness and high spirits prevailed. There was a great deal of noise, good-tempered noise, outbursts of laughter, joking remarks thrown out to passers-by, music, and now and again the explosion of crackers flung slyly among the persons seated at the tables by young urchins.

Groups of guests in the inns were discussing in low tones the event of the day. The terrible story from the Viei-Castou-Nou cast a gloom over more than one face. The people were utterly nonplussed by Odette's disappearance. The affair was so extraordinary that they scarcely trusted themselves to express an opinion upon it. And then though de Lauriac had few friends he was universally feared.

When Jean, after leaving his car in the square, made his way down the street, each one silently removed his hat. They felt sorry for him. They drew back to allow him to enter the Hôtel des Saintes Maries. The proprietor, an old sailor who had become an innkeeper, greeted him with sympathy, but refrained from asking any questions.

"Have you seen Rouletabille?" inquired Jean.

"Yes, monsieur, he was here a little while ago."

"Where can I find him?"

"Upon my word, I can't say. I fancy he must have gone away again."

"What makes you think so?"

"Well, it's like this: When he came in, he asked me if a lady was waiting for him. I tell you this because I know that you are hand in glove with him. I answered that no one had called for him. Thereupon he went out, and came back a little while later. He seemed to have something on his mind. He again asked me if the lady had called, and I told him no. Then he wrote a short note, slipped it in an envelope and said: 'I don't think she'll come now, but if she does, give her this.' So saying he went out and I haven't seen him since; and that's what made me say that he must have left Les Saintes Maries."

"Did the lady turn up?"

"Yes, monsieur, she came not so very long ago and I gave her the note. She seemed rather vexed that Monsieur Rouletabille hadn't waited for her."

"Rouletabille wants to have an interview with Callista," thought Jean. In reality he himself would not be sorry to meet her, if only to dispel every possibility of misunderstanding between them. After his last encounter with her, at which, with the degree of fatalism peculiar to her race, she had shown such perfect resignation, it never entered his mind that she could be guilty of the odious crime which Rouletabille imputed to her. She could not have forgotten all that Jean had done for her, and indeed, after his last gift which had assured her future and which she had accepted, there was nothing with which she could reproach him. She had come to Les Saintes Maries without making any secret of it and told her servants the object which she had in view. Rouletabille's suspicions were sheer imagination.

Jean described Callista to the hotel proprietor, who told him, to his great surprise, that she in no way resembled the visitor. To begin with, the lady of whom he was speaking was dark, while the visitor was fair.

Jean reflected for a while and then suddenly an idea flashed across his mind.

"Did the lady wear a fringe over her forehead?"

"Yes, monsieur, you're right this time."

Jean drew nearer the hotel proprietor.

"The letter must have been addressed to someone," he suggested.

But as the other maintained a discreet silence Jean blurted out:

"Wasn't the letter addressed to Madame de Meyrens?"

The man indicated by a nod that it was so, whereupon Jean left him, his mind increasingly perturbed.

"He can't do without that detestable woman," he said to himself. "What can he want with her at a time like this? And why does he make appointments with her if he doesn't care for her as he pretends?"

Leaving the question for the time being, he went in search of the herdsmen who usually formed de Lauriac's society, for he was pursuing his own train of thought, but when he got beyond the full light of the street and found himself in the partial obscurity of the sandhills, his attention was attracted by two figures, at no great distance ahead, who seemed not unfamiliar to him.

A man and a woman were making their way along the walls. Then crossing a deserted space broken with shadows, they appeared in view once more in the flickering light of a fire outside a caravan.

Many similar fires were alight along the beach, forming sort of semi-circle round Les Saintes Maries. They had been kindled by gypsies from Béziers and Pézenas, who were staying at Les Saintes Maries longer than their brethren, for, after all, these gypsies were in their own country and had no great distance to go to reach the roads along which they were accustomed to live.

Most of these bivouacs were deserted. The younger folk had left them to join in the dancing, and supper was being prepared under the watchful eyes of the old women.

Jean could not repress a faint exclamation when he recognized in the two forms whom he was following Olajaï and the Octopus.

They seated themselves near an old gypsy woman, who, as they approached, stood up and eyed them with some suspicion. But Olajaï spoke, and the old woman nodded her head, and clearly was now receiving the newcomers with the kindest welcome.

Afterwards Olajaï and the Octopus visited several other caravans, and then suddenly disappeared from view as if by magic, and Jean was unable to come up with them again. He went back to the lights of the main street wrapped in thought and greatly excited by his experience, and here he was told that the herdsmen were gathered together at the Little Rhone Inn.

When he entered the inn the herdsmen, who were engaged in an animated discussion, suddenly stopped talking. Jean's gaze wandered from one to the other of these men of rough appearance, set faces and hostile looks.

"You know what's happened," he said. "Do you think de Lauriac did it?"

"No, we are sure he didn't," they replied unanimously.

"Still, he is in prison for it. If anyone saw him on the night in question it might help him. Let him speak out. . . ."

The men remained silent.

"I don't see Lou Rousso Fiamo here," went on Jean. "Perhaps he can give us a little information."

Lou Rousso Fiamo, a man with fiery-red hair, was at one time Hubert de Lauriac's head man. He was well

known for his strength and brutality, and blind devotion
to his master.

"Lou Rousso Fiamo went off to Beaucaire the day
before yesterday to get four bulls branded," a voice
volunteered.

"It's the first time Lou Rousso Fiamo has missed Les
Saintes Maries' fête," returned Jean. "He will certainly
be very annoyed about it."

He left the inn as it was no use persisting, for he knew
that they would all stand together and he would get
nothing out of them. Nevertheless, his journey to Les
Saintes Maries had been far from useless, and he was
eager to see Rouletabille again.

An hour and a half later he joined him at Lavardens.

"Well?" he asked.

"Well, in spite of Olajaï's warning I was determined
to go to Les Saintes Maries," returned Rouletabille, "but
I no sooner got there that Olajaï came to me at a corner
of the street and once more told me that Camargue was
very unhealthy for me. I tried to obtain some explanation, but he left me hurriedly, saying: 'I've chattered
too much already.'"

"So you came back here?"

"Yes, of course; especially as I still had a great deal
to do here."

"And then," went on Jean, with a purpose which did
not escape the journalist's notice, "you did not meet the
person whom you expected to meet."

"I see that you've been told all about it," returned
Rouletabille, frowning.

"In any case, I know one thing," declared Jean in a
strained voice. "While Olajaï succeeded in making you
leave Les Saintes Maries he stayed there himself with
the Octopus, whom you came to see, but did not see.
But I saw them both working at some sort of secret
job which cannot be either to your liking or mine,

seeing that they take such pains to hide it from us."

"Have no fear," returned Rouletabille in increasingly gloomy tones. "Give me another twenty-four hours and neither Olajaï nor the Octopus will prevent me from rescuing Odette."

"I've brought back information which may be of use to us," said Jean, stopping Rouletabille, who made a movement to leave him. "If de Lauriac is guilty, as I believe more firmly than ever, he must undoubtedly have had accomplices, or at least one accomplice. Now, I've just learned that Lou Rousso Fiamo has been away from Les Saintes Maries for the last two days."

"I am aware of it," returned Rouletabille.

He walked away abruptly, giving Jean, as the phrase goes, the slip. The latter did not persist. He took his seat at the wheel again and drove off to Beaucaire. He wanted to know for certain the truth about Lou Rousso Fiamo's absence.

Extracts from Rouletabille's diary at this date:

"Olajaï and the Octopus. Jean may be right. I have not been sufficiently on my guard against the Octopus.

"As to Olajaï, there are times when I am on the point of learning his secret and then just as I seem to fathom it I fall into mystification again.

"The dangers which he prophesies and from which he pretends to wish to save me, fit in too well with the attempted burglary in Paris to make the close connection between them doubtful. The whole thing stands together and yet remains a mystery to me.

"One thing alone is certain: some serious danger is hanging over me. I managed to follow Callista's trail almost step by step since her arrival at Les Saintes Maries, and I know everything that she did in the place

up to the moment when she vanished not far from the
Viei-Castou-Nou.

"Alighting from the train at Avignon, like ourselves,
but twenty-four hours earlier, she was driven by car,
like ourselves, to Arles. But here she left the car,
passed through the town on foot, and took the first train at
Arles-Trinquet wayside station, reaching Les Saintes
Maries at ten minutes to ten. She was clad simply but
stylishly in a nigger-brown velvet costume set off with
beaver, and a hat trimmed with monkey fur. That
was the dress which she wore when she last went out
with Jean and me some days before he broke with her.
Certainly she made no effort to keep in the background.
She at once went to church and began her devotions.
Next she called on the rector and asked him for an invitation for the afternoon ceremony of viewing the sacred
relics. Afterwards she had a look round the town without any apparent object, interesting herself in the many
sights which the gypsy encampments afforded her. At
one moment she went up to a group which at first paid
no more heed to her than to any other passer-by. A
small boy asked her for alms. She spoke to him. A
man seated in front of her at once turned his back on
her, and threw her a look over his shoulder, and then
in a flash stood up before her. He stared her in the
face, took stock of her dress, and flung at her
hoarsely between his clenched teeth in his own language
the worst insults. She did not wince, but answering
him shortly in his own tongue, walked away. When she
was gone the man and the gypsies with him spat upon
the ground.

"Callista seemingly left Les Saintes Maries, and its
swarms of gypsies who had transformed the village into
a zone of squalor, with perfect indifference. She went
down to the most secluded spot on the beach and entered the ruins of a hut, in which she undressed and

soon emerged ready for bathing. After a swim she lay stretched at full length on the sand like a weary animal. "Suddenly there was a movement near her—it was the man! She was expecting him despite his insults. She began to laugh as her eyes met his. He silenced her by pressing his lips to hers in a savage kiss. The man was Andréa, who had chased her two years before, and from whom, to his sorrow, Jean had rescued her. If the finery in which Callista as a gypsy woman was attired just before was the cause of Andréa's raging reception of her, she wore nothing now which could offend his eyes as he gazed at her. The whole incident had been carefully planned. She had found her man. He tried to seize her. She pushed him aside, but what must she not have promised him? He at once gave way to her. She went back to dress, and they left the place on the best possible terms with each other.

"Callista was not present at the afternoon ceremony. She left the village surreptitiously in a cart driven by a gypsy, who dropped her at no great distance from La-vardens, and I lost sight of her. Andréa, too, disappeared from Les Saintes Maries. I lost track of him at Maguelonne-le-Sauveur, but there can be no doubt that I found it again in the dog-shearer mentioned by Estève.

"Andréa was on foot at Maguelonne-le-Sauveur. It is to be noted that neither of them took the train for they would certainly have been seen by the porters, and the train to Arles at that hour was empty. Jean left me and, doubtless, went to Beaucaire to inquire about Lou Rousso Fiamo. After all, his journey will not be wholly futile. We must be prepared for anything in view of the fact that I found the gypsy emblem in Odette's room—a present from de Lauriac! And now I must 'pump' Estève. There is still much to be learned from her. I asked Jean to give me twenty-four hours in which to save Odette—if there is still time to do so!"

CHAPTER XI

IN WHICH ROULETABILLE EXPRESSES A DEFINITE OPINION ABOUT THE MURDERER

Extract from Rouletabille's diary of the 27th May:

I WAS convinced that Estève knew a great deal more than she chose to say. In the end I made her admit that on several occasions during the last month she accompanied Odette to Lavardens woods, where the latter used to meet in secret a curious person whom Monsieur de Lavardens once caught talking to his daughter to his intense surprise. The person in question was an old woman who certainly did not belong to those parts, but lived away from everybody like a hermit, and went to earth in no one knows what sort of burrow.

"Odette told Estève that this old woman had aroused her pity and she had willingly given her a trifle for which she showed her gratitude in a sort of worship of Odette. She often told Odette's fortune, predicting a brilliant future which only made the child laugh. She wanted to tell Estève's fortune, but Estève, who is very superstitious and believes in witchcraft, invariably set herself against it. The old woman had a face that frightened her, and she failed to understand how her young mistress could find pleasure in the company of this old hag who said her name was Zina.

"Zina was obviously a gypsy judging from Estève's description of her. Their meetings, as a rule, took place between Lavardens and Albaron, not far from the cross-

way at La Font. Now I managed to establish definitely
that the car in which Odette was carried off was driven
towards Albaron and was not seen after it reached Albaron. I feel that I am 'getting warmer' and that the
net of my inquiries is drawing closer round the chief
persons concerned in the tragedy.

"What was the part played by de Lauriac in Odette's
abduction? Everything depends on the answer. Does
he know where she is. He may, and I hope he does, but
I am not certain. Was there some understanding between
him and Callista? The thought of his complicity occurred to me in a flash when I discovered the connection
between him and the gypsies which his gift of the jewel
to Odette necessarily involves. But I had my misgivings
about this assumption. I felt too great a need for it—it
squared too easily with my method—for me not to be
attracted by it then and there, regardless of my critical
judgment. And indeed there's no proof of it. The gypsies may have done their work and passed through de
Lauriac's property without any connivance on his part.
It was much easier for them, in fact, to pass from de
Lauriac's place to Viei-Castou-Nou than to effect a direct
entrance into de Lavardens' park, surrounded as it is on
the side nearest the country by very high walls. And
then if Callista with Andréa's help did the deed, she
was not perhaps ignorant of the threats made openly by
de Lauriac, and thus allowed suspicion to fall upon
him.

"The matter is the more difficult to clear up in
this respect as de Lauriac is utterly unscrupulous.
Did he know that Odette was being kidnapped while
he was with Monsieur de Lavardens? I failed
to understand his demoniacal look, followed by a kind
of savage grin, when Jean mentioned Odette. I understood it still less seeing that this look was aimed at
me."

Extract from Rouletabille's diary, 10 *o'clock p. m., 27th May:*

"An incident of the first importance! I compelled Estève to come with me to Albaron this afternoon. From here we retraced our steps to Lavardens and entered the wood. I have a hold on Estève by her fears. I threaten to accuse her of complicity in Monsieur de Lavardens' murder. She pointed out the various places where Odette and she used to meet Zina.

"When we were at the crossway at La Font I heard the sound of something stirring behind me in the foliage. I darted into the thicket. Far too many things have been stirring round me since I came to Camargue, and I should very much like to see what sort of figure they cut! I whipped out my revolver. I was prepared to go all lengths to find out. . . .

"But everything relapsed into a dead silence and search as I might for a trace of the person who had stirred, or him or her who was there a moment before, I discovered absolutely nothing. And yet I had so quickly turned round that I saw the foliage open and close in again. I shook the trees. I examined them from root to branch. Nothing! And yet it was no idle fancy.

"Estève, too, heard the movement, but she had not seen any more than I had: 'Let's go back,' she said, her teeth chattering. 'I feel so frightened.'

" 'Yes, let's go back,' I answered in a loud voice. 'We've nothing more to do here'; and we made for a short cut to Viei-Castou-Nou. But after a few steps, at the first bend, I stopped her by a sign, giving her to understand that we must remain still for a moment and listen. Suddenly there was a stir in front of us among the foliage once more, and this time my eyes encountered another pair of eyes. I sprang forward shouting: 'Stop, or I'll fire!' but someone made off through the thickets and I fired. A cry went up, a kind of moan;

after that nothing. Estève had not moved a limb for she was half dead with fright. I myself went forward and hunted for the person who had cried out and caught my eye, but I was unable to find any one or any trace of him. The ground was soft at this spot and would have retained the slightest marks, for the imprint of my footsteps was plainly visible. It was maddening.

"Without troubling any more about Estève whom I left far behind, I continued to advance not quite knowing where I was going, and suddenly I espied the cause of my scare which was fleeing before me in wild leaps and bounds. I uttered a cry, and leapt forward in my turn. The bear's cub! I recognized Callista's bear's cub.

"I plunged after him among a clump of trees and saw him disappear under cover of the branches in the cavity of a rock where I followed him. I at once found myself in a sort of subterranean cave in which some person with a few planks had created the illusion of a human habitation. The obscurity was so dense inside that it was some time before I could distinguish its inconsiderable furniture such as a trucklebed, a stool, a fireplace which still bore the remains of a recent fire. At last something moved at the back, uttering a moan which I knew full well. It was the bear's cub. It was Balogard, for such Callista called him, which in the gypsy vernacular means 'the thief.'

"I crept towards him with a few friendly words. I was afraid lest I had wounded him, but fortunately I had missed him, and he received me without hostility. Then I discovered that Balogard was squatting on some clothes not unfamiliar to me. Callista's cast-off Parisian wardrobe lay there. I inferred from this that for the time at least Callista had become a gypsy once more, and I had no difficulty in assuming that I was in Zina's retreat to which at first they had transported Odette. . . ."

About six o'clock that same evening a scene of considerable importance took place at Lavardens. The authorities had returned here for a supplementary examination, and de Lauriac had been taken to Viei-Castou-Nou.

Rouletabille appeared while de Lauriac was being reexamined at the very spot where Monsieur de Lavardens' body was discovered. Old Tavan was present.

After throwing a glance round him Rouletabille spoke to de Lauriac direct:

"I know who kidnaped Odette, and you also know," he said.

Thereupon de Lauriac began to laugh in the most sinister fashion.

"Of course I know," he returned. "But I don't know as much about it as you do."

"Monsieur de Santierne is on the track of Lou Rousso Fiamo," went on Rouletabille, in a voice which had suddenly taken a new intonation. "Tell the whole truth, monsieur, and you may still be able to save yourself."

"Monsieur de Santierne would do better to follow the track of Olajaï—of Olajaï who came here twenty-four hours before you," retorted de Lauriac.

"I don't know what you mean," returned Rouletabille, growing pale.

"Oh, yes you do, monsieur, you know very well what I mean."

He continued to grin and shrug his shoulders whereupon the examining magistrate losing patience exclaimed:

"This discussion is intolerable. And your behavior in the matter"—turning to Rouletabille—"is particularly unpardonable. You seem to take a pleasure in making our task impossible when you are not trying to turn it into ridicule. You assert that you know who abducted Mademoiselle de Lavardens. Well, your duty is to denounce the guilty party to the police."

"Give you the names of the criminals," exclaimed Rouletabille, who had recovered his accustomed self-possession, "so that you may let them escape. No, Monsieur Crousillat!"

"Monsieur!"

"I prefer to bring them to you bound hand and foot."

"Braggadocio!" retorted the examining magistrate. "It's on a par with the articles that you have telegraphed to Paris which have just reached us here. Why do you suggest that we shall never arrest the murderer? Do you know him? Perhaps you can give us a sketch of him. Is he dark or fair? Is he fat or thin?"

"Thin, monsieur, as thin as a spike," returned Rouletabille.

CHAPTER XII

ROULETABILLE ON THE ALERT

Extract from Rouletabille's diary:

THIS de Lauriac is an infamous rascal. His attitude at the last examination was such that it seemed as if I was paralyzed by it. At one time I could not see my way clear at all, and was not even aware that Jean was standing behind watching me. I must have cut a sorry figure. And then I recovered my wits and answered the examining magistrate as it behooved me to answer him at the moment. It was then that I saw what a wry face Jean was making.

"When de Lauriac was taken away and Monsieur Crousillat, the examining magistrate, and Monsieur Bartholasse, his unspeakable clerk, who are absolutely furious with me, had left Viei-Castou-Nou, slamming the door behind them, I went up to Jean and asked him the result of his journey to Beaucaire. He gave me a peculiar look and made answer that he had seen Lou Rousso Fiamo, and this paragon of a drover had not left his beasts during the period of the tragedy.

" 'Well, and are you still convinced that de Lauriac is the man?' I asked.

" 'What about you?' he returnd. 'Are you still convinced that he isn't?'

"I told him that it was impossible at present to assert or to deny his complicity. Then in a tone of disgust which was, perhaps, pardonable, but for all that gave me a pang at my heart, he rapped out:

" 'In any case, do you, yes or no, know where Odette is?'

" 'If I knew, she would be here now.'

"He gave me a look which was almost that of an enemy, clenched his fists, and turned on his heel as if I were a person whose presence had become unbearable to him."

At this point in the diary some half dozen lines are repeatedly scratched through as if Rouletabille intended deliberately to expunge them. Nevertheless under the lines three words, "dear little Odette," which have already been noted in the diary, may be divined rather than discerned and after the suppressed lines come the following remarks:

"I have a great many enemies here, but the most formidable has just appeared. It is *suspicion;* the suspicion which at first spied on me from afar and next came and stood before me with its ice-cold eyes; eyes which however wide-open they may be when they stare at external things, reflect nothing but the suspicion which excites them. Yet I have outlived worse things than that. Don't let me be affected by them. This is not the moment."

Rouletabille assumed with good reason that if Callista was to return to Zina's retreat for her clothes she would not run the risk of such a visit until after dark. And here is an extract from his diary recording his vigilance:

"It was about ten o'clock when Callista, dressed as a gypsy, appeared on the path leading to the old hag's haunt. She was quite recognizable in spite of her rags. She had the look of an outraged queen which she sometimes assumed in Paris when Jean or any of his friends treated her with too great a familiarity. As she drew near the cave, which Zina had fixed upon as her abode,

she turned round unexpectedly and the moonlight fell
full on a face which expressed intense exasperation.

" 'Is that you again, Andréa?' she said aloud.

"But it was the form of a woman which came in sight
on the path. Callista made a movement as if to draw
back into the thicket, but before she could take a step,
the newcomer spoke and Callista stood still in amazement. I heard her mutter:

" 'Madame de Meyrens!'

"It was in truth the Octopus who came up to her.

" 'How did you get here?' questioned Callista, breathing quickly. 'What are you here for?'

" 'To see you,' answered Madame de Meyrens. 'Oh,
if you only knew how I've hunted for you! It was
Olajaï who told me that there was some possibility of
finding you at Zina's place, and brought me here.'

" 'Olajaï!' snorted Callista furiously. 'Where is he?
I want to talk to him.'

" 'Oh, you won't find him in Camargue now. He's
not anxious to come up against your temper. But I
promised to pacify you. Callista, are we or are we not
good friends?'

"At this moment they entered Zina's grotto. When
they came out again, ten minutes later, they seemed to
have reached some understanding. Callista was carrying a parcel which I imagined contained her clothes.
Meanwhile, she said to the Octopus:

" 'No, don't ask me anything more. We shall see
each other again. I've told you everything that I can
tell you for the time being. Henceforth be easy in your
mind as I am myself. Neither your Rouletabille nor my
Jean will see this Odette again.'

" 'I shan't be easy in my mind until you tell me she
is dead,' declared the Octopus fiercely.

"Callista shrugged her shoulders and with an ominous
chuckle said:

" 'I assure you that no one will ever see her again.'

"Having thus spoken they became silent. When I could no longer hear their footsteps on the road, I darted into the grotto, which was empty. Even the bear's cub was gone. It was pitch dark inside but I had brought my lantern, and I applied myself to a minute search which I was not at liberty to make on my first visit, for I was disturbed by a noise outside.

"As I guessed, Callista had taken away her clothes. What I was hunting for was not so much particular articles as traces of the possibly deadly tragedy which had occurred there. The last words uttered by Callista filled my mind with dismay. Everything was within the region of possibility with such a woman: 'Neither your Rouletabille nor my Jean will see this Odette again!'

"It was no difficult task, unfortunately, to find in the cave traces of a struggle, of an unmistakable and even desperate resistance which had suddenly ceased. At last while I was on all fours at the fireplace my hand strayed to a small dark puddle which gleamed in the light of my lamp. . . . Blood! . . . And in the blood a knife! . . . They had murdered Odette!

"At that moment I could not repress a cry of rage and a great sob broke in my throat. And then suddenly I burst out laughing . . . wild insensate laughter. . . . The thing that I took for blood was ink!

"And I then discovered a broken ink bottle and an old pen in pieces near an overturned stool. I now understood Callista's silence following a certain question put to her by the Octopus, and a light-heartedness flooded my whole being. No, no. . . . Nothing was lost! No blood was on the ground and the knife bore only a little ink on it. And had they been driven to murder Odette, it was here that they would have struck her down since they possessed all that was needed—the knife and silence!

"What a plucky little thing Odette was! What had

they endeavored to make her write, or sign? . . . Still, nowhere was there any trace of blood. It was not therefore a corpse which they had carried away in the caravan whose trail I had picked up close to the grotto—a trail which joined the road from Arles to Les Saintes Maries and was lost among the tracks of a hundred other caravans proceeding to the four corners of the earth.

"Was I right or wrong, therefore, to refrain from giving the least hint to the magistrates lest they should badger all the gypsies leaving Les Saintes Maries? Who can ever tell the terrors of so great a responsibility. Why, would not it have been tantamount to warning the fugitives of the discovery of their crime when above all the thing was to take them by surprise? With their immemorial cunning they would have played a hundred tricks before handing Odette over to us. Was I not bound to take into consideration that the deed was done some hours before our arrival at Lavardens and that the ruffians had had ample time to take their precautions? No, no! I was right not to lend myself to a problematical pursuit which Odette's abductors must have foreseen. It was through Callista that I should get at Odette if there was still time. And there was still time because she was alive. . . . But Callista had done her utmost to lead the Octopus to believe that Odette was dead. . . . Ah, the Octopus!"

CHAPTER XIII

EXPLANATIONS

ROULETABILLE hastened to return to the château filled with a feeling of elation which he wished Jean to share. He found him stretched on a sofa in his clothes, sleeping a sleep disturbed by nightmares. He quickly woke him up.

"Odette is alive. I feel positive of it."

Jean looked at him haggard-eyed.

"If you are so positive as all that why don't you bring her back to us?"

Rouletabille received the question without flinching. He sat down beside Jean and took his hands in his.

"I can see that what de Lauriac said yesterday made a considerable impression on you. At present it is not de Lauriac who is the villain, it is I. . . . Come, Jean, look me in the face and unburden yourself of everything that weighs on your mind."

Jean could not repress his emotion.

"It's true I'm going crazy," he said. "But you must forgive me. I don't know which way to turn. I am beset with trouble. I've lost my faith in everything."

"Do you still believe in love?"

"I suffer too much from it to disbelieve in it," returned the hapless Jean.

"But do you doubt friendship?" asked Rouletabille in a low voice.

"You must forgive me," repeated Jean, covering his face with his hands.

"Come, come now. Jean. I know that since our last

visit to Lavardens you have entertained hard thoughts of me—hard thoughts which you have striven to dismiss from your mind, but never quite got rid of. And I will tell you why you have never quite got rid of them. It began in Paris. I have very sharp ears which enable me at times to dispense with eavesdropping, and one day as I was leaving you and Callista, I overheard her say: 'Of course you can't go to Camargue without Rouletabille. It's a place which must have a great deal of attraction for young people.' "

"That's true," confessed Jean. "Callista never liked you and she did her utmost to make me break with you. I swear that she never succeeded. Shake hands on it."

They clasped hands.

"Now tell me what you know about Odette," said Jean with a sigh.

Then Rouletabille told him how he discovered the cave, how he kept watch on it, and how he overheard the conversation which passed between Callista and the Octopus.

"The Octopus! . . . The Octopus again!" exclaimed Jean. "Lord, haven't I warned you often enough against her. And she knows Callista! They must have joined forces against us in Paris."

"The odds are in favor of it, certainly," said Rouletabille calmly. "Callista is an adept in arousing jealousy. . . ."

"Oh, don't let's speak of it," sighed Jean. "I only ask you from now onwards to hate Madame de Meyrens as I hate Callista, and we shall both be all the better for it, I assure you. . . . So you followed them?"

"No."

"Why didn't you follow Callista?" asked Jean.

"Because I know where to find her," returned Rouletabille. "After listening to their conversation was it not more important to make certain, before anything else, whether Odette was alive or dead?"

"Did the cave tell you that?"

"That and a great many other things."

"But, after all, if I understand you rightly, the evidence of Odette's safety seems very inconclusive. They may have carried her off to get rid of her elsewhere."

"Where to?" asked Rouletabille, forcing Jean to sit down, for he had risen to his feet, his pupils dilated as though he saw some terrible vision.

"Where to? Why, didn't you say that they took her away in a caravan?"

"And I say it again. To begin with, after the abduction, they drove off in a motor-car with the object of diverting suspicion, but gypsies who come to Les Saintes Maries are not used to motor-cars, and they took her from the car to the cave, and from the cave to the caravan."

"I quite understand, but do try to understand me too, Rouletabille. Did you not say that this caravan took the road from Arles to Les Saintes Maries on the very night when these infernal people were celebrating the festival of Saint Sarah?"

"Do you suggest a blood offering?" asked the journalist quietly.

"You heard, as I did, what old Alari said. Nobody knows what happens in that church crypt on this dreadful night."

"Pull yourself together. As a matter of fact, I considered that everything was possible. Accordingly the first thing I did at Camargue was to make certain that there were no grounds for so horrible a supposition."

"Do you know what happened in the crypt?"

"Yes, I do."

"But how do you know? You told me yourself that you couldn't appear at Les Saintes Maries without being forced to leave again."

"That's why I did not *appear*, my dear Jean. But

when people think that I am far away I am sometimes close at hand, very close at hand. Let's hope that I shall soon be near Odette," he added with a bright smile, taking leave of Jean.

"But where are you going? I'll come with you."

"No, have a good sleep. You haven't slept for a couple of nights."

"What about you? What sleep have you had during the last three nights?"

"But, my dear fellow, I've slept my fill. A quarter of an hour here and half an hour there. As you know, I'm used to sleeping in this way."

"You're not telling the truth, Rouletabille. You haven't slept a wink."

"Well, that's true. Up to now I've had a bad time. . . . But now you'll see that I have fully recovered my spirits. The worthy Monsieur Crousillat, and Bartholosse, his apoplectic clerk, had better look out for themselves. There'll be plenty of scope for laughter and amusement at their expense."

"Let me come with you, Rouletabille."

"No," he returned. "I want you to stay at Viei-Castou-Nou, or at least not to go far away from it because . . ."

"Because what?"

"Because we must know where to find you."

"Who?"

"Someone who will certainly bring you news of Odette."

"You are a magician!"

"Perhaps. . . . Good-by, Jean."

"But, after all, Rouletabille, if you really know the guilty party you can very well give me his name."

Rouletabille wavered a moment and then went up to de Santierne and whispered a few words in his ear. . . . Afterwards he made his escape, leaving Jean completely staggered.

CHAPTER XIV

PANDORA SLEEPS

WAS there complicity? Such was the question which Rouletabille asked himself when he was in de Lauriac's grounds, after clearing the wall dividing the Viei-Castou-Nou from the "shanty," for the authorities had permanently closed the partition gate. Until then he had not lost a moment, pressing forward to do the thing that seemed most urgent. But he felt from the beginning that a thorough search of the place, even if de Lauriac was innocent, might be of the greatest advantage.

And then he had good reason to proceed with caution. Monsieur Crousillat, at the instigation of Bartholasse, his clerk, who had a holy horror of journalists in general and Rouletabille in particular, objected to his setting foot in the house. Seals had been affixed to the door of the room in which so much incriminating evidence was found affecting this de Lauriac whom Rouletabille, to every one's amazement, defended. Moreover, Monsieur Crousillat had posted two gendarmes on guard, who had strict orders to allow no one to come near and to keep the house under observation.

Rouletabille had already seen these two watch-dogs barring the way. He had not persisted. He would leave them gradually to relax their vigilance.

Accordingly he chose to enter de Lauriac's place during the early hours, for he had observed that the gendarme on duty at that particular time gave way to fatigue and sleep. In short, finding the moment a propitious one, he walked round the house, and reached without being observed a light well, into which he crept. Five minutes later, stealing from light well to skylight and from skylight to window, he attained de Lauriac's study. He could hear through the sealed door a resounding and regular snore. It was Pandora keeping watch!

Rouletabille set about ransacking the room with his accustomed thoroughness, convinced that he would not be disturbed. He emptied a small writing-desk of all its documents from top to bottom, and carefully examined each one. The fact that the police had been there first in no way discouraged our journalist—far from it. He was wont to say that the authorities never failed to facilitate his task by constantly neglecting those things which related to the matter in hand, and taking away all else!

Nevertheless he found nothing that morning which had any direct or indirect bearing on the tragic incidents which had so greatly excited this part of Camargue, and he was wondering if he had not wasted his time, when, among the few books which lay on the tables and shelves, he perceived a big book whose antiquated appearance caused him some astonishment.

De Lauriac was in no sense a lover of books. His library amounted to little or nothing. A few of the latest novels, some books of travel and sports magazines, constituted his entire collection. The ancient volume, whose binding, moreover, appeared to have greatly suffered from the ravages of time, was out of place in this modern setting—this study furnished in a manner at once pretentious and ordinary, beloved of those young persons who are anxious to follow the style which happens to be in the fashion.

The only mark of originality in the room consisted in a few uncommon objects brought back from distant lands; bronze masks wearing a savage grin, which took the unsuspecting visitor by surprise, and skins of wild beasts which suggested big game hunting, but had possibly been bought at some bazaar.

But how came the book in de Lauriac's possession? Rouletabille did not fail to examine it in the hope of finding an answer to his question, for he held in his hand a work resembling a book of antiphons and yet it was not a book of antiphons. He was opening it when a kind of dagger slipped out and fell to the floor. He looked down, picked it up, and saw that it was not so much a weapon as a paper cutter.

Thereupon he noticed that a page had been cut out quite neatly at the very place where the book opened. The page was missing. What was the object of removing that page? And, first of all, what was the book? The letterpress in it was unusual, approximating to Greek, Byzantine and even Slavonic typography. He could identify certain characters.

The book greatly attracted him. It was obviously of very considerable value. Why had it been mutilated? And why had the binding, in which a number of little holes could be seen and felt, been disfigured in that way? At first sight Rouletabille attributed these mutilations to the action of time, but now, as he scrutinized the work more closely, he perceived that they were comparatively recent.

He pocketed the dagger and inserted a small sheet of paper in the place where the book had opened; and then closed it and examined the binding from every point of view. He soon came to the conclusion that the cover had been studded with precious stones, for it was a very valuable book. It was illuminated inside with splendid initial letters and tail-pieces in color of a somewhat rude design, an impressive treasure such as is greatly sought after by book collectors. It indubitably contained some kind of ritual, appertaining to a religion which had yet to be determined.

Suddenly, while his attention was attracted by the shape of a hollow space in the cover which must certainly have contained and held in place the iron fastening in the middle, Rouletabille excitedly felt in the inside pocket of his jacket and drew forth the jewel which he had found in Odette's room and thought fit to appropriate to himself.

This jewel, or rather the center ornament of the pendant, fitted exactly into the marks left by the iron clasp of the book. The fatal sign of the cross and crescent, the gypsies' sacred device, was formerly the clasp of the book!

"Whew!" whistled Rouletabille. "It is quite possible that my little visit to dear Monsieur de Lauriac's study will not be absolutely useless."

Five minutes later he had left Lou Cabanou without disturbing Pandora's slumbers.

The chief librarian of the Municipal Library at Arles had barely reached his room, and had not yet had time to take his spectacles from their case when he saw coming towards him, like a whirlwind, a breathless young man, carrying under his arm a weighty portfolio, from which, wthout speaking a word, he drew one of the oldest specimens of the bookman's art which had ever been placed under this worthy official's eyes.

"Here, monsieur, is a little thing which I wish to submit for your expert opinion. Everyone is aware that you possess an unequaled knowledge of whatever pertains to Oriental languages . . ."

"I read them all and speak some of them." interrupted the librarian modestly.

"Well, I have come to the right man. You shall tell me what you think of my 'little diary.'"

The librarian did not even condescend to smile at

Rouletabille's jest. He was already enraptured. His wide-open eyes, gleaming behind his spectacles, his trembling fingers as they traveled over the precious book, bore witness to his enthusiasm, which, though it was restrained, was none the less very great.

"It's a beauty, what?" said Rouletabille.

The librarian did not answer. Though Rouletabille might speak the librarian had no ears for him. His entire being was concentrated on seeing and touching the treasure.

"Well, what do you say?" exclaimed the journalist.

The librarian was reading it. He began at the first page, and was about to turn over the second, seemingly disinclined to skip a line. Rouletabille sat down, prepared, whatever happened, to show patience and good temper. He knew that learned men have their little eccentricities, and, in particular, do not like to be hurried.

He would wait since he must wait. All the more so, as some scholars under an appearance of childish simplicity, conceal a diabolical craft and enjoy to the full, without appearing to do so, a laugh at other people's expense.

However, the librarian, after reading the second page, started on the third. Therefore Rouletabille rose to his feet and in his most imperturbable manner went up to him, drew his "turnip" from his waistcoat pocket, and quietly placed it on the third page under the librarian's nose.

The librarian contemplated the dial for a moment as though it were some strange beast of an entirely unknown species, then raised his head and stared questioningly at the journalist with a look of blank and anxious surprise. His gaze seemed to say: "What does this fellow want with me?" or again, "Who allowed this gentleman to come into my room without knocking?"

Rouletabille gave the learned man one of his most agreeable smiles.

"I should like to tell you, monsieur, that this book contains four hundred pages, and I am showing you my watch to remind you that it is half-past nine in the morning. At what time do you expect to finish reading it? I have a few calls to make in the town. When shall I come back?"

"In a week, monsieur. Come back here in a week's time. This book is a wonder. I want to read and re-read it. If I were rich enough to buy it, you would not see it again."

"And if it belonged to me, I would make you a present of it."

"That's very good of you to say so. What do you want from me?"

"It's a Romany book, is it not?"

"I see that you know what you're talking about, young man. I dare say you 'do a little book-collecting.'"

"No, monsieur," returned Rouletabille, who would not have admitted to a public official for anything in the world his position as a journalist, knowing that as a rule such persons loathe the very name of journalist. "No, monsieur, but I am a bit of a traveler, and I said to my friend from whom I borrowed it: 'I may be mistaken, but in my opinion this book is a Romany book.'"

"What did your friend say?"

"He told me to come and see you."

"He was quite right. . . . Yes, this book is very old, and is written in the traditional gypsy language. . . . But see what there is inside. I find these words on the cover. I will translate them," said the librarian, adjusting his glasses. "This is the Book of Ancestors:

'Whoso shall reverence this Book,
Preserve it if it be in peril,
.

> *Restore it if it be lost,*
> *Shall be given a befitting recompense,'*

and underneath

> *'But whoso shall steal this Book*
> *Or mutilate it,*
> *Shall be chastened and meet the pain of death.' "*

"By Jove!" exclaimed Rouletabille, "they come it a bit strong those ancestors. Fortunately they died before the man stole it."

"Did your friend steal the book?" asked the librarian, gazing at Rouletabille over the rim of his glasses.

"Well, now, he omitted to tell me," returned the journalist, laughing heartily, "but between ourselves he is quite capable of doing so."

"A strange sort of friend," observed the worthy functionary, compressing his lips.

"He is, you understand, a devoted lover of rare books, and book-collecting covers a multitude of sins."

"I doubt if there is in France or Europe, I might even say in the whole world, a more devoted lover of rare books than myself, and yet I have never robbed anyone," protested the librarian, turning purple at Rouletabille's enunciation of a sentiment destructive alike of public and private morals.

"I quite believe you, monsieur. You have the look of an honest man. And as to this book, I intend to discover the truth. My friend shall tell me where and when he got it and if he appropriated it honestly! If he cannot reply to my questions straightforwardly, I shall threaten to denounce him to the Public Prosecutor, unless . . ."

"Unless?"

"Unless he makes a present of it to the Arles Library."

The librarian's expression gradually relaxed into a smile. He held out his huge paw:

"You are a man of wit."

"And so are you," returned the journalist, warmly shaking him by the hand. "But I am not a scholar. What else does the book contain?"

"It contains the sacred text of the rites which govern the consecration of towns, churches, altars, encampments."

While speaking he turned over the pages:

"Here is a chapter which deals with the art of reading omens and divining the future. Gypsies have always been addicted to those sort of practices. The book dates from a period when this nomadic people finally settled down for some centuries in the Near East. From what I can gather, at a glance, I should not be surprised if we had in our possession the orthodox ritual of the gypsies who settled in Europe after their flight from Asia, and eventually established the Patriarchate of Transylvania."

"What you tell me is most interesting."

"Oh, good heavens!" cried the librarian suddenly, as if he had received a blow in the chest.

"What's the matter?"

"Well, a stone is lacking in the edifice. I mean a page is missing from the book. What a vandal, what a ruffian the man must be who tore out this page. It is the more to be deplored as the absence of this page prevents me from reading the continuation of a most curious prophecy which begins on the preceding page."

"A prophecy!" exclaimed Rouletabille, assuming a more serious air, as though an idea had suddenly occurred to his ever-active brain. "Will you translate the actual wording of the prophecy?"

"Here it is literally translated: 'In due time a queen shall be born to the race bearing on the left shoulder the mark of the crown. . . . This child shall be born of a gypsy mother and an alien father. . . .And the race during her reign shall behold once more its ancient prosperity.' "

While the librarian was reading Rouletabille's face gleamed with a strange light. As soon as the last words of the prophecy were uttered, he gave way to his excitement:

"Ah, now I understand," he cried, wildly waving his cap.

"Are you going mad?" asked the librarian. "I should think you did understand, seeing that I've translated the words for you."

"Oh, monsieur, it was not a question of understanding those words. I understand now what I didn't understand before!"

"But I don't understand you."

"You must understand, then, that I see now why my flat was burgled."

And without further ado Rouletabille snatched the precious book from the librarian's hands. The latter bewildered, gave a start, exclaiming:

"Your flat was burgled?"

"I look a bit of a burglar myself, eh? That's what you mean. Well, I'm going to take this book back to where I found it. It scares me. . . . It scares me. Oh, I'm not keen on being sent to an early grave by those ancestors!"

Rouletabille vanished. The librarian, not knowing what he was doing or saying, threw up his arms in the air and groaned:

"Stop thief!"

It seemed to him, indeed, that he himself was being robbed. This incomparable treasure which had no sooner appeared than it disappeared, had unbalanced his mind. He regretted allowing this great work of art to escape him, though it was not his property. The librarian understood now that "book-collecting covered a multitude of sins!"

An hour later Rouletabille was once more in Lou Cabanou. He encountered no greater opposition in returning to it than when he first entered it. He placed the Book of Ancestors in the exact spot where he found it, taking care to replace the paper-cutter in the page in which he had inserted the sheet of paper; and when he had got rid of it his thoughts swelled the veins in his forehead and he murmured:

"Yes, this book scares me. It is the key of the riddle. It is the origin of the trouble. It is through this book that the whole thing has happened. It is to discover the whereabouts of this book that every effort is directed, and de Lauriac, Jean, Odette, Callista, Olajaï, Rouletabille, and even the Octopus are without knowing it drawn within its orbit. This book can tell us everything— more indeed than any of us imagine. And the book will divulge its secret. It will reveal whether de Lauriac is in league with Callista. . . . The book is an evil influence and, perhaps, it has saved us."

After indulging in this soliloquy Rouletabille climbed out of the study through the window; and from the window he slid down to the pantry and from the pantry . . .

Meantime Pandora in the passage continued snoring.

CHAPTER XV

PANDORA'S INQUIRY

PANDORA'S slumbers must have ceased soon for shortly afterwards this worthy representative of the mounted police was observed, not far from the house, questioning a young herdsman. The youngster was asked what the gendarme had said to him. The gendarme had asked him if he had seen, about midnight, a gypsy woman come out of the forest and make for. a grove of tamarisks which lined the road from Arles to Lavardens.

"I was there myself," the youngster returned. "The gypsy woman came along and met a man who was hanging round there for some time. They had a talk and then the gypsy woman left him saying: 'Till this afternoon at three o'clock at Roche d'Ozoul.'"

Thereupon the gendarme left the young herdsman with the remark:

"Capital! The thing still holds good."

Pandora obviously was making some inquiry on the instruction of the examining magistrate for he was seen half an hour later questioning certain persons who were gossiping on their doorsteps. At last on the stroke of midday he appeared at the office of Mᵉ Camousse, the solicitor.

Mᵉ Camousse's practice was admittedly the largest in the town. Generations of the Camousses from father to son had drafted the marriage contracts and held custody of the wills of the most important families in the district. With a reputation which was in some degree hereditary, the Camousses held in their strong-room great fortunes of which they were the faithful trustees. Moreover, the secrets of many a family had been confided to them, and their integrity was not less substantial than their strong room. For over a hundred years they had been the de Lavardens' family lawyers.

"I've come about the de Lavardens' business," said the sergeant, thrusting his fist between the door and the frame at the moment when the junior clerk was closing the office. It was the hour at which work was temporarily suspended and only the copying clerks, who were preparing to go to lunch, remained in the outside office.

"Hullo, another sergeant!" exclaimed the junior clerk as he opened the door, disregarding the protests of the staff.

Nevertheless when the clerks caught sight of the gendarme they became silent, waiting for him to speak.

"You young rascal," said the sergeant, "go and fetch your governor. And look sharp!"

The clerk told him that Me Camousse was about to go to lunch, but that the chief clerk and the liquidating clerk were still there and perhaps could deal with the matter.

"What's that! I didn't ask to see those people. I want Monsieur Camousse personally, so look alive."

Just then Monsieur Camousse, a presentable man about forty years of age, with a somewhat ruddy face and iron-gray side whiskers, came out, inquired what was wanted, and showed the sergeant into his room.

"I am sent to you by the examining magistrate."

"The examining magistrate!" echoed Monsieur Camousse in astonishment.

"Yes, Monsieur Crousillat himself. He is up to his ears in this de Lavardens' business, and has instructed me to assist him in his investigations by putting a few simple questions to you."

"I'm listening, sergeant. Please take a seat."

"Now this is what's what. I've come here about the de Lavardens' affair, eh! The examining magistrate wishes to know the date of Monsieur de Lavardens' marriage. You can answer that question, eh! I suppose you've no objection to that?"

"I cannot refuse the authorities of my country anything. I will make it my duty to help them to the utmost of my power, provided, of course, that I am not asked to violate professional secrecy."

"Of course. That's quite reasonable."

"And you, sergeant, I gather from your accent belong to Rousillon."

"One can't hide anything from you, mosieu. , . . You've guessed right. I was born near Perpignan, at your service. As to professional secrecy, I am a gendarme and know what that means, and I am not the man to ask you to give away anything which, if I may say so, is sacred."

"I mention this to you, sergeant, because hardly more than an hour ago a young man came to my office and asked me questions to answer which would have involved a breach of professional duty."

"Oh, you don't say so! A young man?"

"Yes, he called himself a journalist—Rouletabille by name."

"Rouletabille came here to question you?"

"I might say to ask indiscreet questions."

"I hope you kicked him out."

"Very nearly so, but as you know we are always polite in our profession. Oh, there's a fellow with plenty of cheek! He claimed to be well known. Personally I have never heard of him."

"Don't you read the newspapers?"

"As little as possible. You see, sergeant, either there's nothing in them or there's something in them. When there's nothing in them it is not worth while to read them, and when there's something in them it is always about crimes or disasters; in other words, things which we should do well to remain in ignorance of as long as possible. . . . But you appear to know this Rouleta- bille?"

"I should think I did know him, mosieu! Why, he's a regular nuisance, is this journalist. Monsieur Crousillat shuns him as though he were the plague. Rouletabille never leaves me. He spies on all my movements. I bet you he called about this Lavardens' affair."

"You've won your bet, sergeant, but he lost . . . lost this time."

"When I tell Monsieur Crousillat so, he will be delighted. . . . We were saying that Monsieur de Lavardens was married . . ."

"Listen," said the lawyer, looking through a file of papers. "Here is a copy of the marriage certificate de- posited at the French Consulate in Odessa. You've only got to make a copy of it."

"That's what I was told. He was married in Odessa to a young French girl by whom he had a daughter legitimized by the marriage."

"Be careful! Here we are trenching upon profes- sional secrecy, sergeant. Logically I cannot refuse to let the authorities of my country see a document a copy of which they would possibly have some difficulty in ob- taining now."

"Yes, Odessa is a long way off, and besides, there are Bolsheviks."

"But, you understand, there's no necessity for all the world to know that Mademoiselle de Lavardens was born before her mother's marriage."

"Of course. Have no fear. . . . I'm not the man to go and tell this to Rouletabille."

"You've grasped the point, sergeant."

"It's not for me to praise myself, but everybody says that I am blessed with rather exceptional intelligence. Now one thing more: Have you by chance the child's birth certificate, eh?"

"To tell you the truth, no," returned Mᵉ Camousse, knitting his brows slightly and closing the file of papers.

"Isn't it among your papers?"

"No, it is not among my papers."

"That's a pity, because, as you may have observed, the details of the child's birth-place on the certificate of legitimization are most vague, whereas if we had a copy of the birth certificate that would perhaps . . ."

"What?" questioned the lawyer, nervously tapping the top of his desk.

"Why, perhaps it would be easier to silence scandal-mongers."

"What scandal-mongers?"

"Well those people, for instance, who suggest that this French woman was not Odette's real mother."

"I've never heard anyone say such a thing, sergeant," returned the lawyer, rising to his feet. "I should be interested to know from whom you heard it."

"Why, from some one who is as interested as you are, I assure you. From the examining magistrate himself, and I am instructed by his worship to ask you—he is convinced, by the way, that you know all there is to be known on the subject—whether Mademoiselle de Lavardens was really the daughter of Madame de Lavardens."

"The examining magistrate instructed you to ask me that!" exclaimed Mᵉ Camousse, turning scarlet.

"I swear it by my sergeant's stripes!"

"And I swear that if I were Monsieur Crousillat and wanted to put such a question to Mᵉ Camousse, I should have invited Mᵉ Camousse to come to my office, and spoken to him as magistrate to magistrate, and not sent a sergeant of gendarmes to him. . . . Besides, I'm going," declared the lawyer, putting on his hat.

"Where to?"

"Why, I'm going with you to the examining magistrate."

"Well, I shall go off alone! Don't put yourself out. Hang it all, how you take on—how you take on! What a hot-tempered person you are! I ask you questions and you are free to refuse to answer them. Devil take it, professional secrecy before all. We'll say no more about it."

But do and say what the sergeant might, Mᵉ Camousse was resolved to accompany him to Monsieur Crousillat's. He reached the stairs and street as soon as the sergeant. As he stepped into the street the sergeant looked at his watch, a huge turnip, and declared that he had an important call to make and would leave Mᵉ Camousse to see the examining magistrate alone. And he had already walked a few steps away when two men in plain clothes, appeared from no one knows where, and made a rush at him shouting.

"It's no use putting up a fight. Be good enough to come with us."

"But who are you?" the lawyer asked, turning to the two plain clothes men.

"We are detectives, Mᵉ Camousse, instructed to arrest Rouletabille."

"Do you mean to say this gendarme . . ."

"That's Rouletabille!"

Mᵉ Camousse, gasping for breath, was obliged to lean against the wall to prevent himself from slipping to the pavement.

"This is undoubtedly the greatest event in my life," he murmured.

Meantime people came hurrying up from every side

to see a gendarme marched off as a prisoner by two plain clothes men.

And Rouletabille pulled a long face. . . .

It was obvious that the last scene in the little farce which he had been playing so airily was not included in the program. He dropped his Rousillon accent then and there, and rolling his r's with the drawling pronunciation of a man who lived in the Montmartre district of Paris asked:

"Are you taking me to the lock-up?"

"No, my lad, we're taking you to Monsieur Crousillat."

"Ah, now I feel quite easy," said Rouletabille. "We're going to a café."

The detectives and the little group wnich formed an escort burst out laughing. Monsieur Crousillat, who was undoubtedly the weightiest examining magistrate in France and Navarre, at least in point of adipose tissue, was well known for his unquenchable thirst. The least physical or even mental exertion put him in a bath of perspiration. Accordingly, he was often to be seen conducting his investigations in the shade of the open front of a cafè with a couple of bocks full to the brim before him, which were quite cool when the waiter served them. It was a method of setting to work, however, which greatly tried the temper of his clerk, Bartholasse, a thin man as yellow as a lemon, whose disordered stomach could not stand anything stronger than homely camomile tea.

In short, the end of the incident caused a great deal of merriment around, and Rouletabille, who was not of a nature to stand aloof for long, was soon joining in the laugh. After all, had he not got his way and learned what he wanted to know? Could the worthy Mᵉ Camousse have told him anything more? Had not the excitement which the solicitor betrayed when the last question was put to him with intentional bluntness by the sham Pandora—was Mademoiselle de Lavardens the daughter of Madame de Lavardens?—sufficiently enlightened him? In any case, the family lawyer's attitude coming after the librarian's reading, or rather translation of certain passages in the Book of Ancestors, entitled Rouletabille to assume a great many things suggestive of a development in the tragedy, in which Odette was the center, which until then he alone had suspected. . . .

CHAPTER XVI

ROULETABILLE TELLS A FEW STORIES

ARE the magistrate and his clerk in a vile temper?' Rouletabille asked the detectives.

"You must admit that they have good cause, Monsieur Rouletabille," returned one.

"Lou Fineto is· the most infuriated," said the other. "He is squalling like a cat."

"So Lou Fineto is squalling like a cat! Who is Lou Fineto, my dear fellow?"

"That's the nickname given here to La Finette, the gendarme whom you so smartly relieved of his tunic and cap."

"He had fixed up a very soft and luxurious pillow with this tunic and cap had the worthy La Finette," returned Rouletabille, who had recovered his high spirits, "and I felt considerable remorse at the time for taking them from him, but I did it with the greatest delicacy so as not to disturb his slumbers. What else could I do? Business is business. Why did La Finette wake up so soon? It is entirely his own fault. He ought to have slept an hour longer, and I should have returned his pillow, and he wouldn't have noticed anything. So the worthy La Finette is squalling is he! Well, when he has done squalling he will say nothing. . . . In any case, he doesn't expect to get me sent to penal servitude for life, I suppose?"

"Oh, Monsieur Rouletabille, don't think you're going to get out of it so easily. It's a very serious matter to take a gendarme's uniform away from him."

"Be assured, my dear fellow, that nothing in life is serious," returned Rouletabille in a tone of philosophy, "nothing except death. And then we are no longer here to worry about it."

Chatting in this way, the group reached Monsieur Crousillat's office which, as Rouletabille anticipated, was the cool pavement of a café. The gentlemen from the prosecutor's office were launching into derogatory remarks about newspapers in general, and Rouletabille in particular, when the latter appeared with his escort.

"There he is!" snarled Bartholasse, letting the papers which he had spread on the zinc-top table be scattered by the wind.

"Ah, there you are!" squealed Monsieur Crousillat, after, however, taking time to consume the bock which had just been brought to him.

"I should think so! . . . Peep-Bo! . . . How are you this morning, Monsieur Crousillat? And you, Monsieur Bartholasse? . . . Our dear friend Monsieur Bartholasse! . . . I see by his look that he made the mistake of having another champagne dinner last night."

It seemed as if the clerk was about to have a fit. He was a very short man, and stood on tiptoe shaking his fist in the journalist's face, and predicting that he would come to a bad end.

"Have you engaged the services of the hangman?" asked Rouletabille placidly.

Just then frantic shouts could be heard, and a man in shirt sleeves appeared at the café window foaming with rage.

"Ah, there's our La Finette! We were only waiting for him to complete our little party. I mean what I say. I quite understand, Monsieur La Finette, why you are not pleased, and I offer you my apologies. Besides, it would ill become me not to admit that I was in the wrong. What I did was too bad, and I promise you, Monsieur

Crousillat, that it shall never occur again. I'm not a pig-headed man. . . . Of course, I went a little too far. My business is responsible for that."

"Do you know where your business will lead you?" asked Monsieur Crousillat, silencing the onlookers by a peremptory gesture.

"Yes, monsieur, it will lead me to save you from doing an idiotic thing!"

"Monsieur!"

"I am sorry, monsieur, I certainly did not intend to be wanting in respect. I say that my business, of which you hold such a poor opinion, may really prevent you from making a mistake, and when a man's life depends upon it, it may be worth your while, in return, to pass over the trick which Rouletabille played on the worthy La Finette."

"Oh, what you say won't affect me, and I tell you that your business will land you first in the lock-up, and next before the bench."

"Very well," returned the journalist imperturbably. "I see that this is a prejudice with you. I won't dwell upon it. Waiter, bring me a bock."

And he took a seat.

"He is utterly hopeless," said Monsieur Bartholasse in a harsh voice.

"You, my friend, had better be careful," declared Rouletabille, fixing him with an icy stare. "You would like to kill me with a look. As for you, Monsieur Crousillat, you are the most sensible man here. After all, if there was half the rage in your heart that is choking Monsieur Bartholasse, you might have greeted my arrival with a blow from those fists with which nature has generously endowed you, and it would have been a question only of writing my epitaph. But speaking generally, physically robust men are good men. Therefore it is for your benefit that I wish to tell this little story. . . .

"For instance, it is funny when a murder has been committed in a house and the concierge has sworn to give no information to the newspapers, for a journalist to appear with a police pass signed by police-headquarters, to palm himself off as a detective, and to obtain from the doorkeeper particulars which enable him to find the criminal in a place where the police would never have suspected him of setting foot. That happened to me personallly, monsieur, and the police who, after all, are easy-going fellows with whom, in most cases, we get on very well, bore me no malice. But there was a high official who made a fuss about it; one of those men to whom the result of an investigation is nothing, but the form of it everything. This man was determined to fall foul of Rouletabille the journalist. We must take it that the latter had access to the powers that be, for the pride of this high official was laid low, and he is now living in the country. Do you like the country, Monsieur Crousillat? . . .

"Another story: One day I had to join the Minister of the Navy, who was making a tour of inspection, along the coast, of our torpedo defence. I was late for the naval review, and I found myself refused admittance everywhere. My pass as a journalist was of no avail. As a last resource I sought out the Deputy-Prefect who was about to dress up in full fig. He deputed his valet to see me, and the man received me as if I were a dog at a wedding. He left me in a room and paid no further attention to me. Suddenly I espied on a chair the official uniform which the man had placed there. I slipped into it like a rat in a hole. I jumped into a taxi and drove to the harbor. Ten minutes later I was ushered into the presence of the Minister with all the honors due to my rank!

"What do you think of that? The uniform of a Deputy-Prefect is not less important than the uniform of a gendarme. Well, when he saw me in that rig-out, the Minister, who was a Parisian, or who had become one after he joined the government, entered into the spirit of the joke. But the Deputy-Prefect made the mistake of treating it seriously. He lodged a complaint . . . a complaint in due form. Well, monsieur, this Deputy-Prefect is still a Deputy-Prefect . . . Monsieur Crousillat, believe me, a man of your stamp will live to be a Judge of the Court of Appeal."

Monsieur Crousillat who, as he listened to the first story, began to scratch his head with a preoccupied air, laughed heartily over the second.

"Now then," said he, "off you go and don't let me catch you at it again."

Rouletabille leapt to his feet, looked at his watch, uttered a muffled exclamation: "I shall be late," and scampered away like a hare.

CHAPTER XVII

A DRAMATIC INCIDENT

ROULETABILLE was once more, at Lavardens. He seemed, as usual, in a hurry. He made his way quickly to Viei-Castou-Nou and, darting into the entrance hall, mounted four at a time the stairs leading to the first floor. He encountered a number of persons dressed in mourning, distant relatives of Monsieur de Lavardens who, since the disappearance of Odette, had been keeping an eye on the property, and at length he came upon the woman—the lady's maid—whom he was seeking. He bundled her into a small study and closed the door so that they might be undisturbed.

Estève could not now meet Rouletabille without trembling like a leaf. She held out her clasped hands to him and said:

"I swear, monsieur, that I've told you everything."

"Look here," said Rouletabille, as he pressed down her hands. "I'm going to ask you a simple question, but it is of more importance than you can imagine."

"Good gracious, what is it now?" moaned poor Estève.

"I want you to tell me," explained Rouletabille, bending over the girl who stared at him with ever increasing dismay. "I want you to tell me—don't look at me like that, because my question is a mere nothing—whether Mademoiselle Odette bore any mark on her left shoulder."

"Mark on her left shoulder!" echoed the lady's maid

113

opening her eyes in wonder. "Now that's a nice question!"

"I didn't ask you for your opinion, but for an answer. Was there any mark on her left shoulder?"

"Certainly not. There was no mark either on her left or right shoulder."

"Understand what I mean," persisted Rouletabille. "Some people have what is called a strawberry mark or some birth-mark on the skin. You must often have helped your mistress to undress, and you should have seen it."

"Certainly I should have seen it. There was no such mark. Her skin was as clear as a mirror."

"No mark—nothing?"

"Nothing, I tell you."

"Not even a beauty spot, hang it all?"

"She was beautiful all over, but she had no beauty spot."

"You're not deceiving me? Besides, you have no reason to deceive me."

"What difference does it make to me whether she had a beauty spot or not?"

"Very well," returned Rouletabille, brooding for a while. "That's all I want to know," and he abruptly left her.

"He's got a beauty spot on the brain," muttered Estève.

Rouletabille left the house and was making for the town of Lavardens when he caught sight of Jean coming towards Viei-Castou-Nou. He called him, and Jean ran up.

"I was looking for you," cried Jean. "Do you remember what you told me?"

"What was it?"

"That someone would bring me news of Odette."

"Oh, yes, I remember something of the sort."

"Just think! I have had a most extraordinary meeting, only a stone's throw from here. I've been keeping near Viei-Castou-Nou as you suggested."

"What then?"

"Well, I was seated on a road-side bank thinking of what you said, and feeling very depressed in spite of your optimism; and I was wondering how it was that you could speak with such self-assurance of a matter which seemed to become more and more puzzling and mysterious—so many persons were leagued against us though I could not imagine why—when I saw a little girl in tatters, undoubtedly a little gypsy girl, carrying a few baskets and a bundle of osier twigs. She glanced round her as if she wished to make certain that no one was watching her, and then leaning towards me said:

" 'Are you Monsieur Jean?'

" 'Yes, what do you want with me?' I returned.

"She answered by asking me another question:

" 'Would you like to have news of the young lady?'

"You can imagine the effect which her words had on me, particularly after what you told me.

" 'Why of course,' I said, 'I should be very pleased.'

"She gazed round her once more.

" 'Whatever you do, don't tell anyone you've seen me, or they'll kill me.'

"I assured her that she need have no fear.

" 'Well,' she said in a whisper. 'There's some one who can tell you. Go to . . .' "

"Go to Roseaux plain at seven o'clock," broke in Rouletabille.

"What! Do you know about it?" cried Jean astounded.

"Ought I not to know everything?"

"She walked away telling me that it would be well to go to the place alone, otherwise I shouldn't see anyone."

"I quite believe it."

"As you knew that this appointment would be made for me, I suppose you've come along here to go with me?"

"Not a bit of it! I don't want you to miss your appointment. You must go alone. Off you go—alone."

"Have you any suggestions to make?"

"None. . . . One moment, I suggest that you do not lose a single word of what may be said. Good-by, Jean, and good luck."

Jean looked at his watch.

"I'll be off," he said. "Roseaux plain is some distance from here and I intend to go on foot to avoid attracting any attention."

"Well, go and good luck. While you are away I shan't be wasting time, I promise you."

"Shall we meet again at Viei-Castou-Nou?"

"Get on with it, chatterer! Aren't you longing to know where Odette is?"

Jean left him. Rouletabille took the road in an opposite direction. He seemed somewhat lost in thought when on passing a café in Lavardens, he was attracted by the sound of voices, the voices of the examining magistrate and his clerk in conversation with the owner. Rouletabille bent forward and his eyes fell on the gendarmes seated under an awning at the far end of the café with a bottle before them. La Finette was telling the story how that low-down journalist had sent back his tunic and cap with his best thanks: "Well, the first time I lay hands on him I'll give him 'best thanks.'"

Rouletabille noticed also Monsieur Crousillat's bicycle on the pavement. The sight of it seemed straightway to determine his course of action. He walked up to the "bike," mounted it, and making no attempt at concealment started off at a good speed just as Monsieur Crousillat came out of the café to sit down on the open front.

"My bicycle!" roared the examining magistrate. "Ah, this time he's going too far!"

He called the gendarmes who also had bicycles, and they started to give chase to Rouletabille, shouting at the top of their voices. Rouletabille turned round and beckoning them in the friendliest way to follow him, amused himself by slackening his speed when he was too far ahead. In short, he seemed to take a special pleasure in the uncommon sight of a spreading procession of gendarmes yelping and gesticulating like madness. La Finette, of course, was the most excited of them all.

"This time he shan't escape me," he cried.

Rouletabille kissed his hand to him.

On the stroke of seven o'clock Jean reached Roseaux plain.

The first thing that met his eyes was the little gypsy girl, who, after a friendly nod, disappeared from view, and he did not give her another thought. He continued to go forward. A dead silence enveloped him, and the solitude was beginning to tell upon him when suddenly the reeds in front of him were thrust aside and from behind the screen emerged the form of a gypsy whom at first he did not recognize. Then she drew nearer and fixed him with her blazing eyes.

"Callista!" he cried, instinctively starting back. "You in that dress!"

"Yes," she returned in a tone of defiance. "Why should you be surprised? Am I not a Romany? Though I had forgotten it, you did your best to remind me of it. You took me from the road, and I am back to it again since you turned me adrift. . . . But before we part I wanted to see you for the last time, my love."

And she burst into a fit of wild laughter.

Jean was in the presence of a being who was a stranger to him and whose nature he had never suspected. The Callista of old had been easy-going or affectionate or sulky and sometimes artlessly proud like a spoilt child.

And now standing before him was the embodiment of hate. He had no call to look at her a second time to comprehend that she was the cause of all his misfortunes. And his heart was filled with a savage resentment. He seized her by the wrist with a violence that made her cry out.

"Odette? What have you done with Odette?" he shouted.

She writhed in his grip, but continued her mocking laugh.

"Odette!" she echoed. "What's this Odette? Who's seen Odette? Are you looking for Odette?"

Jean was more incensed by her ridicule than he would have been by her insults, and it seemed as if he would shake the life out of her. Then, foaming with passion, she cried:

"Well, yes, it's true. Your Odette—I took her away from you. And you will never see her again—never, never, never!"

The word "never," as she shouted it at him, seemed to stab him like a knife. Jean was silent and they continued to struggle. Suddenly he staggered and slipped on his knees. It seemed as if some wild beast, some lion had leaped on to his shoulders, for as he collapsed under the impact a kind of growl broke out behind him.

Callista now stood silent while Jean and Andréa, locked in a deadly embrace, seemed to be choking the life out of each other. As they fought they drew nearer the shining surface of the water which shimmered between the tall reeds. The two men rolled towards it, each bent on forcing his adversary into its depths. Callista, panting for breath, was leaning over them. Jean was being worsted in the fight. At the moment when he was about to be hurled into the water Callista uttered a cry, and it would have been difficult to say whether it was a shout of triumph or of anguish.

And then when all was about to culminate in a tragic climax, the scene changed. A new actor appeared on the stage. It was Rouletabille. He gave a shrill whistle and a small body of gendarmes came rushing up, and throwing themselves on Andréa and Callista, made them prisoners.

The two gypsies were so entirely taken by surprise that they allowed themselves to be handcuffed without protest.

"I think it was about time for me to come, what?" said Rouletabille.

"You always come at the right moment," returned Jean, embracing him.

CHAPTER XVIII

IN WHICH MONSIEUR CROUSILLAT DISCOVERS THAT JOURNALISTS SOMETIMES "HAVE GOOD QUALITIES"

MONSIEUR CROUSILLAT returned puffing and perspiring to Arles on foot in a state of mind that may easily be imagined. Monsieur Bartholasse, his clerk, had scored. He had not forgiven his chief for his forbearance towards Rouletabille.

"You never gain anything by sparing a man of that kidney," he said. "Give him an inch and he'll take an ell. The joker's always making fools of us. He began by going off with a gendarme's uniform and you'll see what the end will be."

As the reader knows, the end was that Rouletabille rode off with the examining magistrate's bicycle.

"I'll have him put under lock and key," declared Monsieur Crousillat.

"You say that now, but he'll get round you again with his humbug."

When Monsieur Crousillat reached the Law Courts, to which he had repaired for his official papers, so that he might continue his work on them at home in the evening, for the case kept him on the alert night and day, the first thing that met his gaze was his bicycle propped up against the porter's lodge. He could scarcely believe his own eyes.

"It's yours right enough," said Monsieur Bartholasse.

"Who brought this bicycle here?" asked Monsieur Crousillat.

"Monsieur Rouletabille brought it only a moment ago," returned the porter. "He told me that you lent it to him, and said I was to be sure and take great care of it. He asked me also to say that he was coming back himself to thank you for it."

"The farce continues," muttered Monsieur Bartholasse with a titter, which increased the examining magistrate's exasperation. "Oh, we haven't done with him yet."

Raging within himself, Monsieur Crousillat hurriedly mounted the stairs to his office. Monsieur Bartholasse had some difficulty in keeping pace with him.

"Whew!" breathed the clerk. "We're better off here than in a café, anyway."

"Do you say that for my benefit, Monsieur Bartholasse?"

"No, Monsieur Crousillat, for the benefit of Rouletabille, who has led us a pretty dance."

Just then the office messenger announced Monsieur Rouletabille. The two men gave a start.

"Show him in," ordered Monsieur Crousillat in a threatening voice.

"Monsieur Rouletabille is not alone."

Rouletabille made his appearance.

"Ah, so there you are!"

"Yes, here *we* are. I am very pleased to see you here, as I know that this is your dinner hour."

"I've had enough of your humbug," returned the examining magistrate, who in his wrath not only used his clerk's words, but pronounced them with his accent.

"I am going to teach you that it's an expensive matter to play tricks on magistrates."

"I, play tricks on magistrates!" broke in Rouletabille, with his most frank and open look.

"With whom were you playing tricks then when you ran off with my bicycle under my very eyes?"

"Not with magistrates certainly, because I only borrowed it so as to help you."

"What did I say?" exclaimed Monsieur Bartholasse. "Here he is again with the same old humbug. Listen to him. Listen to him for yourself."

"Yes, listen to me," assented Rouletabille. "I am much obliged to you, Monsieur Bartholasse, for this is the first time to-day that you've made a sensible remark."

"Look here, I had better leave the place, otherwise I shall do something rash," said the clerk.

"Let this man go to his camomile tea," said the journalist, turning his back on him, "but you, Monsieur Crousillat, do you remember what I promised you for your dinner?—the arrest of the guilty parties. Well, don't disturb yourself. Monsieur, your dinner is served!"

With an illustrative gesture which a butler in the days of Louis XIV might have envied, he pointed to the feast which he had prepared: Andréa and Callista standing at the entrance of the door with a couple of gendarmes on either side.

La Finette nudged the two gypsies, who took a step forward.

Andréa folded his arms and gazed with a look of contempt and indifference at the persons present. He carried his head high. As he advanced into the room he spat forth a few words at Rouletabille, consigning him to eternal perdition, and afterwards seemed to take little interest in the proceedings. With his shoulder barely covered with a tattered shirt, and his neck and throat partly exposed, he seemed like the bronze statue of a god.

Callista, on the other hand, had seated herself on the first chair within reach, without waiting to be asked, and was staring at her nails, which had lost some of their luster since she left Paris.

"You were looking for the persons who kidnaped Mademoiselle de Lavardens. Here they are!" said Rouletabille.

"Mosieu, they don't deny it," broke in La Finette. "They've confessed it in our presence. The villains! They brag about it. Yes, indeed, I must tell you, between ourselves, that the young man over there"—pointing to Rouletabille—"pulled off the business very well."

Monsieur Crousillat looked in turn at the prisoner, the journalist, and La Finette. His excitement was such that he was speechless. La Finette went on:

"He's made a fine haul, what?"

"But, confound it," at last burst out Monsieur Crousillat, patting Rouletabille on the shoulder with his huge paw, "why did you not tell me you were going to pull off a thing like this? That would have been much more simple than stea—borrowing my bicycle. I would have given you all the gendarmes you needed."

"No, you would not have given me one. Our dear friend Monsieur Bartholasse would have known how to prevent you. It was much simpler to take the gendarmes from you. And when I borrowed your bicycle I was certain that they would come after me."

Monsieur Crousillat did not persist. He turned to the prisoners.

"So these are the vagabonds who are responsible. Young woman, stand up!"

Callista obediently rose from her chair without apparent emotion.

"You understand, both of you, what the charge is— the murder of Monsieur de Lavardens and the abduction of his daughter. And you say, La Finette, that the prisoners have confessed? . . . Monsieur Bartholasse, please take this down."

"We haven't murdered anybody," declared Callista.

"First of all, who are you?" went on the examining

magistrate. . . . "What are these people? Gypsies, obviously."

"Monsieur can answer you," said Callista, pointing to Rouletabille and still speaking very calmly. "He knows me."

Rouletabille went up to her, lifted the sleeve of her blouse, and disclosed round her amber-colored arm the gold slave-bangle which she had shown him on one occasion.

"Yes, I know you," he returned. "You are the woman who wears on her arm the sign of revenge. You meant to be revenged on Monsieur de Santierne and you carried off the girl he was about to marry."

"But, look here, what does all this mean?" exclaimed Monsieur Crousillat. "Do you know this woman?"

"Oh, Monsieur Rouletabille and I are old friends," said Callista, with a peculiar smile. "He has often dined with me."

"Do people dine with you!" cried the examining magistrate, letting his gaze stray over the wretched garments in which this strange beauty was clad—if the term can be used.

"Madame keeps an excellent cook and lives in a luxurious flat in one of the smartest parts of Paris."

"Do you mean to say that this woman is a Parisian?"

"No, she is a gypsy, but thanks to Monsieur Jean de Santierne, who on one occasion rescued her from this man's brutality—this man who is her accomplice to-day —she became one of the most attractive women in Paris whom I have ever met. I have no wish to forget the hospitality which she and her lover, her bear's cub and her parrot offered me only a few days ago; and I am very sorry that she left Paris to assume these rags. But, as the saying goes, one always returns to one's first love. For my part, I see no objection to that, but she must tell us what she has done with Mademoiselle de Lavardens."

"Never!" cried Callista in such savage tones that a shudder passed through them.

"You forget, madame, that Monsieur de Lavardens has been murdered," continued Rouletabille.

"We had no hand in that."

"It suits you to say so," interrupted Monsieur Crousillat, who had been following the colloquy without intervening, for he was gathering a considerable amount of information. "But the murder was committed at the same time as the abduction."

"And no one can entertain the shadow of a doubt," argued Rouletabille, "that you killed Monsieur de Lavardens because he came rushing up to the assistance of his daughter. You say that you are innocent of the murder. Well, only one person in the world can establish that innocence, and that person is Mademoiselle de Lavardens."

"That's as clear as daylight," added Monsieur Crousillat. "Unless you hand over Mademoiselle de Lavardens to us, it means that you murdered her father."

"Do you understand?" went on Rouletabille, turning to Andréa. "It's Mademoiselle de Lavardens or death for the pair of you."

Andréa did not even unfold his arms. He stared at Rouletabille over his shoulder and, indicating Callista by a sign of his head, said:

"I'm quite ready to die with her."

"It would be much better to live with her," returned Rouletabille in a wheedling voice.

Callista cast a deadly look at the journalist, and then sat down declaring calmly that this attempt at blackmail by introducing a charge of murder was not badly conceived, but would have no result. The magistrate could do with them what he pleased, but he would not learn anything more from them.

As to Monsieur Crousillat, he seemed to be present only

in the person of Rouletabille, to whom from that moment, without being conscious of it, he surrendered the control of the proceedings. It was a part for which the journalist possessed a natural gift, for he was accustomed to do the talking when the police had nothing more to say.

"Callista, I cannot too strongly urge you to consider your interests a little more closely," went on Rouletabille in his softest manner, ceasing to use threatening language. "I have never given you bad advice. If you and Jean had listened to me, we should none of us be in our present predicament. I understand your resentment against him; and you told me that you were meditating some wicked act of revenge. For my part, I don't think that you went so far as to murder Monsieur de Lavardens, but there's no getting away from this murder, and you must take it into account. You won't be able to save yourself in this business unless you restore that child, who does not know you and who has suffered enough through you. What is the use of being obstinate? Even though you refuse to speak I shall take Odette away from you. Give her back to us now."

"It is not within the power of anyone to give Odette back to you now."

"I know what you mean."

"No, you don't."

"To prove to you that I know everything, would you like me to tell you what took place in old Zina's den?. . ."

Callista could not refrain from giving a start.

"And what you did and said?"

"Oh, really . . . I defy you to do so."

"Very well," returned Rouletabille. "Monsieur Bartholasse, please write that Mademoiselle Callista admits going to old Zina's den."

"But I am not here under your orders," protested

Monsieur Bartholasse, incensed by the journalist's freedom.

"No, but you are under Monsieur Crousillat's orders, and Monsieur Crousillat orders you to take it down."

"Take it down," echoed Monsieur Crousillat.

"I say . . . I say," spluttered Monsieur Bartholasse in a choking voice.

"If you do not take it down I shall do so myself, and Mademoiselle Callista will sign it," declared Rouletabille.

Monsieur Bartholasse, mastered, dipped his pen in the ink with such a furious gesture that he almost knocked over the inkstand.

"Mademoiselle Odette de Lavardens," began Rouletabille, dictating to the clerk, "having been carried in a half-unconscious condition to the den of an old gypsy fortune-teller, Zina by name, I went to see her." ("It is Mademoiselle Callista who is speaking," explained Rouletabille, "and if I make a mistake she will have the kindness to correct me.") "My accomplice, Andréa, was with me.

"As soon as Mademoiselle de Lavardens saw us she began to tremble with fear, for she recognized in this man who seized and carried her off, the dog-shearer who accosted her at Viei-Castou-Nou, and this man terrified her. . . . I motioned to Andréa to leave us, and I remained alone with Mademoiselle de Lavardens."

Little by little, as Rouletabille proceeded with his story, Callista who at first affected to listen with contempt, now stared at him with something in the nature of dismay.

"I was alone with Mademoiselle de Lavardens," went on the journalist, "because, in my mind, old Zina was a creature who did not matter. She was less than a servant; she was a slave.

" 'Who are you? What do you want with me?' asked Mademoiselle de Lavardens in a deathly voice.

"I answered that I might become her friend and save

her life if she would fall in with my wishes. I went on
to say that the greatest dangers were hanging over her,
that the persons who had stopped at nothing to obtain
possession of her would not hesitate to make away with
her once and for all if she forced them to do so. She
answered me at first only with a sort of moan: 'God,
am I to die here!' while her faltering eyes wandered round
the hideous dwelling, on the walls of which old Zina had
nailed dead owls and bats. An owl was perched over the
fireplace and a bear's cub was forever strutting about
in a corner. I persuaded her that I would get her out of
this inferno. She ended by placing her burning hands
in mine, for in order to inspire her with confidence I
had indulged in the most honeyed words. 'All this around
me is nothing, but there are rats at night,' she said to
me with a shudder."

Callista, growing more and more perturbed, drew back
her chair from Rouletabille and, white-faced, murmured
in Romany:

"He's the very devil!"

"My dear!" broke in Andréa in a muffled voice. And
he spluttered a few words in the same language which
seemed to comfort her, but Rouletabille had no intention
of allowing his advantage to be lost, and with a masterful
air and a peremptory sign to Monsieur Bartholasse he
continued his story:

"I asked Mademoiselle de Lavardens if, as far as she
knew, she had any enemies. She answered 'no.'

" 'Well, you have one deadly enemy and her name is
Callista.'

"I had no sooner mentioned this name than Mademoiselle de Lavardens hid her head in her hands and
sobbed aloud. Then it was that I determined to strike
a great blow.

" 'She made up her mind at first to have your life,'
I said, 'but I have induced her to relent. Still, there is

one condition; you must do everything I tell you to do.'

"She gave me an anxious look through her tears.

" 'You must write what I am about to dictate.'

"I had with me some notepaper which I bought at Arles, and I slipped a small board on her knees."

"Is not all this absolutely correct?" demanded Rouletabille, still riveting her with his gaze.

"Wizard!" Callista rapped out at him, drawing back her chair still farther.

"Monsieur Bartholasse, please make a note that the female prisoner called Monsieur Rouletabille a 'wizard,' which is in itself a confession," interposed Monsieur Crousillat.

"Zina put on this small board a dirty ink bottle which had recently been filled and I dictated the following letter:

" '*I do not love you, Jean. I know now that Callista is your mistress. I prefer to run away from home rather than marry you. You will never see me again· Good-by!*' "

"Was this not the exact wording?" demanded Rouletabille.

Callista's answer was an ice-cold stare.

"I will continue the story as she offers no denial," said Rouletabille.

"Until then Mademoiselle de Lavardens seemed half-dead and unable to make the least exertion, but as soon as she heard what I wanted she leapt to her feet, upsetting the ink bottle, shattering the pen, and deluging my feet with ink."

"Show your feet," exclaimed the journalist. "Show your feet, madame. The people of the road do not wash their feet every day, and though you brought your bear's cub from Paris you left behind your chiropodist!

Ah, you refuse to show your feet. Monsieur Bartholasse, take this down—write that madame refused to show her feet to the person named Rouletabille, which is equivalent to another confession. . . . I will continue:

"After this outburst Mademoiselle de Lavardens declared to me, quivering all over, that she would never write a word which might make Monsieur Jean de Santierne believe that she did not love him: 'I would rather have my hand cut off,' and I answered: 'Well, my beauty, you shall have your hand cut off.' "

"Do you deny those words? Do you repudiate the knife? No, because they are your very words, and here is the actual knife."

Rouletabille threw a knife with a horn handle on the examining magistrate's table, and added the further detail:

"You bought it on the evening of the twenty-third at Bonnafous', Les Saintes Maries."

"That was to frighten her," muttered Callista, gasping like a hunted animal, at a loss to know when or how the attack was coming.

"Perhaps. . . . Perhaps if she had signed the letter you would not have murdered her."

"Have they murdered her?" exclaimed the examining magistrate, who seemed to have become merely a spectator witnessing the tense excitement of a drama which was being conjured up before him.

"No, but she wanted to murder her."

"That's not true."

"You say it's not true. But this is what happened exactly. When you saw Mademoiselle de Lavarden's determined attitude you said to her: 'I am Callista. Your affianced husband is my lover. You must make your choice: either you give up Jean or you shall not leave this place alive.' A frightful scene ensued from

which, indeed, Mademoiselle de Lavardens would not
have left the place alive if . . ."

"If?" repeated the examining magistrate.

"If at that moment an extraordinary thing had not
happened. . . ."

On hearing these last words Callista displayed so
much agitation that nothing but a fresh intervention
by Andréa succeeded in soothing her. Then while
Rouletabille, who closely followed what was passing
between the two gypsies, went on with his narrative, the
young woman continued to stare at her companion's
demoniacal face.

"Yes, it was, in truth, an extraordinary thing," went
on Rouletabille. "Odette might have been regarded as
lost but for a poor creature, a poor old thing upon whom
until then no one had bestowed any attention, unless it
were to spurn her with a foot or to cast her aside in the
dark, where as a rule she sat cowering . . . . In short,
Zina threw herself between Callista and the child . . . .
Andréa came in again prepared at any moment to assist
his accomplice in her hideous revenge. But neither this
man nor woman persisted in the face of a sign from
Zina, who spoke certain words in a low voice, so low
that no one could hear them except Callista, Andréa—
and Rouletabille!"

Callista and Andréa were now both deadly pale.

"You are lying," she said. "You were too far away
to hear what she said. If you had heard you would have
saved your Odette."

"Zina, who is a witch," returned the journalist, "will
tell you that a wizard can hear things which may be
said at the end of the world, and even in the other
world. . . . I am so well aware of what old Zina said
that I know you have but one fear, both of you—the
fear lest I should repeat her words, for it would be
assumed that you repeated them, and there is not a

Romany in the wide world who would forgive you for that. . . .

"Ah, you hang your head. Well, don't be afraid. I shall not repeat those words spoken in old Zina's den. I fully see now how difficult the position would be for both of you in the event of your wishing to give Odette back to us. Accordingly, I propose a bargain with you. Give me certain information and I will take the entire risk on my own shoulders. As far as you are concerned it will be made public that you refused to speak, even to save your head. In this way I shall save Odette and at the same time save you—provided you are innocent of Monsieur de Lavarden's murder."

Rouletabille's reasoning, as well as the hidden meaning which lay in his words, seemed once more greatly to disturb Callista, but Andréa gave her a peculiar look and she rapped out with a malicious smile:

"As you are a wizard you will soon find Odette without our help."

"Of course, you she-devil," exclaimed Rouletabille, exasperated at the futility of his efforts, "but I would gladly have gained time for her sake and yours by getting a word from you. You know how precious every minute is."

"You are wasting your breath here," returned Callista coldly.

Rouletabille stood up.

"Monsieur," he said to the examining magistrate, "you may have the prisoners taken down to their cell. Nothing more can be done with them to-day."

Monsieur Crousillat was too eager to be alone with the journalist and to ask him certain questions to offer any objection. He motioned to La Finette to remove the prisoners.

"Keep a good watch on them," counselled Rouletabille.

La Finette smiled and twirled his moustache. The

thought that the prisoners might make their escape seemed distinctly humorous. Nevertheless, he took every precaution, so that whatever happened he might have nothing to reproach himself with.

As soon as the door was closed the examining magistrate turned to Rouletabille.

"What was it that this old Zina said to them?"

"Oh, that, monsieur, is not my secret!"

"Do you mean to say that you don't intend to tell me?"

"Neither you nor anyone else."

"You respect the secrets of those ruffians?"

"It's neither Andréa's, nor Callista's, nor even old Zina's secret," returned Rouletabille, plunged in thought.

"Then might I be allowed to know whose secret it is?"

"Yes, monsieur, it is a dead man's secret."

"Monsieur de Lavarden's secret! That being so, the secret died with him."

"No; it is from the secret that . . ."

"All the evil comes."

"All the good, monsieur, all the good. Just think! If Zina had not spoken, Mademoiselle de Lavardens would be dead now."

"They would have murdered her as they murdered her father."

"They did not murder her father."

"They kidnaped the daughter, but did not murder the father. Bless my soul, since you say so, we must believe you."

"You look as if the thought distresses you," said Rouletabille with a smile.

"What distresses me," returned Monsieur Crousillat, not unreasonably, "is that you have the appearance of knowing everything, but tell me nothing. Well, for my part, I shall make less mystery of things than you do.

Granted that Andréa did not commit the murder, we are forced to turn our attention to de Lauriac, and that being so what I have to say is not without importance. It appears that de Lauriac had on his desk a sort of sharp-pointed paper-knife, which cannot be found anywhere."

"That is because you've looked in the wrong place for it. But, I say again, it was not de Lauriac who struck the blow."

"Then if it was neither Andréa nor de Lauriac, will you tell me who it was?"

"You shall know to-morrow morning. Meet me at de Lauriac's Lou Cabanou. Have him brought there and arrange for the divisional surgeons to be present."

"And you promise me? . . ."

"The name of Monsieur de Lavardens' murderer."

CHAPTER XIX

THE MURDERER

NEXT morning the authorities were once more at Lou Cabanou with de Lauriac as desired by Rouletabille. While they were waiting for him, Monsieur Crousillat subjected the prisoner to a fresh and vigorous examination. He had the satisfaction of seeing him turn pale when he spoke to him of the dagger-knife, but as soon as de Lauriac felt certain that this weapon, with which he might have murdered Monsieur de Lavardens, had not been found, his agitation vanished. His change of demeanor was so obvious that the examining magistrate bit his lip and regretted not having begun by declaring to the accused that the weapon had been found. "I made a gross blunder which Rouletabille would not have made," he said to himself. In any case, he was sorry that the journalist was not present to behold de Lauriac's first display of confusion.

At length he was informed that Rouletabille had come with the divisional surgeons, and was waiting for him in Viei-Castou-Nou park at the spot where Monsieur de Lavardens' body was discovered.

Monsieur Crousillat hastened towards them, followed some way behind by Monsieur Bartholasse, who continued to grumble about Rouletabille's unreasonable requests and the easy-going nature of examining magistrates. The gendarmes could be seen bringing along their prisoner.

"Well?" questioned Monsieur Crousillat.

"Well, these gentlemen have brought their report . . . ."

135

"No report of theirs will do away with the fact that Monsieur de Lavardens was murdered."

"These gentlemen have come to the conclusion that Monsieur de Lavardens died from a heart attack."

"A heart attack!" exclaimed the examining magistrate, looking in turn at the doctors and Rouletabille. "But how do you account for the wound on the temple?"

"The wound on the temple does not do away with the fact that Monsieur de Lavardens died from a heart attack," returned one of the doctors.

"I've got it this time," said Monsieur Crousillat, who was making great intellectual efforts to reconcile the fact of murder with the doctor's conclusion. "I understand. . . . The person who kidnaped Mademoiselle Odette attacked and wounded Monsieur de Lavardens. The excitement killed him, and the assailant removed the body to this place." And turning to de Lauriac he went on: "The man must have had very good reasons for not leaving Monsieur de Lavardens' body in Monsieur de Lauriac's grounds."

"No, monsieur, you are wide of the mark," interposed Rouletabille, "and I am here to explain to you what really did happen.

"When the accused threw Monsieur de Lavardens out of his house after the violent scene which the former has described to us, Monsieur de Lavardens came up against the balustrade of de Lauriac's front steps. Then he went down and walked a few paces. . . .

"By this time he must have felt somewhat ill, for he stopped and leant against the wall before entering the partition gate to his own place. At last, collecting his strength, he made his way towards Viei-Castou-Nou. As he crossed his park it occurred to him that he had omitted to close the partition gate, in which he had left the key. Though he was conscious of his growing weakness, he had the pluck to retrace his steps. On reaching

this tree his heart stopped beating . . . he fell forward
. . . and it was then that the 'murderer' intervened . . .

"I told you, monsieur, that the murderer was as thin
as a spike. . . . Here you are!"

Rouletabille removed his cap from a nail in the tree
upon which he had hung it and revealed the 'culprit.'

"In his fall Monsieur de Lavardens' temple was cruelly
pierced by this nail."

Monsieur Crousillat and the divisional surgeons were
by this time at the foot of the tree examining the incriminating weapon. Rouletabille pointed to the blood-
stains on the trunk near the nail:

"A close inspection will show you what sort of rust
is on it."

Old Tavan, who was passing that way, taking stock
of everything out of the tail of his eye, was called. The
police borrowed his pincers, and the inquiry was amplified
by a most material piece of evidence. From that moment,
moreover—and the divisional surgeons expressed their
assent—no one could entertain the least doubt but that
Monsieur de Lavardens' death was brought about in the
manner related by Rouletabille.

"I say, he's been making fools of us," exclaimed
Monsieur Bartholasse.

"Who has?" asked Monsieur Crousillat.

"Why, your Rouletabille," returned the clerk. "Considering he knew that the nail did it, why didn't he tell
us so before?"

"Yes, that's true," agreed Monsieur Crousillat. "You
are incorrigible. It was not worth while to persuade me
to arrest this gentleman"—indicating de Lauriac—"seeing that you knew he was innocent."

"If you make yourself useful to the police this is
how you are rewarded!" retorted Rouletabille. "Why,
my dear Monsieur Crousillat, you forget one thing; while
Monsieur de Lavardens was at Monsieur de Lauriac's

place, Mademoiselle Odette was being kidnaped. I was determined to find out whether Monsieur de Lauriac, even if he were innocent of Monsieur de Lavardens' death, was or was not a party to Mademoiselle Odette's abduction. In allowing the charge of murder to hang over him, I compelled him, in a sense, to confess the less-important assault in order to prove his innocence of murder. It was well to hold over the heads of everybody—that is to say, of all persons who might be concerned in carrying off Mademoiselle Odette—the menace which Monsieur de Lavardens' murder constituted; and not only over de Lauriac, but over the gypsies and Andréa and Callista, and even over old Tavan, who is here, and, I suspect, knows a great deal more about the matter than the length of his face would suggest."

De Lauriac, who had watched the entire scene in silence, interrupted the laughter which greeted Rouletabille's last sally:

"Now, gentlemen, what are you going to do with me?"

"Why, my dear Monsieur de Lauriac, you will be set at liberty," returned Rouletabille.

Monsieur Bartholasse gave a start.

"You don't say so!"

Monsieur Crousillat cast a black look at him.

"What else is possible now, Monsieur Bartholasse?"

"In any case," returned the clerk, beside himself, 'whether the accused is discharged or not is no business of his. If you were to ask my opinion, monsieur, I should say at once: 'Don't release Monsieur de Lauriac until his dagger-paper-knife is found.'"

"If that is the only thing that will please you," interposed Rouletabille, "I will tell you myself where the paper-knife is."

De Lauriac was not the last to follow Rouletabille, who, with a gesture, led the company to Lou Cabanou, and the former's eagerness did not escape his attention.

When the entire party was assembled in the study in which the opening scene of the tragedy was enacted, Rouletabille turned to the examining magistrate:

"You see the disadvantage, Monsieur Crousillat, of failing to rely on the right end of one's judgment in any and every circumstance. What did you do? Starting from a preconceived idea, the idea of murder, you hunted for this dagger-like paper-cutter in every direction where Monsieur de Lauriac might have thrown it after the crime was committed, and consequently your investigations were fruitless. On the other hand, if you had let yourself be guided by 'the right end of your judgment' you would have at once been led to the place where the knife in ordinary circumstances was to be found. Its proper place, if it is not on the desk, is in some book. Monsieur Bartholasse, you may be quite satisfied, for here is the precious paper-knife."

Rouletabille opened a large tome which, in spite of the spoliation to which it had been subjected, was indubitably the finest gem in de Lauriac's library. He let the knife slip out of it.

"As you perceive," he said, handing the knife to the examining magistrate, "there's no blood on it—neither blood nor ink on it. Come, monsieur, sign the order for Monsieur de Lauriac's release. He is innocent."

A few minutes later Monsieur de Lauriac was free.

"It was a piece of luck for you that I found the paper-knife, Monsieur de Lauriac," said Rouletabille. "You must admit that it was a great relief to you. For, when all is said, had you known where that knife was you would have told us, seeing that it had not been used . . . . But *were* you certain that it *had* not been used?"

De Lauriac glared at him.

"Monsieur, I owe my discharge to you," he returned in a hoarse voice, "but as I also owe my arrest to you, you will permit me to refrain from offering you my thanks."

CHAPTER XX

THE BOOK OF ANCESTORS CONTINUES TO DIVULGE
ITS SECRET

Extract from Rouletabille's diary at this date:

MET Jean. He had just learnt that as a result of my efforts de Lauriac was discharged. I did not expect to receive congratulations from him, but it was as much as he could do to refrain from striking me.

" 'You look after that brute and meantime you don't even ask yourself what has become of Odette.'

" 'By the way,' I said, 'are you certain that she bore no mark on her shoulder?'"

"He showed the same astonishment at this question as Estève, and as I could not just then explain why I wanted to know, he reproached me with the utmost bitterness for my way of doing things since I came to Camargue. Strange suspicions are still springing up in his mind.

" 'Don't you want her to be found?' he exclaimed.

"I was so greatly amazed by this 'outburst' that at first I was at a loss for an answer. I feel sure that it s going to be very difficult to work with this youngster. He spends his time either cursing or praising me, which doesn't advance matters. I asked him to put his thoughts into words and tell me once and for all what was in his mind, but he evaded the question:

" 'As you are absolutely certain that she was abducted by gypsies, ought you not to give the authorities a description of her? I quite understand why you avoided asking that bungler Crousillat's help to trace her, but

140

still there are persons in France who might be able to help us to discover her.'

" 'Why, of course, the custom-house people,' I said.

" 'The custom-house people?'

" 'Yes. I feel convinced that the gypsies will make every effort to take Odette over the frontier.'

" 'What then?'

" 'Well, as I am on very friendly terms with a high official at the chief office, I asked him to telephone instructions accordingly. I suggested that those instructions should be carried out with great discretion, in order as far as possible not to arouse their suspicions."

" 'That's the first comforting word that I have yet heard.'

" 'Consequently, for the last four days, every caravan which has attempted to cross the frontier has been stopped.'

" 'Have they not discovered anything?'

" 'They will not discover anything.'

" 'That's just like you. You are so aggravating. . . . Then why did you give the orders?'

" 'To please you. To have some answer to you when you accuse me of doing nothing to find Odette; in short, to make sure that silly asses should have nothing to reproach me with.'

" 'Thank you,' returned Jean.

" 'Don't mention it. But, mark me, the reason why they cannot find Odette is simply because the gypsies make no attempt to hide her. They may not have read Edgar Allan Poe, but they are as clever as the author of "The Stolen Letter"—the letter for which everyone was looking and which was purposely displayed for everyone to see. Dressed in tatters, with a fillet of ornaments round her forehead, and wearing big ear-rings, Odette would look so much the gypsy that she would excite no attention from anyone.'

" 'But still she has only to cry out or make some movement.'

" 'She will not cry out or make any movement. She will be asleep, or at least she will be drowsing. She will be dreaming—perhaps of you, Jean, for, take it from me, those people have at their command every sort of nostrum by which they can numb the will, and every sort of sedative which can allay grief. Neither custom-house officers nor gendarmes will spot Odette de Lavardens. They will see a gypsy girl who may be smiling at them.'

" 'But what you tell me is worse than anything I could imagine. . . . So I shall never see Odette again?'

" 'Yes, you will see her again. But, you understand, you must let me do things my own way.' "

Late in the day, however, Jean had not left Rouletabille, for they were still at Arles, shadowing de Lauriac, whose every step and movement they watched after his release from custody. De Lauriac first met Lou Rousso Fiamo, who seemed to be expecting him, and they had a long talk together in a public-house near the ruins of the Roman amphitheater. Rouletabille was able to catch the last sentence which fell from de Lauriac as he left his old herdsman: "I am relying on you," and the herdsman nodded in a manner which signified *that he could rely on him*. De Lauriac then called on several newspaper shops and obtained copies of the principal papers which had appeared since his arrest.

He at once turned his steps towards Lavardens with his bundle of papers, and reaching Lou Cabanou, leaped over the low wall in his eagerness to get home and shut himself up in his study.

Rouletabille by this time had given up following him.

"Come," he said to Jean, "we needn't disturb him while he's reading the newspapers."

"It is obvious that they must have an immediate interest for him," returned Jean.

"We'll give him a good mark for that."

"Why a good mark?"

"Well, granted that he is eager to learn what has been happening to Odette while he was in prison, I assume that he knows nothing about her, and if he knows nothing about her, depend upon it he had no hand in her abduction."

Chatting in this way Rouletabille led Jean to a wine-shop not a stone's throw from the Arles-Trinquet railway station. He took from his pocket his tobacco-pouch.

"Now we can have a quiet pipe."

"But what are we waiting here for?"

"News of de Lauriac."

Two hours later they were still waiting. Rouletabille after a third pipe fell peacefully asleep. Jean, on the other hand, left the place thrice and thrice returned to it. At last a form swung into sight on the dusty road. Rouletabille at once opened his eyes as though some instinct told him that the person whom he was expecting had come.

Old Tavan stood before him. Rouletabille motioned that he could speak out before Jean.

"Well, he's gone," said old Tavan.

"Tell me everything, down to the least detail."

"There's not much to tell. He didn't stay more than a couple of hours in his house. His servant went off and came back with a small motor-car, and then went in to let him know. Then I saw our man come out with a knapsack in which he must have packed his luggage. He jumped into the car and drove off at a good speed."

"Did you pump the servant?"

"Oh, yes. If our man isn't back within a week he's got to lock up the place and give the key to Lou Rousso Fiamo."

"Is that all?"

"That's all."

Rouletabille took a banknote from his pocket-book and handed it to old Tavan.

"Your intelligence department is quite all right," said Jean, "but what are you driving at with de Lauriac? He is certainly following up Odette's trail. Are we going to let him catch her up before we do?"

Having unburdened himself, he stood fidgeting, and Rouletabille's impassive manner merely had the effect of exasperating him as usual. Rouletabille lighted his pipe once more.

"You say that he is certainly following Odette's tracks, but I am not so sure about it as all that. We'll discuss this again to-night. Meanwhile let's go back."

"Where to?"

"To Viei-Castou-Nou. Now we shan't interfere with de Lauriac's plans. Had he known that we were so close upon his heels he would never have left the place."

"Why not?"

"He would have been afraid of our following him."

"Then you think he was a party to Odette's abduction?"

"I assure you that I don't know."

During the dinner-hour that evening Rouletabille made his way into de Lauriac's house by his usual expedient. He waited, to no purpose, for the servants to leave Lou Cabanou; but taking advantage of their master's absence and apparently wishing to celebrate his release, they gave a supper-party to the servants in the neighborhood. Whatever Jean may have thought, Rouletabille was eager to discover certain things which it was of importance that he should know. In spite of the sounds of festivities which reached his ear from the servants' quarters, he took his risk and was not a little pleased to find himself in de Lauriac's study without disturbing the company in their good cheer.

Close to de Lauriac's desk a newspaper lay crumpled

up among many others. Rouletabille picked it up. It was full of the Lavardens case, and he read the last part of the telegram which had been despatched by its correspondent from Arles:

"The two gypsies made no scruple in admitting that they had effected Mademoiselle Odette de Lavardens' abduction, but they resolutely refused to give any clue as to the place where the hapless young girl was being held prisoner. . . . Callista declared that in this way she was taking her revenge for the alleged treachery of Jean de S——, her lover."

Rouletabille threw down the newspaper and, turning to the bureau, stared at the shelf. The book of Ancestors was not in its place.

An intense joy seemed to flood his entire being, and he left the house without making the least effort at concealment. But his departure did not pass unobserved and the servants raising a great outcry, went in pursuit of him.

He had the start of them. He leaped the wall, but this time the luck was against him. A hand caught hold of him:

"Where on earth are you going?"

It was Monsieur Crousillat, who was taking a short rest, fishing with rod and line, after his exceptional labors.

"After de Lauriac."

"Well I never! So he is guilty."

"No, but he will be."

And he sprang forward and resumed his flight, returning by a roundabout way to Viei-Castou-Nou, where he stumbled up against Jean this time.

"My dear fellow," he said, "not only is de Lauriac innocent of the abduction as I felt certain, but he is not even implicated in it as I feared he might be. This greatly simplifies our task. Fortunately the book has divulged its secret."

CHAPTER XXI

JEAN VERSUS THE OCTOPUS

MONSIEUR CROUSILLAT, the examining magistrate, and Monsieur Bartholasse, his clerk, had returned that same evening—it was the evening of the day after de Lauriac's release—to the prison in which for the time being the gypsies were incarcerated. Monsieur Crousillat had subjected them that afternoon to a further examination, and they had positively refused to answer any question. Monsieur Crousillat had requested to see the governor of the jail.

When he found himself face to face with the governor of the prison, a worthy man in every sense of the word, but a strict disciplinarian and a stickler for rules and regulations, he had little difficulty in making himself understood. As the prisoners refused to say anything in the examining magistrate's office, they would have to resort to other means to make them speak in their cell.

"A prison spy?" suggested Monsieur Mathieu, the governor. "I see no objection to that. But still we shall have to get hold of one."

"What! Haven't you a sharp-witted fellow among your prisoners?"

"I have never troubled about such matters," returned the governor. "There's no mention of them in the regulations, and when in certain cases the police have found it necessary to employ a police-spy they have always obtained one for me. . . . Apply to the Criminal

146

Investigation Department. They've sent their men down here."

"But they are not here now," objected Monsieur Crousillat with a sigh. "They are searching high and low for Mademoiselle de Lavardens, scouring the country for every caravan and they may find her before I get the chance. We're wasting a great deal of time."

"Meanwhile Rouletabille is making game of us," interposed Monsieur Bartholasse acidly.

"By the way," said Monsieur Mathieu, "Rouletabille came to see me."

"Be on your guard," exclaimed the clerk. "What did he come here for?"

"He wanted to go over the prison. He said it was for the purpose of an article—one of a series. It seems that he has visited and described all the prisons in France!"

"Did you agree to let him?"

"No, Monsieur. To me the regulations are the only things that matter, and the man named Rouletabille had no order. He was in no way entitled to visit my prison."

"Oh, don't flatter yourself that that will interfere with his plans," returned Monsieur Bartholasse. "He probably didn't tell you how he visited the Moulins prison during the trial of the Marquis de T——?"

"Good heavens, no. He bowed very politely and I haven't seen him since."

"Well, I'll tell you the story myself. I was in Moulins at the time, and the incident caused a bit of a row. You will remember the famous case. The Marquis was charged with having thrown his son-in-law over a cliff while they were out for a walk. The whole thing was complicated by the extraordinary relations which existed between the tutor and the Marquis. . . . In short, the newspapers of the whole world sent their representatives to the town and they filled the hotels long before the trial began. At that time Rouletabille, almost a boy, was a beginner. Well, he began by a master stroke which brought about a change of prefects, caused the governor of the prison to be dismissed, and the suspension of I don't know how many members of the prison staff."

"The devil he did!"

"There you are! The thing for him was to see the Marquis and interview him before anyone else. Two days before the trial, Rouletabille appeared at the prison record office with a properly-stamped permit from police-headquarters authorizing Monsieur Arnault, anthropologist, to inspect the prisons in the Allier district. . . ."

"I need not say that he had dressed himself for the part, making himself up as a respectable old gentleman, and the governor of the prison saw before him a man of learning as worthy of esteem as were his credentials. He allowed him to go over the entire prison, and Monsieur Arnault had but to express the wish, and he was shown for a moment into the Marquis's cell. In that moment the Marquis uttered three words, and next morning Rouletabille had transformed those three words into three columns!"

Just then there was a knock at the door of Monsieur Mathieu's room and a warder came in to say that a caller, an anthropologist, was in the record office claiming to have received an order to inspect the prisons in the Rhone valley.

Monsieur Mathieu, Monsieur Crousillat and Monsieur Bartholasse exchanged a glance of amazement.

"Bring the person here," ordered the governor in a somewhat broken voice.

During the few minutes which ensued no word was spoken by the three men. They were expecting to see Rouletabille disguised as a scientist. They saw before them a woman.

She was dressed with extreme simplicity, but very

smartly. Her manners were lady-like and, without being beautiful, there was something in her expression which, though hard to define, was curiously attractive. As soon as the door was closed she began to speak, and her voice with its musical intonation, the pleasant and child-like roll of her words and her perfect pronunciation, seemed to suggest that she was of Slavonic origin.

The three officials stood up and she gave the governor who had introduced himself to her, an official document, apologizing for disturbing him at that late hour, but she had an urgent mission to perform.

"Are persons interested in anthropology in such a hurry as all that?" inquired Monsieur Mathieu, on the defensive.

"Yes, to tell you the truth, monsieur, we are, in this instance, in a great hurry. But I feel somewhat embarrassed, somewhat confused, I assure you. I prefer to say what I think—it is better so—and these gentlemen will excuse me, but I should prefer to speak to you in private."

"You can speak before these gentlemen, who are my good friends, and from whom I have no secrets. Allow me to introduce them to you: Monsieur Crousillat, the examining magistrate, and Monsieur Bartholasse, his clerk."

Then turning to them and indicating his visitor he presented:

"Madame de Meyrens."

The governor had just read her name on a letter from the prefect's office introducing the distinguished anthropologist to his notice.

Madame de Meyrens' face expressed the utmost satisfaction.

"The examining magistrate! The clerk!" she cried. "Why, in that case I can speak out. Now this is what I have to say to you, but it must be understood, of course, that I am telling you a state secret." She gave her most seductive smile, and looked towards the door as if to make certain that nobody could overhear her. "Well, I am not an anthropologist, and though I've brought you this official order it is only to 'clear' you, as they say in government service, so that the regulations might not be infringed. This, monsieur, will tell you who I am."

She drew from her bodice an envelope, which she handed to Monsieur Mathieu. He took out a number of documents, including a passport with Madame de Meyrens' photograph, and several letters written on the notepaper of the Criminal Investigation Department. A recent letter from the Chief of the Department was pinned to the papers and produced a decisive effect. He passed the letter to Monsieur Crousillat:

"Well, you are on the look-out for a police-spy. Here is what you want."

"You call a police-spy in French a sheep," said Madame de Meyrens. . . . "I shall be your little lamb!"

It appeared from the papers that the highest authorities in Paris had sent one of their cleverest agents, Madame de Meyrens, to Arles to "pump" the two prisoners and endeavor to extract information which might assist the police, for they had lost every trace of Mademoiselle de Lavardens. We know that the custom-house authorities, on their side, who were set going by Rouletabille, had not obtained any greater success.

A quarter of an hour later Madame de Meyrens was admitted to Callista's cell. The latter could scarcely conceal her dismay when she recognized in the new prisoner, who was to be her companion, the Octopus.

"I am here to save you," said Madame de Meyrens, as soon as they were left to themselves; and she let slip from underneath her skirt a jersey, a bricklayer's overalls, stained with plaster, and a cap.

When the Octopus entered the cell, Callista was crouching in a corner with her elbows on the knees of her ragged skirt, her long pitiless face held in her burning hands, a picture of utter dejection. Any person who had watched her in the examining magistrate's office, holding her own with Rouletabille and displaying an undaunted spirit, and saw her now alone in her cell, no longer playing a game either for her own or others' sake, would have found it difficult to believe that she was the same woman.

She had determined to take her revenge. She had succeeded, but none the less, everything was lost to her. Her love for Jean? Doubtless she believed that she really loved him, but if she could have analyzed her feelings, she would have found that they were made up more of ruffled pride than love driven to despair. . . . Callista had suffered a humiliating downfall. With childish simplicity she imagined, in her inordinate ambition, that she would one day be a great lady and that great lady would be called Madame Jean de Santierne. Such a thought could only have occurred to the mind of a daughter of the road, ignorant of modern conventions and believing that every barrier was overthrown when she was transplanted one day from her native caravan to a flat in the Champs Elysées.

Without saying a word to Jean—for, however artless she was in her ambition, she possessed an instinctive cunning—she had more than once visited Lavardens unknown to him. She sought to view his château and estates from a distance. Possibly in her solitary walks she had encountered Zina, who had settled herself in the district long years before. Possibly she had confided her dreams to her, discovering an ally in this old woman of her own race. Be that as it may, Zina had often said to Odette:

"You should marry, my child."

But, as she gave her the advice while reading the lines of her hand, Odette had merely laughed at her.

And now Odette was not married. Nor was Callista. Though Odette was bowling along to nobody knew what tragedy, who could say where Callista's adventure would eventually lead her? . . .

The prison cell for a number of years, and when she left it—Andréa. Andréa who terrified her and would never let her go.

But at the moment when she believed that everything was lost, the Octopus appeared in her cell to save her. She could not believe her eyes and ears. She drew herself erect, unable to speak a word, or understand what was coming. . . . The Octopus! . . . She had heard that this woman was in the pay of the police. Ought she not to be on her guard against her?

Madame de Meyrens gathered up the garments which she had clandestinely brought with her, and hid them in Callista's straw mattress, and quietly seated herself on the one stool in the cell. She drew a dainty cigarette-case from her pocket and offered it open to Callista.

"Have a fag?" she asked. "You know, my poor dear Callista, we have plenty of time; as much time as I please."

She lighted the two cigarettes and went on:

"You say nothing, my dear. You seem to be surprised, and I don't wonder at it. You would like to know how I managed to get here. I won't keep you in suspense, and you'll see how easy it was. People say that I belong to the police. I belong to the police only when it suits me. . . . I use the police much more than they use me. Do you follow me? . . . Yes? . . . Well, then, I wish to save you, therefore I belong to the police. I have got all my papers in due form. I am put into your cell so as to get you to tell me things—to tell me where Odette is."

"Never! . . . Not to a living soul. Not even to save my life!"

"I know that, of course. Calm yourself, my poor dear

Callista. I am telling you that I belong to the police because I want you to trust me. I am, as they say in
prisons, a police-spy, sent here to get you to give yourself away, but I shall not get you to give yourself away
because I tell you I am a police-spy, but I am not a
police-spy to you."

"I see," said Callista, nodding her head.

"I congratulate you, my dear. With the exercise of a
little willingness one can do anything, you know. I am
supposed, as far as you are concerned, to be a society
lady, a very dangerous museum thief, arrested this afternoon. I'll tell you what it is," she added, bursting out
laughing, "I came to Arles to rob the Roman amphitheater. Doesn't it make you laugh, too? It must. And
now let's be serious.

"As soon as I'm gone and they've brought your supper,
place this stool on your mattress, and you'll find it
easy to file through the one little bar which prevents you
from slipping out of this sky-light."

"What with?"

"With this file."

She fished out a file from the lining of her coat and
handed it to Callista.

"It's a job that won't take you more than an hour
at most."

"But it won't be a bit of good," objected Callista,
throwing her cigarette away. "Is that the only way
you've found of helping me? Suppose I got out of
this yard, I should have to pass through a railed archway, and suppose I got over the railings, I should find
myself in the patrol-path, and to leave the patrol-path I
should have to go past the record office. I say nothing
of the warders that I should meet on the way. I've made
a thorough examination of this prison every time I've
come into it. There's nothing to be done by a prisoner
here."

'That's true, but what about a person who is free?"
"I am not free."
"Yes, you are. Listen to me, my dear but impatient Callista. When you've filed through the bar, you must go to bed and sleep peacefully as though you hadn't a care. Next morning they'll bring you your breakfast, and afterwards bolt the door. Make yourself quite at home. Nobody will disturb you. You can slip off your rags and put on the bricklayer's things that I've brought you. Pull your cap well over your eyes, and you'll be transformed into a bricklayer's apprentice. You know, or you don't know, that just now workmen are repairing the building in yard C where Andréa's cell is. Work starts at eight o'clock. At half-past eight a truck of rubbish will leave this yard C dragged by a workman. He will pass through your yard and stop for a few seconds under your skylight. He won't stop unless he considers that you can clear your skylight without running the risk of being caught; otherwise he will stop a little farther away and not come up to your skylight until the danger is over. . . . So don't hesitate, I tell you, but slide down and place yourself behind the truck to push it while the man in front pulls it. In this way you will get out of the prison safe and sound—you, the truck, the workman—I'll vouch for it. Once you are outside the rest is easy. A motor-car will be waiting for you at the corner of the street, and by the time they've discovered that you've flown, you'll have covered a good distance."

"Can you depend upon the workman?" asked Callista, whose heart was pounding wildly at the picture which the Octopus had drawn of her chances of escape.

"I can depend upon him as I can upon you. The workman is Andréa."

"Well, I never!" sighed Callista.

"Would you have preferred to run away alone?"

questioned the Octopus, with a knowing smile. "I . . . I hardly know."

"I know that you'll need this man. That's why I didn't hesitate to have a file and an outfit, similar to yours, passed through his window by the man in charge of the truck. Besides, Andréa is a necessary part of the scheme. Who would have pulled the truck? Neither the workman whom I bought over nor anyone else would have had anything to do with the matter."

"You think I shall still need this man?"

"Yes, because you have not yet done with Odette."

"Oh, you don't say so."

"Rouletabille and Jean are by this time on her trail, not to mention de Lauriac, who is hurrying after her like a madman, prepared to break down every obstacle, and if you want to keep her, you will both have your work cut out, believe me."

"Our entire nation will guard her," said Callista in a strained voice.

"That's more than is necessary," returned the Octopus, frowning. "More than is necessary—and yet possibly, not enough to get the better of Rouletabille."

An hour later the Octopus came out of the prison and walked towards the market square.

A dark form which never let her out of sight was creeping in her shadow. That dark form was Jean.

He watched Madame de Meyrens enter the Hôtel du Forum. For a few moments he stood gazing at the front of the hotel. Lights appeared in two windows on the first floor.

A little later he perceived through the glass Madame de Meyrens meet Rouletabille and enter into an excited conversation with him, which seemed to end in a "scene."

Then Jean de Santierne made up his mind to act. He left the market square to visit Monsieur Crousillat, the examining magistrate.

CHAPTER XXII

JEAN CONTINUES HIS FIGHT WITH THE OCTOPUS

AFTER what had occurred some days previously at Les Saintes Maries, after what Jean had seen of the underhand trickery of this dangerous and scheming woman, after what Rouletabille himself had told him of the relations which existed between her and Callista, how was it that Rouletabille failed to sever once and for all a connection which, unfortunately for him and the peace of mind of his friends, had lasted only too long?

He seemed never to meet the Octopus without an altercation with her, but these were only lover's quarrels. And in the meantime the wretched woman, pursuing an aim which Jean could not contemplate without bitterness, was stealthily working against them, against every measure which they were taking. The fact that Odette was still held a prisoner was entirely due, Jean was convinced, to the Octopus.

Thus he was unable to repress a gesture of aversion when he suddenly caught sight of her hateful form at a corner of a street in Arles. What was her object in stealing furtively through the narrow streets already darkened by the falling night? He followed her to the prison. He waited nearly two hours before she came out again.

It occurred to him to tell Rouletabille of the incident, and then when she came out he followed her almost involuntarily to the hotel in which she had an appointment with the journalist. Jean realized that this woman held so great a sway over his friend's mind that he could never convince him of her double-dealing. She would find some excuse which Rouletabille, in his infatuation, would end by accepting.

Jean made up his mind, therefore, to strike a decisive blow and without letting Rouletabille know to save him in spite of himself.

He was aware that Monsieur Crousillat, who was a bachelor, was accustomed to dine in a small inn, which bore a reputation for the manner in which it served certain special dishes.

He found the examining magistrate about to begin his meal and little inclined to give ear to a case which had brought him nothing but annoyance. His ill-humor was increased by the fact that the police-spy sent down by the Criminal Investigation Department had effected nothing; and when young de Santierne told him that he had a serious communication to make to him, he would willingly have sent him to the devil.

"Let me at least finish my dinner, my good fellow," he grunted. "What with you and Rouletabille I haven't a moment to myself."

"You will be able to dine later, monsieur," returned Jean, "for I believe that what I have to tell you will not brook delay."

And he revealed to the examining magistrate without further ado the story of the ties which bound Rouletabille to a certain Madame de Meyrens, who was a friend of Callista's. This was enough to suspend for the time being Monsieur Crousillat's formidable appetite.

"This Madame de Meyrens, who is well-known in certain circles by the name of the Octopus, is our worst enemy in this affair and humbugs Rouletabille himself.

"Rouletabille caused Callista to be arrested. I'm certain that nothing would suit Madame de Meyrens better than to bring about her escape. I saw her not long ago go into the prison and she stayed there a couple of hours."

"Good heavens," gasped Monsieur Crousillat, throwing down his napkin, "and we put her in this Callista's very cell! Wait for me here, young man. I'll run over to the prison and be back presently." So saying the ponderous Monsieur Crousillat took himself off with an agility which no one would have expected from him.

Jean waited much longer than the examining magistrate had led him to expect, and as he felt hungry and was pretty well satisfied with himself for having taken the initiative, he ended by eating Monsieur Crousillat's dinner. The latter appeared about an hour later. He dropped into a seat with a deep sigh.

"Well?" inquired Jean.

"Well, young man, I was none too soon," he made reply, mopping his streaming forehead.

"I was right, wasn't I?"

"Were you right? . . . Oh, my friend, just fancy. . . . But where's my dinner?"

"I have eaten it, monsieur."

"I am glad to hear it. Was it pretty good?"

"First rate. I hope you will allow me to offer you another."

"Not at all. It's for me to pay to-night. I am greatly indebted to you. You can pride yourself on getting us out of a serious difficulty. What do you suppose we found in those two ruffians' cells? Files and bricklayers' clothing. The whole thing was prepared in advance—there's no doubt about that. Callista was filing through the bars of her cage when we took her by surprise. She fought like a wild cat. She refused to give up her file. She was like a woman possessed. After threatening the warders with it she tried to use it on herself."

"Poor girl!" said Jean under his breath.

"What's that? . . . Now you're pitying her."

"She was my friend, as you are well aware. Allow

me to feel sorry for her, though when I had to choose
between her and my future wife, I did not hesitate. We
must keep a tight hold on her. She is sure to let her
secret out in the long run. What do you say?"

"I say nothing and I have no wish to say anything.
It's no longer any business of mine."

"What do you mean? What about Madame de
Meyrens, who tried to effect their escape? What are you
going to do?"

"Personally, nothing at all. She has too many friends
in high places, and the matter now rests with the prison
governor, who will act."

"What will he do?"

"Write a report."

"Good morning, monsieur," said Jean, rising from the
table.

Jean at once returned to the Hôtel du Forum, where
he would have liked to encounter Rouletabille. But
neither Rouletabille nor the Octopus were to be seen.
They occupied adjoining rooms, while Jean's room was
on the floor above.

He threw himself, dressed as he was, on the bed, and
was called at daybreak . Thus early he began to keep
a look-out from his window on persons entering or leaving the hotel. At seven o'clock he observed Madame de
Meyrens leave the hotel and cross the square. He followed in her footsteps.

Madame de Meyrens was wearing a dust-cloak over
her costume and a small toque which Jean had not seen
the night before. From all appearances she was about
to start on a journey by motor-car, and he was in no way
surprised to see her enter a garage. She was evidently
expected, for the man in charge placed himself at her
disposal.

A few minutes later she came out of the garage driving a small racing car, which started at a slow pace

down the narrow streets. Jean had no difficulty in keeping up with her. The car picked its way not only carefully but silently and did not sound its horn. Madame de Meyrens steered for the part of the town in which the prison stood.

When she came within a hundred yards of it, she pulled up at the corner of the street. Jean then saw her slip the gear into neutral position, consult her wristwatch, and then stand up and alight from the car with an air of unconcern which was not devoid of a certain charm.

He foresaw that an event of some importance was about to happen, and, taking a roundabout way, went down a back lane leading to the prison.

On the way he met Monsieur Bartholasse, and asked him to inform Monsieur Crousillat that Madame de Meyrens was near the prison with a motor-car and that her movements seemed in the highest degree suspicious. Monsieur Bartholasse answered with a disagreeable smile that his chief had left for a day's fishing in the country and that he, a simple clerk, could not take upon himself the risk of disturbing an examining magistrate.

Thereupon Jean determined to interview the governor of the prison. He was told at the record office that the governor had gone for a day's fishing with Monsieur Crousillat. These interviews and movements occupied some time and it was now eight o'clock. When Jean left the prison the first thing that met his eyes was the figure of Madame de Meyrens disappearing round the corner of the street in which she had left her car.

Jean reached this point in his reflections when he was forced to swerve aside to avoid a truck of builders' rubbish which came out of the archway, dragged by a workman in front and pushed by another behind. The figure of Madame de Meyrens came into view once more at the far end of the street and she seemed to expect the truck to pass her.

Jean clearly saw her speak to the workman, who answered her without stopping. Then the truck turned down the street and Madame de Meyrens followed it.

When she was out of sight, Jean rushed back to the prison and asked to see the official who was deputizing for the governor in his absence.

"Tell him that it has to do with very serious matters."

He was convinced that all that he had seen was connected with the preparation for Andréa and Callista's escape, and he was by no means sure that Monsieur Crousillat and the governor had done their utmost, before they departed on their little fishing expedition, to avoid such a contingency. In view of their discovery the night before they had, to his mind, shown great carelessness in starting off for a day's amusement and leaving behind them Madame de Meyrens free to act as she pleased, for doubtless she had more than one trick up her sleeve.

A quarter of an hour later he left the prison and hastened to the Hôtel du Forum, where he asked to see Rouletabille. The latter soon appeared, looking somewhat annoyed.

"Hullo, there you are. Who told you I was here?"

"I met Madame de Meyrens last night on her way to this hotel, and as you didn't come back to Lavardens I . . ."

"Quite right, I understand. . . . Anything fresh?"

"Let's leave the hotel."

"As you please. But you go first and I'll follow later."

"No, come with me now. Madame de Meyrens left the hotel this morning. Can you tell me if she has returned?"

"Yes, just this moment."

"Well, I want to talk to you before you see her again. What I have to say is very serious."

"As usual."

"No, much more serious than usual."

Though Rouletabille affected to attach no importance to what he called "Jean's fancies," he was somewhat interested and accompanied him to the square. Jean made him hug the hotel in such a way that they could not be seen from the windows.

"What an excess of caution!" said Rouletabille, shrugging his shoulders.

"You'll understand me presently."

Jean took him to the café in which the night before he had eaten Monsieur Crousillat's dinner. They were alone at the back of the room and Jean kept silence until the waiter had brought the horse-shoe rolls and coffee which he ordered. Rouletabille began to display an ever-increasing impatience.

"I will first tell you, old man, what your Madame de Meyrens did last night."

"So this is why you are making so much fuss," said Rouletabille with a start. "Why, I myself can tell you what she did last night. She called at the prison and asked to see the governor."

"What then?"

"Then she presented a letter containing an official authorization from police-headquarters to visit, as an anthropologist, the prisons in the Rhone valley."

"Did she tell you so?"

"There was no need to tell me so, seeing that it was I who sent her and gave her the letter."

"In that case I don't know what your object was, but you are certainly unaware of the fact that as soon as she saw the governor, in the presence of the examining magistrate and his clerk, she disclosed the trick which you suggested to her. She told them that she was no anthropologist, but sent down by the detective service to 'pump' the prisoners. You appear to be unaware that she was admitted to Callista's cell and left behind a file and a bricklayer's overalls."

"Anything else?" asked Rouletabille, fixing him with a curious expression.

"You may or may not know that at the present time the prison is in the builders' hands. She must have bribed one of the workmen who came out this morning drawing a truck."

"No," interrupted Rouletabille in a harsh voice. "She did not bribe that man."

"Allow me to have my doubts about that, for while you were asleep this morning, or perhaps still 'thinking things over,' Madame de Meyrens went to a garage, obtained a car and lay in wait a few hundred yards from the prison, and when the man passed near her she had a talk with him."

"No," again interpolated Rouletabille. "She did not bribe that man. It was I who bribed him."

"You!"

"Yes, and while she was inside the prison carrying out my instructions I, in the meantime, was making all my arrangements outside."

"With what object?" shouted Jean in amazement.

"Not so loud, my boy," said Rouletabille, forcing him by a peremptory gesture to keep his seat. "I will tell you with what object, seeing that you were not clever enough to guess it. . . . But drink your coffee quietly and follow my example by assuming a calmness which is only on the surface, I assure you. I have always told you that the one way of getting at Odette was through Callista. It was to make her talk that I got her and Andréa arrested."

"I haven't forgotten that your intervention saved my life."

"Even if you had been in no danger I should have had them run in just the same, so there's no need to thank me. We are not in the mood to bandy compliments, and I will not keep from you that I fear some egregious blunder on your part, but first of all follow my line of reasoning. By holding the charge of murder over her I hoped to make her show the white feather. When I was satisfied that neither she nor Andréa would give anything away, I was obliged to make a radical change in my tactics. I caused them to be arrested, and I made up my mind to help them to escape, for it was a moral certainty that after their escape they would attempt to join Odette, more particularly as the Octopus would impress on them that we were already on her track. Then we should follow them—I had arranged that no attempt would be made to catch them again—and reach the goal we had in view. But what's up with you? Aren't you feeling well?"

"Rouletabille," murmured Jean under his breath, "I *have* made another blunder."

"I thought as much. What have you done, unhappy man?"

"I came to this very café last night and told Monsieur Crousillat to be on his guard against Madame de Meyrens."

"You did that! You did that!" gasped Rouletabille in a muffled voice. "What else?"

"Then the examining magistrate hurried off to the prison to see the governor and they discovered files and bricklayers' clothes in the prisoners' cells."

"That'll do. I knew it as soon as you opened your mouth."

Rouletabille leant his elbows on the table and covered his face with his hands. Jean was staggered. A dead silence fell and one might have heard a pin drop. . . . At last Rouletabille looked up and said:

"It's no use worrying about it, for you are sufficiently punished by what you have done."

"I am a silly ass," moaned Jean.

"No, you are not a silly ass, but don't sneer at me again. And let me in future conspire with the Octopus as I think fit. Of course, I admit that she is very clever, but I have just shown you that on this occasion, as on many others, if you had not interfered I should have been more than a match for her."

"After what she's done the police will nab her," cried Jean.

"You've said another foolish thing. The Octopus will have no difficulty in explaining to the police that as her instructions were to 'pump' Callista, she could not do better, in order to win her confidence and insure some disclosure, than to agree to help her in this plan to escape —a plan which she will father on to me without a scruple of remorse. No, she will not be embarrassed by the police, but the police, when confronted with the report of the prison governor, will find it difficult to employ her again for some time to come. A good riddance! You think that I am very smitten with her. I assure you that I've had enough of her. I am thinking only of Odette."

The last words rose naturally to Rouletabille's lips, but they were uttered so simply and in such a peculiar accent, and seemed so fully to complete the significance of what he had said before, that they rang with an almost painful echo in Jean's as well as in his own ears.

The latter grew slightly pale.

"I have promised you happiness and I intend to keep my word. And now let's adjourn," he said, passing his arm through Jean's in the friendliest manner. "Callista's escape is essential and we shall manage it. I know the prison thoroughly and have been considering other methods."

They left the café.   Rouletabille could feel Jean swaying against his arm.

"What's the matter now? You're not going to faint?"

"I feel inclined to put an end to myself," sighed Jean.

"Don't do that," said Rouletabille, pretending to burst
out laughing. "Don't put me under the necessity of
breaking such unpleasant news to Odette."

"Oh, my dear fellow, even now I haven't told you
everything. I called at the prison this morning."

"Well?"

"Well, Andréa and Callista are not there now."

"What's that?"

"An order to transfer Andréa and Callista to Aix
prison was signed last night by Monsieur Crousillat and
the instructions were carried out this morning."

"Hell and fury!" shouted Rouletabille. "Hell and
fury, that's the limit. We've come a mucker. . . .
Have you anything more to tell me? No? . . . Thanks!

" . . . Well, now, old man, we must part. I've taken an
oath and I'll stick to it in any case. I'll make you the
gift of Odette, but on one condition: that you swear
not to attempt to come after me, and not to budge from
Lavardens until you receive word from me."

"Oh, forgive me," said Jean, with tears in his eyes.

"I forgive you, you ass!"

Rouletabille shook hands with him quite stiffly and left
him standing there in the street, while he turned on his
heel. But at the corner of the street he looked round
and shouted:

"If you meet the Octopus, don't tell her which way
I've gone."

CHAPTER XXIII

ROULETABILLE AND LA FINETTE

IT was Sergeant La Finette who received orders to conduct Andréa and Callista to Aix prison, and as he was called upon also to take two horses, which had just been purchased at Arles, to the Gendarmery of the ancient Roman town, he did not feel disposed to suggest that a journey by railway, even if it involved a circuitous route and the unpleasantness of frequent changes, would have saved a great deal of worry and fatigue.

He took his comrade Cornouilles with him, and from early dawn they had been riding, one on each side of the road, with their handcuffed prisoners walking between them.

Neither the gendarmes nor the prisoners spoke. Cornouilles seemed to be still asleep, and La Finette was smoking his pipe. Andréa was watching Callista out of the corner of his eye with a look of mingled gloom and love. Callista, on the other hand, proudly erect, stepped forward along the dusty road seemingly leading the way for the little company. Nothing could be heard but the sound of their footsteps, the clank of the horses curb-chains, the cry of the peewit as it flew through the inexorable blue in quest of an infrequent pool.

The gendarmes themselves were feeling thirsty. Cornouilles' first words when he awoke were:

"It will be all right at Salon."

And, in fact, they had to pass through Salon where they would halt, in order to make an official call, and

167

breakfast. La Finette emptied his pipe against his boot, and echoed with emphasis:

"It will be all right at Salon."

And they relapsed once more into silence. Suddenly the road made a bend, and as they passed a clump of tamarisks a number of strange figures appeared before them on the road-side bank.

They were dark, glossy-haired, amber-skinned and splendid in their squalor. They seemed the very monarchs of destitution as they stood in the pride of their rags and stature.

They had no fear of gendarmes, for somewhere in their caravans lay hidden passports with every country, which gave them a few weeks respite during which they could reach the frontier and disappear into space.

Three men and two women and five little imps of gypsies stared in silence as the procession moved over the dusty road. Their eyes were fixed on Andréa, and they betrayed neither astonishment nor concern when they beheld his manacled hands and woeful plight.

The gypsies watched the little party march past. Nevertheless there was one person whose eyes were fixed upon the gypsies, and when a few minutes later they went back to their encampment, this person went straight up to them. It was a certain youth with the amber skin and black mustache of a Hungarian violinist. He emerged from a small wood of chestnut trees which threw their shade over the first slopes leading to the village next to Salon.

The gypsies squatting round the remnants of a highly-flavored sheep condescended to look up.

The newcomer acted in a somewhat mysterious manner, stepping now and again on tiptoe to see if anything fresh was happening on the road in the distance.

The gypsies began to eye him with obvious hostility, when he drew from his pocket a certain clasp fixed to a chain which at once made the impression upon them which he clearly expected from it.

"The sign!" mumbled the gypsies in their jargon, and stood up politely. Of course this youth with the amber skin and black mustache of a Hungarian violinist had gypsy blood in his veins.

He led them to understand, in a few words, that he was one of themselves, and his object or rather his mission was to liberate Andréa and his companion. Their eyes at once lit up. They all knew Andréa. The woman was a stranger to them, but there was no possibility of doubt that she was their *shaia*, their sister. The young man explained that he would "see to the gendarmes" but that as soon as he had relieved Andréa and Callista of their guards they must look after them. He had come a long way round by car knowing that the party would pass through Salon. He then took them to the wood of chestnut trees and showed them his small racing car:

"This is where you must bring the prisoners as soon as they are free," he said.

When the entire plan of campaign was fully understood he added:

"And now go. . . . Make haste. . . . Don't let the gendarmes out of sight, but try to keep *out* of sight yourselves. They must not see you."

"What about you?"

"You will find me again here. Don't worry about me."

They separated, scampering away with the utmost speed, and their bare feet made no more sound on the road than a flight of sparrows skimming over the tall grass. . . .

On the outskirts of the village, La Finette turned round in his saddle. He caught the sound of a bicycle and straightway shouted out his famous *"Quésaco?* What's that?" whereupon the entire company looked round.

"Well, upon my word, if it isn't Rouletabille himself!" said La Finette.

"You've hit it in one, fathead," rapped out the journalist as he leapt from his bicycle. "Whew! It *is* hot on these Provençal roads. I thought I should never come up to you."

The reader will recall that La Finette and Rouletabille since their expedition to Roseaux plain had become the best of friends.

"This is a surprise!" cried La Finette. "To what do we owe the pleasure of your company?"

"I learnt this morning of our prisoners' attempt to escape, and the order to transfer them. I said to myself. 'Those dogs will stick at nothing, and besides, are as clever as monkeys. They might play some trick on my friend La Finette.' "

"I say, you don't mean it!" cried La Finette, scarlet with indignation. "Do you take me for a baby? Never on your life! You don't know Lou Fineto, Monsieur Rouletabille. If you only knew Lou Fineto!"

"Calm yourself, La Finette. I have the utmost confidence in you; the truth is that I have a little business which takes me to Aix, so I thought that we might do the journey together. . . . Don't you feel a bit thirsty, La Finette?"

La Finette possessed, as the saying goes, a bulbous nose. . . . The party had arrived outside a small inn of high repute in the countryside, where on Sundays and holidays, visitors from Salon came to make good cheer and play bowls. The fare was excellent, but the charges were higher than some pockets could afford, and it would never have occurred to La Finette to stop there if Rouletabille, who was very considerate and tactful, had not invited him and his comrade to lunch with him.

"All right," said Cornouilles simply, while La Finette would have liked to embrace Rouletabille.

"Wait a bit! What are you going to do with the prisoners?" asked the latter.

"Well, my boy, I'll fix them to my boots if necessary, but they shan't get away, I give you my word."

The two gendarmes had already dismounted. They tied their steeds to a ring in the stable wall near the manger. After assuring themselves that the animals wanted for nothing, they turned their attention to the prisoners. On the suggestion of the proprietor, they locked them in a kind of lean-to built of brick, and used for the storage of wood. The door possessed a substantial lock. Clearly the two prisoners would have no chance of escape during the short time in which they would be kept there. Moreover, their handcuffs were not removed even for their frugal meal, which Cornouilles had brought with him in his haversack; and the door of the lean-to stood exactly opposite the cool little room in which Rouletabille had ordered the table to be laid. The prisoners were within reach and within sight.

"Lord bless me, did you notice what a face they pulled when they saw you?" asked La Finette as he entered the inn.

"Yes, I'm no friend of theirs! What do you say to some of this saveloy, an omelette, a rabbit, a nice little salad, and a bottle of wine of Provence?"

"Only one!" cried La Finette and Cornouilles in unison. "What should we do with one bottle?"

"Well, let's say a couple, but no more. I don't want anyone to get 'tight.' Let me tell you one thing, La Finette: Three-fourths of the cases where prisoners escape would never occur if the guards hadn't got drunk beforehand."

"Beforehand! Perhaps you're right, young man," agreed the sergeant with a somewhat doleful air. "Beforehand! . . . . We'll be satisfied with a couple of bottles."

"But there'll be coffee and a liqueur brandy."

"Only one!" cried the representatives of law and order once more.

"Let's make it a couple, and we'll say no more about it. And now for lunch."

"What are you going to do outside?" asked the sergeant, seeing Rouletabille make for the woodshed in which the two prisoners were confined.

"I want to make sure that our birds can't fly away."

"There's no window and I've got the key of the door in my pocket," returned the sergeant, bursting out laughing.

But Rouletabille seized the handle and gave the door a vigorous shake, eager doubtless to ascertain the truth for himself.

"It's all right," he said.   "We can be easy in our minds."

Just then the waiter put the first bottle on the table.

"Speaking of guards who drink too much," he said, taking his seat, "I must tell you a little story."

"This devil of a Rouletabille! He's always got a yarn to tell," exclaimed La Finette with a laugh, as he poured out his first bumper and cut himself a fair-sized slice of saveloy. "That comes of being a newspaper man. Ah, these journalists! A regular lot of jokers!"

"Have you ever been to St. Martin-de-Ré?" asked Rouletabille.

"Never. I'm not a warder."

"Oh, there are gendarmes in the penal settlement. At the time I speak of there were, in fact, two very well known, shrewd gendarmes, and it was 'no good trying it on with them' as one might say of you and our worthy friend Cornouilles."

"What then?"

"Well, this is what happened . . ."

"Wait a moment, if you don't mind. I seem to hear someone stirring near my prisoners."

La Finette rose from the table and went outside and listened at the door of the lean-to, then walked round it, cast a glance in the vicinity, and came back with a worried look.

"I thought I caught sight of some of those wretched people."

"Oh, really. . . . The gypsies on the road. I saw them too," returned Rouletabille. "You do well to be suspicious. All these people back each other up. But what do you expect them to do against two gendarmes like La Finette and Cornouilles, I wonder?"

"What were they doing when you came across them, my dear Rouletabille?"

"Upon my word, they were having something to eat quite peacefully under the shelter of their caravan, and they didn't even look at me. . . . Take care, La Finette, you'll soon be emptying the bottle."

"We were speaking of St. Martin-de-Ré," went on the gendarme. "Have you ever been there?"

"Yes, to inspect the convict prison. It was when Chéri-Bibi was caught and sent back to the penal settlement for the third time. You must understand that there is never any such thing as an escape in St. Martin-de-Ré; that is when Chéri-Bibi is not there, but when Chéri-Bibi is there! . . ."

"What did he do, your Chéri-Bibi?"

"He helped five men to get away."

"The devil he did."

"What I'm telling you is quite true. The governor of the prison himself explained to me how the thing came about. At that time they had at St. Martin-de-Ré the very pick of the convict settlements—five blackguards

whose reputations were known throughout the penitentiary establishments. These were: Cochot, who said to
the governor: 'You ask me if, when I am committing my
crimes, I am ever arrested by the fear of punishment.
Sure enough if I hadn't been arrested by anything but
fear you would never have had the pleasure of my company at St. Martin-de-Ré.' . . . Petit, who was captured
at Abbeville, and warned the mayor of that delightful
city that he intended to leave the prison next day as it
didn't seem to him a comfortable place to live in, and
as a matter of fact he was as good as his word. . . .
Piercy, who once made his escape from a departmental
prison by faking a warder's uniform out of paper and
putting it on before the eyes of the men whose business
it was to take him and his fellow-prisoners to the exercise yard. . . . Fanfan, who was the terror of the prison
warders—he had escaped seven times—and had but to say
aloud: 'My feet itch to get away' to throw the entire
penitentiary into a state of consternation. . . . Arigonde,
who had a genius for disguise. Fregoli, the quick-change
music-hall artist, was a mere child compared with him.
But Arigonde was a clown, for instance, and he would
make up his hair and whiskers, deface the special marks
by which he was identified, and slip on a suit of clothes,
whatever it was, before the professional mime could take
off his tie. I knew Arigonde very well. . . ."

"Was he a newspaper man?" asked Cornouilles.

"No, he was employed in a private inquiry office, but
they made the mistake of paying too little for his ability.
. . . Finally, there was Chéri-Bibi, the most wonderful
of them all.

"When he learnt that the five of them were there,
he made up his mind to play a trick on the administra-
tion by helping the whole lot to escape. . . . Chéri-
Bibi always maintained relations with the outside world.
On such and such a day and hour a launch lay waiting

for the convicts in a little creek some distance away, as
luck would have it, from the 'wild coast' whence it would
be easy for them to reach the mainland. During the
night they dug near the fort, a hiding-place as they called
it, in which they concealed sailors' clothes, peak caps and
sou'westers which they were to put on, once they left the
prison, in order to get to the spot where the launch was
moored. The escape could only be attempted in broad
daylight. It took place at a quarter past eight in the
morning; the hour at which bricklayers started their work
on a wall in one of the prison yards."

"Look here, that was the trick that was being tried
on behalf of our gypsies!"

"There's nothing new under the sun," went on Rouletabille imperturbably. "How did Chéri-Bibi and his five
comrades manage to plan the affair? One thing is certain: a gang of five workmen entered the prison at eight
o'clock and came out again at a quarter past eight. . . .

"The ruffians knew that there was some risk of their
escapade being discovered a few minutes later. Accordingly they were eager to get to the hiding-place, and
wait events there until the right moment for slipping
out. Unluckily, two gendarmes stood opposite the hiding-place, the two very artful gendarmes whom I mentioned just now—the La Finette and Cornouilles of the
Ile-de-Ré. . . . Well, these two gendarmes saw a man
whose head was covered with a colored handkerchief
coming up the road towards them. He was dragging a
wheelbarrow containing a pick-ax. He was walking at
a moderate pace, and when he was on a level with the
representatives of law and order who wished him 'Good
morning,' he stopped for a moment.

"What idiots!" exclaimed La Finette. "I bet it was
Chéri-Bibi."

"You've guessed right, La Finette."

"Oh, he wouldn't have had me like that."

"They began chatting. The man told them that he had just drawn his pay and meant to have a little time off. . . . In short, he invited the two gendarmes to have a drink with him at a small public-house which was not exactly next door to the 'hiding-place.'

"The gendarmes plied their glasses in that public-house with such good will that when they tried to stand up their legs shook under them. . . . Chéri-Bibi had to help them to get to St. Martin. He had the kindness to take them to the prison, and when the door was opened, he said: 'I've brought you a couple of gendarmes slightly "sprung."'"

"'Gendarmes! What do you expect us to do with them?' he was asked.

"'Leave them outside if you like, but I'm sure you've got room for me here.'

"He removed the handkerchief from his head and was at once recognized. You can imagine the warmth of his welcome! The entire island was turned topsy-turvy when it was discovered that he and five fellow prisoners had made their escape. Still they consoled themselves for the loss of the five by the presence of Chéri-Bibi. When the warders expressed surprise at his carrying out such superhuman labor only to return and give himself up he made reply:

"'As for me, you know, there are times when I long for the penal settlement.'

"I need not tell you, to conclude the story, that our two gendarmes were reduced to the ranks with all the ceremony due to their position. . . . To allow themselves to be brought back to the prison by a convict— here was something out of the common. Well, gentlemen, won't you have another drink?"

While Rouletabille was telling his story the lunch drew to a finish. Coffee was served, and they were at the stage when they had before them a glass of brandy of the

Province called by the peasants *grappa*. It is a liqueur which is wonderfully cheering, warming the inner man and expanding the heart with gladness.

After the second glass was consumed La Finette leered at the bottle with a look of desire.

"Remembering what I told you just now, it would be unpardonable to have any more," said Rouletabille.

"Yes, of course, young man," La Finette broke in bluntly. "Beforehand! You are right. But as long as that confounded bottle is on the table . . ."

"I'll take it away," declared Rouletabille, and left the room with the dangerous object.

Any one who might have had the curiosity to follow him, would have seen him a minute or two later pour the contents of the bottle into the horses' manger which he had just replenished.

"I don't like to see gendarmes the worse for liquor," he muttered between his teeth. "But as to their horses, well, that's another story!"

CHAPTER XXIV

IN WHICH EVENTS COME TO PASS AS ROULETABILLE
FORETOLD

THE departure from the inn was made without any incident worthy of mention. With the exception of the prisoners the entire party—Rouletabille, the gendarmes, and even the horses—seemed in a lively mood. The horses in particular looked very spry, which was by no means displeasing to La Finette and Cornouilles, who had laid claim to be first-rate horsemen.

"They seem somewhat restive," observed La Finette simply as he mounted his steed. "You, Cornouilles, must have given them a good feed of oats, what? . . . Are you coming, Monsieur Rouletabille?"

"I notice that one of my tires has burst," he answered. "I'll put it right and soon overtake you."

Thus they set out.

Their mounts began to indulge in strange antics.

"Perhaps these horses are not free from vice," suggested Cornouilles. "We're not used to them, you know."

"But they were so very quiet before lunch. What's the matter with them," exclaimed La Finette, almost thrown from the saddle, for his mount shied with a suddenness which he was far from expecting.

"Come now, you silly brute," growled Cornouilles in his turn. "Aren't you going to stop your pranks?"

His mare had, in fact, started to prance and rear as though she intended to complete the journey on her hind legs.

"Give her a whack on the nose. There's nothing like

178

it when they go frisking about," advised La Finette.
But his own horse had started to curvet. Angrily he
proceeded to give it a thrashing.

"I'll show her the stuff I'm made of," shouted Cornouilles from his side.

Then the horses dashed off at a breakneck speed and
were lost to sight with their riders in a whirl of dust
like those mythological heroes or demi-gods who were
hidden from the view of ordinary mortals in the cloud
which Jupiter hurled to their support.

When the cloud had passed away and the eyes of
ordinary mortals could discern La Finette and Cornouilles, it was to discover two riders unhorsed, disabled,
dejected and bruised, dragging themselves along the road,
uttering inarticulate cries, gazing frantically now towards
the setting sun, in the direction of which their infernal
horses had fled, and now towards the east where the road
spread out before them likewise deserted; that is to say,
containing no sign of the prisoners intrusted to their
keeping. . . . Then they climbed the road-side bank
moaning like children who had lost their mother. They
would be able to find their horses again—but their prisoners! . . .

"Perhaps Rouletabille is on their track," murmured
Cornouilles.

"We've none the less disgraced ourselves," returned La
Finette, in a broken voice.

At the same moment the excited company of gypsies
who had gathered round Andréa and Callista and relieved
them of their handcuffs, turned into the lower road
behind the wood of chestnut trees where the car, with
its driver with the amber skin and black mustache of
a Hungarian violinist, was waiting for them. He was
already seated at the wheel ready to drive off.

"This is the man who brought us here and arranged
everything," explained the spokesman of the party.

"He has the sign."

No further explanations were offered. Andréa and Callista stepped into the car which drove away at its utmost speed. They were jolted roughly against each other, and at last Andréa with a sudden gesture silently clasped his arms about Callista, who yielded to him without demur. The driver threw them a rug which they wrapped round themselves.

Half an hour later he slackened speed, turned round, showed the sign which Andréa saluted, and fixing him with a direct gaze through his goggles, asked:

"Where am I to take you?"

Callista replied in one word, or rather mentioned the name of a small railway station on the frontier; they reached this place that same evening after an uneventful drive.

Here, they alighted from the car and Callista thanked their unknown benefactor. He offered to take them still farther, but they declined his suggestion. They no longer had anything to fear. The police would not suspect that they were already on the frontier. . . . There was no need of passports in Switzerland; and they might as well take the first train, which started in half an hour, if this unknown rescuer would give them some money.

"This is what I have been asked to give you," he said, as he slipped a few banknotes into Callista's hand.

"You can tell whoever sent you that we are now quite safe," said Callista. "Besides, I hope that we shall meet again soon. Our festivals are close at hand," she added, casting a mysterious glance at him.

"Soon," returned the other under his breath. . . . "At Sever Turn."

Callista put her finger on her lips and departed with Andréa to the station. . . . The chauffeur sprang into his car and disappeared at full speed round a bend in the road.

Half an hour later Andréa and Callista had taken their places in a third class carriage. . . . Callista was wrapped in a shawl which concealed her tatters. She closed her eyes and appeared to sleep. Andréa did not remove his gaze from her. She had returned among her people; they had obtained their freedom; she would be his.

He would soon be her husband in accordance with gypsy rites, and their marriage would be celebrated one night, now near at hand, under the everlasting canopy between the moss-grown pillars of the tall trees illuminated by the lamps of heaven. He was so greatly engrossed in his dream that he failed to notice the face which showed itself in the triangular pane of glass in the partition dividing the compartments.

Extract from Rouletabille's diary:

"Here I am at last at the point which I have so much desired. I am in the train which is taking Callista to the place where Odette is to be found.

"If I put the facts which I learnt from Mᵉ Camousse side by side with the remarks which I overheard both in the church steeple in Ozout and Zina's cave, and compare them with the contents of the Book of Ancestors, I am bound to conclude that Odette is, on her mother's side of gypsy birth, and is being carried off to Sever Turn as the queen whose coming is foretold in the sacred writings.

"And yet the Book of Ancestors mentions a birthmark on the shoulder, a mark in the shape of a crown. Now it seems certain—I may even say that it *is* certain, for I have no reason to doubt Estève's assertions—that Odette had no such mark and has no such mark. Consequently I am necessarily led to believe that Zina faked the mark so as to save Odette's life. These old hags have secret means of their own of producing stains or marks on the skin which appear indelible. . . . And she must have satisfied Andréa and Callista that Odette was the gypsy queen.

"This inference I drew from the course of events, and

it was my strength and safeguard . . . I knew, from that moment, that our Odette was in no danger from the gypsies and that she would be treated as though she were of royal birth. But I was unable to impart this consolation to Jean.

"I wonder indeed—were he acquainted with it—how he would receive the fact which to-day seems obvious to me: 'Odette is a gypsy girl. She is not the daughter of Madame de Lavardens.' No! Until it is absolutely necessary I am not entitled to divulge that information to a soul, and least of all to Jean.

"Why should I conceal from myself the fact that he does not always look upon me with friendly feelings? The suspicion which preys upon him would, doubtless, lead him to regard such a disclosure as an abominable invention on my part, made for the purpose of separating him from our Odette. In short, I did well to say nothing.

"What a number of things the Book of Ancestors has revealed to me!

"First, it told me the reason why my flat was broken into. Ever since de Lauriac robbed the gypsies of the book they have been searching for it.

"I can imagine now the commotion which was caused in gypsy-land—Sever Turn—by my article in which I set down the exact wording of the prediction in which the coming of the queen with the birth-mark on her shoulder was foretold.

"They were straightway convinced that it was I who possessed the book and I who had stolen it from them. Hence the visit of scant ceremony which I received one night and the disorder in which I found my study.

"Now I learnt the wording of the prophecy simply through Olajaï, who repeated it to me one day when I was discussing with him the debasement into which his race had fallen. Like every good gypsy he knew the text by heart.

"But though my burglars did not find the book in my flat, it did not take them long to discover that I had a Romany in my service. Hence Olajaï's precipitate departure for Les Saintes Maries. He must have received the order to explain himself, and he had no alternative but to confess that my knowledge of the gypsy secret was due to his indiscretion, an indiscretion which subsequent events were to render particularly serious.

"The race, indeed, was expecting the destined queen that very year, and it would, perhaps, be still waiting for her but for the intervention of Zina. In any case, Mademoiselle de Lavardens' abduction, Zina's disclosure to her kinsfolk concerning Odette's birth, the coincidence of Monsieur de Lavardens' tragic death—these things were so many incidents which rendered the position of the Romanys in Camargue, after the appearance of my article, one of the utmost difficulty.

"It accounted for Olajaï's terror when he met me in the Province. It accounted for the entreaties and threats by which he sought to make me leave it. My presence there was not less dangerous to him than to myself. He might be taken for my accomplice.

"And his brethren, the gypsies, seem still to be keeping an eye on him, for he has not been seen since he left Camargue. . . . They have undoubtedly compelled him to accompany them.

"Thus everything is explained and it all fits in.

"The Book of Ancestors had told me something else.

"The question suggested itself to me to find out if de Lauriac was in league with Callista. He had traveled in the gypsies' country, he had purloined the Book of Ancestors, the precious stones in which must certainly have formed a considerable portion of the fortune which he brought back from abroad. . . . I knew that he spoke and read the gypsy language. He was aware, therefore, of the great reward which awaited the person who restored the book to its owners.

"Had de Lauriac been Callista's accomplice he would have left the book in the place to which I had carefully returned it, and hastened to the spot where he knew that Odette was to be found. In that event, it would have been easy for me to follow him, but his chief concern was to take the book with him, the book whose restoration would entitle him to a reward; and there is no doubt that, as his reward, he would ask only for Odette's freedom. Therefore the disappearance of the book told me that de Lauriac was not an accomplice.

"What was his destination? Obviously Sever Turn with the least possible delay—Sever Turn, where the man who held sway over the entire race dwelt. Therefore I could ignore de Lauriac and concentrate myself on the search for Odette, who was being carried off to Sever Turn by the most devious ways, for the Romanys would take no risks; the Romanys know that I suspect the truth and certainly realize that in recovering Odette I should be robbing them of their queen. . . .

"Callista grasped the meaning of my allusions to this matter in the examining magistrate's office; and her infuriated retort: 'You will never see Odette again,' confirmed me in my belief that it was no use looking for her on the direct road to Sever Turn.

"And now Callista herself will show me the way and deliver her into my hands. . . . And now I am eager to get to work. I have played my last stake. If I have lost, Odette will reach Sever Turn before me, and then no power on earth will be able to restore her to us.

"I know this people. They would rather die to the last man with their queen under the walls of their temple than surrender her. . . . But I have not lost . . . I have won. . . .

"Oh, but this is a disaster!"

CHAPTER XXV

OF THE RISKS INCURRED BY A TRAVELER WITH
TOO FINE A BEARD

THE train stopped at a wayside station. The stout woman who was nursing her child stood up and the child awoke. The worthy woman wanted to alight. The man with the fine yellow beard returned his notebook to his pocket and opened the carriage door. The woman passed her son to the accommodating passenger and descended to the platform, and then turned and held out her arms to receive her offspring.

At that moment the young imp was gazing with undisguised admiration at the fine golden yellow beard of the man who was lifting him out of the carriage, as though he were the most precious but embarrassing charge. Let us at once say that he was eager to be rid of his burden.

As ill-luck would have it, his impatience was not shared by the child. Such wonderful golden yellow beards are not met with every day in third class carriages, and when we have the good fortune to travel with one, we tear ourselves away from it with sorrow! The youngster laid hold of the flaxen appendage and the traveler uttered a cry. The child cried out too, and the mother cried out louder than either of them, for the train was starting again.

These cries attracted Andréa and Callista to their carriage door, and they caught sight of a stout woman excitedly clutching a child who held in his clenched little fist a splendid beard, which shone like burnished gold!

The carriage door was violently slammed from the inside with a bear-like growl.

185

Callista ran to the partition window and saw a raging gentleman without a beard and recognized him. The latter hurriedly left the compartment and went into the corridor to find some spot where he could be out of the gypsies' sight, but, as we have said, it was too late. Two creatures flung themselves on him like savages and toppled him over on to the permanent way. . . .

Extract from Rouletabille's diary:

"It is a dire moment when you fall from a train, particularly if you have been somewhat brutally thrown out, and you see coming towards you a goods train whose sole mission seems to be to reduce you to pulp. But if you are not dead, take it from me that what remains of life in you will be sufficient to bring you out of danger! . . .

"I contrived to make a leap which shot me outside the track while the 'steam-roller' passed alongside me, furiously puffing and snorting. . . . I should probably have lain there some time if a youthful goat-herd who had witnessed the incident, had not come to my assistance. He showed me a mean-looking inn standing alone on the edge of a wood, as if lost in this deserted neighborhood, and I had sufficient strength to drag myself to it. I was taken to a room on the first floor, where I received first aid.

"I was a mass of bruises, but happily no bones were broken, though it seemed that my left shoulder was dislocated. I was particularly enraged by my misadventure. It was so unforeseen and stupid.

"Nevertheless, I did not give way to despair, because I knew the name of the station to which *they* had taken tickets, and it was no great distance from the place where I was. I learnt that this place was called New Wachter, and the inn, Prince Joseph. As I realized, however, that I was pretty well done for, I got the young goat-herd to send a telegram to Jean: 'Met with accident; come im-

mediately,' adding the address, but no further information. I felt certain that he would lose no time in coming
to me. I determined, moreover, not to wait for him if I
felt better a few hours later, but to hire a car, at whatever cost, and overtake my two rascally birds. . . .

"As I lay stretched on my bed, I suddenly heard
through the open window the sound of a *gusla,* which
was accompanying a strange melody. I dragged myself
to the window and from my observatory—the inn was
on rising ground—I beheld in the middle of a clearing
a gypsy encampment of some dimensions. The gypsies
seemed to be making merry, and were dancing round a
number of fires.

"I had an intuition which sent a thrill through me from
head to foot. I called out and a young girl came to my
room. Pointing to the distant gypsy encampment I said:

" 'Every gypsy is more or less a bone-setter. Couldn't
you go and see if there's one among them who can set
a dislocated shoulder?'

"She set out at once. I closed the window, drew the
curtains so that the room should be in semi-darkness,
altered the appearance of my face, and waited. . . ."

At this point the diary comes to a stop, as though it
had been suddenly suspended. Then, on the next page,
are these lines written in a feverish hand:

"An old woman came to me. I artfully asked her
a number of questions. . . . It was Zina! . . . It was
Zina! I could swear that it was Zina. . . . And Odette
is here—here within a few hundred yards of me. I am
positive of it. . . . Odette! . . . Odette! . . . My dear
Odette, whom I love as a dear frail young sister. . . .
You are saved! . . ."

And then there are a few words written quickly in
scarcely intelligible letters:

"But who is this banging so loudly on the inn door
at this late hour?"

CHAPTER XXVI

"WHO COULD SAY IF SHE WERE AWAKE OR ASLEEP?"

SHE lay on the tattered bedclothes which the gypsies had flung there so that she might rest awhile in the cool twilight. Their hearts were alike sad and glad. They were leading home to the sacred city their young queen who had been lost and was found.

She turned her head when anyone came near her.

"She is thinking of her own country," mumbled the aged Oliva between her loose teeth.

"A Romany woman has no country," broke in the harsh voice of Suco, who was patching up the harness of his old hack.

But Sumbala, the chief of the tribe, a tawny old man with a beard gray with dust, said:

"Sever Turn will become the queen of nations. Through this child she will arise from her desolation and astonish the world. What is written is written."

Olajaï stopped poking the flickering fire, drew himself up and interposed:

"The dark mist in which the gypsy nation is shrouded will pass away. The glorious day for which we have so long waited, will dawn at last, our brethren will be united once more, and we shall be great and free. Our victorious ranks will march against the enemy filled with one proud thought and strong in one faith!"

But Olajaï's intervention was not a success. His words fell on deaf ears, for he had been in the service of an alien, and they had abundant reason for mistrusting him.

188

Then the youthful Ari, who was but sixteen years of age, stopped trimming her rushes.

"If she is not asleep she is thinking of the alien whom she loves."

They all turned their blazing eyes upon her and a few oaths whistled past her ears. She had brought them upon herself, but she did not lose countenance.

"One cannot help falling in love," she said. "I've seen him. By Saint Sarah, he is handsomer than Suco."

There was a laugh, but Suco, who made pretentions to good looks, threw a stone at her and called her *usheia*—"a slut."

"I will denounce you to our chief when we get to Sever Turn."

Sumbala quietened them by pointing to Odette asleep. . . . She was not asleep. She was thinking of *him*, of him and her father, of whose tragic end she knew nothing, and of all those who had loved her. What were they doing? Why did they not come to her rescue? Was it possible that she had been carried off, as the wind blows away a feather, and taken across the frontier under their very eyes, without the least effort on their part to protect her? Was it possible that she had traveled in a caravan for days together, as though it were an ordinary occurrence?

The gendarmes had visited the caravan, the customs-house officers had come, and they had gazed at her. They had seen her and said nothing. Nor had she said anything. By what manner of witchcraft had the thing come to pass?

All her young being was stirred to its very depths, all her energies were summoned up to shout aloud to them: "Save me!" and with Zina's eyes on her she had not moved a limb or uttered a sound. . . .

This Zina, this wicked little old witch of a woman—she had at once taken a liking to her. When the street boys of the village turned away from the old woman setting up an outcry, when the girls of Camargue fled from her making the sign of the cross, she went up to her, impelled by some strange, indefinable power. . . . And she had returned to the cross-roads, where the old creature was waiting for her, without any previous understanding between them. . . .

Was Zina her good or evil genius in this terrible experience? This wicked little old witch of a woman a good genius? And yet she had saved Odette's life. Without her intervention she would have received her death blow from Callista and the savage Andréa. What could she have told them? What could she have shown them? What was it that they all stared at beneath the wrap round her shoulders? . . . They called her their queen, their young queen. What was their motive? What had she to do with these people? She was Odette de Lavardens—and behold now she was a queen in a caravan!

These gypsies were all magicians. The whole world was aware of it. She was bewitched by this wicked little old hag of a woman with the hook nose, whom she hated and who was forever sighing and clasping her in her arms against her rags. . . .

She hated her, but was afraid when she knew that she was not hovering round her, and the refuge of her trembling, scraggy arms was not open to her. Make of it what you will, it was so! When Odette wept in silence, she was conscious of a warm breath at her feet. It was Zina who worshiped her. . . . Odette believed now in fairy tales.

Suddenly a kind of uproar caused her to open her eyes. Then she leapt to her feet and hastily retreated to the caravan, uttering a cry like a wounded animal.

Callista! Callista, her bitterest enemy and the savage Andréa were there!

They had just come within the circle of gypsies revealed by the tongues of fire which licked the sides of a cauldron. And they gathered round them with words of welcome and signs of delight, all talking together.

Odette could feel and hear her heart throb in her chest like a hammer on an anvil.

Oh, this Callista, this Callista whom her Jean used to love, and perhaps loved still! She lifted the curtain of the little window, but let it down again with a gesture of rage, and it was torn.

Callista was looking at her. . . . She was fixing her eyes on the caravan in which Odette was imprisoned— They were wicked eyes; though assuredly men loved eyes like that, since Jean had loved them.

Jean had kissed those eyes as he had kissed hers. Jean had lied to her. She no longer loved him. . . .

She gave a cry, starting back with horror. Callista and Andréa were coming towards the caravan, laughing.

Odette darted to the door, calling: "Zina! Zina!"

And it was not Olajaï, the mysterious Olajaï, who from the beginning of the journey had been watching her by stealth, without once speaking to her—Olajaï, whom all the gypsies mistrusted, and whose face was not entirely unfamiliar to her—where had she seen him months, perhaps years, ago?—assuredly it was not he who would thrust himself between Callista and the prisoner and save her as Zina had done, for he seemed anxious, shy, frightened at the least thing, even to look at her in secret and show pity for her.

And suddenly she caught the sound of Zina's voice. She sprang to the caravan window. It seemed as if a meeting of fiends had gathered round the panic-stricken Zina.

The silhouette of Zina's scraggy arms seemed to be summoning every gypsy in the camp and pointing to the menacing spot on the horizon near the inn. . . . Odette

could not comprehend what they were saying in their
hateful language. As to Callista and Andréa, they exchanged glances as they listened to the old woman.

No further interest had been taken in Olajaï, who,
hidden behind a tree, lost no word of what was said. But
Callista caught sight of his crafty face, which a sudden
gleam from the fire caused to stand out in the obscurity.
He made a movement to slink away, but she rushed at
him, and handed him over to Andréa, who forced him
into the center of the camp; and then, throwing a few
words to the crowd, she disappeared in the darkness towards the inn.

CHAPTER XXVII

THE MAN WHO KNOCKED AT THE INN DOOR

ROULETABILLE felt much better after the visit of the old gypsy bone-setter. He no longer had any pain in the shoulder; the fever had subsided; and even his foot ceased to trouble him. He slipped out of bed, and, standing at the window, his gaze strayed over' the tops of the fir trees and encountered the figures in the clearing flinging themselves round that fires in the forest.

Zina! It was Zina who had been brought to him, had tended him to begin with in her own way, by deafening him with her weird incantaions. She told him that she was called Zina. He did not move a muscle, and while she massaged his shoulder with the art of long experience, he cleverly put a number of questions to her in order to make certain that she was indeed Zina. And great was her agitation when he mentioned the de Lavardens tragedy, which he pretended to have read about in that morning's paper. . . . She did not wait to hear more! She bound up his shoulder in a trice, and scurried away into the darkness like an old owl.

It may be that he ought to have been more careful. But he wanted to make doubly certain that it was Zina, for if it were Zina it meant that Odette was not far away.

He would not lose sight of her now; of the poor young prisoner and the band which had carried her off by force; and her release would be a matter of twenty-four hours, the time which it would take him to inform the authorities at New Wachter. Nothing could be more simple. With

193

this object he asked to see the proprietor, one Otto, a German-Swiss, a heavy-witted man who always seemed half asleep; so much so that to rouse him fully nothing was so effective as to prove to him that in those difficult times, when paper money had assumed a world-wide significance, one did not travel without a purse well lined with monetary devices which did not come from the printing presses of Vienna or Moscow.

Nevertheless, the man gave his visitor to understand that it would be impossible to disturb these gentlemen until the morning. A grievous piece of ill-luck! Rouletabille none the less took his precautions so that these "gentry" should be told as soon as possible. Meantime, he would have to rely upon himself, as usual.

.   .   .   .

Rouletabille put on his clothes and loaded his revolver. He took care not to press on his left foot which once more began to hurt him, and he discovered with dismay that, short of hobbling on one foot, he would be unable to get to the camp which he intended to keep under close observation.

Just then the young goat-herd who had helped him to reach the inn passed his window. He called him and made him understand that he would pay him well if he would keep a sharp lookout on the gypsies' movements, and come and tell him when they started their preparations to break camp.

He crept to the window and looked out. . . . The man who was shaking the door was wrapped in a great cloak and his face was hidden in a wide-brimmed felt hat. Rouletabille gave a start. A sure instinct warned him that the stranger's nocturnal arrival was not unconnected with the tragedy which had brought him, too, to New Wachter. He collected all his strength and went downstairs. As a matter of fact, after his foot was bandaged he could use it, and the pain was not more than he could bear. On the other hand the dressing with which the old witch had rubbed it was beginning to take effect. His shoulder was much easier and he could now move his arm. . . .

He descended the stairs and entered the public room as the proprietor, carrying a lamp, opened the door after parleying with the man outside. The newcomer's face could be clearly seen: it was Hubert de Lauriac.

Hardly believing his eyes, Rouletabille drew back into the shadow. Otto put the lamp on the table and closed the door. De Lauriac seemed worn out with fatigue. He sank into a chair, threw down his hat and exclaimed:

"Give me something to eat."

Otto made answer in a mixture of bad French and bad German that it was very late and he could only provide him with a few scraps.

De Lauriac fell upon them, and when his hunger was appeased, asked:

"Have these gypsies been in the place long?"

"A couple of days," returned Otto, "and I wish the devil would take the whole lot of them. They prevent me from sleeping at night."

"How do you mean?"

"I'm afraid they'll rob me. These people stick at nothing. Still, I must admit that up to now they've paid for everything they've taken."

"What are they doing here?"

"You should ask them yourself. They don't blab much."

"I'll tell you what they're doing here," said a voice from the darkness.

De Lauriac turned his head in the direction of the voice, and Rouletabille stepped forward with outstretched hand:

"How are you, Monsieur de Lauriac?"

De Lauriac shot up as if he had received an electric shock.

"You! . . . You here!"

"Well, you are here. Why shouldn't I be here?" returned Rouletabille, drawing up a stool to the table and ordering a bottle of hock: "Rudesheimer, and the best you've got!"

While Otto went down to the cellar, Rouletabille said to de Lauriac:

"You made a mistake, Monsieur de Lauriac, not to take the hand that I offered you just now, because we are friends, or at least we shall become friends. Would you like me to tell you what these gypsies are here for?"

"That's not necessary," returned de Lauriac in a hoarse voice, a look of hostility in his eyes. "I know why."

"And, doubtless, that's why we are having the pleasure of meeting here," said Rouletabille with his most ingratiating smile.

"The pleasure is entirely on your side," retorted de Lauriac with a bear-like grunt.

Rouletabille burst out laughing.

"You are so bad tempered that you won't let me touch you with my hands or even with a pair of tongs, here or anywhere else. What a grudge you must have against me!"

"It was you who had me 'touched' with the handcuffs," he rapped out. "I can't forget that."

"That's obvious. But as to the handcuffs, remember that it was I who had them taken off, Monsieur de Lauriac. Come, play the game. We are both of us here with the same object. We are pursuing the same goal. You for your own sake and I for my friend Jean's sake. Let us join forces—that's the best thing we can do. First of all, it is to our interest to deliver Odette from the hands of those brigands. That outweighs every other consideration. Afterwards we can talk. What do you say?"

Just then the proprietor came in with the hock, and his dog could be heard barking outside.

"I believe it's those cursed gypsies prowling round my rabbit hutches," he said.

He walked over to the window, opened it, and looked out upon the impenetrable darkness, which had once more relapsed into silence.

"Leave the window open, the room is stifling," said Rouletabille.

The man lit a lantern:

"Excuse me, I'm going to have a look round."

"Well?" questioned Rouletabille, when Otto had left the room.

"Well," returned de Lauriac, "I've thought it over. It's a bargain."

"As you say!"

He had reflected, chiefly, that he could not do other than accept Rouletabille's proposition. Obviously both were embarrassed by meeting in that place when each hoped to arrive alone; but, after all, their temporary alliance would have the immediate advantage of enabling them to keep an eye on each other.

"Then we are friends," said Rouletabille, offering his hand once more.

"Friends," echoed de Lauriac, shaking hands.

"I say, how is it that you are here?" asked Rouletabille, greatly perplexed, for according to his calculations and inferences de Lauriac should have been on the direct road to Sever Turn.

"Well, and what about you?" retorted de Lauriac, who, despite his protestations of friendship, had no intention of giving himself away.

"Look here," went on Rouletabille, "don't let us try it on with each other. I should get the better of you. You are clever enough to know that as well as I do. We must both feel certain that we shan't do any good if we cross each other. The gypsies would reap the advantage."

"Pooh!" returned the other with an air of indifference. "What can they do now that we have come up with them? They will have to hand Mademoiselle de Lavardens over to us. I shall inform the authorities first thing in the morning."

"That's unnecessary. I have already sent to New Wachter," broke in Rouletabille. "All the same, don't make any mistake. The matter will not be so easy, perhaps, as you think, and I will at once tell you why. First, it's the business of these gypsies to trick the police, and then we shall be up against two persons whom you have evidently left out of consideration."

"Who are they?"

"Andréa and Callista."

"Andréa and Callista!" cried de Lauriac. "Why, I thought they were in prison."

"I helped them to escape."

"You? But why did you do such a thing? Have you forgotten that they swore to see Odette dead before they gave her up?"

"I did so because I wanted them to show me the road by which they were taking her."

"Then you followed them?"

"Yes, of course."

"Now, that's too bad."

"Hang it all, it's not at all bad," said Rouletabille modestly. "And now that I've told you everything it's your turn to speak out. You started to go to Sever Turn, didn't you?"

"How do you know?"

"By a process of deduction. Oh, don't be so inordinately surprised, and try to realize that what I don't know now I shall find out to-morrow. So it's not worth wasting time, is it?"

De Lauriac gazed at Rouletabille for a moment in silence. Such a display of self-assurance somwhat disconcerted him. Was he speaking seriously? At last he made up his mind.

"Well, I have no objection to tell you that I did in fact set out for Sever Turn with the object of seeing the Patriarch, whom I know. You will be aware that the Patriarch of Transylvania is the chief religious dignitary, and even, if one may say so, the political head of the entire Romany race. I intended to beseech him to ntervene on behalf of Mademoiselle de Lavardens, pointing out the danger of this reckless act of abduction, and the unfortunate effect which it might have, for the Romanys, throughout Europe."

"Excellent! I follow you," interrupted Rouletabille with the gravity of a priest. "I know now the reasons why you set out for Sever Turn. And then? . . ."

"And then when I was within a day's march of Sever Turn I met a gypsy on horseback who was coming away from it. He seemed very fatigued after the distance covered by him. We stopped at an inn and fell into conversation. I must tell you that to get to Sever Turn, and pass through territory which I knew to be deliberately hostile to aliens, I put on an old suit of gypsy clothes."

"A wise precaution," said Rouletabille. "I can see that you know how to travel."

"In spite of his fatigue, this man was in a state of religious frenzy and he invited me to rejoice with him. He told me that the time was at hand when Sever Turn would have its young queen. I let him talk, listening but absent-mindedly to his fanatical tirade. Then he mentioned two names which startled me: Andréa and Callista. He asked me if I knew Andréa. I answered that I certainly knew him, for he was a good friend of mine, and some years previously we had made the pilgrimage to Les Saintes Maries together. In short, I gained his confidence so completely that he told me that Andréa and Callista had been entrusted with the *queyra* whom they were bringing to Sever Turn.

"Thus the Patriarch had christened her whom they were seeking and whose coming they awaited—the messenger of God. . . . The *queyra* means in gypsy parlance the Messiah. In short, the high priest had appointed this gypsy to convey certain secret instructions to Andréa and Callista at New Wachter, where they would certainly be in camp for the time being."

"So they did not know at the Patriarchate of the arrest of these two people?"

"That is my impression. But what I cannot describe, I assure you, is the state of mind into which I was thrown by this man's confidences. Remembering Andréa and Callista's admissions, I could not doubt for a moment that the girl whom these brigands of gypsies were carrying off to Sever Turn was Mademoiselle de Lavardens. But then, how explain this story about a young queen. De Lavardens' daughter the queen of the gypsies! I was quite at a loss, and even now I can't make it out."

"Nor I," said Rouletabille ingenuously. "The whole thing is extraordinary."

"By the way, you were often at the Viei-Castou-Nou and must have seen Mademoiselle de Lavardens in evening dress, have you ever noticed any birth-mark on her shoulder?"

"I've never noticed any such mark," declared Rouletabille. "But why do you ask?"

"Nothing—or rather for this reason. I call to mind that the gypsy—I left him to continue his journey alone, for I was bent on arriving here by another route before he did—I call to mind that he mentioned that Les Saintes Maries gypsies had discovered their young queen thanks to this birth-mark on the left shoulder. And that is why

I asked you if you were certain that Mademoiselle de Lavardens bore no such mark."

"None at all, I assure you. Her shoulder is as white as snow; at least as far as a young girl's low-necked dress enables me to say positively. But between ourselves, I imagine that a birth-mark on the shoulder would not suffice to transform the heiress of the de Lavardens' into a gypsy."

"I can only repeat what that man in his excitement told me."

"You were quite right, monsieur, because this extra-ordinary story at least shows the necessity of rescuing Mademoiselle de Lavardens from this band of fanatics without loss of time."

"Of course," returned de Lauriac, becoming suddenly wrapped in thought.

.   .   .   .

Just then the barking of the dogs broke out again. Rouletabille crept to the window and gazed into the darkness of the night, already beginning to lift.

CHAPTER XXVIII

IN WHICH OLAJAÏ IS SORRY FOR TALKING TOO MUCH

ZINA took advantage of Callista's temporary absence from the gypsy camp to proceed to the caravan, where she found Odette in tears, trembling with fear and dismayed by the unexpected appearance of the two gypsies.

Before her eyes there flashed the vision of the scene in the cave, and the upraised knife with which Callista so cruelly threatened her.

Zina took her in her arms, covered her hands with kisses, seeking to comfort her, vowing that her life was sacred and no one would dare to touch a hair of her head. "Don't cry. Don't cry. A great surprise awaits you in a new land. . . . Every door will be open to you, and every head bow down before you. . . ."

They both spoke at the same time. Odette answered Zina's caresses by flying out at her and repeating for the thousandth time that she wanted to go back to Lavardens. But the old witch continued her sooth-saying in a state of exaltation which rendered her insensible to the child's outbursts.

Suddenly she rose from her tripod, for Callista's voice could be heard, and the tumult broke out anew round the caravan. Entreating Odette not to budge, Zina went outside.

Odette at once ran to her observatory, and ventured to open slightly the small window, hoping that she might catch a word or two which would disclose the meaning of this unwonted excitement among the gypsies.

In her heart of hearts she thought that some attempt

202

was being made to rescue her. That was her one insistent thought, the thought that caused her to wake with
a start in the night and give ear to the mysterious sounds
of the countryside. Oh, when would she awake from this
horrible nightmare! . . . And then suddenly a word, a
name, uttered by gypsy lips, fell on her ears:
"Rouletabille!"

In her astonishment a cry broke in her throat.

Rouletabille! Rouletabille! She was no longer trembling with fear but with hope. Rouletabille! . . . The
name was repeated quite near her by Callista, who was
holding a stormy consultation with Andréa and Sumbalo.
The latter had given orders for the camp to be struck,
and every caravan warned of the danger with which their
precious child was menaced.

Callista, put on her guard by Zina, had been lurking
near the inn, and recognized standing at the window
of the low room their most formidable enemy. . . .
Therefore, they would never be able to shake him
off! . . .

There was but one method of saving themselves from
the danger, and that was to show that they could be
more cunning than Rouletabille himself. And to do
this, there was but one course to take; old Sumbalo and
the entire tribe must resolutely remain where they were
while she, Callista, and Andréa made off with Odette
concealed in another caravan, which would have the start
of him and travel only by night. They must not waste
a moment. The camp was even now, perhaps, under
observation.

Sumbalo was at last persuaded and gave fresh orders,
which, however, the gypsies accepted much against their
will and after many protests. Some of them indulged in
threats and cries of rage. At length a fresh incident
caused a general outburst of fury.

Olajaï, availing himself of Andréa's inattention, had

slipped away. Andréa noticed it just as Rouletabille's former servant was stealthily leaving the circle illuminated by the fires.

He swore an oath and shouted: "Olajaï!" and Callista grasped the situation. Both rushed after him, followed by others. They would have to recapture their hypocritical brother at all costs.

Olajaï had a foreboding that his "goose was cooked" now that Rouletabille's presence in the vicinity had become known, and his chief concern was to escape the evil fate in store for him. It may have been, indeed, that he was on his way to warn Rouletabille.

"Rush after him! Take the path to the inn," shouted Callista.

She conducted the chase with amazing strategy, surrounding the wretched man, compelling him to flee from thicket to thicket like a hunted animal, and finally to rush headlong into the arms of Andréa, who lay in wait for him behind a tree.

Andréa gripped and crushed him in his powerful arms as though to choke the life out of him, dragged him back to the camp a human wreck, scarcely able to breathe, more dead than alive; and, flinging him among the gypsies, exclaimed:

"I make you a present of him. Do with him as you please. He is a traitor. Had he not betrayed us, we should not be in our present plight. He is the cause of our troubles. If they rob us of our queen one day, it will be his doing."

A kind of roar burst forth round Olajaï, who raised himself, and, attempting to stand on his feet, drew himself up with a look of unspeakable terror. A stab in the back with a dagger felled him to the ground.

Odette, with ever-increasing excitement, watched the occurrence from her caravan and uttered a shriek of horror. At that moment the door of her prison opened

and Andréa flung himself on her, threw a rug round
her, and carried her off as though she were a feather.
Zina ran after him in silence, wildly waving her arms.
Callista brought up the rear.

Some minutes later a scene was enacted in that part
of the forest round a fire, the embers of which had been
revived by the race whose immemorial fanaticism in
matters of vengeance knew no bounds—a scene was
enacted which would need the brush of a Goya to portray
in all its peculiar and potent vividness and horror.

Fantastic creatures, fiends, specters or monsters
swarmed round the fire which was scorching human
flesh. An abominable odor, which seemed to intoxicate
these beings escaped from another world, spread from
the forest.

The youthful Ari, whose beautiful bright eyes reflected
her fifteen summers, lay stretched on the grass, holding
her chin in her amber-colored hands and smiling at
Olajaï's torment. He must have bitterly regretted that
the dagger had not inflicted a death-blow as the fire burnt
his feet. Smiling at him with her three loose teeth, Oliva
had thrust a scrap of her shawl in his mouth to suppress
his ineffectual outcries.

Sumbalo, seated on a step of his caravan, presided over
the execution in silence, with a dignity which might have
been envied by the Grand Inquisitor. . . . A dozen
youngsters danced round this little private diversion with
the hop and skip peculiar to the imps of the road.

Suco, the blacksmith, held the prisoner's ankles in such
a grip that the latter seemed as if he were a willing
victim. Suco's hands were of iron and feared no
fire. . . .

And Olajaï's feet, which had become soft in the service of the aliens, supplied the necessary fuel.

Part II

CHAPTER XXIX

IN WHICH OLAJAÏ IS STILL SORRY FOR TALKING TOO MUCH AND TAKES HIS REVENGE BY TALKING MORE

THE young goat-herd hanging to the branch of a tree like a squirrel had watched Olajaï's sufferings.

It was half-past three in the morning. The inn door stood ajar, and he saw Rouletabille in the yard arguing with Otto about the hire, for the day, of a couple of old crocks which had been his beasts of burden for fifteen years.

He called de Lauriac, who proceeded to dress. When he appeared and saw the animal intended for his use he pulled a wry face.

"We haven't any choice," Rouletabille shouted. "Let's be off. The gypsies have already cleared out."

The young goat-herd trotted in front of them. When he came to the border of the wood, the youngster pointed to the road which they would have to take to reach the gypsy encampment by the shortest way, and claiming his reward, scampered off like a hare.

A few minutes later the two horsemen were arrested by the sound of moans and groans.

Rouletabille went a few steps into a thicket, pushed aside the branches and shouted for de Lauriac. . . . Between them they carried out a poor fellow who was bleeding from several wounds and unable to stand.

Olajaï opened his eyes. He recognized his master.

206

Rouletabille put his flask between his teeth while Lauriac lifted his head. . . . There was a running brook near by, and he bade de Lauriac soak a handkerchief in it; and holding the gypsy in his turn said:

"They struck at you because of me, didn't they?" Olajaï made an affirmative motion of his head.

"Take care!" Olajaï breathed. "They will serve you the same one day. Go back . . . go back to Paris!"

"And Mademoiselle de Lavardens?" asked the journalist anxiously.

"She is the young queen," he said, shaking his head. "They will never give her up."

De Lauriac was on his knees beside the wounded man preparing to bathe his wounds. He heard Olajaï's last words and gave a start. Rouletabille observed his agitation.

"Look here, Olajaï," he said, "don't give away to despair. We may still, perhaps, save your life. We will send assistance to you at once, but my friend and I must overtake the caravans. . . . They went off by this road, didn't they?"

By a supreme effort Olajaï lifted himself. The fire of revenge flashed in his eyes.

"They've taken her in another direction."

"Who are *they?* . . . Andréa? . . . Callista?"

"Yes, and Zina. . . . But I can tell you . . . I can tell you where they must all meet again."

He closed his eyes for a moment as if he were about to draw his last breath.

"Olajaï! . . . Olajaï! . . . Where are they to meet?" whispered Rouletabille.

He uttered a name in a breath which was like a death rattle.

"Temesvar Pesth."

"Let's go," cried Rouletabille. "Temesvar is too near

Sever Turn, and if Odette once gets inside Sever Turn she will never leave it."

To his amazement de Lauriac answered:

"You go, and I'll follow later. I can't leave this poor fellow here."

"Good-bye, Olajaï," said Rouletabille, casting a look of suspicion and menace at de Lauriac and disappearing under the trees.

He felt that Olajaï was stricken to death, and after all he had not come thus far in order to save him though he had been a faithful servant. First and foremost he must not lose track of Odette. . . . The hapless Olajaï was the first to be sacrificed . . . nor would he be the only victim. Was he not himself marked down? It was a formidable and cruel enterprise, and he must needs have an iron heart.

Left behind with Olajaï and certain of remaining undisturbed, de Lauriac continued eagerly to question him. Rouletabille's flask contained water, but de Lauriac's contained fire—brandy—which considerably revived the dying man. His thoughts were now concentrated upon his master: "He was very good to me. Some years ago he saved my life. I have laid down mine for him. But let him beware! I warned him at Camargue. And I warned the Octopus also when she came."

"Who is the Octopus?" questioned de Lauriac.

"Don't you know? My master and Callista are friends of hers. She came to Les Saintes Maries. . . . She wanted to see Callista. . . . I took her everywhere where Callista was to be seen. The Octopus promised in return to take Rouletabille away from Odette . . . far from Odette. . . . If I had only known when she came to the flat in Paris!"

"Who came to the flat?"

"Odette. They are all crazy about her. It will bring them bad luck."

"Did Odette come to Paris?"

"Yes."

"To Rouletabille's flat?"

"Yes."

"Was that long ago?"

"No. . . . You are his friend. Just see! . . . He must forget her. She is the queen foretold in the sacred writings."

"But she has no birth-mark on her shoulder," said de Lauriac, eying him greedily.

"Yes, she has," Olajaï returned. "She has the birth-mark on her shoulder . . . the sign of the crown."

"But Mademoiselle de Lavardens is not a gypsy," objected de Lauriac with a catch in his breath.

"Yes, she is pure Tsigane by birth. I knew her *raya,* her mother, her real mother. Monsieur de Lavardens used to live in Sever Turn. . . . He married there according to our rites. . . . The *raya* died in giving birth to a child, and Zina was the child's foster mother. Zina will tell you everything. The father fled with the child as it was written. That child—was Odette."

De Lauriac leapt to his feet and started at a run to the inn, leaving the unhappy man in his death agony. . . . Fortunately a cart happened to be passing at the time.

CHAPTER XXX

"HELP, LITTLE ZO!"

THE gypsies were by no means easy in their minds after Callista and Andréa had taken Odette away. Not that they lacked confidence in the two gypsies, and in particular Zina, who went with them, but they feared lest some wretched accident should befall their young queen which would cut her off from them for ever.

Rouletabille did not pursue them. Enlightened by the few words which he was able to extract from Olajaï, he followed the tracks of a single caravan which made a detour in order to keep as far away as possible from the main road. For nearly two hours he guided his horse through paths of unwonted difficulty, wondering how a caravan could cover such ruts without being overturned, when suddenly he caught sight of the caravan in the middle of a dense wood some hundred yards ahead. It had pulled up.

Andréa and Callista must have felt confident of safety at least for a few hours, and were resting their jaded horses.

Rouletabille slipped from the saddle, tied his horse to a tree, and revolver in hand stole beneath the branches. His foot still pained him, his shoulder was still inflamed, but he none the less displayed the swift and sinuous cunning of the serpent. The moment for action was at hand, and he was confident that victory would be his.

Rouletabille had now attained the edge of the narrow open space in which this cabin on wheels had come to a stand. Before his eyes stood the two-winged door, the upper half of which was glass, and hung with squalid curtains—the door which was reached by steps or rather the few rungs of a ladder.

That was Odette's prison! It was the palace of the queen of the gypsies. . . .

The horses had been unharnessed and must be resting not far away, close to some stream. Rouletabille was on all fours. He rose to his feet, revolver in hand, his heart beating wildly. He crept up to the steps, and suddenly hurled himself against the door breaking it in with a tremendous blow from his knees.

"Hands up!"

Nobody there! The cabin was empty. . . . The caravan was deserted, and the words "Help, little Zo," written with a knife on the side, brought the tears to his eyes.

"Little Zo!" She knew, therefore, that he was there, he thought. Or else without being certain that he was there, she was hoping that he was shadowing her and waiting for a favorable moment to release her. When all was said and done, she had not ceased to put her trust in him, and it was to him that she was calling.

He left the hateful prison. . . .

Rouletabille picked up the trail of the thieves—a trail of twists and turns, which he followed and lost and picked up again, and which harassed his mind for many hours. . . .

And suddenly a man in the fullness of his strength and arrogance appeared.

Rouletabille recognized Andréa. He leapt to his feet, brandishing his revolver. The other gave a scornful laugh.

"What are you doing here?" he said in a ringing voice. "What do you want with us? Why are you following us?"

"Because you are child stealers."

"The child stealers are those who robbed us of our queen. You will never see her again. She is in a safe place now, and I lured you here because I have a last word to say to you, a last piece of advice to give to you if you value your life. . . . Go back westwards."

"You tried to kill me once, but I'm still alive," returned Rouletabille, in no way impressed by the gypsy's threatrical language.

Andréa made no reply, but shrugging his shoulders turned on his heels, and dived into the forest.

"As a matter of fact, he is right," muttered Rouletabille, who had remained motionless. "I have followed these people long enough. Now I shall go ahead of them."

CHAPTER XXXI

IN WHICH THE BOOK OF ANCESTORS APPEARS ONCE MORE

DE LAURIAC had mounted his horse and ridden direct to the inn. He darted up to his room, opened his knapsack and drew out a venerable book of some size. He sat down and turned over the leaves.

At length he found the place for which he was seeking —the page containing the prediction whose wording he could almost remember. He turned over the page and found that the next page was missing. He cursed himself for maltreating the book. Not only had he stolen the precious stones which made it one of the most valuable memorials of religious book-making which lie hidden in sacred places, but he had also removed pages containing priceless examples of the illuminators' and miniaturists' art for which enraptured book-collectors would pay untold gold.

Suddenly he made up his mind what to do, replaced the book in his knapsack, descended the stairs, and without even listening to what the innkeeper was saying to him, mounted his horse and rode at a gallop to New Wachter. He entered the post office and dispatched a telegram:

"Stevens, Art Dealer, Rue La Boétie, Paris.
"Wire me if you still possess the illuminated page of Romany printing, decorated with miniatures, you bought from me."

He added his name and address.

He passed the remainder of the day waiting for a reply. At last, in the late afternoon, a telegram was brought to him which he eagerly read. . . .

A traveler had just come in. His back was turned, and he was bending over his bag, taking out some linen. De Lauriac came down and banged the table. The traveler turned round. It was Jean de Santierne.

The recognition was mutual. Each confronted the other with a glare of hostility. Jean was the first to speak.

"How unexpectedly people meet," he said contemptuously.

"Yes, people always meet again," returned de Lauriac in a harsh voice.

Just then the door opened and Rouletabille came in.

"Ah, Jean, there you are at last."

"It seems to me that I haven't wasted much time," said Jean, shaking hands. "How goes the injury?"

"Quite well! . . . I treat an injury with contempt. That's the way to cure it." Then turning to de Lauriac. "I hope that you are pleased to see Monsieur de Santierne. It was I who got him to come here. Yesterday there were only two of us. To-day there are three. The gypsies had better look out for themselves! It's our business to save Odette. Let us bury the hatchet and think only of her safety."

"Very well," agreed de Lauriac.

"What is the present position?" asked Jean. "And what about Odette?"

"We're all right. All goes well. But we must work together."

"Personally, I don't intend to leave you," said Jean.

"In that case, we shall have to take leave for a day or two of M. de Lauriac who will perhaps be kind enough to accept the job of crossing the frontier and keeping an eye on the gypsies. In any case, we shall all meet again in Temesvar."

"Might I ask whether there is any real reason why we should part company now, seeing that you appear to have done your best to bring us together?" asked de Lauriac, uneasy and suspicious.

"I've got to make a little trip to Innsbruck," returned Rouletabille, casting a side glance at de Lauriac, who gave a start.

"Innsbruck!" he echoed.

"Yes, I want to meet the correspondent of our paper who settled down in Temesvar during the war. He might tell us a few things and give us valuable advice."

"How lucky!" said de Lauriac. "I, too, have got to make a little trip to Innsbruck, and for the silliest reason imaginable—to get some money. I must cash a check there."

"If you want any money, monsieur . . ." began Jean.

But the other flatly interrupted him. He fixed him with eyes in which an undying hatred gleamed.

"Keep your money, monsieur. I have no wish to be under obligation to you."

"Come, come," said Rouletabille. "That's all right. We'll all take the train to Innsbruck in the morning. Of course perfect confidence prevails between us," he added with ironical good humor. "Otto, let's have supper."

De Lauriac did not open his lips during the meal. Rouletabille told Jean everything that had happened since he left him, explaining the later events and his pursuit of the caravan in the wood. Jean listened in a fever of impatience. He quickly finished his supper, and the two men left the table.

"We're going to take the air before we turn in," he said.

De Lauriac did not even reply.

"What a bear!" exclaimed Rouletabille.

"What I fail to understand," said Jean, when they were out of hearing, "is why we should let Odette slide and go to Innsbruck seeing that we are so near her."

"Oh, you're not going to break out again. . . . To begin with, I am not letting Odette slide because I haven't yet got hold of her; but I am certain of finding her in Temesvar. I'll tell you why I am going to Innsbruck. I went to New Wachter a couple of hours ago. I managed to find out what de Lauriac was doing in my absence, and I bribed a man at the post office to give me a copy of a telegram that our worthy friend received. Here it is:

Jean read:

"Sold Romany page to Nathan, Art Dealer, Innsbruck.—STEVENS."

"Do you understand?" asked Rouletabille.

"Indeed I don't."

"Don't you realize that de Lauriac will go to Innsbruck even if we do not?"

"What I don't understand is why we should go to Innsbruck. What has this 'Romany page' to do with us?"

"That's true," admitted Rouletabille. "And I think that the time has come for you to know what it means. Do you really love Odette, Jean?"

"How can you ask me that?"

"Well, you shall know the truth."

He told him the whole story. When Jean learnt that Odette was not Madame de Lavardens' daughter but of gypsy birth, he could only murmur "Poor child!" Rouletabille shook him by the hand. When Jean fully comprehended the significance of the tragedy which was being enacted at that moment, and the last act of which was to be played at Sever Turn he groaned and said:

"They may kill me, but they shall not have her."

He realized at once the importance of the Book of Ancestors, and the immediate necessity of discovering why de Lauriac was so keenly interested in this Romany page.

Next morning they reached the capital of the Tyrol. Rouletabille called on Nathan, whose shop was in the old town.

"I understand that you have an interesting specimen of Romany work," he said.

"Very interesting, monsieur."

Nathan raised no objection to showing it to him.

"How much do you want for it?" asked Rouletabille.

"I'm sorry. A collector bought it by telegram."

Rouletabille could not help rapping out an oath.

"Might I at least ask what the text means?"

"I can't read Romany," replied the dealer.

Rouletabille went back to the hotel where Jean was waiting for him.

"We've been done. Where's de Lauriac?"

"He left me a few minutes ago," returned Jean, and added, when he heard the result of the visit to the dealer. "There's no doubt our luck is out."

A few minutes later de Lauriac rejoined them. He wore a look of self-satisfaction which spoke volumes. As he came towards them the janitor handed him a letter. He stopped to read it. It was worded thus:

"Be on your guard against Rouletabille, who is playing a game which he keeps to himself. If you wish to learn more, be at the entrance to Rose Park to-night at ten o'clock."

The missive was unsigned and de Lauriac put it in his pocket.

"I am going to keep an eye on you, old fellow," muttered Rouletabille.

De Lauriac was at the entrance to Rose Park at the hour fixed for the secret meeting. A slowly driven closed carriage stopped before him. The blind was lowered, and a young woman wearing a light veil, looked out. She beckoned him. She opened the door and he stepped in, and the carriage drove off again.

CHAPTER XXXII

THE MEETING

YOU wonder who I am. Everyone will tell you that I am an old friend of Rouletabille's. He has behaved infamously to me. My name is Madame de Meyrens."

De Lauriac did not speak. The name had produced an impression on him.

The carriage was now proceeding at a smart pace.

"Where are we going?" inquired de Lauriac.

"Where we shall be able to talk undisturbed."

When they entered one of the busiest streets in the town, Madame de Meyrens pulled up the blinds. The carriage stopped at a large building, open during the night, which was a restaurant and dancing and music hall combined, and was crowded. De Lauriac was amazed.

"It is only in a crowd that one passes unnoticed," she said. "And besides, there are private rooms upstairs where we shan't be disturbed and can have supper, for I am ravenous, old thing. I have eaten nothing since my arrival in Innsbruck."

"When did you get here?"

"At the same hour and by the same train as you."

She pushed him before her through a dense crowd which was coming out of the theater, for it was the interval. Then they went upstairs, and a head-waiter showed them into a spacious room.

Madame de Meyrens made herself at home, shed her cloak, took off her hat, stood before the mirror, smoothed her hair, and put a little rouge on her face. And

219

she did full justice to the first dish that was served.

"Excuse me, dear."

She ordered champagne, and meanwhile drained a liquor brandy in the Russian manner. De Lauriac lit a cigarette, but did not eat anything.

"You are no gossip," she said, wafting the smoke of her Turkish cigarette in his face.

"I came to listen to you," he returned. "And then I am looking at you and wondering how it happened that you traveled this morning by our train."

"Because I am after Rouletabille. I learnt that Monsieur de Santierne was to join him. I followed de Santierne to New Wachter, and I followed you all from New Wachter to this place.

"I spent my time keeping you under observation—following up your trail. I have never lost sight of you. I have in particular kept an eye on Rouletabille. You are aware that he no sooner got out of the train than he hurried to the art dealer on whom you yourself called afterwards. It must have been something very important to take him there before you. I have no idea what his object was, but I know my Rouletabille."

She began to laugh maliciously, showing her sharp little teeth.

"I know what his object was," returned de Lauriac. "Fortunately I was able to secure the thing by telegram."

"Yes, you dished Rouletabille without knowing it. He tricks everybody. I've been done by him."

"In what way?"

"In serious matters," she returned in a strained voice. "But I'll make him suffer for it. And to be even with him I want . . ."

"What do you want?"

"If I told you, you would ask me to have some mercy on him."

"You are very cruel, you know."

"That's no news to anyone."

She drained a full glass of champagne.

"Look here, old thing, that youngster has made a fool of me. He has behaved like a knave. He never loved me. And that stripling has turned me into ridicule. It's awful. And I thought that he loved me. He loves only Odette."

"Ah, I always suspected as much," cried de Lauriac.

"That shows that you are no fool. It's pathetic, you know, to see the three of you joining together to rescue a young girl whom each of you eagerly desires for himself. And when I think of Jean's blind confidence in that little wretch! He believes that Rouletabille is working on his behalf, but Rouletabille, with all his frank and open manner as a good fellow, has never worked for anyone but himself. He has sworn to marry Odette. . . . And I have sworn to be revenged on him. Odette may not become Jean's wife, but she shall not marry Rouletabille. You want her, Monsieur de Lauriac. I give her to you."

"Madame, I accept," returned de Lauriac, offering her his hand. "It is not so much Odette that I accept from you as the alliance which you offer me in these very difficult circumstances. It may be of great use to me, for in truth Rouletabille is a formidable adversary. But have no fear about Mademoiselle de Lavardens. She cannot escape me now."

"I should be delighted to think so," said Madame de Meyrens, by no means convinced. "But are you not deceiving yourself?"

"Not at all."

"What makes you so confident?"

"Ah, that's just it. You are asking me to reveal my secrets, and I haven't yet made a single request to you."

"You are not of a naturally trusting disposition, Monsieur de Lauriac. Well, what is it that you want to know?"

"This: Have you any evidence of Rouletabille's trickery with his friend Jean—and with Mademoiselle de Lavardens?"

"I have something better still. I have proofs of the complete understanding which exists between Mademoiselle de Lavardens and Rouletabille."

"You don't say so!" exclaimed de Lauriac, rising from the table. "Convincing proofs?"

"Proofs beyond dispute."

CHAPTER XXXIII

TWIN ACCOMPLICES

SHE drew from her corsage a kind of satchel in the shape of a pocket-book, which appeared to contain a number of valuable papers, and went over and sat down beside de Lauriac.

"You see these two letters?" she said, taking them from the satchel. "They are short, but when you have read them you will cast aside your doubts."

"Who wrote them?"

"Odette."

"May I ask how you managed to get hold of them?"

"I stole them from Rouletabille one day when his flat was broken into."

She handed de Lauriac the letters.

His hand shook as he took them. They were written on two thin sheets of notepaper which bore Odette's monogram and the engraved heading "Viei-Castou-Nou."

He had never received letters from her like these. And this is what he read. It was the first in date:

"MY DEAR LITTLE Zo,—I made up a story for father. I leave here in the morning and shall be in Paris the day after to-morrow; I can't hold out any longer. I must see my little Zo. No one will know anything about it. Be careful not to come to the station to meet me. . . . Secrecy and prudence! . . . Let there be no one at the flat, and keep it from Jean. You are my last hope.
                              Your little ODETTE."

223

"Ah, this Jean, I hate him."

"Indeed," said Hubert, as he wiped his streaming forehead. "This, of course, seems to me conclusive, and agrees entirely with the disclosures which were made to me recently by a dying man."

"A dying man?" questioned Madame de Meyrens.

"Yes, Rouletabille's man-servant."

"Olajaï. Be careful of Olajaï. He would go through fire for Rouletabille."

"He has already gone through fire for him, madame," returned de Lauriac with a grim smile.

"Read the other letter."

The second letter was equally brief, but its significance was not less than that of the first:

"My DEAR LITTLE Zo,—I arrived home safely. Father's suspicions had been aroused. In the end he made our poor 'mama' speak out. There was a violent scene and he dismissed her. I cried a great deal, but I don't regret anything. Only my little Zo can comfort me. We shall meet again soon, I hope. Happy times will come back to us."

"This is too much of a good thing," snorted de Lauriac, loosening his collar. His face was scarlet. He swallowed a large glass of water. He loathed Rouletabille now more than he did Jean.

"Well," he went on, handing back the letters to Madame de Meyrens, who asked for them and carefully put them away in their receptacle. "Well, I can tell you one thing neither Jean nor Rouletabille shall have her, and I will now give you proof of that."

"Ah, confidence is restored."

"We have joined forces. We are guided by a common interest. A woman like you and a man like me must inevitably win, particularly as the game is already half won," declared de Lauriac, taking from the inside pocket of his jacket a piece of carefully folded parchment. "You are aware, perhaps," he went on, "that the reason why the gypsies set so much store on Mademoiselle de Lavardens is because they wish to make her their queen."

"Yes, that story is beginning to be spread everywhere. But why Mademoiselle de Lavardens?"

"Because she was born under conditions foretold in the Book of Ancestors—that is, her mother was a Princess of Sever Turn, and her father a noble alien—none other than Monsieur de Lavardens."

"Very interesting," said Madame de Meyrens, who was listening avidly to every word. "But I don't see where you come in."

"You'll soon see. One of the pages of the Book of Ancestors is missing, a page which contains the sequel to this prediction, and this page was in the hands of the art dealer at whose shop you saw me call not long ago."

"And at whose shop I saw Rouletabille call earlier."

"Exactly. That page is now in my possession."

"It's a splendid piece of work. What a pity you folded it," exclaimed Madame de Meyrens, who had the artistic sense and could appreciate beautiful things.

"Unfortunately I can't carry it about in a frame. It would be too cumbersome and not sufficiently secret. But such as it is will serve its purpose. Besides, I intend to sew it into the lining of my coat to-night for greater security."

"But what does the page contain? Do you understand Romany?"

"Yes, I will translate the contents to you."

He translated into Madame de Meyrens' ear the Romany page torn from the Book of Ancestors.

De Lauriac could be easy in his mind, for Madame de Meyrens alone heard him, and he had reason to be satisfied with the effect which he produced on her.

"Now I understand," she cried, beaming. "I follow you. . . . I congratulate you, old thing."

De Lauriac added a few words in her ear. She nodded her head in token of agreement, and he returned the page to its place. A quarter of an hour later they left the festive scene where both had done such excellent business.

The carriage which had brought them was waiting outside the music-hall. Madame de Meyrens took leave of de Lauriac, saying aloud:

"We shall meet again—you know where."

They shook hands and the carriage drove off. De Lauriac returned to his hotel on foot, reflecting on what the evening had brought forth, and feeling that his time had not been wasted. He failed to perceive a dark form which was shadowing him.

That dark form was Jean.

Let us hark back a little in point of time; in other words, let us, with the help of Rouletabille's diary, set down the events as they occurred a few hours earlier.

Rouletabille and Jean continued to watch de Lauriac closely. They wondered with a vague misgiving, what the purport of this letter was, which had been delivered to him at an hotel where, only at the last moment, they had decided to stop.

"Perhaps the art dealer has written him a line," suggested de Santierne.

"That's what we've got to find out," returned Rouletabille. "Meantime I will question the page-boy."

The boy told him that the letter was brought by a messenger whom he did not know.

While Rouletabille remained in the hotel to keep an eye on de Lauriac, Jean called at the dealer's, and artfully questioning him, learnt for certain that the letter did not come from him. He returned to the hotel.

"De Lauriac has not left his room. He seems very restless, almost anxious. He has read the mysterious letter several times," said Rouletabille.

Just then de Lauriac came out of his room and suggested a stroll. They went together to the old town, admired the ancient buildings with their many contrasting colors—yellow, green, pink, blue—and their queer looking corbeled windows, broke forth into raptures over the famous mausoleum of Maximilian I, in the Church of the Franciscans, and then retraced their steps to the hotel.

Now and then Rouletabille entered a shop to make a purchase, for his mishap in the train had bereft him of everything, since Andréa and Callista had omitted to throw his valise out of the window after him.

They dined together on the best of fare, seemingly forgetting their anxieties. After dinner de Lauriac wrote a long letter which he took to the post. Rouletabille and Jean went with him.

"I would give a great deal," said Rouletabille to Jean, "to know the contents of that letter. He is taking too many precautions. It must be the answer to the letter which he received a little while ago."

De Lauriac declared at nine o'clock that he was done up, and being "in arrears with his sleep," was "going to catch them up." He shut himself up in his bed room, and a quarter of an hour later could be heard snoring loudly.

Jean's room was divided from de Lauriac's only by a partition. Rouletabille's room was opposite Jean's on the other side of the passage. Hence he had command of both doors. When he heard de Lauriac's snore, however, it seemed to him that he might tell Jean that the day's work was done.

Jean did not agree with him.

"He may be shamming sleep," he objected.

"Well, if he stops snoring come and tell me." And he retired to his room.

Jean took off his boots noisily, threw himself on his bed, making the mattress creak, and stealthily putting on his boots again waited events.

A few minutes later the snoring ceased and a door was opened slightly.

"Certainly Rouletabille is getting played out," thought Jean, and priding himself on having foreseen the trick, soon made sure that de Lauriac had left his room and was descending the stairs with as little noise as might be.

Jean left his room in his turn and opened Rouletabille's door. The latter was in his shirt sleeves and Jean rapped out:

"De Lauriac is scooting. I'm going after him."

Then without waiting to hear what he had to say, Jean darted after de Lauriac, who had not yet had time to leave the hotel. And so he followed him without being observed to Rose Park. And so, a quarter of an hour later, he saw the carriage drive up and de Lauriac step into it .

Jean caught a glimpse of a feminine form, and wondered if he had not wasted his time by merely witnessing a lover's assignation of no interest to him. On reflection he came to the conclusion that de Lauriac was in no mood to think, so to speak, of gadding about with any woman, and he hastened after the carriage which was proceeding at a slow pace.

An empty cab was coming towards him. He stopped it, and told the driver, to whom he promised an extra tip, not to lose sight of the cab ahead of them. Thus when he drew near the music-hall he saw de Lauriac enter it with the mysterious stranger.

She had lowered her veil, but at the first view of her figure Jean recognized her.

"The Octopus!" he said to himself. "That's the Octopus!"

He pushed his way through the crowd after them. He saw them go upstairs to the private rooms, and decided to wait and "make assurance doubly sure."

He saw them again as they left the music-hall. It was the Octopus right enough. He watched them say goodbye, and again followed de Lauriac when the cab drove off at a smart pace.

"The wretches!" thought Jean, "I wonder what they have been plotting together. The Octopus here! And with de Lauriac. That explains why he wanted to come to Innsbruck—he had an appointment with the Octopus. And Rouletabille had no suspicion of it."

De Lauriac walked slowly away smoking a big cigar.

"Perhaps he is not going straight back to the hotel, and his movements might tell me something," Jean thought.

But after turning down a few dimly lit streets in which, moreover, he seemed to have gone astray, he got back to the hotel. As soon as he was again in his room Jean made one leap to Rouletabille's door.

He found him admiring himself in his new pajamas, and performing his breathing exercises in front of his wardrobe mirror.

"Ah, there you are," said Rouletabille, when his eyes fell on Jean. "But you look quite upset. What's happened?"

"Do you know who's here?"

"Indeed I don't."

"The Octopus."

"What's that!"

"The Octopus. I say that the Octopus is here."

"Why, it's out of the question, or else it's a pure accident. In reality we have no reason to get excited over it. What is it to do with us?"

"Ask de Lauriac, who had an appointment with her at

Rose Park tonight, and was with her nearly a couple of hours."

"That's more serious," said Rouletabille, who had stopped his gymnastics. "Yes, that's much more serious, because she didn't know him, and obviously it was not to discuss the weather that they arranged to meet."

Wrapped in thought he began to fill his pipe as was his wont when some particular train of thought obsessed him. He would fill it . . . fill it . . . until he saw the position clearly. Then he would light it, and have what he called a "delightful smoke." But he did not light his pipe that night.

"It means that I am no longer a favorite with the Octopus," he observed at last. "We didn't part on very good terms, you know."

"Let me tell you that this woman will ruin you as she has ruined so many others. Haven't I said so often enough?"

"Meanwhile, don't let's waste time in futile chatter," broke in Rouletabille. "We've something better to do than that tonight."

"What is that?"

"Go to bed."

"Is that all you can suggest? To think that while de Lauriac and that woman were plotting some fake or other against us, you were trying on your new pajamas!"

"Still don't take me for a bigger fool than I am.

"I ransacked de Lauriac's room, his luggage, his haversack, and hunted high and low for the Romany page without finding it, of course, because he dare not let it out of his possession. But I had a look at the Book of Ancestors again, and something can always be learnt from it though I don't understand a word of its contents."

"If the Book of Ancestors which you are for ever talking about is invaluable to de Lauriac, it must be equally invaluable to us."

"Be assured that the Rouletabille of today is just as good as he was yesterday. Why, this book has become as useless to us as it is to de Lauriac—nay more, it is a positive danger."

"Explain yourself."

"Well, of course, since you don't yet see through it. When de Lauriac left for Sever Turn with that splendid old book, he placed his hopes in the 'recompense' which was promised to the person who restored it. He felt certain, in his mind, of obtaining Odette's release through the intervention of the Patriarch, but he learnt on his way that Odette was being received with open arms as a gypsy princess and was to be crowned queen. His hopes founded on the book fell. They would grant him anything he pleased save Odette. Therefore he turned back hot foot to Odette, intending to try to rescue her by his own resources."

"With the assistance of the Octopus," exclaimed Jean.

CHAPTER XXXIV

"DON'T WORRY"

OUR three travelers arrived at Temesvar Pesth some days before the gypsies, in accordance with Rouletabille's new plan of preceding instead of following them, and they spent their time in fully taking their bearings. In those districts, where gypsy caravans invariably halted before the last stage of their tramp from or to Sever Turn, the local authorities had allotted certain places, away from the towns, where the wanderers could halt and pitch their camps.

In these circumstances it was easy for Rouletabille, Jean and de Lauriac to study the country minutely, and to consider beforehand how best to turn their knowledge to account.

The partnership still held good, but as the crucial moment drew near it seemed as if the mistrust which loomed over the little community had become accentuated. Jean found points in Rouletabille's conduct which bewildered him and roused a feeling of uneasiness. Why, for instance, was he so insistent from the first on their acting alone, without recourse to the local police? Why, in this respect, did he share the opinion of de Lauriac, who had good reasons, obvious to them both, for appearing as little as possible in a business in which he reckoned, by hook or by crook, to be the only one to benefit?

When Rouletabille left Temesvar Pesth he sent his horse at the gallop over the Puszta towards the inn where the three men had established their headquarters. It was the inn at which de Lauriac had stopped with the gypsy from Sever Turn, when he learnt of the *queyra* for the first time.

Just then Jean cast a last glance at the two horses which were tethered at the inn door. The three allies had bought three fine, wiry, vigorous animals, capable of a sustained effort and having a nice turn of speed. They preferred to buy horses rather than a motor-car in a country wherein roads were scarce and badly maintained, especially as they would probably have to take action in the Balkans, which were not far away, and in which they might have a breakdown at the first impediment.

After making sure that the horses had had their provender, Jean went into the general room, which was empty. Almost immediately a door facing a staircase was opened, and a man appeared whom Jean did not at first recognize, mistaking him for a gypsy.

As a matter of fact he was dressed like Andréa, with weapons in his belt and wide breeches held in by top boots. His sunburnt face was adorned with a pair of flowing black mustaches. It was de Lauriac, who began to laugh.

"Well, Monsieur de Santierne, what do you think of me?"

"A capital disguise, but what's the object?"

De Lauriac took a seat, lit a cigarette, crossed his legs, and said:

"I am the only one among us who can speak Romany, and the only one who can get within reach of Odette. They will take me for one of themselves. Trust me!"

Jean turned very red at de Lauriac's statement: "I am the only one who can get within reach of Odette." He threw a fierce look at the man who seemed to be setting him at defiance.

"Unfortunately, I don't trust you, Monsieur de Lauriac," he said.

"You make a mistake," returned the other, in no way disconcerted. "Of course, in trying to set Mademoiselle Odette free, I am working in my own interests, but have no fear, I have no intention of marrying her by force. Besides, there are two of you to prevent me if needs be. Act, therefore, or rather let me act, as if you did trust me, Monsieur de Santierne."

"I don't trust you and I will tell you why, since an explanation has become necessary between us."

"I am in no hurry, you know. We might just as well defer it for the time being."

"Monsieur de Lauriac, you wish to betray our confidence, but you won't succeed. I followed you the other night in Innsbruck."

De Lauriac could not refrain from giving a start. Nevertheless, he soon recovered his composure and began to smile.

"I saw you with Madame de Meyrens," Jean continued.

"Well, what about it?" exclaimed de Lauriac, turning right round and keeping his eyes fixed on Jean's face.

"Madame de Meyrens is our worst enemy."

"Oh, you don't say so. That's very strange. I thought she was only Rouletabille's enemy."

"That ought to have been enough to prevent you, in present circumstances, from keeping any appointment with her."

"Look here, Monsieur de Santierne," returned the other with increasing calmness. "I did not know the lady, and I swear on Mademoiselle de Lavardens' life, which is at least as dear to me as to you, that I was unaware of her presence in Innsbruck. She followed you when you left France, feeling sure in this way of again seeing Rouletabille, whom, from what I can gather, she loathes. To my great surprise she wrote me a letter at Innsbruck asking me to meet her."

"What then?" asked Jean, impressed by de Lauriac's tone of sincerity.

"Then I was naturally curious to know what this woman, a stranger to me, had to say."

"Your conversation must have been interesting," said Jean sarcastically.

"It was quite interesting," returned de Lauriac emphatically, with a grim smile. "Madame de Meyrens merely wished to tell me that your friend Rouletabille was not working in this affair either for you or, of course, for me, but solely for himself. He is in love with Odette."

Jean's cheeks blanched.

"It's an infamous lie," he flung out in a hoarse voice.

"That's pretty well what I told her."

"I doubt it, monsieur," said Jean, scarcely able to control the rage which made the blood dance in his veins. "I doubt it, for if my memory serves me, you used certain language during the magistrate's examination—it is odds on that this examination would have been fatal to you if the man whom you slander to-day had not proved your innocence—which might have made me suspect Rouletabille's good faith and friendship. Fortunately I have known him long enough to feel that he is incapable of such treachery."

"The peculiar circumstances in which I found myself," returned de Lauriac, whose self-possession contrasted more and more with Jean's excitement, "made me use language the meaning of which I did not fully realize. I was the victim of both of you, and the injustice to me, which was your doing, lay heavy on me, and led me to say things which certainly were not intended to be agreeable to you, but between that and making any charge against Rouletabille there is a wide gulf. Madame de Meyrens made the charge against him. You were curious to know what she told me. I have accurately reported her conversation."

"And, of course, you entered a protest . . ."

"I asked for proofs."

"And she gave them to you?"

"Exactly."

"You have either said too much or too little. I am entitled to know all. What were the proofs?"

"Are you aware that Mademoiselle de Lavardens went to Paris a few days before the tragedy at Viei-Castou-Nou?"

"Paris! . . . What nonsense! . . . I should have been the first to be informed. I knew that she went on a visit."

"Well, she went to Rouletabille's flat."

"Rouletabille's flat! If Madame de Meyrens told you that she lied. What an abominable woman!" cried Jean, sitting down. De Lauriac's story began to dull his brain and beads of perspiration trickled down his forehead.

"I should have taken good care not to believe Madame de Meyrens' word," returned de Lauriac, with a cruel smile, "but she showed me two letters from Mademoiselle de Lavardens—one telling Rouletabille of her coming and begging him to say nothing to you about it, and the other letting him know of her father's anger on her return. This last epistle expressed the hope that their happy hours together might return."

Jean knew Odette, her young girl's pride and honesty. What he now heard was so astounding, so utterly impossible, that he refused with all his might to give credence to the disgraceful story. It was past belief. Madame de Meyrens had gone too far. That Monsieur de Lauriac, who did not know Odette as he did, should allow himself to be deceived was quite possible. But he was not deceived. In choosing between Madame de Meyrens and Odette there was no room for hesitation.

"Those letters were fakes. That is my one answer.
". . . Ah, here comes Rouletabille. Don't let us speak
again of this awful story. I shall not insult my friend by
repeating it to him. And as you say that you, too, love
Mademoiselle de Lavardens, forget these scandalous assertions. You must keep silent for her sake, for the
sake of her honor, for ours, and for your own, monsieur, if you have any left."

"Monsieur!"

"Monsieur!"

They stood erect face to face, measuring each other
with a look as if about to come to blows. Then Rouletabille rode up, and quickly dismounting, flung himself
between them. In spite of de Lauriac's disguise he at
once recognized him.

"Gentlemen, what's the matter?"

"Nothing," returned Jean, making a mighty effort to
recover his self-possession.

True, he needed to keep calm with Rouletabille before his eyes—most of all with Rouletabille before his
eyes—for, notwithstanding his chivalrous and generous
attitude, de Lauriac had inflicted a wound upon his heart
which was far from being healed.

"It strikes me that I arrived just in time," growled
Rouletabille. "You must know that it is forbidden to
quarrel in the face of the enemy."

"Monsieur de Santierne took offense at my disguising
myself as a gypsy so as to enter the camp, speak to
Mademoiselle de Lavardens, and thus facilitate her escape," explained de Lauriac coldly. "I speak Romany
fluently. I am confident of success."

"Yes, but I have no confidence in you," retorted de
Santierne.

"That's the second time you have told me so."

"Hold your tongue, Jean, if you don't mind," cried
Rouletabille. "Odette's life is at stake. You have ac-

knowledged me as your leader. I am the one to give orders and make decisions—by your own choice. . . . The Temesvar Pesth police refuse to interfere in the matter. We have to rely upon our own resources. In these circumstances, Monsieur de Lauriac's scheme in my opinion is an excellent one. Had he not disguised himself as a gypsy I should have suggested such a course to him. . . . Go ahead, monsieur, and may you succeed, quickly. We will follow you. We shan't let you out of our sight. Not that I mistrust you, but we must be ready to give each other immediate assistance whenever a united effort is essential to insure the safety of her who is dear to us. You have only to call out for us and we shall hear you. Now, gentlemen, to horse."

They mounted their horses. It was now quite dark. A cold wind from the mountains drove the ever-thickening clouds across the sky and obscured at times the effulgent moon.

"We couldn't hope for a more favorable night. We can hide ourselves and watch by turns."

Jean, losing patience, put spurs to his mount. Rouletabille leant over and clutched the bridle.

"Wait a bit. . . . Good luck, Monsieur de Lauriac."

De Lauriac went ahead of them and vanished in the darkness.

"Look here," growled Jean, losing all patience and quivering with annoyance at being held back. "Are you here in his interests or mine?"

"I am here in Odette's interests. Think a little less of him and yourself."

"But he will take her away from us."

"I sincerely hope so. I want him to take her away from us so that we may take her away from him."

"Well, then, let's go after him."

"No," said Rouletabille. "Come with me."

And as they had reached a crossway he turned back

eastward, which led them away from the road followed by de Lauriac.

"You are taking the road from Sever Turn," exclaimed Jean. "You are taking the road which leads to the gypsies, while de Lauriac will avoid them if he gets hold of Odette, and we shall never see him again— neither him nor his victim."

"Do as I tell you if you want to see Odette again."

"Rouletabille, you must be mad—or rather you are too clever—too clever for me, you know. I prefer not to say any more. You want us to part company. That's what you want, isn't it? Well, we will go our separate ways."

"Jean, I entreat you to listen to me," said Rouletabille, making a last appeal.

"I have never had any confidence in de Lauriac and now I have no confidence in you." And digging his spurs into his horse, he rode off in the direction taken by de Lauriac.

"Well, this is about the limit," cried Rouletabille, taken aback. "What on earth has come over him? Now I am left to deal the final blow by myself. Ah, where are my friends of old, my faithful comrades in adventure—Le Candour and Vladimir? Still, my dear old Rouletabille, we must win through in spite of them. Come, don't worry."

And he passed out of sight at a gentle trot, gloomily filling his pipe.

CHAPTER XXXV

"HE COMES WHOM SHE DID NOT EXPECT"

DE LAURIAC reached the Romany camp without further disguise, having ridden post haste. He was at once surrounded by men and women of the tribe, who plied him with a hundred questions in one breath.

He told them that he wanted to speak to their chief. Thereupon Suco, the blacksmith, led the way to Sumbalo, whom the horseman saluted in the gypsy manner. Then de Lauriac leapt from the saddle and, still holding the bridle of his horse, explained that he came from Sever Turn, delegated by the Patriarch to have speech with the *queyra*.

The group gathered round him gave vent to demonstrations of satisfaction and begged him to tell them what was happening in the sacred city.

He described the state of impatient expectancy and delight which prevailed there. In the Temple all was festivity, the citizens had put out their carpets, the bells were ringing continuously. The Great Chief—the man who carried the whip across his shoulder, with which he inflicted punishment—had had a gorgeous costume made for himself; the Patriarch had dispatched messengers to all the principal cities round about. As for himself, he was intrusted with a message from the chief priest to the *queyra*, and after he had delivered it he would continue his journey westward to carry the glad news to the People of the Road.

Sumbalo himself took him to Odette.

Odette had remained in her caravan in a state of prostration after getting rid of Zina. She had, of course, heard the commotion caused by the arrival of the messenger from Sever Turn, but had become so accustomed to these shouts and sounds that she paid no heed to them. Fresh groups of gypsies were forever flocking to meet her, to form part of her retinue, and to ask for a sight of their queen.

Thus when she heard the door open behind her she made ready to welcome the newcomers with the same favor with which she had received Zina a little while before. She turned round with an angry gesture, and remained in blank amazement before a man who was certainly no stranger to her. The small lamp fell full on the face of the newcomer.

"Do you not recognize me, mademoiselle? I am Hubert de Lauriac."

She leapt to her feet.

"You . . . you here!"

De Lauriac had explained to Sumbalo, adducing the Patriarch's authority, that he had to speak to their young queen in private, and the chief saw no objection to leaving him alone with her for a while.

"Yes, it's I," he returned. "Cannot you trust me?"

She did not at first answer. Nevertheless, she knew that de Lauriac was madly in love with her, and his object in coming to her could only be to rescue her from her captors. Afterwards they would see! Greatly touched, breathing quickly, she asked after her father.

"It was he who sent me," returned de Lauriac, taking advantage of her ignorance of her father's death.

"What about Jean and Rouletabille? I know that Rouletabille was at New Wachter."

"Jean is remaining in France," declared de Lauriac. "As to Rouletabille, he was seriously wounded at New

Wachter in an attempt to save his servant from the vengeance of the gypsies in charge of you."

This last statement corresponded so exactly with the facts within her knowledge that she could not doubt de Lauriac's word. But it struck a chill to her heart to learn that Jean had remained in France and made no effort to rescue her. . . . In very truth, she could depend only on de Lauriac, who, in spite of every obstacle, had succeeded in coming to her at the risk of his life. He was her last hope; and that very fact was in itself a torment. She was silent.

"It won't be easy to escape," he went on. "We must put a bold face on it."

Odette had made up her mind. In a voice which she vainly strove to make firm she said:

"Monsieur, I shall not be lacking in courage."

"Thank you, Odette," murmured de Lauriac with emotion. "I shall be worthy of your trust. My life, you know, belongs to you. And now I swear to succeed."

His last words rung ominously in Odette's ears. She ascribed a meaning to them which left no room for misunderstanding.

"Don't let there be any mistake. My life does not belong to you."

De Lauriac grew pale, bowed, and said:

"Mademoiselle, I ask nothing but to be allowed to restore you to your father."

Odette gave him her hand. He put his lips to it with great deference, and she felt much easier.

"This is what you must do when I leave you," began de Lauriac, after looking behind the door to make sure that no one was eavesdropping.

*   *   *   *   *   *   *   *

Callista lived only for the bitter satisfaction of revenge. In the days when she was a "Parisienne" she would never have believed it possible to take up again

so easily the life of the road, with its free and easy intercourse. She had submitted once more to gypsy habits
without revolt and even without repugnance, as though
she had never tasted the refined enjoyments of modern
society. At moments she was surprised at herself, but
she attributed so much complaisance to the intense satisfaction which she felt in knowing that she was wreak-
ing her revenge. The sight of Odette's misery was a
sufficient reward. She never wearied of seeing her in
tears, and the thought of Jean's despair made her heart
leap.

How that man had played her false! What a fool he
had made of her! What a thing of little account she was
in his eyes!

That was it! But she had dragged down Odette with
her. Let him come and take her away from her. The
gypsies of the world would be ranged against him. The
peculiar fate by which the entire race had become her
accomplice in this act of revenge delighted her as though
it were a smile from the gods. . . . It was written! . . .

She stole into the wood and the fresh cool breeze blowing from the distant hills caressed her face. She crept
forward, trampling under her osier sandals the thin, dry,
tall grass, sprinkled with wild flowers.

She turned back and found herself confronted with
a motionless shadow. But she perceived that it was the
shadow of a man, and at once recovered her composure.

"Oh, it's you, Andréa," she said in an angry voice.
"What do you want now? Can't you leave me in peace
for a moment?"

"Listen to me, Callista," returned Andréa gently in
a trembling voice. "You know what was agreed between
us, and you know I love you. I have done everything
you wished me to do. You must have pity on me. I tell
you I love you."

"And I tell you I don't love you."

A silence ensued.

He made a grab at her and remorselessly dragged her back to him.

"No more of this nonsense. If you don't love me I'll make you. You've played with me long enough."

She tried to push him aside.

"At Sever Turn," she snapped. "You know what I said: At Sever Turn."

"You'll never see Sever Turn again if you don't give in now."

He was like a savage. She struggled furiously. She saw the gleam of a knife in his hands.

Then, when he saw her in his arms accepting the inevitable, he seated her gently beside him and began to caress and kiss her and stroke her hair.

She closed her eyes to shut out the sight of him. To all appearances she was submissive. He pressed a kiss upon her icy lips.

Suddenly the sound of voices broke forth from the camp, and there was a mad rush to the woods. The despairing cries brought them to their feet. Someone passing in the darkness shouted:

"They've carried off the *queyra*."

CHAPTER XXXVI

AT SEVER TURN

EVENTS followed the course prepared by de Lauriac. We know that the three men had had time to study the ground and take their bearings before the gypsies arrived upon the scene. De Lauriac, warily working in his own interests, had made up his mind how to effect Odette's escape. She was ready to accept his suggestions. For that matter the scheme was a simple one.

When he left the caravan, he held a brief conversation with Sumbalo, who desired him to stay to supper and spend the night in the camp, but de Lauriac fell back on the orders which he had received, and declined the invitation.

He heard a whistle and saw to his great surprise that Jean was alone. Jean told him that Rouletabille was endeavoring to inspect the farther side of the camp, and he asked anxiously after Odette.

"All goes well," returned de Lauriac. "The gypsies suspect nothing, and I am to return across country and wait at a certain place, where Odette will come to me. She will be accompanied, I expect, by old Zina. I will get away with Odette and come back to you."

"I will come with you," said Jean.

"That would jeopardize our success. The camp is well guarded. I may be recognized. As far as I am concerned there is no risk. I should tell them that I had returned because I had forgotten something that I had to say to the queen, and I should spend the night in camp,

245

waiting the first favorable opportunity that offers."

"Go ahead, and may God be with us," said Jean.

Half an hour after de Lauriac's departure Odette opened her caravan door. Zina saw her and went up to her.

"Would you like to have something to eat, light of my life?" she asked.

The old hag displayed unspeakable joy when Odette accepted some black bread and milk. She expressed a wish to wander round the camp before going to bed. Zina threw a wrap over her shoulders and went with her.

Odette stole forward under the trees with a careless step, plucking the tall ferns.

"I want to sleep in the open to-night. I'm tired of your little old witch of a woman's trucklebed."

Zina, a slave to her whims, eagerly loaded herself with ferns. Suddenly, raising her head, she realized that Odette was gone. There was a stir in the foliage ahead. She uttered a cry . . . shouted for assistance. The cry was taken up and the air resounded with oaths. "They're carrying off the *queyra*," they yelled. An indescribable uproar and confusion ensued; the men flew to their arms, and rushed madly in all directions. Callista, followed by Andréa, panic-stricken, ran up. . . . Ah, this Callista, how quickly she had leapt to her feet! With a scream of rage she flung Andréa aside:

"You swore to watch over her. I owe you nothing now."

It was, in truth, poor Zina who suffered the most grievous time. She was abused and beaten and bruised without mercy.

Jean heard the shouts and shots and assumed that de Lauriac had been successful. He made ready to join him, as much to lend him a helping hand as to avoid leaving him alone with his beautiful captive.

He stood on the summit of a conical hill which

served as his observatory, and strove to penetrate the gathering darkness. The moon appeared between two clouds, and he beheld the gypsies' headlong race as they instinctively made for the road to the east. And while he saw them, he too was seen.

A general outcry greeted the sight of him. It would seem that they took him for the abductor, and he scarcely had time to gallop back to the plain. They flocked after him, urging each other on with fierce shouts. They did not yet fire on him, fearing lest their shots, aimed at the equestrian shadow fleeing before them, might strike down the queen on whom all their hopes were set.

Jean at last reached the road, but he realized that he would be overtaken, and suddenly in desperation he flung himself into a willow plantation on the bank of a swamp.

Here he did not hesitate to abandon his horse. He leapt into the water and succeeded in reaching the opposite bank, after untold efforts to save himself from being engulfed in the sand.

Then, utterly exhausted, he lay down among the reeds waiting the course of events. He could hear the mad shouting of men beating down the tall grass. Lights flickered to and fro.

De Lauriac had not budged. He was hiding in a tree with Odette. His horse, tethered in a gully, was eating his feed of corn from a nosebag which his master had fastened to his collar before leaving him, and was too busy to make himself heard.

When the clamor near the camp began to sober down, and the horsemen had vanished into the night like madmen riding the darkness, he descended from his refuge, carrying Odette in his arms.

Soon he came up to his mount. He put Odette in the saddle and led the horse by the bridle. Thus they advanced, making a number of winds and turns in the forest. He did not hesitate in his course. He knew exactly where he was going. From time to time he recognized a landmark and quickened his pace.

Then he mounted his horse. With one arm he held Odette seated in the saddle before him, and his heart throbbed as he felt the contact of her young form against his breast.

He put spurs to his horse, and the pebbles on the road flew under the furious clatter of the hoofs.

At daybreak they reached a sunken road leading to an ancient tower, in part demolished, from which, as they drew near, a host of pigeons took flight.

Odette had not yet uttered a word. She slid down from the horse, and de Lauriac led the way.

"Here is your palace, my queen."

But Odette did not smile. De Lauriac in a polite mood frightened her. She cast a glance at him, averted her head, and colored as she caught the passion in his eyes.

At first Odette had received de Lauriac as her deliverer, but now that she was alone with him in that old tower, in that lost wilderness in which she could hope for no succor, she wondered anxiously whether it would not have been better for her to remain a prisoner of those gypsies, who had surrounded her with every mark of honor and respect.

Everything had been made ready by him in this small room so that they might spend some hours in rest and refreshment. A sort of fireplace had been built with a heap of fallen stones, and a wood fire was ready to be lighted if Odette felt cold. A bed of ferns, on which lay a blanket, was prepared for her use. Lastly, de Lauriac had produced a small spirit lamp, and was boiling the water for tea.

"Do you think we are now safe?" she asked, so as to say something, for she felt that silence between them was more painful than words.

"I think so," he assured her. "We have thrown those

infernal gypsies off the scent. To insure greater safety we shall travel only at night. To-morrow we reach a town. We will take the train and be in France in a couple of days."

"In France!"

Her thoughts turned to Jean, but she dared not utter his name. She spoke of her father.

"He is very ill," said de Lauriac. "Your abduction was a crushing blow to him. Moreover, we had a terrible scene the day before. Though I was wrong to write that letter, you were wrong to show it to him. Still, when I heard of this incomprehensible abduction, I hastened to him and apologized and placed my services at his disposal. Monsieur de Santierne was with him. There was an explanation between the three of us. Matters had reached the point when your father made no secret of your birth: 'The gypsies have retaken her because she is a gypsy princess,' he said. 'Her mother was a Sever Turn gypsy.'"

"Good gracious, so it is true," cried Odette in a strained voice. "I am the daughter of a gypsy."

"Why, are you ashamed of your birth?" asked de Lauriac quietly. "Your mother was, it seems, of high rank, and it is this fact which is the cause of your trouble. But I have sworn to make you happy."

After these last words there was an oppressive silence. Odette could hear the wild throbbing of her heart.

"Monsieur de Santierne did not wait to hear more," de Lauriac went on. "He left us, declaring that a de Santierne could never marry a gypsy girl, a child of the road."

Odette leant against the wall and covered her face with her hands. She would have fallen to the ground had he not held her.

"He was unworthy of you," he murmured. "Have

you not already judged him. . . . Odette, I alone love you. I have always loved you."

She sobbed aloud. She did not notice that she lay in his arms, and suddenly relaxing his hold with a gesture which he was unable to control, he caught the beloved face, bathed in tears, and madly kissed her lips, parted in an expression of despair.

His burning kiss at once restored Odette to the full possession of her faculties. With an irresistible movement she flung him aside, and it was as much as he could do to save himself from a grotesque fall.

"So it was for this that you came to my rescue," she cried fiercely. "Understand: I prefer the gypsies."

She stood before him as brave as a lion. He could hardly believe his eyes. She sprang towards the door, but he was before her and, seizing her in his powerful arms, threw her back with unspeakable violence into this lair to which he had brought her, and, with a jeer charged with menace, cried:

"You prefer the gypsies! . . . Let your fate take its course, Odette."

CHAPTER XXXVII

"IT'S ALL ROULETABILLE'S FAULT"

JEAN had fallen asleep. Fatigue had overcome him. He did not wake up until daybreak. Memories of the events of the day before crowded upon him. He crawled carefully for a few minutes among the reeds. No sound could be heard near him. He felt reassured and stood up. The danger was past. . . . But what had become of Odette? Had the gypsies recaptured her? And if de Lauriac had succeeded in getting away with her, what had become of de Lauriac? . . .

He had lost everything. His horse had undoubtedly fallen into the hands of the gypsies. The thought of de Lauriac and Odette obsessed him. Where had they taken refuge in their flight from the enemy? His gaze strayed over the plain, and he observed a few hundred yards away on the right a small wood, which, save the willow-grove surrounding the marshes which he had just left, was the sole spot in which it was possible to hide.

His eyes scrutinized the track for tell-tale footmarks, as he had often seen Rouletabille do, but nothing specially worth noting attracted his attention. . . .

The memory of his conversation with de Lauriac rankled in his mind. Rouletabille's attitude seemed more and more suspect and impossible to understand. He no longer believed in anything and had lost faith even in Rouletabille.

Jean seated himself in the solitude of the wood on a a fallen tree-trunk which bared his irresolute steps, and began to reflect. Reflect upon what? In reality he could think of but one thing, a thing of which he was absolutely certain—he was the most miserable of men.

Suddenly he raised his head. He seemed to hear a sound. The branches were thrust apart and a man stood before him. It was Andréa.

"Ive found you at last," said the gypsy.

He had appeared in this same way to Rouletabille in the wood at New Wachter, but his purpose then was to get rid of him. On this occasion he seemed in no hurry to part with Jean.

"Do you recognize me?" he asked.

"No," returned Jean. "People of your race mean very little to me. But I am not sure that you are a friend of mine."

"I am the man who loved Callista. You stole her from me," said Andréa harshly.

"Well, we are quits. I am not in love with Callista, but I am in love with a girl whom you forcibly kidnaped. Andréa, for that's what they call you, do you want to make your fortune? As far as Callista is concerned, you can be easy in your mind in the future, for I shan't take her away from you again, but if you will help me to find Mademoiselle de Lavardens I will make it worth your while."

Andréa received the offer with a loud guffaw, to which other guffaws not less significant echoed in unison.

Jean turned his head and perceived standing round him a number of armed gypsies, who took stock of him with a look of bitter hostility.

He made a movement to withdraw from the circle which enclosed him, but came up against a solid wall of men who repelled him by a waving of arms.

"You are our prisoner," declared Andréa.

"We shan't go back to camp empty-handed," broke in Monoko, the tinsmith, in a strong Pézenas accent.

"You are a fellow-countryman," said Jean, turning

to him, "and we may be able to come to an understanding if you are more amenable than they are. What you have just said shows that you haven't succeeded in recapturing Mademoiselle de Lavardens. Tell me what I want to know and you won't regret it."

The man gave a shrug of his shoulders and turned on his heel.

"Now then, come with me," ordered Andréa.

Jean was obliged to accompany them.

It was evident that Odette had managed to elude them. . . . The thought that she had been rescued by de Lauriac was anything but an unmixed joy to him. . . .

The gypsies traversed the wood by the most out-of-the-way tracks, in order to avoid the roads and even the least semblance of a path. They did not reach the camp until nightfall.

Consternation still prevailed in it. When those who had remained behind saw their brethren return without the *queyra* they gave vent to yells of fury and terrible threats against Jean and then broke into loud lamentations. The women put ashes on their heads. Zina seemed as if she were possessed of a devil.

After a while they harked back to Jean with fierce clamor. Callista suddenly came upon the scene and was not less implacable than the rest. Sumbalo was obliged to intervene when she began to incite them to wreak their vengeance there and then on their prisoner. Jean no longer recognized this hell-cat.

Was this the young, fantastic, easy-going mistress whom he had dressed like a doll for a couple of years, and imagined that he had transformed into a "Parisienne"?

Sumbalo went up to him:

"There is only one way for you, stranger, to get out of this trouble: tell us where to find our queen. You must know where she is."

Jean did not even answer him. Then Sumbalo, greatly perturbed, also left him. It was the most disastrous incident in his life. To allow the *queyra* to slip out of his hands! Fortunately he was taking one of those aliens to Sever Turn. The wrath of the people would fall upon that man.

He was determined that his prisoner should reach Sever Turn alive. Thus he gave orders for food to be supplied to him.

Jean wrapped himself in a horse-rug which had been thrown to him. He was conscious that he was being guarded, and that any attempt on his part to escape was bound to fail, at least for the present.

He closed his eyes and strove to sleep. . . . A hand was placed on his shoulder. He looked round. Callista lay beside him and whispered to him with her lips almost touching his ear.

She explained that her rage against him was but a bit of play-acting intended to deceive her people. If he liked . . . if he was willing, he had but to say the word and nothing was lost.

"In losing Odette I have lost everything," returned Jean, who knew how much he was making her suffer.

She dug her nails into his hands and he almost cried out.

"You must be mad," she whispered. "Why aggravate me? I am your last hope.

"One word and we will escape together.

"You have no idea what they will do to you. You don't know what is in store for you in Sever Turn."

"And you will escape with me?"

"I should have to go with you, of course. What does it matter to you? You used to love me. Have we not spent many happy hours together? Remember, Jean! Remember! And I shall know how to make you forget your Odette."

Suddenly she was caught in an iron grip and thrown violently away from him like a bundle. And the volley of gypsy oaths which followed were accompanied by kicks which made her rise in part and gasp with fury. And then a mighty box on the ear flung her to the ground again where she lay sobbing loudly, cowed.

She had taken advantage of the slumbering Andréa to go to Jean, but her muffled pleadings had at last wakened him, and he intervened in his own peculiar fashion. There was no argument. It was the way of the gypsy world. Callista had received her deserts.

She considered it useless to offer any protest.

In the morning they struck camp and proceeded towards Sever Turn. Jean was taken off in the caravan in which Odette had been held captive.

CHAPTER XXXVIII

THE SCARECROW AND THE FLY

THE first thing that caught Jean's eye were the words which Odette seemingly had cut with a knife: "Help little Zo!" It was a cruel moment, the bitterest moment that he had yet experienced in the course of this adventure.

And so, in her hour of distress, her thoughts had turned to Rouletabille!

Little Zo! It was a pet name which she used with apparent innocence at Lavardens, because this diminutive of Joseph, his Christian name, amused her, and Jean in his simplicity had regarded it as perfectly straightforward. How they had laughed in their sleeves at him! At that time he was mainly concerned about de Lauriac, and de Lauriac was a saint compared with the crafty Rouletabille.

Let the gypsies do with him at Sever Turn what they pleased. Life had become intolerable to him. He asked nothing better than to have done with it.

He would have been still more convinced of the vanity of friendship had he known that Rouletabille, at the very moment when he was cursing his treachery, saw him pass, a prisoner in the gypsies' power, a pitiful figure pressing his face against the carvan window, but otherwise seemingly unconcerned. Rouletabille exhibited no particular emotion at the sight of him. He made no attempt to follow him. . . . Under this date, indeed, we find the following entry in *Rouletabille's diary:*

"Jean has just passed me guarded by gypsies. He has allowed himself to be nabbed, the ass! He would have done better to come with me as I begged and implored him to do. But no! My gentleman insisted on acting solely upon his own judgment; he had had enough of mine. A fine result! Here I am deprived of all my forces. I no longer have any troops, and I shall probably have to fight a world of enemies.

"The result will depend on what will happen very shortly. I have been waiting for de Lauriac for some thirty-six hours. He is bound to be here soon. I have come to this place leaning, as ever, on 'the right end of my judgment,' which told me that I must look for him on the road to Sever Turn. Whatever our Jean may have said, it is here that de Lauriac will indubitably come *with her*. He must pass this way. I am positive of it.

"I was unable to give Jean my reasons for feeling so positive. I thought it well over, but knowing him as I do, it would be utterly impossible. He ought to have accepted my word, but if a person is to believe in me that person must be in sympathy with me. Jean does not like me any more. My one consolation is that he will be worshiping me in another fortnight.

"Meantime there is a distinct lack of modern comfort here. I am hiding in an old hut. The plain stretches before me. The hills lie behind, and behind them again is the Patriarchate. I am on the threshold which Odette must not be allowed to cross. It is the threshold of the grave for her as the poet might say.

"Fortunately de Lauriac does not expect to see me here, nor can he have any suspicion that I am expecting to see him. I shall have the advantage of taking him by surprise. I must win the fight before he is aware that I am making an attack. Otherwise—I should cut a poor figure against him. He can shoot a swallow on the wing; with one twist make a bull roll in the dust; and he can handle a horse like a veritable Centaur!

"From my position the eye can take in the road before me for about a league. I shall see the gallant horseman ride up with Odette more or less bound in front of him.

"To be sure, he has no need now to worry himself. His only risk is lest he should encounter gypsies—gypsies returning from Sever Turn, and they if needs be, would come to his assistance. Yes, but this is the position: I have prepared a nice little surprise for him.

"If there were no danger of killing or wounding Odette I should fire my revolver as he passed—his offence this time is obvious—and I fell that his abrupt departure from this life would not keep me awake at nights. But for Odette's sake I must play a safe hand, that is to say, shoot point blank at him. And herein lies the difficulty. The road is on a level with the plain until we reach the frontier. Up to this point it is almost entirely open country on my right and left. My hut stands on the first spur of the mountain, much too far away to enable me to remain hidden in it. That is the crux of the problem. It is essential for me to be on the road-side, but there is no place in which I can take cover, and yet de Lauriac must not see me. . . . So what was I to do?

"Well, there is a cornfield by the road-side. The corn is still green and quite short, and in the cornfield, near the road, stands a scarecrow.

"Yes, an ordinary scarecrow placed there to keep away the birds. . . .

"It came in splendidly. This scarecrow was dressed in a peculiar frock-coat, or rather a tattered overcoat, which imparted to it an altogether sumptuous appearance. Its arms were outstretched and seemed to be calling down a blessing on the harvest to come. Finally it

wore a hat, a soft felt hat with turned down brim, which
gave to the whole conglomeration a somewhat doggish
air.

"The reader must have grasped the situation. . . .

"I slipped into the scarecrow's clothes. I rammed
the hat on one side so as to hide my face. I stretched
out my arms, and, be assured, I held in the scarecrow's
sleeve, which fortunately was a little too long for me, a
Browning revolver at full cock ready to fire.

"My man will pass close to me, and almost touch
me without suspecting the least thing, and I . . . I shall
blow out his brains. And there you are! It's as easy
as shelling peas. The problem is solved. Our dear
Monsieur de Lauriac will sprawl in the dust. Odette
will be saved. We will discuss matters afterwards if
he is still alive. Take care! . . . I discern a slight cloud
of dust on the road in the distance. . . . And now for
the scarecrow!"

.   .   .   .

Rouletabille's diary breaks off here and begins again
the next day. We extract a few lines which complete
the story of the scarecrow. Rouletabille sets down the
facts as if they were happening there and then:

"I have been standing for a quarter of an hour with
outstretched arms as motionless as though I were carved
in wood. I begin to have cramp. Will he soon be here,
the brute? I speak of de Lauriac's horse, which he
must be riding at a walking pace after covering a considerable amount of ground. . . . De Lauriac is now feeling safe. He allows his horse to recover his wind. Still,
I am in a very fatiguing position. He might hurry up
a little. I am feeling the cramp . . . cramp.

"I hear the sound of horse's hoofs on the road. The
brute—this time I mean de Lauriac—has put him to the

trot. . . . And now I have pins and needles in my feet. Hang it all, de Lauriac has slackened to a walking pace again.

"What infinite patience one requires to be a successful scarecrow!

"Now he is on the trot again. This time I shall have him. I steady my revolver in my right hand. . . . A few moments later I hear the horse's breathing. . . .

"Hell and fury! As if it were not enough to have pins and needles in my feet, a fly, a gnat, a flea, a mere nothing alights on the tip of my nose just at this moment, and with an involuntary movement of my left hand I administer a resounding thump. . . . A shot rings out. A bullet sends my hat flying."

CHAPTER XXXIX

A FIGHT

ROULETABILLE was so intensely annoyed by the grotesque incident which nearly cost him his life, that his comments on the fight which ensued are exceedingly brief, and it would be difficult to piece the facts together from his diary alone. But in a chatty mood he told all of the exciting story.

"I felt the whiz of the bullet, and I was so flabbergasted by my own stupidity that I remained bareheaded, exposed to de Lauriac's shots for, of course, he recognized me.

"He did not consider it necessary to kill me though he might have done so without detriment to himself, for the scarecrow's sleeve had completely slipped over my right hand, which held my revolver, and I was unable to extricate it. De Lauriac was mounted. I was on foot. He assumed that I was without a horse, having abandoned mine somewhere, and in order to get rid of me, he had only to put both spurs to his mount which he straightway proceeded to do.

"Odette, who was lying across the saddle in front of him, had not uttered a cry. I concluded that she was gagged or, possibly, had fainted.

"After throwing off, not without difficulty, the miserable scarecrow's clothes, the use of which I had regarded for the moment as one of the finest ideas that had ever occurred to me, I started to run. Seeing me come hot foot behind him while his horse was galloping at full speed, de Lauriac gave a laugh—a jeering

261

laugh which he sent me by way of a last good-by.

"It was in this way that the ruffian reached the hills where he stopped to take his breath after the encounter. Then he continued his way for about half an hour at an easy jog-trot. I repeat that he could consider himself safe, inasmuch as the frontier was within a few hour's march, and there was not a person in the district who would not fly to his assistance at the first summons.

"Suddenly there was a great clatter on his left. He turned round and saw me making for him like a whirlwind. This time I, too, was in the saddle.

"I had hidden my horse between two undulations of the ground, behind the first spur of the hills, in what I venture to say was an excellent strategic position, for a goats' track led me straight to it, and another ran down from it, intersecting, a little farther away, the road which wound round the side of the hills. . . . Consequently we were flung against each other as soon as de Lauriac once more put his horse to the gallop.

"The ridiculous result of the first manœuvre had rendered me mad with rage. I was determined to make an end of my man, who was more than I could stand.

"The impact was tremendous. Our horses reared, and neighed, and foamed at the mouth as if they were about to tear each other to pieces, and it was this which for the time being saved me.

"I hoped to unhorse him because I dared not use my revolver lest I should hit Odette, but he fired at me point blank. The horse received three bullets in the chest, and other shots merely grazed me as I rolled in the dust beside him. I leapt at the nose of de Lauriac's horse. This time I had the advantage, for my adversary had exhausted his ammunition and was deprived of any means of attack.

"I called upon him to surrender, leveling my revolver at his horse's head, but, he gave me a savage kick in the chest which caused my weapon to swerve, and threw me violently to the ground.

"I was blinded with rage. I was worsted in this absurd encounter.

"Meanwhile de Lauriac passed out of sight with Odette hanging as though lifeless on his arm.

"Then I caught sight of him again on another ridge of the mountain. A band of gypsies was running up to him. He spoke to them, flinging out his arm in my direction. I crept into a crevice in the rock; a sort of cave, the mouth of which I hurriedly concealed with a few brambles.

"I dragged in my impedimenta—I mean my toilet necessaries rolled up in my rug. I determined to die in this hole if I were discovered."

CHAPTER XL

A DARK PRISON

SEVER TURN! The ancient city with is moldy and tumble-down houses, tottering walls, broken roads, discolored frontages, crumbling palace, antiquated court house, and gloomy towers guarding the sanctuary which throughout the centuries, despite devastating revolutions, invasions and plagues, had maintained its immemorial traditions and sacred ceremonies —the aspect of this ancient city was changed from the first proclamation of the glad news.

Let us hark back to the early hours of the enchantment. Never was there such a display of carpets, flags, banners. The bells pealed; the people made merry. The country folk flocked from distant lands, their donkeys laden with children waving flowers. Men on the ramparts discharged their weapons, and young girls brought baskets of fragrant flowers to the public squares.

The city as far as the new European quarter—so the gypsies called it as though they were still a barbaric tribe of Asia—was crowded with travelers and tourists who had come out of their way to witness the fateful event.

The Hôtel des Balkans, which was close to the caravanserai, wore a new pink coat; its shutters were newly painted green; the windows of its banqueting hall newly cleaned. The flagstones of the entrance lobby shone like marble; the hotel flew the large new flag of the Consul of Wallachia—an important person occupying the best rooms on the first floor as befitted the representative of

264

the whole diplomatic corps—and might almost be taken for a palace. Here was the center of modern society while across the street dwelt the life of the middle ages.

Let us enter the temple. Let us cross the courtyard of this stronghold alive with priests and people thronging the porch in a multi-colored mass. The rich are clad in their red shirts and yellow tunics and steel waistbands inlaid with gold and silver; and yet the ragged and tattered have their rich hues which vie with the red shirts and yellow tunics, in this bewildering and varied scale of civilization.

Under a blazing sun the priests, all in black with long veils like women in mourning, come and go, holding aloft golden ikons. . . . A great joy is depicted on every countenance. . . . They have come! . . . They will see their young queen! . . . They repeat the prophetic verses from the Book of Ancestors, the book which was stolen from them. . . . They are waiting for their *queyra*. . . . At last the long iron doors of the temple are opened and the people flock into it. . . .

Suddenly a mighty clamor bursts forth under the sacred roof, and the messenger of misfortune arrives. He is covered with dust and, in the last stages of exhaustion, sinks in a huddled heap at the feet of the Patriarch.

"The *queyra* has been carried off by aliens," he cries, and has strength to add: "But we are bringing you one of the kidnapers."

A tremendous silence fell in the temple, a silence more terrible than words can picture, forming an awful contrast to the yells of despair which began to break forth from the four corners of the ill-fated city.

The Patriarch did not deign to cast a glance at the messenger. He drew himself up and waited, motionless as a statue; and it seemed as if he were surrounded by other statues, by others who had become old men like himself. He stood thus until the great chief who had just entered the temple led the prisoner up to him. . . .

"Well, that fellow won't make old bones," said Monsieur Nicolas Tournesol in an undertone, behind a pillar as he watched the prisoner pass before him pursued by the murderous gestures of the rabble.

Monsieur Nicolas Tournesol was a commercial traveler. He was, perhaps, the only commercial traveler who had ever set foot in the Patriarchate where, moreover, he did an excellent business in his particular brand of champagne and tins of preserved meat. He was the sole representative in Sever Turn of trade with Europe, just as the Consul of Wallachia was the sole representative of the diplomatic corps of both hemispheres.

.   .   .   .

But we must return to the prisoner who was none other than Jean de Santierne. He was in a pitiful state. When he reached the city gates he was almost torn to pieces. His captors were compelled to make a detour and effect an entrance through an ancient disused watercourse which led to one of the courtyards in the temple. And here he escaped being stoned only because the great chief walked beside him, for the people of Sever Turn feared and esteemed their war minister. . . . Not that he had won many battles, but he had a way of handling the whip which enforced respect. . . .

Jean was covered with blood. Supported by the great chief, he clambered up the steps amid the hooting of the populace to where the Patriarch stood surrounded by his choir of old men who had fallen back into curule chairs. Sumbalo, Andréa, Suco the blacksmith, and others who had assisted in his capture, brought up the rear. Zina was nowhere to be seen, for, since the disappearance of Odette, she was like a living corpse.

Callista remained behind watching without taking part in the proceedings. She was in a state of mind which caused her greatly to suffer because, in her heart, her execration of Jean contended with a feeling of remorse for having led him with her own hands to the brink of the abyss into which he was to be hurled. Even that form of hatred went by the name of love. . . . But what had she come there for? To hear sentence pronounced on him, without the shadow of doubt. But assuredly it would not be the satisfaction to her which in the pitiless ferocity of her original resentment she had promised herself. The heart of a woman, we know, is made up of inconsistencies.

"Here is the criminal," said the great chief, thrusting Jean before the Patriarch.

The dead silence which prevailed in the temple was broken by a thousand voices shouting "Death!" and the shout was taken up and echoed by the people outside. It came like a thunderclap which, following the terrible silence of a few minutes before, when they learnt of the loss of their queen, sent a shudder through the bravest heart.

Monsieur Nicolas Tournesol himself, who had seen many worse things in his life, muttered sadly:

"Poor fellow."

Callista was almost fainting.

"Death! Death!"

Was it true that her Jean was to be put to death? . . . Suddenly the enormity of her deed broke in upon her. She had willed Odette's death, and it was Jean who was about to die. In an impulse of which she was unconscious she went up to the Patriarch and threw herself at his feet.

"Mercy for this man!" cried she who, in very truth, was Jean's executioner.

A tremendous clamor and a blow from Andréa's fists silenced her. He pushed her roughly down the steps, sending her sprawling on the stone floor.

Then the Patriarch spoke:

"Do you deny your complicity in the abduction of the *queyra?*" he asked.

Jean did not reply, for he was unable to understand the question which was put to him in the Romany tongue. Andréa translated it, and Jean made answer that, as a matter of fact, he had done his utmost to rescue his future wife from the hands of those who had stolen her from him, and if he were free he would do the same again. They did not expect so complete a confession. It was more than enough.

The tumult broke out with renewed vigor. There was a serious commotion, and the guards had as much as they could to keep order.

The Patriarch lifted his hand, and silence was restored:

"Remember that you and your people have committed the greatest crime that it is possible to conceive, and if you do not help us by making amends, the consequences will fall entirely upon you."

"I do not attach much value to my life," returned Jean, "but I may as well tell you that I am a French subject, and you will be held responsible for my death."

"Our answer will be that your death was but an act of justice. . . . Come, take time to think. Listen to the threatening cries of the people, who are losing patience. We shall discover our queen wherever she may be, wherever you may have hidden her. Her fate is written, and yours is in the very course of being written. Do you intend to help us?"

Jean shrugged his shoulders. The gesture was an affront to the dignity of the high priest and the temple.

The prisoner's insult produced another outbreak of passion. Shouts of "Death!" were mingled with cries of "Torture!" Some demanded that he should be burned in a slow fire; others that he should be drawn and quartered; others again that he should die on the cross. The doorkeepers fought with the crowd to keep them from the sacred building, but were borne down with the crush.

The Patriarch, incited by the fears of the elders, hastened to pronounce judgment:

"We condemn you to death by starvation."

The sentence was generally regarded as a mild one, and many protestations were made, but some persons explained that it was a wise sentence, for apart from the fact that starvation was a painful death, it would give Jean time for reflection, and he might make up his mind to tell them where the *queyra* was hidden.

He was at once taken by guards to the underground part of the temple and marched through dark, stifling passages hollowed out of the rock to the palace dungeons. A door with iron bars half-way up was opened, which apparently had not been used for a considerable time, for a crowd of rats inside scampered away with a great noise.

It was a hideous cell. The great chief pushed Jean into it. It was in this place that he was to die.

CHAPTER XLI

IN WHICH NICOLAS TOURNESOL MAKES LOVE

A FEELING of gloomy dismay followed the enthusiasm which had stirred the city. In a little while the scene was changed. The gorgeous finery with which the buildings had been dressed disappeared as if by magic, and the dreary, faded, wrinkled face of the ancient city looked down anew upon its suffering people. The flowers in the streets were trampled under foot. Gone was the music; gone the decorations. On the towers of the temple arms were uplifted, imploring divine mercy; but suddenly the heavens became stormy and were wrapped in an ashen mantle under which, it seemed, all earthly hopes lay buried.

Monsieur Nicolas Tournesol sauntered back to his hotel with a somewhat dejected air. He had greatly relied on the coronation fêtes to establish, once for all, his fortune. He received a large commission, particularly on the sale of champagne, and had set his hopes upon an almost unlimited consumption. Unfortunately, events were against him, and his stock would be left on his hands.

It was therefore in a somewhat dejected mood that he stepped into the deserted hotel lobby, for the visitors had left to see the sights. Nevertheless, Nicolas Tournesol hated dull care. He decided to fight against it with the help of a few special gin cocktails, in the making of which he was an adept pupil of Vladislas Kamenos, the proprietor, who was his own barman.

He settled himself on a high stool before the mahogany counter at the back of the room, and with a long metal spoon was preparing to make music with the glasses, when a lady of lively appearance dressed simply but smartly entered the room.

They looked at each other. The lady went on her way and Tournesol got off his stool.

"Why, I've seen that face somewhere!"

The newcomer went over to a small table on which lay an inkstand, and was beginning to write a letter when she saw standing before her a stout young man with a good-humored face, who bowed very low.

"I beg you to excuse me, madame, but there's no one in Sever Turn or anywhere else in the Balkans to introduce me. Let me therefore introduce myself. I am Monsieur Tournesol . . . Nicolas Tournesol."

"My goodness," returned the lady, smiling. "I see no reason why you should not introduce yourself."

"Don't you recognize me? Tournesol, traveler in champagne, the friend of princes, dukes, and particularly of bars. . . . We spent one evening together with some friends of yours in a palatial bar."

"Really, monsieur, I never go to such places."

"Anyway, someone took you there that evening. Look here, it was about five years ago. Aren't you Madame de Meyrens?"

"You are quite right. . . . Yes, yes, of course, I remember now. Gracious, how funny you were. You were making declarations of love to all the ladies."

"Did I make a declaration to you, madame?"

"Indeed, you did not."

"There's plenty of time," returned Nicolas Tournesol imperturbably, seating himself without further ado beside Madame de Meyrens. "Vladislas, two cocktails—here! . . . Will you allow me, madame, to offer you a cocktail? Do you know you look very charming?"

"I say, you are going it, Monsieur Tournesol."

"I fear nothing as long as we enjoy ourselves. Pardon, madame, my intentions are strictly honorable. I know to whom I am speaking, and I shall not be lacking in respect for you if you like my style."

"What are you doing here?"

"What are you?"

"I will tell you presently."

"Well, I will tell you at once what I am doing here. The war ruined me and I am doing anything I can. I sell things. I am the channel of communication, if I may say so, between the manufacturer, the agent and the wholesale merchant; the *vade semper* of the duplicate entry, the unsalable article, and the surplus stock; the purveyor loved by the packer, the cartage commissary, and the drayman; the god of the hotel-keeper, the despot of the dinner table, the boss of the smoking-room, and the darling of the ladies."

"Spare my blushes," said Madame de Meyrens. "But I can't allow you to smoke a pipe."

"Oh, it's easy to see that you are a woman of fashion. . . . Have you been here long?"

"I've only just come. I came to see the queen, but it seems that there is no queen."

"They've found her again," yelled Vladislas, running in from the street.

He hurriedly gave orders to the servants to lay the carpets on the balconies again, to hang the flags out of the windows, and to place flowers everywhere. Tournesol, turning scarlet, made a grab at him.

"Is it true?"

"I tell you that she has been found again. A horseman has just brought her in. He took her away from the aliens. The city is once more in a commotion. There! Listen to the bells."

And indeed they were again ringing a full peal. It

was a tremendous symphony, a song of gladness resounding above the tumult of rejoicing.

"I'm going to see what's happening," said Madame de Meyrens, making for the door.

"Wait a bit and we'll go together. We won't lose sight of each other," said Monsieur Tournesol, placing his arm in that of Madame de Meyrens, who did not appear to raise any great objection. Nevertheless, a few minutes later she slipped away in the crowd, but Tournesol swore to find her again.

CHAPTER XLII

THE MISSING PAGE

WE shall make no attempt to describe de Lauriac's triumphal entry into Sever Turn. He was escorted by a band of gypsies, who proclaimed the news before they passed the ramparts. Odette had been given a draught of their own concoction which would have resuscitated a corpse!

She lay in de Lauriac's arms without power of resistance, and from the saddle he showed her to the people as though she were a new Pallas and Sever Turn a new Troy. A few patriotic and impressive words in Romany accompanied this exhibition of the queen, foretold in the sacred writings, and increased the delirium of the crowd. They took de Lauriac for a gypsy and a brother.

"The queen is here! The queen is here!"

The first person to throw herself at the feet of the idol when she entered the temple was Zina. Odette was half carried and half led to the Patriarch, who received her with outstretched hands, trembling with respect and emotion. He gently assisted her to the ivory throne set aside for her, and when she was seated, knelt before her thrice, murmuring the time-honored ritual.

Following his example, the people knelt down thrice and thrice stood up, singing the song of victory which concluded the hymn to Debla, the saint of the day.

Then de Lauriac went up to the Patriarch and asked to be allowed to speak.

Andréa stepped forward in his turn:

"This man is an impostor and guilty of sacrilege. He

274

is not a gypsy. He is an alien belonging to Les Saintes
Maries, and Sumbalo, the chief, and Suco, the blacksmith, recognize in him the queen's real abductor."

Having thus spoken, he laid violent hands on de Lauriac's disguise, tearing the false beard from his face
amid a scene of wild disorder.

De Lauriac remained impassive despite the affront,
and folding his arms, said:

"I knew that a plot was being formed against the queen
by aliens. . . . I took part in the plot so that it might
fail and that I might restore her for whom you are waiting."

"What was your object in so doing?" demanded the
Patriarch.

"Do you ask me that?" exclaimed de Lauriac. "Have
you forgotten the sacred text: 'The prediction must be
fulfilled.' "

The Patriarch lifted his handsome gray head, while
his face was illumined with a sudden inspiration.

"This man speaks the truth. This man is the messenger sent by St. Sarah," he declared.

"Look at me," went on de Lauriac, appealing to the
elders. "Two years ago one of you, struck down by
the plague, entrusted the book to my keeping. . . . If
he is alive, let him speak: if he is dead, let him come
forth from the grave."

"So it was you," cried one of the elders. "It was
you of whom my old friend Father Autischine spoke
before he died. It was you to whom he entrusted the
book?"

"Where is the book?" asked the Patriarch.

"The book was stolen from me by an alien, who fled
the country," returned de Lauriac. "I have searched for
him in vain, but I was able to find the most precious page
in it, which had been torn from it."

Then the Patriarch read in a sonorous voice, which

could be heard as far as the forecourt of the temple:

"'The Daughter of the Race will be marked with the sign of the crown and be stolen by aliens. . . . And an alien shall restore her to the city, and she shall be proclaimed *queyra*, and he, king. And thus, by their union, the race shall be regenerated.'"

A wild outburst of applause greeted the reading of the sacred text and ten thousand voices cried: "It is written! It is written!"

The Patriarch took de Lauriac by the hand and led him to Odette.

"The King of the World has made him the king of this land," cried the Patriarch. "This man shall be your husband."

At this juncture a sort of meteor whirled through the building amid the shouts, protests and cries of women and children thrust aside and thrown down in its passage. The meteor did not stay its course until it was before the Patriarch. It was Rouletabille.

"I am sorry, Monsieur le Patriarch," he said, "but I have something to say before the ceremony begins."

CHAPTER XLIII.

THE SIGN OF THE CROWN

AN immense tumult ensued.

Andréa, Callista, Zina, and the rest of Sumbalo's tribe were all speaking together, or rather shrieking at the top of their voices, threatening Rouletabille with clenched fists.

Odette seemed to come to herself from the languor which had taken possession of her and stood up, flinging out her arms to this hope of salvation—Rouletabille!

The great chief, with his fiercest expression, walked over to the intruder who had dared to violate the sacred precincts.

When the disorder was at length stilled, they began to talk, but could not understand each other. Rouletabille spoke the language of the *gaschi*, the vile aliens, which was unintelligible to most of them. The Patriarch called for the services of a spectacled old bookman, who had spent a lifetime in libraries and knew many languages; and with this official interpreter to help them the people were able to grasp the meaning of the colloquy.

Rouletabille, like Cassandra, who had the evil eye not less than Zina, predicted that the gypsy race would suffer untold calamities if the Patriarch and Council of Elders brought to a conclusion the criminal work on which they were engaged. He declared his conviction that the God of the Romany's, who was also the God of the Christians, and in particular of the French—the French were the first to dedicate a temple to St. Sarah, who was a blessed servant of God and the guardian of her people—had im-

277

bued the mind of the high priest with too much wisdom, and the hearts of the Council of Elders with too much goodness, to permit them to become accomplices in an act of sacrilege.

"This young man talks like a diplomat. We must be on our guard," said the Patriarch, turning to the Council. And aloud, he went on: "You speak of sacrilege. The only sacrilege that I am aware of is that which was committed by you in entering these forbidden walls."

"St. Sarah will forgive me, for she knows that I have come here solely to speak the truth."

"You seem to be on very good terms with St. Sarah," returned the Patriarch cuttingly.

"Those three people," said Rouletabille, pointing to Andréa, Callista and Zina, "appealing to a sacred text, take advantage of the credulity of a people and lead them to believe that the moon is made of green cheese."

"The moon is made of green cheese! What does that mean?" asked the Patriarch gravely.

"It is a figure of speech," explained Rouletabille, "and means that you are taking Mademoiselle de Lavardens for the *queyra* foretold in your sacred writings. Now, Mademoiselle de Lavardens is the victim in this matter of Callista, who is jealous of her and in love with her future husband."

"Lies! Lies!" shouted Callista.

"If it was to talk such *sobradas* (nonsense)," interposed one old man, "may the *zarapia* (plague) take you!"

"You must in any case be told why you are being deceived, and I can only explain myself by speaking out clearly," went on Rouletabille, incensed at the contempt with which his accusations were received. "But for this particular twaddle Mademoiselle de Lavardens would still be in France, her country which is claiming her, and from which you had no right to take her."

"Mademoiselle de Lavardens is a Romany and subject to Romany law."

"She is French and subject to French law."

"Her mother was a gypsy."

"I knew her mother," several old men declared.

"I held her mother in my arms when she was a child," said another.

"When her mother died I became her mother. The foreigner stole her from us. . . . I went with the foreigner," said Zina.

"You went with the foreigner," shouted Rouletabille, "but for all these years you held your tongue, though you knew that your gypsy brethren were searching the world for their princess. Had you known that she was really the *queyra,* would you have remained silent?"

A dead hush greeted this unanswerable argument. Every eye was fixed on Zina, who, breathing hard, did not speak. And yet she knew that her silence was her condemnation. She hid her face in her hands, and a threatening murmur arose round her.

"I begin to see 'the right end,' " said Rouletabille to himself; "let me take advantage of it. Forward with the 'right end of my judgment' and strike hard."

"I will tell you why you kept silent for so many years," he yelled with all his might. "It was because you knew that the child could not be the long-expected princess, because she did not bear on her shoulder the predicted birth-mark, the mark foretold in the Book of Ancestors. Mademoiselle de Lavardens was not born with a birth-mark of the sign of the crown."

A loud and mournful wail echoed through the building. The people had by now given way to despair.

"No birth-mark! No birth-mark!" they murmured sadly.

"No birth-mark?" echoed Callista, stepping between

Rouletabille and Zina, who seemed about to faint. "You say she has no birth-mark!"

At that moment a soft, low voice, a golden voice, seemed to come from the mouth of ivory. Odette drew herself up, and, as though she were walking in her sleep, went up to the Patriarch and in her soft voice said:

"Birth-mark? I have no birth-mark."

Then Callista sprang upon the child like a fury, and with a single gesture, tore off the light wrap that hung over her shoulders.

"Look!" she cried. "See whether she has the sign of the crown or not."

The only person who had remained calm during this last incident was the Patriarch himself, who, before seating Odette on the throne, had taken the precaution to satisfy himself that she did indeed bear the sacred mark. In his opinion, the sign should not be shown to the people until the coronation day, but events were too strong for him, and he realized that it was necessary to allow them to judge for themselves.

"She has the birth-mark. We may rejoice, for the birth-mark is there."

Then the people made a rush forward. They wanted to see the sacred sign. They wanted to see this seal of a divine union, to have proof that the birth-mark was not an illusion, nor a tattooed mark, nor a clever counterfeit, but in very truth a birth-mark which was one with the flesh and born of the flesh.

And when they had verified the falsity of the accusation, they turned to him who had tried to deceive them, but he had disappeared.

CHAPTER XLIV

ODETTE AND ZINA

ODETTE was taken to the women's apartments. Bowed down by the weight of her amazing experience, terrified by the hideous mystery of this royal birth, in which nature appeared to have become an accomplice, she allowed herself to be dressed by the women, as insensible as a doll dressed by children for amusement.

And now she lay on cushions in the darkness of the old palace, which had become silent again.

She stood up and walked towards the fountain whose plaintive music bewitched her. Her bare feet, round which slavish fingers had placed gold bangles, stole over the polished flagstones and drew her, almost against her will, to the charmed basin.

The basin was of some size and lay between marble steps, and the water looked as black as a grave, the water which would presently close in upon her, lifeless and cold, while the fountain with its water lily would continue to sing above her head its cool, silvery song: "She is dead, is Odette, the impetuous young girl from Camargue, whom the witchcraft of the little old hag of a woman rendered more languid than an eastern idol. She is dead because he to whom she had given her heart did not love her."

That, too, was written in the book of fate. Odette placed her foot on the first step which led to the depths of this black lake filled with the waters of oblivion. . . . Oh, how cold it was! How icy-cold it was! And

281

then, how it gave forth the odor of death. . . . Death
had seemed so beautiful from afar. . . . But courage
was needed to face death. . . . She had never been
lacking in courage.

She took another step, murmuring softly Jean's name.
Her heart leaped wildly, as though it could escape from
her breast, like the last flutter of a bird dying in its
nest. She too, she too would die, since Jean did not love
her. . . . And then a hand drew her back and she caught
the sound of a sob.

It was the little old witch of a woman.

"Come, you shall not die. I will show you someone
you love."

Odette opened her great eyes in wonder.

"You will show me Jean?"

"I will show you Jean at once."

"You really mean it? At once? But I don't trust
you, you little old witch of a woman. I know that you
can do many things because the *heka* (the devil) is in
you, and you are always telling fortunes. Are you going
to show me Jean in a glass of water or in the tea-leaves
in a cup? Look! Jean is there, down in the water. I
see his face as it used to be when he loved me, and I am
going to join him."

"My dove, he still loves you. Swear that you will
live if I show him to you."

"If you show him to me alive and he loves me, I swear
to live, Zina," said Odette, breathing unevenly, and clasping her hands in a gesture of hope and entreaty.

"Why shouldn't he love you?" went on Zina hurriedly,
leading Odette away under cover of a deafening flow
of words. . . . "If you only knew what he has done—
all that he has done for you!"

"But where is he? Where is he?"

"Here."

"Take me to him. Oh dear, I feel now as if I were

going to die of joy. But can I believe it? Can I believe it?"

"Hush! Calm yourself, my little dove. Alas, he is in prison."

"In prison. Poor thing! But why is he in prison?"

"Because, like a madman, like the bravest of men, he hurried after you to rescue you and was taken prisoner. That was how he showed that he didn't love you!"

"Oh, my Jean," she cried, bursting into tears, but tears of joy this time. "You will save him, for if you don't they will have to put me in prison too. Besides, I am the queen. I am the *queyra*. They must do as I tell them. . . . Stop kissing my feet, you dear little old witch of a woman, and take me to Jean, so that I may release him from his cell! . . . Now, tell me, is it really true that they have put him in prison? You are not making game of me?"

She continued to chatter. Life, which had been strangely dormant for so many days, had come back and was flowing in her veins once more.

She was a queer creature was Zina, pretending to be Odette's slave and yet doing with her what she willed. A look, a word, was enough to transform the handsome child. Zina had the power to change her into a statue. At one time, Odette felt herself turned to stone under the cold gaze of the terrible little old woman, and at another she felt herself yielding to her in all the innocence of her heart, as though Zina were her real mother. Her resistance was but the caprice of a child and powerless against the occult power which mastered her, even when the little old woman was not present and walls separated them.

Zina took her hand and she let herself be led through dark passages, whose twists and turns were almost unknown even to those who were familiar with the mysterious places of the palace. She had to stoop low, descend and mount many stairs, and descend again into the bowels of the earth, in order to make her way along the huge foundations of the temple; foundations which dated from the times of the Pelasgians, and upon which civilizations, long since disappeared, had erected their first sanctuaries. In this way, Zina and Odette reached the dungeons, enclosed with iron rails like cages, in which were incarcerated prisoners condemned to death. Outside one of these cages Andréa stood on guard.

CHAPTER XLV

THE KISS IN THE TOMB

SO far Odette had not been lacking in courage, but her courage was in reality an expression of joy: she was about to see Jean.

Zina threw a light veil over Odette's face, and led her along at a quickened pace, but it was not at a moment when she was hoping to see Jean that she would allow her eyes to be veiled. She tore off the wrap and uttered a cry of horror. Almost immediately afterwards she caught sight of Andréa. He seemed to be the all-powerful guardian of the inferno. . . . Her horror gave way to fear.

Zina gathered her to her breast and placed her arms round her, while Andréa took a step forward, and in a threatening voice asked the old woman:

"What are you doing here with the *queyra?*"

"I've come to ask you to unlock the door of the cell in which the stranger is imprisoned," was the calm reply.

"You must be mad, Zina," exclaimed Andréa. "What is your object in asking such a thing?"

"I would like her to see him before he dies. It would be a kindness to both of them and St. Sarah would be pleased."

Andréa burst out laughing. . . . Zina bent forward and whispered a few words in his ear. . . . Andréa ceased laughing, but his face wore a smile, and the smile was more hideous than his laugh. He took a bunch of keys from his belt and, pointing to one of them, handed her the bunch and walked quickly away.

285

When his footsteps had died down Zina turned to Odette.

"Don't be afraid. He's gone," she said, and she carried rather than led her to Jean's cell.

Zina now kept watch in the darkness of the passage in which dwelt so much anguish and torture. . . . She stood on guard while Jean and Odette mingled their tears of happiness and despair.

"And I thought you didn't love me any more," sighed the poor child in a faltering voice.

"Do you not know, my love, that anyone who is put in these dungeons never comes out again?"

"But I shall make you king," she cried.

"My love, hasn't Zina told you?"

"What? What? She hasn't said a word. But you must tell me. I must know everything. I am the queen. I am entitled to know everything."

"Well, they have imprisoned me here for life."

"Don't say that. It's ridiculous. I am the only one to command here. What sentence did they pass on you?"

"They sentenced me to death."

She uttered a cry.

"Don't! Don't! You are my Jean. You are my love. They may have sentenced you when I was not here, but now that I am here everything will be changed. I have only to say the word. If you knew how these people worship me! They fall at my feet. They kiss the hem of my robe. They shout 'Hosannah!' when I pass. . . . I have but to lift a finger. . . . Oh, it was a fine idea of de Lauriac's to bring me here! Providence, you see, willed it so. The good God is with us. It was written, as the dotards in the cathedral say. It was written that I should save your life, my dear Jean. . . . So they sentenced you to death! Well, they're going to be nicely disappointed. I can picture to myself de Lauriac's face when he knows! But kiss me and don't look so glum. Do I look glum? . . . Oh, and to satisfy my curiosity, tell me what sort of death they sentenced you to?"

She asked him the question with a smile.

"Zina!" she cried.

The old woman came up.

"Run and get some bread—milk—preserves   Anything you can find."

"I promise to fetch something for him after you've left," said Zina, scared. "But I must first take you back to your apartment. Someone may have heard you calling."

"But I don't want to go at once. Besides, I won't go without Jean. . . . Fetch the Patriarch and the Council."

"Silence," ordered Zina, straining her ears to catch any sound from the underground passage. "Someone is coming. I hear footsteps. They're coming down the stairs. Take care!"

She made another movement of her head and once more dived into the darkness to keep watch.

Odette threw herself into Jean's arms:

"To die of starvation!" She was crying now on his shoulder. "Oh, my dearest, I swear to eat nothing until they've given you something to eat. If you die, I shall die too. May my father forgive me!"

Jean gave a start.

"Your father, my Odette! Don't you know?"

"What do you mean? My father? Tell me about him."

And as Jean said nothing:

"Your silence makes me fear the worst. If it were not so, you would say something. Do speak, Jean," she entreated in a smothered voice. "I didn't think that any other misfortune could happen to me."

Jean told her the story of the terrible tragedy at Lavardens.

"Nothing is left to us but our love," she murmured.

.   .   .   .

Andréa had gone to see Callista. She was far from expecting him, for she knew that he had volunteered to keep guard over Jean and be responsible for him.

Stretched at full length on the carpet, she was drugging herself with perfumes burning in the ornamental vases. Her thoughts were of the condemned man and not of his warder, of whom she stood in greater fear every day and whose fierce love filled her with dread, or rather with a strange misgiving, which sent a shudder through her whenever she saw him. She undoubtedly hated him still, but she no longer despised him. She pictured him as he was in Temesvar woods with a knife in his hand, ready to slay her if she continued to repel him. A casual incident had saved her, but at that moment on that day he was her master.

"It's you," she said in a sulky voice, when she recognized him in the shadow as he drew near. "What do you want with me now?"

"You don't seem very pleased to see your future husband," uttered Andréa coldly, sitting down beside her, crossing his legs, and picking up the narghile which she omitted to offer him.

"We are not married yet," she said curtly.

"I bet that I should have been more welcome had I given you the message: 'The stranger refuses to die until he has seen you.'"

Callista rose as though she had received an electric shock.

"Did he say that?"

"May I never see the face of *Debla Temeata* (the mother of God) if I am not telling the truth," he replied. "The stranger asked me three times. Apparently his last hope is in you, Callista, or," he added with a grin, "perhaps he genuinely loves you, and wants to ask your

forgiveness for the despair which has taken possession
of your heart. Anyway, the cursed fellow is longing to
see you."

"No more speeches, Andréa. What was your answer?"

"What do you suppose my answer was? He appealed
to the kindness of my heart. I am a baby when anyone
touches my feelings. I answered that I would pass his
request on to you, and you were free to do as you liked.
Of course, I knew that you would be pleased. You will
reward me for it, perhaps, with a smile, and for a smile
from you I would sacrifice my mother."

"All right. All right. We'll see about that later on.
So you're going to allow me to go to him?"

"Have I ever refused you anything?"

"Are you really going to take me to him?"

"Yes, now he is condemned to die," returned Andréa
with emphasis, rising to his feet and making a movement to set out.

She accompanied him in a state of great excitement.
Suppose it were true that Jean still loved her!

And they descended to the dungeons.

It was the sound of their footsteps which Zina had
caught on the steps, but she assumed that Andréa was
returning alone. It was she who had suggested the
diabolical idea of letting Odette go to Jean in his cell, as
an act of revenge on Callista, who still loved Jean, and
as a cruel trick with which Andréa could amuse himself
afterwards by telling Callista the story, a story which
would disgust her with aliens for the rest of her life.
But Zina did not imagine for a moment that Andréa
would have the audacity to bring Callista to witness the
scene. She said to herself: "Meantime Andréa will be
making love to Callista, and he will have a good laugh
when he thinks of the trick he is playing her."

Zina was terrified when she saw Callista with him.
But before she had time to utter a word, Andréa sent

her sprawling to the ground, after taking the bunch of
keys from her, and they went on to the cell.

A mysterious glimmer of light which emanated from
no one knew where broke on the moldy walls, and thrust
its beam between two bars. . . . Two forms behind the
bars were locked in each other's arms. . . . The scene
was suggestive of a mezzotint, powerful and yet extremely delicate—etched by a Reynolds. . . . And it was
a sight which filled Callista with rage.

CHAPTER XLVI

THE PATRIARCH'S FIRST AND SECOND PLAN

CALLISTA almost swooned, for it is possible to swoon with rage as well as with happiness. But when the first feeling of surprise was over, she recovered her strength and inclusively threw herself against the bars which she shook in a sort of frenzy.

She saw before her the dismay of the surprised lovers; she heard behind her Andréa's laughter and Zina's cries. And then came the sound of warders running up hot-foot to discover the cause of the tumult.

Andréa hastened to open the cell door. Doubtless he thought that Callista would wreak her fury on Jean. It was an error of his somewhat crude psychology, for a woman's anger is always vented upon the woman in the case. . . . Callista made a rush at Odette, but she encountered Jean, who stepped between them.

Odette did not flinch—far from it. She flew at Callista, deprived for the time being of her power of doing mischief by Jean, whose hands she bit. . . . The struggle continued until the warders came up, and taking Odette out of the cell, carried her off in spite of her cries. . . . The cell door was closed once more on Jean.

Callista, eager for revenge, turned round on Andréa, who put the blame on Zina as alone responsible for the plot. And then it seemed from Zina's shrieks as though she were being cut in pieces. Meantime Odette was shut up in her apartment, and the Patriarch informed of the occurrence.

He came to her an hour later, thinking, doubtless, that

291

by this time she would have recovered her calmness. De Lauriac was with him.

They found her crouching on the divan in a passion and in the sulks. . . . Not far away a number of plates and dishes and glasses lay smashed on the floor; the dishes containing her food were scattered on every side.

The Patriarch gazed at the results of the royal anger with a twinkle in his eye, and it was with the utmost respect that he asked the *queyra*, de Lauriac acting as interpreter, if she were not hungry.

"I should think I was hungry!" returned Odette, "but I will not eat anything. I want to be left in peace. I intend to die of starvation like Jean."

She lifted her adorable face slightly, which wore a look of obstinacy, and threw words at de Lauriac which expressed very clearly her state of mind towards him.

"And, you understand, I shall die happy because I've seen Jean and know that he still loves me. And now you can go! Go, I say. I order you to go. I have nothing more to say to you or your Patriarchs. This is the door! I insist on your doing as I say. I am the *queyra*."

De Lauriac, utterly helpless, translated her words to the Patriarch. But the latter had already grasped their meaning, for her voice and gesture left nothing to the imagination. He shrugged his shoulders and, speaking very calmly, said:

"You will live, because what is written must be fulfilled." After that he withdrew full of admiration for the young queen.

"She is a true *gitana*," he said to de Lauriac when they were alone. "She is undoubtedly of gypsy birth. It is a delight to see and hear her."

"I feel less pleasure than you in that respect," returned de Lauriac bitterly, "and I cannot help being surprised at your delight, for after all, I don't see how the prediction is to be . . ."

"I observe with satisfaction," interrupted the Patriarch, "that the sacred writings occupy your mind. Well, there are two ways of making them come true. The first way depends upon you."

"What is that?" asked de Lauriac with an eagerness which may easily be understood.

The Patriarch made no reply, but slipped into de Lauriac's hand the key to Odette's apartments.

De Lauriac bowed without speaking, and walked a few steps towards the apartments, and then stopping for a moment, turned to the Patriarch and said:

"You did not tell me what the second way was."

"I will tell you if the first does not succeed," returned the Patriarch.

De Lauriac went back to the *queyra's* apartments. He found no pleasure in entering them again. He imagined that the key which the Patriarch had placed in his hands was not yet the longed-for key of happiness. Even if his last conversation with Odette had not enlightened her he knew her too well to hope, however he approached her, for any change in her attitude towards him.

Odette was sobbing with rage on the divan at the far end of the room where she had taken refuge after the Patriarch had left her.

She was no longer thinking of de Lauriac. She had expressed herself to him once for all, and he must know that she could never be his wife, for she was promised to Jean, whose life she would save at all costs. When the door opened she hoped to see Zina, who in these last few days had proved to be her only ally, and she was startled to see de Lauriac again.

He came in silently and obsequiously, carefully locking the door behind him; then leisurely turned to her. She started up, retreating to the corner of the wall.

He took a step forward with hanging head and harsh expression.

"Don't come near me," she cried.

Then he looked up and saw her; saw a black shadow of a dark wrap which Zina had thrown over her shoulders before they started on their expedition in the underground passages. Under this ominous covering he beheld only a poor little waxen face with great eyes dilated by the dread of what was about to happen.

"I am not afraid of you," she returned, her teeth chattering with horror. "I have never been afraid of you."

"You have only to say the word, and you will never have a more devoted slave than myself."

"I don't want a slave. . . . Go! . . . Why have you come back. I turned you away. I don't want to see you again. . . . Go, or I shall cry out."

De Lauriac gave a wicked smile.

"You are smiling like a coward. . . . Don't come near me. Don't come beyond this carpet . . . or I swear . . ."

A long breast-pin with a jeweled head held her wrap in place. She had taken it out, and, pushing aside the wrap which covered her shoulders, pressed its steel point against her heart. . . . She was no longer trembling. She feared nothing. It was clear that she was not afraid to die.

De Lauriac stopped, and sat down with a hollow groan.

"How you must hate me," he said.

"You are a miserable wretch," she said. "Think of all your attempts to deceive me. . . . A conversation with my father, after he was dead! And all your lies about Jean!"

"That's true," he returned, shaking his head, "but

it was you who made me so. I was not like that years ago when you were in love with me."

"What nonsense you talk! I was never in love with you."

"Don't say that. Don't say that, Odette. Think of the time when I went away. Remember how grieved you were. Just think how happy we were together when we galloped our horses through the vineyards until we were out of breath; when Camargue existed only for us two. You were delighted to be with me then."

"You dare say that! . . . You . . . You . . ." she cried indignantly.

He lowered 'iis head dejectedly, and said in a strained voice.

"I would have fled to the other end of the world with you, had you been willing. But you spurned me. Then I brought you here, convinced that these people would discover you in any case, and you cannot fight against your fate."

"All the same you didn't forget that it was written that I should be given to the man who brought me back here."

"That's true, Odette. . . . It is written that we should be married, but I had no need to read the book to know that. The fact was written in my heart on the day when, for the first time, you applauded my triumphs at the branding fêtes in Les Saintes Maries. Yes," he repeated, without lifting his head, "we are bound to be married, and nothing you can do will prevent it."

"Never . . . Never . . . I swear it."

He fell on his knees and with clasped hands went on:

"And I, Odette, swear that when we are married I will respect you as though I were the humblest of your servants. I, Hubert de Lauriac, the king of Camargue herdsmen, swear to come near you only as your slave. . . . A sign from you and I will go away."

"Then go away now," she cried, incensed by a declaration which might have roused her pity, but in which, with the cruelty of youth, she could see nothing but hypocritical chatter intended to disarm her.

Then de Lauriac rose to his feet with a savage look.

"Is that your last word?"

"Yes, my last word before my last deed."

She brandished the long breast-pin. He cast a fierce glance at her, a hoarse cry broke in his throat, he clenched his fists, and his hard face turned crimson as though he were about to have a fit. . . . She thought he would fly at her, but he turned quickly and went out of the room. He was like a drunken man; and it was in this pitiable condition that he once more faced the Patriarch, into whose presence he had been taken.

"I see at once that the first plan has failed," said the Patriarch, gazing at him with a look of pity. Then with a peculiar smile, he added: "Give me back the key, my young friend."

De Lauriac threw down the key with a gesture which was anything but courteous.

"Calm yourself," said the Patriarch gently, "because if the first plan has succeeded only in putting you in this state, what will happen to you when you know what the second is?"

"I am here to ask you to tell me what your second plan is, and whether it depends upon me," growled de Lauriac.

"Unfortunately for you it does not depend upon you, my dear friend."

The Patriarch rose as he uttered this enigmatic sentence and made a motion with his hand. A man came in and showed de Lauriac out, increasingly distraught at the Patriarch's change of manner.

As he entered the apartments in the palace which had been reserved for him, the first person whom he encountered was Callista. She seemed as excited as he was cast down. She had lifted her veil so that he might recognize her.

"Monsieur de Lauriac," she began in a low voice, after making sure that they could not be overheard, "you know who I am. You love Odette. I hate her. I will do for you from hatred what you wish to do for yourself from love. I want you to marry Odette. You must not hide from me what happened between you and the Patriarch. What did he say?"

De Lauriac stared at Callista for a moment. She too was an interested party, was Callista. The thing that the Octopus had promised to do through jealousy of Rouletabille, Callista proposed to do through jealousy of Jean. But, when all was said, neither the one nor the other had helped him in any way. He had heard nothing further from Madame de Meyrens. And what could Callista do for him? He shrugged his shoulders and plucked up courage to laugh at himself.

"Everybody wishes me to marry Odette," he said, "but the unfortunate thing is that Odette doesn't wish to marry me! Faced with this fact neither you nor I nor the sacred writings are of any avail."

"What about the Patriarch? What did he say to you?" she asked impatiently.

"He has, it seems, two plans by which the prediction in the book may be fulfilled."

"What are they?"

"Well, he placed the first in my hands, and it failed," returned de Lauriac with a sinister grin.

"What about the second? Did he tell you what the second was?"

"He told me that it did not concern me."

"Well, I am here to discuss it with you. . . . But, first of all, I must know . . ."

"You must know that Odette is ready to kill herself

rather than give way. That is my present position. . . . I am willing to listen to you. . . ."

"Let me tell you, then, that before giving you the key of Odette's apartments the Elders met in council, and decided to provide Odette with a husband as foretold in the book. If that husband cannot be Hubert de Lauriac, then it will be another . . . that's all."

De Lauriac rose to his feet, and with a fierce gesture seized Callista's hand.

"Another? . . . What do you mean?"

"Well, *the* other whom she loves."

"Jean?"

"Yes, Jean, because she won't have anyone else."

"I refuse to believe it," gasped de Lauriac. "Look here, have you come here to make a fool of me? Mind what you're saying!"

"Nothing is impossible if Jean will consent to live here as Prince Consort. . . . They will arrange for Odette to escape for Jean to bring her back here. It's as easy as can be. . . . You see, he won't hesitate when it's a question between Odette and death."

De Lauriac gripped Callista's hand.

"Callista, you didn't come here to tell me this without having something in your mind—some scheme."

"My scheme is as simple as theirs," she said quietly. "Jean must die to-morrow morning."

CHAPTER XLVII

THE LIBRARIAN

Extract from Rouletabille's diary:

WHAT a turn this Sever Turn gives me! If we ever come forth from it alive it will be a piece of luck. I am well aware that I have a Romany gem which acts as an 'Open Sesame' in this diabolical maze, but I have already made pretty free with it, to say nothing of the fact that as we all know, it is much easier to get into a maze than out of it. The chief trouble in this dreadful business is that there is a sign, which is disastrous to us—as disastrous as the other is useful—I mean the sign of the crown. Whatever one may say it exists in every deed. And it is by no means invisible. It is even bigger than a chick-pea. It consists of a royal crown, very plainly marked, and is about the size of the top of one's little finger—a royal crown which our poor Odette bears above the left shoulder-blade.

"That strictly speaking she had never seen it, may be conceded, for Lavardens is not a place where persons have at command a play of mirrors such as are met with in Paris in the dressing-rooms of coquettes; but that no one should have enlightened her on this peculiar mark, that her maid should never have breathed a word about it, that Estève should have lied to me on this point—these things require consideration.

"I must think it out. I now have the time. . . . I barely had time to make myself scarce after the scene in the temple! . . . To be sure, had the gypsies been less

299

absorbed by their *queyra,* my life would not have been worth a, moment's purchase, but in the language of strategists, I had taken the precaution to assure a line of retreat, and I had already located a certain winding staircase inside the third pillar on the left, by means of which I was enabled to effect a speedy retirement.

"In this way I knew I could reach an emplacement whence I could slide down into a small yard connected directly with the outside.

"There were about twenty steps to mount. My good or evil star willed that, at the moment when I rushed to the staircase, I should hear above my head the tramp of a heavy footstep, and instead of mounting the stairs I descended them. I descended them until I found myself in the basement, and as I continued to hear the threatening footstep above me, I slipped into the first passage which presented itself. . . . Through passages and subways I reached, in a few minutes, the Palace of the Patriarchs. This huge structure must be as old as the hills. At all events it justifies everything that may have been written on the subject of underground architecture in mediæval castles, and also on the precautions which the lords of these castles took to enable them, in crucial times, to dive down into the vaults, and if needs be to take flight into the surrounding country.

"Of course, it was sinister to a degree down there, with its peculiar odor of sulphur which I have never experienced anywhere else. The subterranean part of Sever Turn is a very devil's cave! But I have seen many worse things in my time. . . . Here and there was the dim light from a lantern hanging to the wall; and then suddenly I came upon a door, or rather a grating, behind which I could discern a staircase from which I concluded that this passage was frequently used. In this hope I awaited events, hiding in a small recess into which I crept.

"I waited an hour. . . . Yes, I waited until some one came and opened the grating which divided me from Odette. I waited, leaning, as far as possible, on the right end of my judgment, which for a moment had almost eluded me, but upon which I now lean again more firmly than ever.

"And there was something else upon which I leaned not less firmly, to wit, my revolver, for at last I heard the tramp of footsteps once more.

"Upon my word, here comes a dignified old man who is not entirely unknown to me. Bless me, if it isn't the worthy librarian, the distinguished linguist, the chief scholar in Sever Turn. . . . He is doubtless returning home after the ceremony for he is still clad in gala dress —a long loose vestment with wide sleeves and a cap with fillets—a dress which imparts to all these Elders of the Council the appearance of Byzantine demons. . . . And behold the magnificent finery which would not disfigure an exhibition in the Faubourg Poissonnière, and may be of some service to me until it becomes an agreeable memory! . . .

"Shall we be able to come to an understanding? I hope so for his sake.

"It is worthy of remark that these great dignitaries, notwithstanding the solemnity of their office, preserve in their demeanor and character an indefinable something suggestive of the cunning and raillery peculiar to the race. I had already observed the same thing even in the Patriarch himself. Though he is the Patriarch it must not be forgotten that he is the patron saint of the *balogards,* a tribe of gypsies who have no equal among the entire human race for deceit. As to the gray-beard for whom I waited, his expression had nothing formidable in it. It proclaimed a knave, rather than a rascal, it was marked more by craft than cruelty. His dark keen eyes, his bold look, the sardonic smile which he invariably

wore, imparted to his countenance a subtle air which reassured me. Before he became a librarian, he was, perhaps, a horse dealer. At all events he must have been
well known in the fairs and market places. Let us have
a chat with him. . . .

"Well, our worthy librarian straightway understood
us—my revolver and myself. He merely asked me to
bind him hand and foot, so that no accusation could be
brought against him of complicity in my project; and
he furnished me, thanks to his somewhat elaborate costume and his fillets, with the bonds essential for the
operation. He made me promise, too, when I had taken
him to the recess in which I had until then found refuge,
to come back to him as soon as I possibly could, and
return his vestment to which he seemed to attach some
value, and not to breathe a word about the incident if
subsequent events showed that it need not be noised
abroad.

"When I conceded all his stipulations he repaid me by
giving me, in addition to the key of the iron gate, certain information which I found very useful in wandering about this maze. . . . 'Good-by for the present,
and thank you.' "

At this point there is a blank in the diary, and then
come the following notes:

"I go everywhere without let or hindrance. . . .
Enormous excitement in the Palace. . . . Settling the
queyra comfortably in her apartments has put the house-
hold in a flutter. I take advantage of the confusion to
steal through these rooms. I reached them at the moment when Callista was 'doing for' Zina. She left her
lying outside the women's quarters, to all seeming dead.
If only she had not killed her outright! . . . No, she
still breathes. . . . These old women are wonderfully
tough! . . . I lift her up. I do my utmost for her.

She opens her eyes, and I make myself known to her.
" 'Each has in turn tended the other. You remember
New Wachter.'

"While I hastily dress the old woman's injuries, I
have a very interesting talk with her. She tells me what
happened in the condemned cell. . . . Poor Jean! . . .
But I must, as usual, think first of Odette. . . . And
Zina whom I support, leads me as best she can, through
the kitchens to the *queyra's* rooms. . . .

"I have seen Odette!"

Here a few lines have been carefully erased as often
happened when Rouletabille expressed too impulsively
his feelings with regard to Odette.

"I leave Odette with Zina in spite of her entreaties,
for Zina has aroused all her fears again. In truth, the
old woman with her loose and disordered hair, her bleeding wounds, her wild eyes which begin to hypnotize
Odette, is a terrifying sight. . . . I wanted to stay, but
it was she who turned me away: 'Go! Go! I need to
be alone with her.' And I fled so as no longer to hear
the poor child's wail of anguish, and her uneven breathing, no more able to withstand Zina's gaze than the dove
can resist the hawk's direct and penetrating eye."

Another blank and then:

"Callista again! I caught a glimpse of her as she
came away from a meeting with de Lauriac, who seems
to have taken up his abode here. They were joined by
an old woman of the same type as Zina, who kissed
Callista's hands and feet, while spluttering from her
toothless jaws a few raucous words like the croak of a
toad: 'You can be easy in your mind,' said Callista to
de Lauriac. 'As for her, she will anticipate our desires,
If she could make the foreigner die twice she wouldn't
let the opportunities slip.'

"It is obvious that I shall have to turn my attention to Jean. . . . Yes, we must strain every nerve to gain time. . . ."

A blank space and then:

"I haven't wasted my night. . . . I risked everything to have two words with Jean through the grating of the condemned cell . . . two necessary words.

"This morning I saw the page-boy at the Hôtel des Balkans deliver a letter to de Lauriac. . . . Beware . . . beware of the Octopus!"

CHAPTER XLVIII

ONE WAY IN SEVER TURN OF DESPATCHING A PRISONER

ON the morning following the day so crowded with events, Monsieur Nicolas Tournesol was shaving in his room in the Hôtel des Balkans when his door was abruptly opened and Rouletabille made his appearance.

"Are you Monsieur Nicolas Tournesol?"

"Monsieur Rouletabille!"

"Ah, you know me."

"I know everybody, and it would be very surprising if I didn't know the most famous journalist in Europe. . . . Won't you sit down? I saw you in the temple yesterday, and I am very glad to see you to-day, let me tell you, for I rather thought that I should never see you again! You know as well as I do, monsieur, that these people are anything but well disposed towards you, and I cannot too strongly advise you to take the air."

"The air?"

"Yes, take the air—do a bunk, if you know what I mean."

"Oh, yes, yes. . . . Very nice of you. . . . I beg your pardon."

"Not at all—a slight joke of mine. I am the last of the commercial travelers. . . . I sell everything. . . . I am the channel of communication between the manufacturer, the agent and the wholesale merchant; the *vade semper* of the duplicate entry, the unsaleable article, and the surplus stock. Have a drink, will you? . . . May I ask to what I owe the pleasure of this visit?"

"A serious matter, monsieur. I have come to see you in your capacity as a Frenchman. You represent France here, Monsieur Tournesol."

"Good lord," exclaimed Tournesol, forgetting to boast for the first time in his life. "I represent still more an excellent brand of champagne."

"I will come to the point, and you will at once understand me. As you were present yesterday, I need not tell you that Monsieur Jean de Santierne, a Frenchman, was sentenced by the Grand Council to die of starvation."

"I was not present when the thing took place, but I know the young man. I arrived at the temple while the people were acclaiming their young queen, and you were raising your voice in a vigorous protest."

"Two abominable crimes are about to be committed."

"That is quite likely," said Monsieur Tournesol, arranging his tie, and making grimaces in the glass. "Everything is possible where state affairs are concerned."

"I have just come from the Wallachian Consul, and he told me, as you do now, that everything is possible where state affairs are concerned. It was an answer which, I may say, in no way surprised me."

"You are right there, monsieur. If we were to interfere in the internal affairs of every country, international intercourse would be impossible. Trade would be at a standstill."

"The sale of champagne would be interrupted."

"You needn't tell me that, worse luck! Politics have already nearly ruined me. Luckily they have recovered the queen."

Rouletabille rose to his feet and made a movement to leave the room. Tournesol caught hold of him.

"Don't go like that. If I can be of any use to you I assure you . . ."

"You cannot be of any use to me. When I left the

Wallachian Consul I inquired at the hotel if there was a Frenchman in the town: 'Yes, there is one—Monsieur Tournesol,' was the reply. Well, they were mistaken. There isn't a Frenchman here, though there is an international commercial traveler. As I don't want to buy anything from you, I'm going. Good-by, Monsieur Nicolas Tournesol."

"Don't, I entreat you, leave me like this," cried Monsieur Tournesol, overwhelmed by remorse, for in reality he had a good heart beneath his somewhat cynical manner. "I agree that what is being done is abominable, and I wish to be your friend. I wish to help you whatever the consequences may be to myself. What must I do?"

Rouletabille turned back and shook his hand.

"You are a very decent fellow," he said, "and I don't hesitate to confide in you. I understand your position. It so happens that without your being in any way responsible, your interests directly conflict with ours."

"Don't speak of my interests. I am ashamed of remembering them when it's a matter of saving the lives of two young people—both French. As sure as my name is Tournesol I am your man."

"I entirely rely on you. A Madame de Meyrens is here, isn't she?"

"A delightful woman with whom I am on rather good terms. Well, I have no wish to be indiscreet. I will not hide from you that if I am rather careful in my personal appearance it is because . . ."

While speaking, Monsieur Tournesol poured a little scent on his handkerchief.

"Well, Madame de Meyrens is my worst enemy."

"The devil she is! Now that's most unfortunate."

"If you were better acquainted with the lady, you would wonder what she's doing in Sever Turn."

"To tell you the truth, I am not a very inquisitive

person, and as long as a woman is charming and doesn't mind being told so . . ."

"I see. I see. But as I know that she is here to bring about the ruin of me and my friends, you will understand that I look upon the affair in a different light. Don't be jealous if I venture to ask you to tell me what room this charming lady is occupying, and if I go and see her and ask for an explanation which I hope may be a final one."

"The fact that you had only to push my door to come in here, shows that it was ajar, and the fact that it was ajar while I was shaving, shows that I was keeping an eye on Madame de Meyrens' door," returned Monsieur Tournesol frankly, but with a touch of regret, for after all, Rouletabille's appearance would disturb many of his plans. "Her door is the second on the other side of the passage."

"Thanks," said Rouletabille. "Whatever you may hear, I beg of you not to interfere."

"Oh, I shan't hear a thing. I'm going downstairs in a moment, for I should be sorry to stand in your way. I only ask you not to tell this lady who, as I said, has been charming to me, that I gave away where her room was. . . . But, in fact, I don't suppose that you called on me merely to get this information, which you could have obtained from any of the servants."

"That is so, Monsieur Tournesol. I wanted to place this letter in your hands for safe custody."

Rouletabille gave him a packet of some size, carefully sealed, bearing the inscription. "To the Minister of Foreign Affairs, Paris. To be delivered personally."

"You must know," explained Rouletabille, speaking very calmly, "that since my arrival here I have not been able to communicate with the outside world, and in the decisive struggle which we are about to wage with this effete barbarism, it is ten to one that my friends and I will go under. Thanks to you, my country will be in-

formed of the crime committed against three of its subjects, and the world will know the fate which befell
Monsieur Jean de Santierne, Mademoiselle Odette de
Lavardens and Monsieur Joseph Rouletabille, your humble servant."

Touched by the trust reposed in him, Monsieur Tournesol was about to utter a few heartfelt words, but Rouletabille had turned on his heel, and was already knocking
at Madame de Meyrens' door. Tournesol saw him enter
the room.

"Well, now, something very disagreeable is going to
happen, but it is no business of mine. My mind is with
Rouletabille, but my heart is with Madame de Meyrens.
All said, I have no reason to be very pleased with my
morning."

After putting the precious missive under lock and key,
Tournesol went downstairs to the bar, feeling by no
means anxious to be brought into a matter in which, he
thought, his good nature had already involved him too
deeply.

He had consumed two or three cocktails pursuing
vaguely his train of thought when, through the open
window which gave on to the medley of the caravanserai,
he caught sight of Madame de Meyrens standing under
an archway before a display of silk goods, bargaining
with a Syrian Jew over the price of some piece of
material.

"Hullo, the explanation is 'over," said Tournesol to
himself.

He was on the point of joining her when he saw her
leave the Syrian Jew and touch the shoulder of a stranger
who had some difficulty in clearing a passage for himself
through the crowd. . . . He seemed, moreover, to be
making for the hotel. . . . The two at once entered the
hotel. Madame de Meyrens had turned down her veil,
and they were walking quickly. They passed close to

Monsieur Tournesol without as much as seeing him, so engrossed were they. And there was not the shadow of a doubt in Monsieur Tournesol's mind that Madame de Meyrens had taken the stranger to her room.

"I am the only one not to go to her room," said the luckless Monsieur Tournesol to himself. And then suddenly he struck his forehead: "Why, I know the silly ass! It's the man who brought back the *queyra*. What can Madame de Meyrens have to do with that impostor?"

The first thing that Madame de Meyrens said to de Lauriac when they were in her room, after carefully closing the door, was not in the nature of a compliment.

"I asked you to come and see me because I know what is happening at the Palace, and you do nothing but blunder. You will never win Odette by force, my friend."

"Neither by force nor by another way, I verily believe," returned de Lauriac bitterly, "but we shall have our revenge."

"What good is revenge going to do you if you lose the battle?" objected the Octopus. "I will tell you how to win Odette. You have only to say to her: 'Jean is condemned to die a most frightful death. Every form of torture will be inflicted on him, but if you consent to become my wife his life shall be saved. I will at once have him set at liberty.'"

De Lauriac leapt to his feet as she uttered these last words.

"If only it is not too late!"

"What do you mean?"

"Callista is to give him some poisoned bread this morning."

CHAPTER XLIX

"REVENGE IS SWEET"

DE LAURIAC made a dash to leave the room after the Octopus had given her advice which filled him with a new hope. Madame de Meyrens barred the way.

"Calm yourself, Monsieur de Lauriac," she said. "If Callista is the only person who is seeking to do away with Jean, he is not yet dead! She is torturing him, but you will see that she will none the less find some means of saving him. Give de Santierne poisoned bread! Why, at the last moment she will poison herself. Wait and see!"

"You don't know her. She thirsts now for vengeance. What if I told you that the thing was done this morning?"

"What thing?"

"At the instance of Callista poisoned bread was taken to Jean."

"What then?" questioned the Octopus.

"Jean refused to touch the bread."

"Well, that's all the better for you. Why this excitement? You see yourself that there is still hope?"

"But unfortunately you don't know what Callista has planned. When she discovered that her first attempt was a failure, she decided to repeat it by sending Jean the bread with a message from Odette."

"And did Callista send the message to him?"

"She must have done so by now."

"Well, go at once," said the Octopus with a shudder.

311

Monsieur Nicolas Tournesol, who had remained standing rather dejectedly at the bar with his fourth cocktail before him, did not fail to observe with a certain satisfaction the reappearance of the strange person who had been shut up with Madame de Meyrens, for Monsieur Tournesol felt himself increasingly attracted by her in spite of all that he had heard against her.

The stranger crossed the room almost at a run and made a dash through the thick of the crowd in the caravanserai, pushing aside and drawing down upon himself the curses of a gypsy mob who were watching two gamblers settling their differences and even their debts with the knife. Then he mounted his horse and rode down every obstacle that stood in his path.

Just then Monsieur Tournesol observed Rouletabille standing beside him.

"He seems in a bit of a hurry does this gentleman," he said, pointing to de Lauriac, who was being followed by the shouts of the populace. "But what about yourself, you look very pale? What's the matter?"

"The matter is that I have just overheard a conversation between Madame de Meyrens and that villain," returned Rouletabille in a lugubrious voice. "I want you to know who this man is so that if later on things go badly and I am not here, you may be able to give your evidence. His name is Hubert de Lauriac, and he is well known in Camargue. . . . As you were present at the *queyra's* arrival I need say nothing about that. But I must tell you, if you have not already guessed it, that he is assisted in his nefarious plot by the woman whom you consider so charming—Madame de Meyrens."

Extract from Rouletabille's diary:

"At the moment I can do no more than bow to fate. With Odette on the one hand and Jean on the other, fate

must take its course. They are either dead or in safety.
I am at the end of my tether. Either I have succeeded
in the attempt that I made yesterday or my effort proved
fruitless. Why should I be in so much of a hurry?
Alas, I fear the worst. It did not occur to me that they
would conceive the infernal idea of asking Odette for
that letter. Did Jean send the food away in spite of that
letter? Everything depends upon that. . . . I still hope
so. . . . When I learnt of Callista's and de Lauriac's
horrible intention, and had the luck last night to speak to
Jean for a few moments through the grating, I said to
him: 'Don't touch any meal that may be brought to you
in secret. They are trying to poison you.' But if they
take food to him with a letter from Odette what will he
do? Perhaps all is over even now. . . . And Jean's
death means Odette's death. She will never again call
me to her assistance. She will never again cry: 'Help,
little Zo!'

"I have, I feel, the mind of a fatalist. It seems to me
that I, too, am sailing between life and death with an
appalling indifference. It is all one to me now that I
have done my utmost. What a strange fate! Odette and
Jean's safety lies now in de Lauriac's hands. . . . If
only he is not too late!"

At that very moment de Lauriac arrived at the Palace
like a whirlwind, and made a dash for Callista, who refused to see him, but he forced his way in despite the
protests of excited servants. He scarcely recognized the
woman before him with her wild eyes, her stony face,
her inert, motionless body lying flat on the floor like a
statue that has been thrown down. She riveted him with
a gaze that burned with unutterable hatred. He comprehended that the crime had been committed, and she would
never forgive him for bringing about Jean's death.

"Is it over?" he cried, gasping for breath.

She made no reply. She did not stir. But for the scorching look in her eyes he might have thought that she was a corpse. And, indeed, after all, perhaps she had poisoned herself, and was waiting for her own end while Jean lay dying.

"We have missed everything through our own fault," he cried. "We have been foolish. I ought to have promised Odette safety and liberty for Jean if she would give in. Is it too late?"

She shot up like an arrow from her couch of beflowered rugs and cushions on which she was stretched in anguish, and called and gave orders to her women, who went out in a panic. And an under servant with heavy eyelids, drooping lip and obsequious movements, wearing a cap turned down over his ears, came in. And then they knew: Jean had read Odette's letter and taken the bread. He had hidden it under the straw in his cell for, at that moment, a warder and Andréa hove in sight.

Callista uttered the same cry as Madame de Meyrens.

"Go at once," she said in a hoarse voice. "Denounce him to the warder so that the bread may be taken away from him. If he has eaten it, you are a dead man."

Jean at that moment, perceiving that the warder had walked a few steps in the darksome passage, read Odette's letter once more:

"MY DEAREST,—We must not give way to despair. We are not without friends even in this benighted country. I am able to send you a little food. I am told that you refuse to eat anything. But I order you to eat. You must live for my sake as I am living for yours. God will not forsake us. I will appeal to the people if the Patriarch will not listen to me. I am the *queyra*. You, too, must do as I say. The whole thing, my Jean, is but a frightful dream. Don't forget that there is someone who is not far away from us. I have confidence in him. I love you!"

Jean kissed the letter, slipped it into his breast pocket, and dived under the straw for the bread. Then he began to eat. . . .

CHAPTER L

THE CHOICE

CALLISTA and Andréa were loaded with honors for the craft with which they had rescued the *queyra* from the aliens and brought her to Sever Turn. Callista, who had conducted the undertaking, was treated like a princess, and given apartments in the Palace and a troop of women to wait upon her. Her authority was considerable; her protection was sought; and nothing was so greatly feared as to be in her bad looks. She was as quickly obeyed in her desire to save Jean, as when she found, without difficulty, accomplices in the crime which she had prepared, but which, when she learnt that it had been committed, filled her with despair.

She waited in a dead silence and an agony of dread for the rascally servant to come back with news from the cell. As soon as she saw the man, however, she knew that Jean's life was safe, or he would never have dared to show himself again, though he had acted as her faithful slave.

This man had reached Jean's cell in time to snatch the poisoned bread from his hand; indeed he had barely tasted it. But Callista demanded full particulars, for she wanted to make certain that the prisoner's health had not suffered.

Then, sending every one away except de Lauriac, she turned a radiant face to him. Just before she had loathed him for driving her to take Jean's life, and now she was immeasurably grateful to him for contriving

a plan which would bring about even yet a happy ending. Odette would consent to marry de Lauriac, and
Jean would be thrown into her arms—Jean whom she
would herself set free and acquaint with Odette's betrayal of him.

The figure of Andréa lurked in the background, but
for the time being she left him there. She had other
things to think about. Moreover, if he continued to
make himself unbearable, was there not a loaf of bread
somewhere which had not been used? They could make
a gypsy cake of it, an engagement cake, heavy and highly
indigestible! But come what might, Odette would have
to lend her willing assistance to the realization of this
Machiavellian scheme.

"We've got to persuade her," she said. "I rely on
you for this, though she does not seem to like you
overmuch, but I'll give you a little advice which may
be useful."

She followed up her advice by handing him a small
box which the worthy graybeard, the steward of the
Palace, had given her the day before to divert her
thoughts. Thus fortified, they made for the *quevra's*
apartments. De Lauriac would speak to Odette with less
constraint than on the first occasion, and, he thought,
with a greater chance of success. . . . Callista caused
the doors to be opened, crept behind him, and arranged
to listen to the conversation behind a moucharaby.

When Odette saw de Lauriac again she called one of
the women and ordered her to show him out; but he
explained, in language which the others did not understand, that it was a question of saving Jean from the
worst tortures, and she must grant him a moment's
conversation.

As she still wavered, he brought out her letter to
Jean which had been taken from him.

Then she allowed him to draw near, but she ordered

her women to hold themselves in readiness to come to her at the first call.

"You make a mistake to treat me so badly," he began. "I will show you once more that I am your real friend. If it were not for me Jean would have been poisoned. The worst of it is, Odette, that it would have been your fault."

"My fault?"

"Yes. He refused the food which Callista and I tried to send him secretly—Callista because she cannot forget all at once how good he used to be to her, and I because I know that you would never forgive me if Jean died; and besides, I am not a monster."

"So he refused to eat anything?"

"Yes, and it was lucky for him, because Andréa in his mad hatred had determined to get rid of him at the earliest moment, and sent him poisoned bread which he refused to eat, as he did when other food was offered to him. It was then that they appealed to you and got you to write the letter which I have here—the letter which induced Jean to eat this poisoned bread."

Odette gave a shriek, and the women came running into the room. But de Lauriac quickly reassured her that he had arrived in time to save Jean, who had scarcely partaken of the bread. He had relieved him of both the bread and the letter. . . . Now the letter had been read to the Council of Elders and passed over to de Lauriac by the Patriarch, because a wife's correspondence is the property of her husband.

"You know as well as I do that I shall never marry you," cried Odette, who listened to his speechifying, a prey to a thousand torments, for she was wondering what he was trying to lead up to.

"Send the women out of the room," said de Lauriac, in no way perturbed by her outburst. "They are in the way. You must know, Odette, that when the Council of Elders handed me this letter they made me a present, for your benefit, of a box which I wish to show you."

Odette waved her hand and they were alone once more. De Lauriac took the box from under his cloak.

"Stand with your back to the light," he said, "and take a look into this box. I have never seen anything quite so extraordinary."

As he spoke he held the box on a level with her face. She looked through the eye-piece, and started back with a dull moan.

"It's awful," she exclaimed. "Why do you show me this?"

"You haven't seen anything yet," he returned, "and it is essential for you to look once more. That is the express wish of the Council, who have instructed me to make you acquainted with a certain intention which will only become clear to you if you look again into the box."

"Go!" she exclaimed. "Can't you see that your mere presence horrifies me. It is quite unnecessary to show me this thing."

"On the contrary it is absolutely necessary. I tell you that Jean's life depends upon it. This box contains a valuable lesson which may decide his fate."

"I don't understand. Explain yourself."

"The explanation in all its details lies in this box. There, just look once more—only once—and you will have nothing more to learn."

He again offered her the box, and she summoned up courage to take a second look.

This time she did not possess the strength to cry out. She shrank back with quivering lips, terrified eyes, and hands upraised before her as though to shut out some terrible vision.

It was indeed a terrible sight. The box was a kind

of stereoscope containing photographs which revolved
by means of a mechanical contrivance, and thus showed
the successive phases of the most frightful tortures.
The photographs had been brought back from China
by a gypsy, who had taken them himself while the torturer with a rough and ready skill flayed the limbs, removed the flesh, laid bare the bones, leaving but the
trunk alive, and continued his fell work until his victim,
not one of whose facial distortions in his sufferings was
lost, ended his martyrdom in a last breath.

"You know how fanatical gypsies are," went on de
Lauriac. "I need not tell a Camargue girl who has lived
in the shadow of St. Sarah to what lengths they are
capable of going when their 'religion' is at stake. The
prediction in the sacred writings must be fulfilled. You
have just seen the torture to which the Council of the
Elders has condemned Jean unless you consent to marry
me. On the other hand, I have been granted his life and
liberty if you marry me. . . . Now it is for you to make
your choice."

CHAPTER LI

THE OCTOPUS' JOY

THE Octopus was as blithe as a lark; and indeed, the entire city was rejoicing. The Council of Elders had issued a proclamation announcing to the populace that the coronation would take place on the morrow and be followed by the marriage. The *queyra* had at last given way before the law and the sacred writings and agreed to marry the alien, who had brought her back to Sever Turn.

The glad tidings were received with rapture, and fittingly celebrated in the ancient Romany city and the new European quarter.

The worthy Monsieur Nicolas Tournesol was in the seventh heaven. Now and then he wondered what had become of Rouletabille, who had not been seen for three days, but he confessed that the exhilarating presence of Madame de Meyrens was of a nature to make him forget, for the time being, this startling disappearance.

They remained together; danced together, dined together, drank together. She was indeed a delightful woman! "Always bright, always lively," said Monsieur Tournesol to himself, admiring her animation and strength of mind.

He made steady love to her but she merely laughed at him.

"She does not care a fig about love," thought Monsieur Tournesol.

Between two cocktails, as she blew the smoke of her cigarette in his face, she asked him point blank:

"What did Rouletabille tell you the other day?"

Nicolas Tournesol blushed to the roots of his hair.

"Tell me?" he echoed, trying to play the innocent. "Why, nothing."

She burst out laughing.

"You are a decent fellow and a simpleton, Monsieur Tournesol. You don't know how to tell a lie."

"I don't even know what you mean," he stammered.

"Do you deny that he was shut up with you in your room for over a quarter of an hour?"

"Oh, you mean the young man who . . ."

"Yes, I mean the young man who . . . Of course you didn't know it was Rouletabille! That won't wash, my dear fellow."

"Well, he forgot to give me his name. . . . After all, he may possibly have mentioned it, but you were uppermost in my mind, you know, and when I am thinking of you, guns might go off and I shouldn't hear anything."

"Still, Rouletabille or not, this youth was in your room for some definite object."

"Certainly! I seem to have gathered vaguely that he was getting ready to leave the Patriarchate and wouldn't be sorry to have a fellow-traveler. But as I had made up my mind not to leave Sever Turn as long as you remained here, dear Madame, I must have given him to understand that I was not the man he was looking for."

"Well, I will tell you, big story-teller that you are, what he called on you for, your Rouletabille. He came to give you a sealed packet containing documents which you were to deliver to the Minister of Foreign Affairs in Paris if any accident happened to cut short the life of Europe's most famous journalist."

Nicolas Tournesol, flabbergasted and turning redder than ever, lowered his head.

"Hush! That's a secret, a secret between him and me," he stammered.

"Before he called on you he went to see the Wallachian Consul, who refused to take charge of the letter, and told me all about it. As I already knew through Vladislas Kamenos, the obliging proprietor of the Hôtel des Balkans, of a stranger calling on you that very morning after leaving the Consulate, I had no difficulty in picturing to myself Rouletabille making this appeal, which the Consul had turned down, to you."

"Obviously there's no keeping anything from you," returned Tournesol. "What I fail to understand is why a Consul should refuse the poor man so small a service which, when all is said, comes within the scope of his duties."

"He refused just because he is a Consul, and if you had ever been in the service you would have done the same thing. The Consul asked Rouletabille's permission to open the packet to see what was in it, but Rouletabille declined to allow him, and the Consul naturally enough answered that he could not undertake to deliver a document of whose contents he knew nothing. What could have been more straight-forward?"

"Well, I am no diplomatist, and I speak my mind openly. If anyone asks me to do him a service, I do it."

"Fathead!"

"Madame de Meyrens, I am madly in love with you."

And placing his arm round her waist he forced her to dance a shimmy with him, and the result was so comical that she laughed till the tears came.

Monsieur Tournesol, rejoicing in his success, became more and more insistent, and he had great difficulty in tearing himself away from Madame de Meyrens when he saw her to her room at two o'clock in the morning. She pointed to his own room at the end of the passage, and breaking away from him reminded him that the hour of repose had long since sounded, and the best of friends must part.

Monsieur Tournesol sighed as though his heart would break.

"I feel very weak, incredibly weak," he said. "I have had supper sent up to my room, which I can't possibly eat alone, and I foresee that if you don't join me I shall undoubtedly faint."

"Unfortunately I am not hungry," said Madame de Meyrens. "Still . . ."

"Still what?"

"Still if you have anything particular to say to me, you may come and say it in my room."

"Oh, you are a dear!"

"On one condition."

"I agree to all your conditions."

"You must bring the packet which Rouletabille handed over to you."

"Devil take it!"

Madame de Meyrens made no reply, and retired to her her room leaving Monsieur Nicolas Tournesol standing irresolutely in the passage.

He slowly regained his own room, closed the door behind him, sighed at the sight of the unnecessary supper with its two covers on a small table, sighed once more, took out his keys, and opened the small safe in the wall.

The packet lay before him in the safe.

Tournesol stretched out his hand, but just as he was about to seize the precious trust, he abruptly closed the safe, inwardly cursing himself.

He went to bed supperless in a rage.

CHAPTER LII

CORONATION DAY

IT was Coronation Day. The Palace was crowded with busy servants. In the women's quarters the women were engaged in dressing the *queyra*, for whom they had brought out the richest treasures of the past and age-old jewels.

Odette let the women do what they pleased with her, submissive to their skillful hands, uttering no word of protest, and wholly indifferent to what was passing round her. Had they been dressing a dead body for a royal funeral they could not have had before them a more immobile princess.

. . . .

On your feet—the hour has come! The brazen voices of the bells peal forth their fateful notes; the processions are ready, and the incense is burning on the altars. On your feet, Odette! . . .

Her costume is so heavy that she has to be lifted; her young form so frail that she has to be supported. But suddenly some strange power causes her to draw herself erect in an attitude of dreadful rigidity.

Zina is but a shadow, a poor decrepit shadow whom a breath might destroy, but her eyes gleam with a fire that gives life to others. And the life in her eyes seems to go out to Odette and to impart to her superhuman strength. . . .

And now the statue moves. . . . Honor to the *queyra!* . . . She arrives at the temple for the wedding. The bridegroom is waiting.

CHAPTER LIII

AN INTERRUPTION

MEANTIME Jean in his cell was awaiting events. He did not give way to despair. The incidents of the last three days had given him renewed courage to bear the strain of his hideous captivity. The sudden appearance of Rouletabille in the dress of an Elder of the great council, and the few words that he had spoken, showed him that nothing was yet lost, and that Rouletabille was busied in preparing his escape.

Moreover, the time spent with Odette had filled his heart with immeasurable joy.

They had tried to poison him, but Rouletabille had supervened in time, and now Zina was visiting him regularly, bringing him food, while the warders, bribed by Callista, were sufficiently accommodating to allow her to do as she pleased.

Zina partook of the fare which she brought to him, thus showing that it was harmless; and whenever she visited him she dropped a few enigmatic words in which he seemed to discern that his miseries would soon be over and Odette and himself united once more.

"It is to be to-morrow," the old woman said definitely the night before.

What did she mean? . . . His release? . . . Obviously.

He had not seen Rouletabille again, but he no longer entertained any doubt that he was working for him in secret. He had reached the point when he could not hear the sound of a footstep in the passage without a feeling of agitation.

And suddenly he started up in his cell. A dark form stood before the grating and put a key in the lock. . . . He was surprised not to recognize Zina's figure. . . . Who was this woman? She came in.

It was Callista. A dull exclamation escaped his lips.

"Come!" she said.

He did not stir and she repeated:

"Come, you are free."

He looked at her in an agony of suspense. He was at a loss; it was not she whom he expected to see. She was the origin of all his troubles. He was on his guard. She could only be meditating some new act of treachery. At last he asked:

"Why are you here?"

"To set you free."

"I don't believe you."

"Come with me and you will see."

"Where are you going to take me?"

"Wherever you like. You are free. Come, you have nothing to fear. I have obtained a pardon for you from the Great Council. The Elders allowed themselves to be moved to pity on hearing my pleading. I told them how good you used to be to me, and how much you had suffered. I promised them that you would leave Sever Turn, never to come back to it. And here is the order for your release."

She gave him the order. He read it by the light of a lantern which shed a gleam from the other side of the grating. So it was true! He was free!

"I shan't leave Sever Turn without Odette," he said.

"Don't rely upon that. And if you will take my advice, forget Odette. She has forgotten you."

"I don't believe it. That's just like you. I know that you can never come near me without trying to hurt me. Besides, nothing you say is of any use. I don't know why I listen to you. I am free. Good-by."

"Good-by, Jean."

He made a movement to go, and it was she now who remained in the cell. He turned back.

"All the same, if I owe my liberty to you, you have made amends for many things, and I forgive you, Callista."

"Forgive me, because anything I may have done was done out of love for you. Whatever you may do or hear, remember that you have no more devoted slave than Callista."

"Nor a more deceitful one. Why tell me that Odette has forgotten me? You must be crazy."

"I am not crazy. Go! . . . And anyone you meet will tell you the same thing."

"Explain yourself. Are you hiding anything from me?"

"I am not hiding anything, though I am not anxious to explain what will probably cause you further pain. You would only turn against me again. I'm tired of your outbursts of temper."

He left the cage. No one was in the corridor. He did not know which way to take. He went back to Callista, who was leaving the cell and closing the grating.

"Let me show you the way," she said. "It will be better for you to leave without attracting the attention of the Palace guard; otherwise they will want some explanation. I know an underground passage which leads to the temple. Once there, no one will take any notice of you, for a great state ceremony is taking place, and you will be able to reach the European quarter without difficulty."

"Are there many people in the temple?"

"A tremendous crowd. Just think, this is the *queyra's* wedding day."

"What *queyra?*" cried Jean in a hoarse voice.

"Well, I only know one, my dear. Odette is being married to-day."

"Odette is being married to-day." The words dulled Jean's brain to such a degree that he was unable to utter a denial or a murmur.

It seemed to him that his heart had ceased to beat and his life and life around him had come to a standstill. Nothing remained in the world but the frightful words: "Odette is being married to-day." Odette was to be the wife of another!

He did not doubt Callista's word. He understood now why she had set him free.

Moreover, was she not, by way of precaution, herself taking him to the ceremony? With what delight she must have hastened to him! He had never felt so much hatred or contempt for her. . . . When he recovered somewhat from the blow which she had struck him, he took a mean revenge. He uttered the word *uschein* that conveyed the worst insult in the gypsy language, and spat on one side in the manner of a gypsy in a passion.

She scarcely resented it. She shrugged her shoulders, and casting a look of pity on him, walked away. . . . They went through the corridor which had previously been traversed by Rouletabille. At the iron gate she stopped to open it.

Then Jean said:

"I know Odette. She loves me. Even you cannot doubt that. You came upon us exchanging a kiss in the cell. When one kisses like that it means that love will last for life."

"Odette is still alive and she is being married," retorted Callista harshly.

"She was undoubtedly forced into it. I am not blaming Odette. She is a child and too young to suffer."

"That's the very word: she is a child," said Callista. "An honest child, in my opinion, but a child who doesn't know her own mind. She began by falling in love with de Lauriac, then she transferred her affections to you, then she had a sort of fancy for Rouletabille, then she came back to you again, and finally she has made up her mind to marry de Lauriac her first love."

"You will never make me doubt her," returned Jean. "If she marries de Lauriac it will break my heart, but I shall forgive her because they are forcing her to marry a man whom she detests."

"Pah! It doesn't look much like it," said Callista in a bitterly sarcastic tone. "Of course I don't suggest that she is marrying him with enthusiasm, but, after all, she is allowing herself to be led to the altar without reluctance by the handsome herdsman who captured her fancy as a young girl."

"You wretch!"

"I don't mind your insults. I accept all you say to me in good part. I am not like Odette. I have loved one man in my life; no other man has ever been anything to me, and if I were threatened with the worst tortures I should submit to them with joy rather than marry any other man."

They had reached the narrow spiral staircase by which Rouletabille, a few days earlier, had descended to the underground part of the Palace, and Jean mounted them, after Callista, a prey to a thousand fresh torments.

He entered the temple just as the *queyra*, at last making her appearance, was being greeted by deafening applause.

The Council of Elders stood up, and the Patriarch, taking her hand, conducted her to the ivory throne. Odette walked like an automaton. The entire audience shouted joyfully: *"The queyra! The queyra!"* Then a great silence fell and a door in the apse opened, and de Lauriac came in dressed in a simple tunic but wearing the priceless royal chain.

He was uncovered, and the expression of his countenance was severe and almost fierce. In a few minutes Odette would be his and he would wear a crown. But at that supreme crisis he could not forget the strange fate which had flung him from one extreme to the other, and cast him down when, as he thought, he was in sight of the goal.

Such as he was, he appealed to the gypsies who greeted him also with applause as their ruler. As the Patriarch had led Odette to the throne, so the Chief led de Lauriac to his place.

Odette did not look at him nor did he look at her.

The service began—the strange service whose ritual was derived from every religion and every age. It was frequently interrupted by dances as in biblical times. . . . And it was thus that whirling round and round under her light drapery, Callista suddenly came into view.

She had never danced so beautifully. The assembly imagined that she was dancing for the *queyra*, but it was to Jean to whom she was devoting her frenzied art. She sank at the feet of Odette in a religious transport, and after the prostration into which the intensity of her love had thrown her, she was brought back to life again by new movements in which her leaping and swaying form seemed in turn to pursue and renounce the delights of life.

She knew that she had captivated him by the pagan audacity of an art which was inborn, and in which her imagination had devised unexpected symbols expressive of her eager, sensual mind, a slave to love and vindictive to the verge of barbarity.

Was it possible for him to witness so rare a sight without recalling how others in the past had ended— the delight with which he had thrown his trembling arms round and imprisoned the half-swooning beauty?

Alas, Jean did not even see her. He had no eyes for anyone but Odette and de Lauriac, seated side by side, as if the marriage were already accomplished. As he had told Callista, he did not blame Odette for this frightful surrender of her love. He had but to look at her to see that the despair which petrified her on the throne, in the royal finery which weighed her down, was at least as great as that which wrung his soul in the shadow of the pillar where his sufferings passed unperceived.

He no longer had the strength to wish for de Lauriac's death. Things were as they were. They could do no more. As the gypsies said: It was written! It was written that Jean should never marry Odette, and that she should be de Lauriac's wife. They were all the blind victims of an inevitable fate. Their efforts had been of no avail. Jean was only sorry that he had not been left to die in his cell.

The ceremony proceeded, for him, as in a dream, as in a nightmare which became more and more terrifying, and at last when he saw the Patriarch join de Lauriac and Odette's hands to bless them, a groan escaped from his lips.

Turning to de Lauriac the Patriarch spoke a few words which Jean did not understand, but he guessed their meaning, which may be thus expressed:

"Always remember that you are king only by the pleasure of our queen. You must take oath that you will serve her as the most faithful and humblest of her subjects, and have no other will but hers. Swear that you will follow in all things the advice of the Elders and devote yourself body and soul to the service of the Patriarchate."

Then turning to the *queyra,* the Patriarch said while the young girls drew near with the royal diadem:

"And you, my daughter, you who are of our race and

already consecrated in the sacred writings, receive this crown from the hands of your people."

It was at this juncture that the event which de Lauriac so greatly feared occurred. Rouletabille appeared among the choir, coming from no one knew where, throwing the entire ceremony into disorder.

"You have been deceived," he shouted. "This girl is not a Romany. She is not the promised *queyra.*"

He uttered these sentences in the Romany language in a ringing voice. It was afterwards discovered that he had learnt them from Zina so that the assembly might understand them.

The confusion which ensued was even greater than that at the time of his first intervention. It was now an act of sacrilege, for it had been officially established that Odette bore "the sign." Thus the storm that broke out against the madman who had the incredible recklessness to repeat his first story at a moment like that, knew no bounds. The guards seized him. Andréa in a transport of fury was already aiming his revolver at him, but Rouletabille managed to slip through the hands that were rending him while the people shouted: "Death to him! She does bear the sign! She does bear the sign!"

Rouletabille sprang towards Odette, who, bewildered, had risen to her feet, while de Lauriac stood before her. But de Lauriac was thrown to the ground, and Rouletabille, snatching aside the royal cloak, lay bare her shoulder.

"See! . . . See for yourself!" he cried. "She does not bear the sign now."

And indeed the sign of the crown had disappeared. No mark could be seen upon her snow-white shoulder. Those who had gazed at it a few days before could scarcely believe their own eyes. The Elders passed their trembling hands over the spotless skin to make certain that they were not the sport of some subterfuge by which the sacred sign had been concealed under powder and paint.

In an ever-increasing uproar the people shouted for Zina, the witness whose word had already been challenged by Rouletabille, and they recalled to mind the reasoning adopted by him.

"If the young princess bore the sign of the crown as a birth-mark, why had her foster-mother kept silent, and why had she who had accompanied her in all her alien travels delayed so long to inform the gypsies of the birth of the *queyra* foretold in the sacred writings?" And they called with one voice: "Zina! Zina!"

Then Zina appeared. She could scarcely stand. It was Rouletabille who conducted her to Odette, at whose feet she fell, and then wringing her hands she made her confession:

"It is true she is not the long-expected *queyra*. I was lying. She had no birth-mark. I produced it by trickery. I took it away by trickery. I lied . . . I lied."

"Desecration!" cried the Patriarch.

The faithful turned the full weight of their fury upon Zina. The sacred precincts were rushed by the people, and while the chief actors in this political and religious drama, including Jean, who at the outset hastened to Rouletabille's side, were hurried by the Patriarch into the Great Council's room, the hapless old woman was swept away in the angry swirl of the rabble tide.

CHAPTER LIV

A STORM

Extract from Rouletabille's diary:

WHEW! . . . I've pulled it off . . . I think we
are now out of the wood. It was no easy task
and it was not without risk. I may as well confess as much now. When I loomed up in sight during
the coronation, I was running a big risk, for I was not
quite certain that the mark had entirely disappeared.

"Zina assured me that during the last three days it
was gradually vanishing, and by coronation day no
vestige of it would remain. I was not quite at my ease.
In any case, I could save myself by relying on Zina's
confession, but would there have been time to explain
matters if any trace of the mark had remained? I doubt
it. One must not juggle with fanaticism. One must be
absolutely in the right in the eyes of the most prejudiced.
One must be jolly clever to hold one's own.

"In very truth the whole affair savored of black magic.
It would have been so considered in the middle ages.
This birth-mark which appeared and disappeared at the
will of a gypsy woman—how could it be explained other
than by the intervention of the *beka* (devil), as they say
still in Sever Turn; and I am convinced that in the minds
of the gypsies, who brought about Zina's wretched fate,
the poor creature was in league with the powers of darkness—an everyday superstition with the Romanys. The
gypsy race, more than any other, is susceptible to suggestion. For hundreds of years these people have prac-

335

ticed auto-suggestion. No one doubts the existence of the evil eye, and hypnotism is of daily occurrence in their lives. Modern science has taught us that there is nothing supernatural in these things, but to the credulous mind such phenomena are associated with occult power. . . .

"I had to discover some explanation of the birthmark on Odette's shoulder. When I became certain that she never had any such mark, when I got to know the relations between Odette and Zina, when I at last learned that Odette was a gypsy by birth, and, from that very fact, more susceptible than anyone else to Zina's hypnotic powers, I was bound—leaning on the right end of my judgment—to come to the conclusion that it was Zina who had made manifest this royal mark on her shoulder, in order to save her from Callista and Andréa's deadly attempts on her life.

"But in that case, since she had caused the mark to appear, she would be able to get rid of it. When everything seemed to have come to grief in Sever Turn, nothing remained but to rely on Zina to save us. I had the good fortune to extract a confession from her at the moment when, escaping from Callista's murderous hands, she was but a poor sufferer, thinking only of revenge. So I had no great difficulty in making the old woman understand that if Odette were to be queen and the wife of the man she loathed, she would as surely die as if Zina had allowed her to be struck down by Callista's knife.

"And the inverted suggestion began. . . . And there was no longer any *queyra!*

"Though we were filled with a feeling of deep delight at the upshot of affairs, there were those who were by no means pleased—the people of Sever Turn. Thus we shall not remain long in the city. In fact we are leaving it this very night, in accordance with the advice of the Patriarch, who has shown a fair and conciliatory spirit throughout, and is not sorry, perhaps, to retain for himself alone supreme power.

"While waiting to make our departure, we ordered an excellent dinner at the Hôtel des Balkans. I walked over for a moment to the window, just for a breath of fresh air, and because I am always interested in what may be passing round me. Who was that I saw over there stealing through the caravanserai, with that look of a savage old bear seeking something, or rather someone whom he may devour? Why, it was our old friend Hubert de Lauriac! . . ."

We may turn aside from Rouletabille's diary, which contains but few observations on the repast which united Jean and Odette, after their many painful experiences, for he treats all too briefly a radiant scene of happiness, in which the two lovers forgot the disastrous past. Lovers are invariably self-centered. Did Rouletabille imagine that they were too absorbed in themselves and devoted too little attention to him? It is quite possible. The best men have their weaknesses. And yet Jean had spoken from his heart in the few sentences in which he sought to express the unbounded gratitude with which he was brimimng over towards his magnanimous friend.

"Thank me?" interrupted Rouletabille bluntly. "But why, old man? It's nothing, I assure you. Forget it."

And Jean, tears in his eyes, relapsed into silence, Odette, on the other hand, embraced her "little Zo" with such ingenuous and yet ardent affection that he turned pale.

And then it was obvious that the lovers were wrapped up in themselves. They sat with clasped hands, their eyes fixed upon each other. . . . Rouletabille walked over to the window to breathe the air, muttering: "What a queer dinner! No one is eating anything, and a fellow is here who has been living on dry bread and water for a week."

The "fellow" was Jean, who had just learned the full extent of Odette's sacrifice and was choking with joy at the thought that she had consented to the horrible marriage only to save him from the pincers of the torturer.

"You did that for me . . . for me!"

"He hadn't the sense to guess it," said Rouletabille to himself, shrugging his shoulders. "What an ass! There's no doubt about it, men in love are fools. Don't let me ever fall in love!"

It was then that the sight of de Lauriac diverted his thoughts, which naturally enough find little or no echo in his diary.

De Lauriac's appearance on the scene meant a renewal of the fight, and possibly danger to them. Rouletabille was in a state of mind to wish that it might be so. To have someone to fight against; to have something to do while the two lovers were making love behind his back! He could hear Odette saying: "My dearest, my dearest, what you must have gone through!"

"Well, and what about me? Does she think that I was enjoying myself when they were preparing that infernal marriage?"

Rouletabille suddenly decided to slip away. He left them. "Hell and fury," he rapped out, "how hot it is here. I'm going to have a look round."

Once out of doors he began to hunt for de Lauriac, whose presence near the Hôtel des Balkans boded no good. It was the erstwhile herdsman who had come out of the adventure most hurt, and Rouletabille was sufficiently acquainted with him to know the sort of balm with which he would try to staunch his wounds.

He must be maneuvering some scheme of revenge which would compensate him for his discomfiture. In his present state of fury, some nice disaster which would engulf them all, himself as well as the rest, would not be unwelcome to him.

A few hours earlier this man was all-powerful, and now he was a nobody. It was in the nature of things that he should dream of involving the aiders and abettors of his ruin in his downfall. Moreover, the grim face that Rouletabille had set eyes on carried its own warning. . . . And meantime Jean and Odette continued to be engrossed in themselves.

Rouletabille did not mention what he had seen, for he had no wish to interrupt so charming a duet, but since he had become, after such efforts, the author of their happiness, it was incumbent upon him to watch over his work. He was too disposed to reproach himself for certain inward sentiments, and his nature was too honest to hesitate to fly to their assistance when danger menaced them.

Where was de Lauriac? He walked round the caravanserai without seeing him. He went back to the hotel and met Monsieur Tournesol, who stopped him.

"I'm glad to see you and congratulate you," said Monsieur Tournesol. "Allow me to offer you one of my own special cocktails. You are now well out of your difficulties. I saw the whole thing and it was a fine piece of work. But I rather fancy that you won't hang about here very long. Shall I give you back your little packet?"

"Well, no," returned Rouletabille, who was opening every door and looking into every room. "Until I am actually in France, keep the letter. One never knows what may happen."

"Quite right. Be on your guard. I know a certain gentleman who has no great love for you."

"Have you seen him about here?"

"I think I caught sight of his ugly face near the Syrian dealer's shop. But he soon made off."

Rouletabille left him. Tournesol called him back.

"It's my turn to ask a question. Do you know what has become of Madame de Meyrens?"

"I don't really. So you are still smitten with the lady's charms?"

"Upon my word, I believe that she, for her part, rather likes me, but she insists on things incompatible with certain old-fashioned notions which my late father inculcated in me."

"Might I ask what those notions are?" inquired the journalist, who had slipped behind the window-curtains, whence he could observe, without being seen, the caravanserai from end to end.

"They are notions on the question of honor, Monsieur Rouletabille."

"Might I ask what she wanted from you?"

"She wanted me to pass over to her the packet which you entrusted to me, that's all."

"What an awful woman! . . . I beg your pardon, Monsieur Tournesol, but I must go upstairs and see if by chance our man is playing round Madame de Meyrens."

Some quarter of an hour after this short colloquy, Rouletabille came rushing like a whirlwind into the room where Jean and Odette were still exchanging sweet nothings before a dinner which they had scarcely touched.

"My friends," he cried, "we must make ourselves scarce without delay."

"What's the matter?" asked Jean, greatly vexed by Rouletabille's sudden appearance.

"The matter is that I have just seen de Lauriac and Madame de Meyrens together."

"Here?"

"Yes, within hearing. . . . I was able to listen to their conversation. De Lauriac is on the point of playing us a nasty trick. I heard him say to the Octopus, who tried to find out more about it and pressed him to explain himself—these were his own words: 'You will be satisfied, I promise you, and so shall I. We shall have our re-

venge within an hour.' So hurry up . . . hurry up,
children, and let's go."

"Let's go," repeated Jean.

"Oh, yes, let's get out of this hateful country," agreed
Odette. "My goodness, and I thought that all our
troubles were over!"

"But how shall we let the drivers know? Besides, we
can't go without horses."

"We must go on foot. Let us get away as best we
can," urged Rouletabille, walking over to the window.
"Do you hear this uproar?"

The uproar rose to a storm, which broke loose with
incredible violence. The caravanserai, silent and deserted
ten minutes before, was filled with a frenzied mob,
armed with rifles, shouting at the top of their voices, led
by Andréa and Callista, while standing at one of the
hotel windows of the room in which Jean had thrown his
light luggage, was an Elder of the Grand Council, whom
Rouletabille recognized as the famous librarian with
whom he had already had trouble. The Elder was waving a large volume, which was equally well-known to
Rouletabille—the Book of Ancestors.

It was easy to guess what the gray beard was shouting
to the people as he pointed to the book, which had at last
been found.

It was the aliens who had stolen it! . . . And where
had he found it. In Jean's luggage.

Standing behind him they saw de Lauriac's pallid and
ominous face. Rouletabille had no need to look round
or to hear what was said to grasp the situation.

"Well, we are in a pretty pickle."

CHAPTER LV

IN WHICH ROULETABILLE DECLARES THAT HE CANNOT LEAVE WITHOUT HIS "DRESSING-CASE," AND WHAT CAME OF IT

THE caravanserai might be likened at that time to a huge vat seething with an infuriated rabble. The gypsies in the Patriarchate had undergone such extremes of enthusiasm and despair that it needed but an incident like the theft by the aliens of the Book of Ancestors to drive them to the worst excesses.

The extraordinary business of the *queyra* had left them with the dismal and maddening conviction that they had allowed themselves to be duped. And by whom, if not by the aliens?

Zina was merely their tool in an affair in which, when all was said, they had endeavored to palm off upon them a sham queen.

The *lingurari*—makers of spoons and wooden vessels —and the *liaessi,* who were the most poverty-stricken, but also the most turbulent among the tribes, for they had nothing to lose, returning from their wanderings as empty-handed as when they set out, joined together to demand the immediate expulsion of the aliens and the confiscation of their property; and they found the Patriarch somewhat disposed to sign a decree of this nature in order to avoid even greater disasters.

It was then that de Lauriac, realizing that Jean and Odette were about to escape him, devised the "theft" by slipping the Book of Ancestors into Jean's luggage. . . . Callista, supported by Andréa, put herself at the head

342

of the movement, which threatened to carry all before it. The town-guards declined to interfere, and the *balogards* shut themselves up with their riches.

The Council of Elders were in permanent session at the Palace. The librarian proved the theft. The Patriarch was thus placed in a serious position, and he wondered how he could overcome the difficulty without giving the order for blood offerings, which would indubitably bring down upon him the wrath of foreign powers. He fervently hoped that Rouletabille and his friends, whom he had advised to make themselves scarce, had been able to effect their retreat. . . .

"We are in a pretty pickle," cried Rouletabille.

But as, in accordance with his custom, he had made himself acquainted with the ramifications of the hotel in which they were staying, he at once took Jean and Odette to a staircase which led to the rear of the hotel, away from the caravanserai. . . . The rooms in the ground floor were by now invaded by a shouting mob, and the sound of blows with the butt-ends of rifles on the doors, which still stood firm, could be heard.

Just then the little group of three was reinforced by Monsieur Nicolas Tournesol, the very picture of despair.

"They're going to fire the hotel. Let's get away at once," he gasped.

"What about Madame de Meyrens? Are you going to desert the poor lady?" asked Rouletabille in a bantering tone.

"Madame de Meyrens can go to the devil. She and that infernal de Lauriac are the cause of all this trouble."

"Hell and fury," cried Rouletabille, "I've forgotten my case."

"What case?" asked Jean, astonished to see his friend stop and make a movement to turn back.

"Why, my dressing-case," said Rouletabille, preparing to dart up the staircase again.

"Look here, this is absurd," Jean broke out. "In another minute it will be too late to get away, and yet you bother about your 'dressing-case.'"

"This is the second time, old man, that I have had to provide myself with shirts and things. I am not a millionaire. Wait for me here, and be sure and do nothing without me."

So saying, pushing Jean aside without much ceremony, he disappeared up the stairs into the hotel.

"He has lost his head," cried Jean irritably. "Let's make a move, Odette."

"He told us to stay here. We had better wait for him," she returned.

"But we can't afford the time. Do you hear them? They're coming. . . . . Listen, here they are!"

"All the more reason," returned Odette, who seemed to have made up her mind, and sat down on a stone bench with an air of resignation. "All the more reason. You wouldn't wish to get away and leave Rouletabille in their hands."

"And all this for a dressing-case!" exclaimed Jean distractedly.

Meantime Monsieur Nicolas Tournesol, who had not forgotten the bag containing his own most precious articles, including the packet which Rouletabille had confided to him, hurriedly made off across a tract of waste land which brought him to a cemetery, whence he hoped, under the shelter of the dead, to reach the open country.

A harsh fate willed it, however, that he should fall upon a procession taking a *balogard* to his last resting-place, and at the sight of the alien the mourners made a rush at him, with the result that it was a question, a few minutes later, whether they should bury the living along with the dead. There are crucial moments in the life of a people when fanatics exert all their powers to devise new methods of making respectable citizens suffer.

Luckily for Monsieur Nicolas Tournesol, none of his debtors were among those upon whom his fate depended, otherwise his life would not have been worth a moment's purchase, and his accounts would have been settled there and then. By promising them to throw open his stock-rooms in the caravanserai he was able to postpone an adverse fate, and was taken back to the city little the worse for the encounter.

It was then that he beheld the march past, amidst the excitement of the populace, of three prisoners, who were none other than Rouletabille, de Santierne and poor Odette.

"Do you know these people?" one of the party asked Tournesol, pointing to the three prisoners, who were apparently being escorted to their execution.

"I've never seen them before," declared Tournesol, without turning a hair.

"Those are the people who stole the Book of Ancestors. They'll have to pay the penalty."

"They deserve it," exclaimed Tournesol.

"And woe betide their accomplices."

"I quite agree. I never heard of such impudence. Steal the Book of Ancestors! Why, some people respect nothing. These tourists think they can do what they like. If they had their way, they would pull down the temple for the sake of adding one of its stones to their collection. It's disgraceful. There's a limit in all things. You are quite right to make an example of them, believe me."

"May Rouletabille forgive me," said Tournesol to himself, trying to discover an excuse for his odious conduct and at once finding it. "May Rouletabille forgive me. But I am bound to chuck him over if I am to have a chance of delivering the packet which he entrusted to me. . . . Another job which you, my poor Tournesol, could very well have done without. But you always were led astray by your good heart."

Meanwhile a body of men, sent by the Patriarch, had come to rescue the three prisoners from popular fury, and they conducted, or rather threw, them into one of the rooms of the Palace, where they were to remain until they received sentence. The three of them were in a state of consternation. Rouletabille, in particular, was a sorry sight. He seemed in a greatly dejected mood, and he opened his mouth only to bewail the ill-luck which had deprived him of his "dressing-case," for, despite all his efforts, he had failed to get it, or rather there was no time to get it.

"And that's all you can say at a time like this," exclaimed Jean. "Why, it's your fault that we are here."

CHAPTER LVI

ROULETABILLE PLAYS HIS GAME

ROULETABILLE was not unduly disturbed by the reproaches. It was to no purpose that Jean, beginning to lose his temper, told him that his wonderful shrewdness was only equaled, at certain times, by his blind obstinacy—he dared not say blundering. Rouletabille expressed no regret for what had happened. And yet "no language could adequately describe" what had happened, declared Jean. To think that he had risked his own and his friends' lives for the sake of a dressing-case!

Odette, worn out with fatigue, endeavored to calm Jean, but it was no easy task, for they heard the journalist mutter, as though in a dream:

"I ought to have taken the other passage and then I could have come back by the servant's staircase, after getting hold of my 'dressing-case.'"

"Oh, shut up with your 'dressing-case.' I tell you straight, that had Odette been willing to come with me I wouldn't have waited for you."

"Well, old man, you ought to have made off. What do you expect? Personally, I can't get used to the idea of going away without my tooth-brush."

Conversation carried on between Rouletabille and Jean in this strain would drive them both to acts of desperation. Fortunately—or unfortunately—it was interrupted by Andréa and his armed band, who came to fetch the prisoners and take them before the Patriarch.

The latter was waiting for them in a small room adjoining that of the Grand Council, from which it was divided only by heavy purple hangings.

Two Elders and the librarian were with him. They wore an equally gloomy expression as they gazed upon the sacred book, which had been recovered from the aliens in such a pitiable condition. They observed with infinite distress that its iron clasp and its precious stones had been torn from it. And the deadly remarks which they exchanged among themselves boded ill for the barbarians who had not hesitated to mutilate this great work of art.

Outside the menacing shouts of the people, "Down with the vandals!" broke upon them in great gusts when a door was opened.

The Patriarch addressed himself to Jean, and asked in a stern voice, the librarian acting as interpreter:

"What have you done with the precious stones which embellished this book, the priceless illuminated letters with which it was decorated, the clasp which held it together and protected it from the wear and tear of hundreds of years?"

Jean protested that he knew nothing about the book, that he saw it for the first time, that it was never in his possession, and that he was the victim of an abominable plot.

His denial was listened to with obvious disbelief, and Rouletabille interposed:

"It is true," he said, "that my friend never had this work in his possession. But it is not the first time that I personally have seen it, and I may tell you that I am in a position to give you back one of the ornaments removed from it."

A great commotion. . . Rouletabille with a sudden gesture dived into his revolver pocket. Andréa sprang towards him, but Rouletabille drew from his pocket with a smile an object which he handed to the Patriarch.

It was the chain with pendant bearing the fatal sign, the cross and crescent, which had at one time formed the clasp of the book. The Patriarch and the Elders recognized it. Odette herself remembered it. Why had Rouletabille produced this object the possession of which would tend to incriminate them more than any other adverse fact?

He was questioned. Where had he obtained it if he did not himself purloin it? And in the calmest of tones he made answer:

"I found it in mademoiselle's room."

He pointed to Odette, who blushed and was startled by this direct attack from her "little Zo," which she was far from expecting. Jean grew more and more non-plussed by Rouletabille's attitude, and observing Odette's embarrassment strove to assist her by denying Rouletabille's assertion.

"I have never seen Odette with it," he said.

"And I say again that I found it in Mademoiselle de Lavardens' room."

In the midst of general bewilderment, Odette asked to be allowed to speak. In a trembling voice she said:

"It is true that this ornament was in my possession, but I would never have believed that Rouletabille would accuse me. When it was given to me, I threw it into a drawer, and the fact that it was found there proves that I forgot about it. I attached no importance to it, I assure you," she said, turning with a grief-stricken expression to Jean.

"But who gave it to you?" asked Jean.

"I'm very sorry, Jean, but it was a present from Hubert de Lauriac."

"There!" exclaimed Rouletabille. "She acknowledges it herself."

"On the other hand," said Jean bitterly, "Hubert de Lauriac made you a present, Odette, and you kept it."

"You shut up, old man," rapped out Rouletabille. . . . "Gentlemen, it's my turn to speak. Besides, I will not detain you for any length of time. And you will understand the whole business. This ornament, torn from the Book of Ancestors, was given to Mademoiselle de Lavardens by Hubert de Lauriac. Now I take my oath that I saw the Book of Ancestors in his house. He brought it back from the Patriarchate where he was traveling recently, and he slipped it into my friend Jean de Santierne's luggage. Hubert de Lauriac is the thief. Do you follow me?"

"Let de Lauriac be brought here. He will show these impostors up," broke in Andréa.

But when the Patriarch assented to the suggestion, which seemed natural enough, Rouletabille implored him not to proceed with it.

"If de Lauriac is brought here he will not show us up, he will deny it," he explained. "And I, for my part, in making these positive statements, will not be able to confound him either. The evidence of the rascality of which I accuse him, must come neither from him nor me, but possess in the eyes of a council of wise men, such as I see before me, sufficient weight to carry conviction. Listen, therefore, to what I have to say. There is a woman in this city of whose presence you are unaware, but who knows all there is to be known about Hubert de Lauriac. It is this woman whom I should like to hear."

"The Octopus again," thought Jean. "What assistance can he hope to obtain from her?"

He tried to dissuade Rouletabille from his intention, reminding him that she had joined forces with de Lauriac at Innsbruck, and come to Sever Turn solely to inflict upon them a final blow.

But Rouletabille did not even listen to him.

"I must find this woman," he said. "Give me one hour's liberty."

Jean shrugged his shoulders.

"You don't suppose that they will allow you to slip away like this."

"I leave my friends here as hostages," Rouletabille went on. "If I do not return within an hour you may do as you please with them."

"Very pretty," said Jean, astounded by the simplicity and effrontery of the proposal. "Ah, he intends to leave us in the lurch!"

"Let little Zo do things his own way," said Odette in her soft voice. "We have no right to take offence. One never knows what his scheme is until afterwards. You will see that he will get us out of our difficulties."

The Elders held a whispered colloquy. Rouletabille's departure would not inconvenience Andréa; on the contrary he sincerely hoped that he would not see him again, and they would then make short work of Jean. However, the Elders decided that Rouletabille should be provided with an escort.

He accepted without demur the three men appointed by Andréa.

"Before the hour is over I will bring them back again," he said to the Patriarch, pointing to the three guards. "But promise me, on your part, to keep de Lauriac here."

"Where is he?" asked the Patriarch.

"Here!" exclaimed Rouletabille, lifting in a flash the purple hangings behind the Patriarch's chair. "Here he is. He has been listening. I should say that he has found our conversation highly interesting."

De Lauriac had heard every word.

"Go, monsieur, go and fetch Madame de Meyrens," he said with a grim smile. And he turned his back on Rouletabille, so confident was he of the result.

The journalist darted out of the room. The guards had some difficulty in keeping pace with him. Outside the shouting of the people had increased.

Extract from Rouletabille's diary:

"And now we come to the great performance. It is the one thing that can save us. But it is terribly dangerous for me because there are persons who will never forgive me for this particular game. Things must obviously have reached their worst point when I do not hesitate to deprive myself of the most powerful weapon in my armory. Well, the hour has struck to throw that too on the scrap heap. Alas, I shall leave this old curiosity shop, Sever Turn, a poor man for some time. But I must get out of it, and above all get the others out of it. . . . Come, let me take courage. . . . To the Octopus! . . . . The Octopus!"

The guards who accompanied Rouletabille were ordered not to let him out of their sight but to obey him in all things. But they were to be back at the Palace with their prisoner within an hour.

They arrived at the Hôtel des Balkans, where Vladislas Kamenos greeted him with a thousand curses.

An attempt had been made to fire the hotel, and the proprietor held him and his friends responsible, if not for the conflagration which had not occurred, at least for the pillage which had taken the place of it. His visitors, of course, had fled without paying their bills.

"Even Monsieur Tournesol?" questioned Rouletabille.

"Even Monsieur Tournesol, and he is not likely to come back. They have plundered his store rooms as they have plundered my cellars. . . . Another man who has much to thank you for!"

"Did he go away alone?" asked Rouletabille, who seemed as calm as Kamenos was excited.

"What do you mean?"

"You know very well what I mean, guvnor. We are here, these gentlemen and myself, with the object of getting from you the latest news of the young lady traveler to whom Monsieur Tournesol paid such devoted attention."

"You mean, I suppose, Madame de Meyrens."

"Exactly. What has become of her?"

"I might reply that it was no business of mine to keep a watch on her still, as her luggage is in her room."

"Don't worry about that. You will be paid, Monsieur Kamenos," returned Rouletabille, making quickly for the first floor.

"By whom?"

"Monsieur Tournesol."

"Where are you going now?"

"To Madame de Meyrens' room."

"But I tell you she is not in her room."

"How do you know? I want to make sure."

"I won't have you go to her room. . . . I am responsible . . ."

The hotel proprietor made a dash after Rouletabille and his escort.

"Besides, the door of her room is locked," he cried.

"Here's the key," said Rouletabille, taking it from his pocket.

"How do you come to have Madame de Meyrens' key?"

"Don't ask indiscreet questions," he returned in a bantering tone, putting the key in the lock.

Monsieur Kamenos expressed his intention of entering the room with Rouletabille.

"Either Madame de Meyrens is or is not there," said Rouletabille firmly. "If she is not there I shall come out again at once; if she is there, I have been entrusted by the Patriarch to make a communication to her which is no business of yours, Monsieur Kamenos."

Rouletabille must have found Madame de Meyrens in her room, and doubtless he had important things to say to her, for ten minutes elapsed, then twenty, then thirty, and still he failed to show himself again.

Monsieur Kamenos was not alone in betraying certain anxiety at the journalist's extraordinary behavior. His guards began to grow impatient at his long absence.

Growing more and more impatient, the man inquired of the hotel proprietor whether the room possessed other doors or ways out, and when he learnt that it was possible to leave by a servants' staircase which led to the backyard and the rabbit hutches, he did not hesitate to break in the door; but he found neither Rouletabille nor Madame de Meyrens in the room.

A rabbit and a cabbage leaf!

Meanwhile the guards returned to the presence of the Patriarch, the Elders—and Rouletabille! Rouletabille was there in the flesh as smiling as the others were astonished.

The guards bent their heads. In their conscience they appeared to think that their orders had only in part been broken.

"Fortunately," continued the Patriarch in a grave voice, "our prisoner is an honest man, and returned of his own accord."

"Bringing with me the lady of whom I was in search," interposed Rouletabille.

"Madame de Meyrens!" exclaimed Vladislas Kamenos. "So she was in her room."

"Certainly, monsieur."

"Well, I'll confess the truth. I thought she had left with Monsieur Tournesol."

Rouletabille shrugged his shoulders.

"Monsieur Tournesol! Madame de Meyrens was always laughing at Monsieur Tournesol. The reason why she was in her room to-day was because she was expecting to see me."

"In that case, you will pay her bill."

"No," returned Rouletabille. "Neither I nor Monsieur

Tournesol will pay her bill. That will be settled by another friend of hers—I mean Monsieur Hubert de Lauriac. . . . Gentlemen, I ask that he be confronted with this lady."

As Rouletabille surmised, de Lauriac heard their last words uttered before the Patriarch, and it was not without a feeling of dread that he saw the moment arrive when he would be face to face with the Octopus. True, he felt confident of her.

If they could only have a few minutes private conversation! And besides, the Octopus was probably better informed than he was. . . . Thus he could not repress a start of joy when he saw Madame de Meyrens in the entrance hall of the Council room in which they were both about to be admitted. Moreover, by the happiest of chances the entrance hall was for the time being empty. De Lauriac hastened to the Octopus.

"Why did you let yourself be brought here?"

"I'm done for. Rouletabille got me here by a trick, and I am now a prisoner. It's all your fault," she said with growing anger. "If you had chosen to get rid of Rouletabille some time ago . . . but you thought only of Odette . . . and Jean. You ought not to have put the book in Jean's luggage but in Rouletabille's."

"Don't let us waste time in useless recriminations. It's they who'll be done for if we act together. What do they want from us?"

"They want me to tell them all that I know about you. That's the price they set on my liberty. Rouletabille has managed to convince the Patriarch that it was you who put the book in Jean's luggage."

"But they have no proof of it," protested de Lauriac in a muffled voice. "Do you take me for a fool? I assure you that not a soul saw me . . ."

He had no sooner uttered these last words than the hangings near which they were standing were thrust aside, and a company of gypsies made a rush at them, shouting: "Death to both of them!"

De Lauriac was seized by Andréa, and the band was preparing under the eyes of the Patriarch and the Elders to lay violent hands on the Octopus, when in a trice she removed hat and veil and wig and appeared before their astonished gaze with the features of Rouletabille!

CHAPTER LVII

MISERERE! MISERERE!

THE tragedy had reached its logical climax in farce. The Patriarch and the librarian had lent themselves to the performance. After bringing from the hotel the puppet-like weapons which Rouletabille needed to carry the one piece of artifice which would save them to a successful issue, he had not hesitated to take the Patriarch and the librarian into his confidence, and in so doing he felt intuitively that he was on the right road. The Patriarch, as the head of the state, was nothing loath to hand over to popular fury, which demanded its scapegoat, a victim less known than Rouletabille and of less mark in the diplomatic world than de Santierne—he had already received a visit on his behalf from the Wallachian Consul—not to mention that the death of these two young men would involve a queen in spite of herself. The responsibility lay only with the plotters. . . . Moreover, was not the Patriarch himself in part to blame in this adventure?

Here were more reasons than were needed to make truth in the end prevail. It stood forth triumphantly, but in so unforeseen a fashion, that taking advantage of the confusion into which Rouletabille's disguises had thrown some of the company, de Lauriac was able to shake himself free from Andréa, make a grab at a window ledge, and leap into a garden, drawing in his wake a maddened band of gypsies, whose pursuit of him was encouraged by word and gesture by the Patriarch himself.

357

Meanwhile, what was Odette doing? She was laughing at Rouletabille, who had not yet had time to rid himself of his skirt, and clad partly as a man and partly as a woman was the drollest sight imaginable.

"I told you that we had only to let little Zo do things his own way."

"So that was why you were so anxious about your luggage? So that was what you were thinking about when you spoke of your dressing-case? You had already thought out your little scheme. Your disguise was ready to hand. Why couldn't you tell us so?"

"What do you think?" grunted Rouletabille. "It is the old story. Suppose I had said: 'Wait for me, I'm going to fetch Madame de Meyrens' hat and veil and things,' you wouldn't have waited had Odette not been with you."

"Yes, but I was there," said Odette, "and I had no intention of going without little Zo."

"Odette is a dear," said Rouletabille.

"What about me?" asked Jean.

"You are an ass, like all lovers."

"Thank you. . . . Well, the ass will give you a piece of advice, for I imagine that when Madame de Meyrens discovers the trick which you have played . . ."

"Never mind about that. Have no fear. We don't intend to hang about here for ever," said Rouletabille.

And now that he was himself again, he went before the Patriarch and addressed him more or less in these terms:

"If they do not overtake the guilty man he will escape! In any case, there is nothing to keep us here now, for in the first place we are not anxious to witness his execution, and secondly it would be a pity if, after you have acknowledged our innocence, we were to witness our own execution!"

The Patriarch considered that this was the language

of wisdom, and at once set to work to assist Rouletabille and his friends to leave the city without delay. Moreover, he disguised their hurried departure by straightway promulgating a decree of expulsion.

In the meantime, the pursuit of de Lauriac was continuing and he had the opportunity, in those tragic hours, of employing all the resources and strength and courage which heroes in ancient and mediæval times have displayed. History repeats itself, which is more or less tantamout to saying that nothing changes, and that time itself is but an illusion. And this fantastic horseman enveloped by a swarm of foes, whom he discomfited by mighty blows struck in a twilight of blood, even as he struck mighty blows under the blazing sun—we have seen this fantastic horseman on the plains of Troy, in the amphitheaters of death in the *Chanson of Roland,* and on the golden plains of Camargue—before he fell and was swallowed up in the insidious depths of a morass on the borders of the plague country.

Hubert died like a hero, whom love had enslaved and death regenerated. It was a splendid fight. How he leapt at the stallion and unhorsed his rider, charging his foes like a meteor, throwing them to the ground and forcing them to retreat! . . . And then he passed through the gates of the city into the open country, the gathering darkness, and, seemingly, life and liberty.

But it was not to be. After his fight with men he encountered the rush of wild bulls, who made an end of him. The bottomless pit drew the four hoofs of his horse and did not give back its prey. And he, too, riding to his death, sank into the abyss. A struggle did but hasten the end.

De Lauriac died for love of Odette, who had no love for him. He died for a smile from her who refused to smile on him. Whatever his sins: *Miserere! Miserere!*

CHAPTER LVIII

IN WHICH WE ARE BROUGHT TOGETHER IN PARIS
FOR A CONVERSATION

A MARRIAGE has been arranged between Monsieur Jean de Santierne and Mademoiselle Odette de Lavardens, but in consequence of a recent family bereavement it will be celebrated privately. The ceremony will take place in the church in Lavardens."

Rouletabille, who was back home again in the Faubourg Poissonière, re-read the brief announcement which appeared in the morning's papers. He re-read it as he smoked his pipe, without any greater betrayal of the feeling with which he was stirred than a certain quickness in inhaling the smoke and in blowing it out again through his nostrils. Obviously that was a sign which could not be taken as an expression of any great satisfaction. But why not? In what respect was he dissatisfied? Did he himself know? What more could he hope for? Was not his task completed? Were not the few lines that danced before his eyes the crown of his efforts? He had assured the happiness of his friends. What more did he want? That was the question which he asked himself and to which at length he made answer aloud: "Nothing!"

Just then his study door was opened and Jean came in.

"Well, Rouletabille, you ought to be very pleased," began de Santierne. "The papers are full of you."

"Oh, my dear fellow, the papers contain some mention of you, too," returned Rouletabille, making an effort to hide the emotion to which he had yielded when his friend entered the room.   And he pointed to the announcement of the forthcoming marriage.

"Well, yes, they mention me and Odette too, of course. But you are the hero.   You are the *deus ex machina*. . . . The man who triumphed over fate and tricked the people of Sever Turn—is you.   I've come to say that Odette and I are eternally grateful to you.   Once more, thanks!"

"I have already told you that it is not worth mentioning. . . . Come, old man, shake hands and go back to Odette."

"Do you want to get rid of me?"

"No, but I thought that Odette was waiting for you."

"That's true."

"There's nothing the matter with her?"

"No.   What a question!"

"Oh, I asked, you know, because I thought she might have come with you."

"She wanted to come, but I found some excuse . . ."

"To come by yourself?"

"Yes. . . . But she won't be bored.   She is going shopping with her old governess—the woman, you know, whom Monsieur de Lavardens dismissed in such strange fashion after Odette and she paid a visit to her aunt," said Jean, turning scarlet.

Rouletabille gazed at him steadily and sat down with his normal composure.

"Yes," went on de Santierne, looking more and more uncomfortable, "I decided to come here alone because I wanted to talk to you about Madame de Meyrens."

"Is it really about Madame de Meyrens that you want to talk to me?"

"Yes . . . the Octopus . . . and also about another matter connected with the Octopus—another matter which I ought to have discussed with you some time ago, but I said nothing out of delicacy, because I know that you are above certain possibilities and certain people. Besides, you are above all these things. Do you follow me?"

"No, I don't follow you, and I should like you to explain—to explain clearly what you mean," returned Rouletabille in increasingly icy tones.

"Well, old man, after all I should prefer to do so. I am perhaps an ass, but this is what came into my mind. I said to myself: It is out of the question for Rouletabille to have invented that fake at Sever Turn on the spur of the moment."

"What fake?"

"Well, your disguise as Madame de Meyrens—unless you had been used to doing it. Am I right?"

"Go on, I am interested," returned Rouletabille stonily.

"The fact that de Lauriac was so easily taken in at Sever Turn proves that he saw before him the only Madame de Meyrens he had ever known—the woman whom he met at Innsbruck. And the woman whom he met at Innsbruck was Rouletabille disguised. Have I guessed the truth?"

"You do yourself an injustice in considering yourself an ass. You show remarkable intelligence," said Rouletabille.

"Well, let's have a good laugh over it, old man. I am delighted to have guessed it. . . . Why don't you laugh?"

"Before I laugh I want to know if you guessed anything else."

"Hang it all, you were playing a pretty game with us. And I was under the impression that Madame de Meyrens crossed the frontier after we did and joined forces with de Lauriac. The devil she did! She joined forces with de Lauriac and wormed all his secrets out of him! Oh, you are deucedly clever. . . . And I was playing

the spy on you—and got frozen waiting in the street for
you!—I who went back to the hotel and found you in
your pajamas. You had just got rid of Madame de
Meyrens' skirt and veil, you villain! And you stuffed
me with all sorts of stories about the way you were
occupying your time, and your visit to that devil de Lauriac's room. All the same, thanks to your trick, you learnt
the meaning of the Romany page."

"A wonderful inference," said Rouletabille.

"You then found out that de Lauriac—he told you
so himself—had everything to gain by getting hold of
Odette and handing her over again to the gypsies, and
that was why you decided to look for her on the road to
Sever Turn."

"What must be very gratifying to you is that there
is no need to explain anything to you," said Rouletabille
with the utmost gravity.

"But there is," returned Jean. "I am going to ask
you to explain something. That loathsome de Lauriac
told me that Madame de Meyrens . . ."

"Ah, now we are coming to the point."

"That Madame de Meyrens—in other words you—
showed him two letters from Odette, proving that she
came to your flat in Paris. You will understand how I
received his statement. I refused to hear any more.
I gathered afterwards that you were obliged to show him
these so-called important letters so as to induce him to
show you the sacred book and in order to convince him
absolutely of the reality of the supposed Madame de
Meyrens' ill-will towards Rouletabille and myself. But
I can positively assure you that I felt certain from the
beginning that the letters were not real, but concocted
by you for the necessities of the case."

"Have you ever spoken to Odette about these letters?"

"No, that would have been an insult to her. Nor did
I speak of them to you for the same reason."

Rouletabille rose from his chair and gripped Jean's hand.

"You are a very decent fellow. But this time you have not guessed right. The letters exist and were not faked by me. Here they are," he added, not without a certain emotion, taking them out of a drawer. "I have not had an opportunity of returning them to Odette. I give them back to her future husband."

Jean was in an indescribable state of excitement.

"Odette came here to your flat!"

"Yes, here to my flat."

"And I knew nothing about it."

"You knew nothing about it. Calm yourself, Jean. I command you to calm yourself. Look me in the face and don't play the fool. Odette came here half mad with jealousy. . . . She was like a little savage—a being who frightened me, for I was unaware then that she was a gypsy. Oh, I assure you that she loves you, for it was on account of Callista that she hated you! She hated you for a time, and her old governess and I had great difficulty in restoring her peace of mind. Remember, she caught sight of you in the street driving in a car with Callista. At last she began to cry. Then it was easy to reason with her. I showed her letters from you, from which it was as clear as noonday that you had been wanting to break with Callista for some time. Finally I was able to take her to the train with her governess, and, ashamed, she made me promise never to tell you of her trip to Paris. Now you know everything, old man. What more can I do for you?"

CHAPTER LIX

IN WHICH WE ARE BROUGHT TOGETHER IN LAVARDENS FOR A CEREMONY WHICH WILL NOT SURPRISE THE READER

WHEN Rouletabille and Jean were not wrangling with each other they were the best of friends. Jean was so delighted with what he had just learnt, and his personal affairs seemed to have taken so favorable a turn that he embraced Rouletabille.

"You are a most wonderful friend," he cried.

"Why 'most wonderful'?" protested Rouletabille, gently releasing himself, "I am your friend, that's all."

"That's all! What splendid words," said Jean, solemnly wiping his eyes. "Now, I'll tell you what it is . . ."

"Don't tell me," interrupted Rouletabille, opening the door. "You can't have anything else to say to me. Odette is expecting you. Go to her. . . . Give her my love. . . . Good-by."

"What do you mean, 'good-by?' Aren't you coming to Lavardens? Don't you intend to be present at our wedding?"

"Well, old man, I want to take a holiday somewhere hereabouts—in America."

"If you ever do that . . . if you go to America before we are married, well . . ."

"Well, what?"

"I shall begin to think . . . No, I won't think that," he said quickly, for Rouletabille stood before him deathly pale. "But do stay."

"All right," said Rouletabille, giving him an ice-cold hand. "I will stay."

Jean hurried away.

"I will stay since they want me," Rouletabille said to himself, and he closed the door, threw himself into an arm-chair, and lit his pipe. "He is very nice. She is very nice. They will make a charming couple."

Just then the door was opened and Jean ran in panic-stricken.

"Rouletabille, she's here."

"Odette?"

"No, Callista . . . Callista is back."

"Oh, is that all?" said Rouletabille, dropping into his chair once more. "I knew that."

"What! You knew it and kept it from me. Why, Callista can't have returned to Paris with any good intentions."

"You may depend upon that," said Rouletabille. "But be easy in your mind, my dear fellow. I took good care that she shouldn't come to Paris alone. Poor Callista! She might have been dull here."

"What then?"

"What then? . . . That's all. . . . Never mind about her. Or rather, take Odette to Lavardens at once, and don't worry, but get married."

"I shan't feel safe unless you come with us."

"Well, I'll come with you. Are you satisfied now?"

"Odette will be satisfied, too. But, tell me, is there nothing to fear from Callista?"

Rouletabille shrugged his shoulders.

"As soon as I learnt that Callista was in Paris—and I expected her—I made arrangements for Andréa to join her here. He arrived this morning. He has already got her in hand, and, I can assure you, he won't let her go."

"Oh, Rouletabille, you think of everything. How shall

I ever be able to show my gratitude. . . . Look here,
old man, if the Octopus becomes a nuisance—for it
strikes me that she will want to be revenged for the freedom with which you made use of her identity in Innsbruck and Sever Turn . . ."

"How well you put it: 'made use of her identity. . . .' "

"Now you're chaffing. . . . Well, give me the hint
and you will see that I shall be ready. . . ."

"That's only what I expected from you, old man. I
rely on you. . . . Hell and fury, the Octopus had better
look out for herself!"

.   .   .   .

A few days later Jean and Odette's wedding took
place in the church at Lavardens, which was all too small
to hold the many friends who had come without being
invited; old friends from Camargue, Crau and the Arles
country.

The many herdsmen from the surrounding farms, and
the fishermen from Les Saintes Maries, were bent on
offering their good wishes to the little lady of Viei-
Castou-Nou, whom they remembered as a child hanging
to the manes of the colts let loose in the meadows. Some
of them recalled that she was not in those days accompanied in her gallops by a young man from town. All the
same, de Lauriac's name was not mentioned. . . . There
are fairy-like forms which are far above the deserts of
some men. . . . It is a risky thing to try to ride after
them, outside one's own morass. . . . Somewhere there
is a morass which opens and engulfs one. There is a song
by a great troubadour which goes something like this:
"I love the sense of space, and yet I am held in bondage.
I go barefooted among the reeds. Love is a gift of the
gods, but love is corruptible; and after the frenzy of the
struggle comes disillusion."

In truth Jean de Santierne was a handsome bride-

groom, thought the gossips. "There is a great difference
between a stable-man and a man like Jean, so elegantly
attired, so refined, and so wealthy, my dear. . . . I can
understand how proudly one would walk arm in arm
with him." . . . Take a look at Odette as she passes.
. . . That day from house to church, as the poet sang,
the birds no longer recognized her, dressed all in white.
"Who is this little witch?" they piped, and taking alarm
were inclined to be suspicious, and then as they eyed her
more closely thought better of it, and greeted her with
their joyous twitterings.

.   .   .   .

   Thus Jean and Odette's wedding passed off very
quietly. Was it indeed quiet? Yes, because Rouletabille
of course had foreseen every contingency, and bound
Andréa to Callista; for, in the shadow of a column,
while the beflowered procession filed past, some one was
there, or rather a girl was there, who, like many another
onlooker, was not an invited guest. See Callista's deadly
profile, her blazing eyes, her trembling lips, her clenched
teeth! Something shines in her hand. It is not the
first time that the flash of a knife, held in that hand, has
menaced Odette. . . . But once again the flash dies down.
Andréa's formidable paw clutches and closes round that
slender wrist, and the Man of the Road takes his prisoner
away for good. . . .
   For good! She knew it now. She did not even offer
any resistance. Her life with the west was over and
done with. . . . He flung her at the foot of the caravan.
She submitted to his ill-treatment with an expression of
happy amazement. Why had he not mastered her before? She put on again, for good, without demur, the
gypsy rags which she ought never to have renounced.
Her adventure was the offspring of pride rather than
love. She was mistaken in herself. How could any

alien understand her? Oh, this weariness, this pleasing sense of exhaustion after the fight—this delight in surrender. Near at hand were arms trembling and open to receive her—arms which she had always spurned because she longed for the life of the town. Absurd! Absurd! . . . She had been a society lady, and she used to shut herself up in her boudoir to sing to herself, to the strains of a guitar bought at a bazaar, the old songs of the road, or to conjure up in silence the night encampments on the outskirts of the forest when she fell asleep stroking the nose of Chuco, the grandsire of all the dogs with the tribe—Chuco, whose white hair she was wont carefully to comb every morning. Well, Chuco was still alive, for he knew that she would return. And her old *guzla,* the one-stringed instrument to the music of which she had danced her first steps, was still hanging in the caravan. . . . Andréa took down the venerable instrument and its string began to vibrate as his fingers strummed an old-time melody.

He came over and sat down beside her. . . . And she wept tears of submission and acceptance of the inevitable. And in burying her head on that heaving breast which she had so often repulsed she was not unhappy because she knew that he would be her master.

CHAPTER LX

IN WHICH ROULETABILLE AND MADAME DE MEYRENS
INVITE THEIR FRIENDS TO DINNER

SOME weeks after the happy ceremony, the Paris
newspapers contained a number of references to a
person who appeared to have played an important
part in the abduction of Mademoiselle de Lavardens, now
Madame de Santierne. After mentioning this person
under her initials, which, of course, were sufficient to
enlighten everybody the papers ended by giving the name
in full. The person in question was Madame de Meyrens, whose adventurous life was recalled, and it was
represented that she had played a most rascally trick on
the powers that be—the public was left to guess which—
and as a result the Chief of the Criminal Investigation
Department had sent in his resignation. A journalist
well known even among the gypsies—look out for yourself Rouletabille!—was seriously implicated in the scandal. It was stated even that the Chief of the Criminal
Investigation Department had sent in his resignation only
because the arrest of Rouletabille was refused. Moreover, it was added that the police had raided Rouletabille's flat, and placed his papers under seal, confiscating
a certain diary, in which the name of Madame de Meyrens, alias the Octopus, appeared on most of the pages.

The *Epoque* published a vague denial which deceived
no one. In press circles bets were exchanged as to
whether the Chief of the Criminal Investigation Department would be dismissed. Rouletabille must have considerable influence with his paper and Madame de Meyrens! One fine morning it was learnt that this Chief

had been appointed Governor of one of the most important possessions in French West Africa. Rouletabille had scored, but the Chief had nothing to complain of; in short, everybody concerned was satisfied. At the same time an examining magistrate, in a small town in the south, of the name of Crousillat, was appointed, no one knew by what act of special favor, judge in the Department of the Seine. It was rumored that Monsieur Crousillat had rendered signal service to Madame de Meyrens.

As to Madame de Meyrens, she was not to be seen anywhere and people were wondering whether, as a measure of precaution, she had not left France, when certain persons in the world of letters and law, and some of Rouletabille's friends, received a card by which they were informed that "Madame de Meyrens and Monsieur Joseph Rouletabille" invited them to dinner.

The incident caused a considerable stir. It was no longer possible to doubt that Rouletabille was parading his friendship with Madame de Meyrens. And it need scarcely be said that such an attitude was severely criticized. Jean de Santierne, who received his invitation on his arrival home from his honeymoon, flew into a furious rage. His anger was roused less by the scandal of the little dinner party, than by Rouletabille's audacity in inviting Odette as well as himself.

He felt greatly inclined, moreover, to say nothing to his wife, for she would wish, whatever happened, to accompany him. . . . He went alone to Ville d'Avray.

It was at Ville d'Avray that the party was to meet together in a well-known restaurant facing the lake. . . . A lover's party, in short, to which Rouletabille had invited his friends—"perhaps," said Jean to himself, "to announce his marriage." And he added with a sigh, with upturned eyes:

"Alas, poor Ivana!"[1]

[1] See "The Phantom Clue" by Gaston Leroux.

The first person whom he encountered when he entered the fashionable restaurant was Monsieur Crousillat.

"Hullo! You here, Monsieur Crousillat. Were you invited, also?"

"Why not? I see no reason why I shouldn't be invited."

"You, a respectable magistrate, going to dine openly with Madame de Meyrens!"

"It looks as if they are to be married," returned Monsieur Crousillat gruffly. "In that case, people will have no further cause to blame them."

"Ah, I expected as much," said Jean in consternation.

"I don't see why you people should be so much affected as all that. Some half-dozen of Rouletabille's friends in the hall facing the water are pulling a long face over it. But as Rouletabille and Madame de Meyrens are in love with each other, we must reconcile ourselves to it, you know."

Just then a stout fellow, whose expression must have been in the ordinary way bright and good humored, but who seemed then somewhat dejected, came up to Jean and greeted him by name. Jean returned the greeting, wondering where he had seen his face before.

"Don't you recognize me?" asked the newcomer. "Let me introduce myself. I am Monsieur Nicolas Tournesol. . . . No, doesn't that tell you anything? . . . I am the channel of communication between the manufacturer, the agent and the wholesale merchant. . . . Nicolas Tournesol, who was in Sever Turn when so many misfortunes beset you. I met you at the Hôtel des Balkans with Monsieur Joseph Rouletabille."

"Yes, of course. Delighted to meet you in Paris. But where is Rouletabille?"

"He has not yet turned up. But for that fact I should have already left, after giving him back a small package which he entrusted to my keeping."

"Did you not receive an invitation from Madame de Meyrens?"

"I may tell you, Monsieur de Santierne, that Madame de Meyrens did not invite me to the lunch, which seems to be an engagement lunch, but Monsieur Rouletabille was good enough to remember me."

"Then stay."

"No, Monsieur de Santierne, because I paid some attention to Madame de Meyrens in Sever Turn."

"You don't mean to say so."

"And I value Monsieur Rouletabille's friendship."

"Yes, of course. It is a delicate position. You are very tactful, Monsieur Tournesol. But, as it happens, here comes Madame de Meyrens."

"I'll be off."

It was too late. Madame de Meyrens, who had in fact come in, caught sight of Monsieur Tournesol, and hastened to thank him for giving up all else in order to be present at her little dinner-party. As she spoke she pressed his hand in a very significant manner, so that Monsieur Nicolas Tournesol could not help changing color as he thought of poor Rouletabille's honor in jeopardy. . . . There was no longer any question of tact. . . . After all, there was nothing of the Joseph about him! All was fair in love and war. . . . War in lace and ruffles, of course.

Nevertheless, when the entire party was assembled in the dining-room which overlooked the lake, Monsieur Tournesol was inclined to think that Madame de Meyrens was going a little too far in asking him, to the amazement of all, to take a seat beside her, and starting in the most downright way to press his foot under the table. Downright is the word, for she had a substantial foot, the shameless creature, and did not spare Monsieur Tournesol's chilbains, so that he was suffering tortures.

"Rouletabille might well say that she is a dangerous woman," he thought.

The extraordinary part was that Rouletabille had not yet arrived, and Madame de Meyrens, thinking that they had waited for him long enough, ordered the dinner to be served without him. Such free and easy manners threw a constraint over the little company. Still Jean said nothing any more than the other guests, who were feeling sorry that they had come.

The only person who was really at his ease was Monsieur Crousillat, who had lost nothing of his tremendous appetite, and as soon as the *hors-d'œuvre* were served, threw himself with zest upon a Russian salad, to which he did full justice as if it had been a special Provençal dish.

La Candeur, one of Rouletabille's colleagues on the *Epoque,* sat facing him, and watched him with some emotion, for he, too, was not given to quarrel with his food, and yet he ate nothing . . . he ate nothing because the forthcoming marriage of Madame de Meyrens and Rouletabille had taken away his appetite. He ate nothing because Rouletabille was absent and he missed him. As to one Vladimir, another of Rouletabille's journalist friends and companions in arms, he rose from the table.

"What is going on is incomprehensible. I must telephone to the office and inquire what has become of Rouletabille."

And he darted out of the room.

"That good-looking fellow makes a mistake to worry," said the charming young Madame de Meyrens in her drawling voice with its musical intonation. "Rouletabille will be here presently. The reason why he is a little late is because we have both definitely made up our minds to part for good and all."

An "Ah!" of surprise which, it must be said, was at the same time an "Ah!" of satisfaction, greeted this

unexpected announcement, and Monsieur Tournesol grew
a deeper crimson as Madame de Meyrens made still
greater play with her foot.

"And it was agreed between us that he should not
come here until after I have gone," continued Madame
de Meyrens. "Gentlemen, I am therefore saying 'Good-
by' to you. I shall never see you again. . . . No need
to offer any protest. I know what many of you think
of me. I bear you no ill-will. Fate has decreed that I
should never love a man without bringing upon him misfortune. . . . There is only one man here whom I do
not inspire with fear—I mean Monsieur Nicolas Tournesol. Our hearts are very near to each other, and I will
also confess that our feet have not ceased contact since
this dinner began! That is one more reason why I
should disappear. I wish to save Monsieur Tournesol
from myself. We have had enough disasters. Gentlemen, I did not invite you to an engagement party, but
to a death performance. . . . I am about to commit
suicide."

The entire party rose to its feet. A look of horror
passed over the face of each one. Monsieur Tournesol
wept. Monsieur Crousillat gasped for breath and implored La Candeur to pat him on the back. . . . That
was not the moment to play a trick upon them. . . . To
commit suicide after such an excellent repast!

Jean had said nothing for some time, but eyed Madame de Meyrens as if he ended at last by understanding
something which had been at the back of his mind from
the beginning but which he had thrust aside as being too
far-fetched.

Madame de Meyrens retained her marvelous composure in her speech, and it was with a truly tragic
gesture that she gave the order:

"And now let the undertaker come in."

"When Lucrezia Borgia announced to the noblemen

of Ferrara that they had been poisoned and had but an hour to live, she could not have produced a more deadly effect than Madame de Meyrens when she called for the undertaker; and each guest was asking himself whether this strange woman to whom they attributed a thousand fantastic actions, had determined to commit suicide before them, when a sight of the undertaker dispelled the gruesome supposition. The undertaker was no other than Vladimir himself, who was wearing the time-honored glossy silk hat pertaining to important funeral ceremonies, and grinning in the most cheerful manner conceivable. By way of a coffin he was carrying under his arm a small box, which he laid on the table, and which bore the inscription:

"Here lies Madame de Meyrens, alias the Octopus."

Just then Madame de Meyrens was seen to divest herself, in a trice, of her wig and feminine finery, and when finally her dress slipped off, Rouletabille stood revealed in his well-known check-suit, amidst the yells and guffaws of the assembled company.

Jean alone, who had already witnessed a similar quick change, was not unduly impressed by it. And he would doubtless have suspected the whole truth from the beginning had not the dinner at Ville d'Avray been fixed by Rouletabille at an hour which shrouded him in the kindly gloom of twilight. Moreover, the dinner which was held in the room facing the lake was lit up only by a few candles.

Rouletabille quietly deposited what remained of Madame de Meyrens in the little coffin brought in by Vladimir, closed it, and straightway began his funeral oration:

"Madame de Meyrens was shot for espionage in the trenches at Schlusselbourg, and was buried where she fell. When I made my last trip to Petrograd I managed to secure her papers, and with their assistance I was able to bring her back to life again. She was very useful in my dealings with a department which had few secrets from her and none at all from me. I was playing a dangerous game, so much so that when I mentioned in my notes or diary the name of Madame de Meyrens or the Octopus, I invariably referred to her in the third person. In this way I protected myself against the department in question, for I always dreaded some inopportune search of my study.

"In this last affair with the gypsies, I was obliged, disguised as the Octopus, to deceive not only the police but many worthy persons to whom I make humble apology here and now. . . . I apologize to Monsieur Crousillat. I apologize to poor Monsieur Bartholasse, whom I did not invite to this function, fearing lest he might suffer an apoplectic stroke as a result of such a cruel disclosure. These worthy persons will understand that I was able, by means of this disguise, to learn many things which, without it, would have remained a lasting mystery. Moreover, was not Madame de Meyrens in a position to wander about Les Saintes Maries and question the gypsies at a time when Rouletabille could not show himself in Camargue under pain of death? Do not, therefore, be surprised any longer, Monsieur Crousillat, that Rouletabille was so fully aware of what happened in Zina's cave. And do not yourself be surprised any longer, my dear Jean, that despite your stormings, I continued to visit the terrible woman whom you hated the very sight of."

"Look here, what are you talking about?" objected Jean. "You now tell me that you disguised yourself as Madame de Meyrens from the beginning of this business. But I saw you and Madame de Meyrens at one and the same time. I saw you talking to Madame de Meyrens."

"No, my dear Jean, you are mistaken. You saw Rouletabille disguised as Madame de Meyrens talking

to—don't look at me like that—well, yes, you shall know
the whole truth. That day, or rather than evening, I was
having a game with you. I left Arles prison in my disguise as Madame de Meyrens, and you saw and followed
me. . . . I was extremely annoyed, and I wondered
whether you had any suspicion of the strange farce which
I was playing. For some years this secret of the sham
Madame de Meyrens had been too valuable to me, and
also too dangerous to allow me to make a confidant of
any person whatever, and above all of an impulsive person
like yourself, my dear Jean. I was determined, therefore, to keep the secret to myself—myself alone—and I
made up my mind to dispel your suspicions if by chance
you entertained any. I got back to the Hôtel du Forum.
You remained in the square watching my windows. I
saw you. My room was still in darkness. . . . Quickly,
with a clothes-peg, a bolster, my own jacket and cap, I
made up a dummy which I seated in a chair with its
back to the square; and I switched on the electric light
as if I, Madame de Meyrens, was entering the room in
which Rouletabille was waiting to receive me. That is
how you saw Madame de Meyrens talking to Rouletabille.
Do you follow me now?"

"Ah, I should think I did follow you now. I've got
it this time. We all understand now."

"Well, and what about me?" asked Monsieur Nicolas
Tournesol. "Do you think that I don't understand!"

This time the company burst out laughing. He made
such a comical face did poor Tournesol.

"When I think," he went on, "that from the beginning
of this dinner he has been stamping on my chilblains!
Oh, I shan't forget my conquest in Sever Turn!"

"You have this consolation, my dear Tournesol," said
Rouletabille. "You have made a friend in me, and it
is better sometimes to find a friend than a wife, and besides, as Madame de Meyrens I feel that I should have

been unfaithful to you. . . . She was shot once, and to-day we are about to drown her. I hope that after suffering capital punishment twice she will be really dead."

And, in fact, they drowned her—first in an ocean of champagne and then in the lake in which they threw the box after filling it with stones to make sure that she would never again come to the surface.

The little ceremony was hardly completed when the telephone bell rang. La Candeur made a dash for the adjoining room, and came back again almost at once.

"This time the thing is serious," he said. "It's the governor himself who has telephoned from the office: 'Tell Rouletabille to come here at once. It is a question of clearing up an affair which has just come to a head and is most mysterious.' "

"Of course," returned Rouletabille, rising from the table, "I should be surprised if it were not, but he might have waited until to-morrow. What a profession!"

"Stow that," cried La Candeur. "You live for it. . . . But you must take me with you in this affair."

"And me too," interposed Vladimir.

"What about you?" asked Rouletabille, turning to Jean with a smile. "You don't ask to come with me."

"No," said Jean, pressing his hand. "I am returning to Odette."

"Give her my love and make her happy, my dear Jean, or you will have me to deal with."

"Don't worry. Thanks to you nothing can disturb our happiness unless . . ."

"Unless what?"

"Unless the terrible Callista . . ."

"Have no fear. I have suggested to Andréa a means of taming her."

THE END